Aftershocks

WILLIAM LAVENDER

Aftershocks

HARCOURT, INC.

Orlando   Austin   New York   San Diego   Toronto   London www.HarcourtBooks.com

Library of Congress Cataloging-in-Publication Data
Lavender, William, 1921 Dec. 23–
Aftershocks/by William Lavender.—1st ed.
p.   cm.
Summary: In San Francisco from 1903 to 1908, teenager Jessie Wainwright
determines to reach her goal of becoming a doctor while also trying to care
for the illegitimate child of a liaison between her father and their Chinese maid.
[1. Sex role—Fiction.   2. Fathers and daughters—Fiction.   3. Sisters—Fiction.
4. Conduct of life—Fiction.   5. Chinese Americans—Fiction.   6. Earthquakes—California—
San Francisco—Fiction.   7. San Francisco (Calif.)—History—20th century—Fiction.]   I. Title.
PZ7.L416Aft   2006
[Fic]—dc22   2005019695
ISBN-13: 978-0-15-205882-1   ISBN-10: 0-15-205882-6

Text set in Perpetua
Designed by April Ward

First edition
A C E G H F D B

Printed in the United States of America

To Mary, my partner from start to finish
And to Debbie, whose work is present on every page
With special thanks to my agent, Barbara Markowitz,
and my editor, Karen Grove, for believing in this book

Part One

One

Friday, May 22, 1903

I can't believe I'm stuck in my room writing in my journal when I could be having a good time over at Hazel's. And all because I was looking in the window at Huston's Medical Supply. The cold fog made me shiver, but I couldn't stop staring at the surgical instruments in their display—they're so amazing! And the smart medical bags that the doctors carry when they make house calls—I do crave one of those.

Not that I need one yet. But someday I will, of that I'm certain.

I thought Papa would be seeing patients at the hospital this afternoon, but I was wrong. As I stood gazing through the window, he and his friend Dr. Arnold came out of the tailor shop next to Huston's and almost ran me down.

Papa's face turned as red as his hair. I think he quite scared Dr. Arnold, who tipped his hat and hurried away. It turns out Papa knew I was supposed to be at Mama's tea party. I tried to tell him there was still plenty of time for me to greet her friends, but he wouldn't listen. He positively forbids me even to slow down on the street when I walk home—he calls it "loitering like a common street girl." The way he practically dragged me home, I felt like I was eight years old, not fourteen.

To Papa, there is no greater disgrace than a disobedient child. Except, perhaps, one who talks back. As we stepped into the foyer, he growled that he'd "deal with" me later. I expect he'll lecture me on how shameful it is for the daughter of San Francisco's most eminent physician to "carry on" the way I do. At least I hope that's all he'll do.

Luckily for me, Ching Lee was polishing the bronze lamp on the upper landing. My getting in trouble with Papa is nothing new to him. When I told him what happened, he nodded in his wise way. He said this might be one of those days when we need Mrs. O'Reilly to whip up Papa's favorite pie. He slipped down the back stairs to see about it.

I heard Papa grumbling to himself as he stood outside the parlor door, straightening his tie. Then he put on his friendly doctor smile and went in to greet the ladies. Right this minute, he's probably admiring the crocheted doilies they make for Mama's charities.

I know that sounds sarcastic, and I don't mean it to. Mama's ladies truly do good for the needy. It's just that I can't help wondering how they keep from getting bored with all that handiwork.

Oh, why didn't I go with Hazel when she asked me to help take care of Claire and Ellie this afternoon? I bet no one would mind if I'd missed Mama's tea to play with sweet little twin girls. After all, a young lady's supposed to want lots of children. I'm sure marriage and babies would be very nice, but there's something else I want more than anything. I can't say it. In fact, I'm not even supposed to think it.

First things first, Mama always says. And right now, that means getting Papa to sign for me to skip ahead of my class and take biology in the fall. Maybe if I tell him I'm taking it just to meet boys, he'll go along. After all, he doesn't know I mean to keep up my schooling after high school. And he has no idea that when there's another Dr. Wainwright in our family, it's not going to be my dear brother, Corey.

It is going to be <u>*me*</u>*.*

JESSIE BLEW LIGHTLY on her page until the ink was dry, then closed her journal and stood up. She was surprised at herself for putting her secret down in writing. She had never breathed a word to anyone, except Hazel. *It still counts as a secret if only your best friend knows,* she thought.

Going to her bay window, she pushed back the rose-colored curtain. Her mother's ladies were departing now, their familiar voices floating up on the late afternoon breeze. Letting the curtain fall back into place, she sat down on one end of the window seat. When she was small, she would curl up there and gaze out over the hills and rooftops, pretending she and her golden-haired doll, Mademoiselle, were princesses in a castle.

Now she reached for Mademoiselle, who sat primly at the other end of the seat with her trusty companion, Chester, an elderly stuffed bear. Holding Mademoiselle and Chester always made Jessie feel happy—and sad at the same time. Chester had been the favorite toy of her own little sister, Amy, and Mademoiselle would have belonged to her someday, too. But Amy had been taken from them when she was only three. One day, they were playing together; the next, Amy had caught a chill and grown so very tired. And then she was gone.

Soon afterward, Jessie had seen a housemaid throw Chester into a donation bag in Amy's room. For the five years since the night Jessie crept into that now-silent room and rescued him, he had brought her steady comfort. And Chester always reminded Jessie of the promise she'd made herself to become a doctor when she grew up, so she could save sick children like Amy.

Impulsively, Jessie got to her feet, tossed Chester and Mademoiselle gently onto her bed, and pulled the cushion off the window seat. She lifted the lid to the storage chest under the seat, breathing in the delicious scent of cedar-wood lining that rose up to greet her. Lifting the bottom board, she placed the leather-bound journal in the secret compartment below. Then she restored the board, the cushion, and the toys to their places.

Good, that's safe, she thought. Now she'd try to make herself especially presentable for supper. Crossing to the tall armoire that dominated one end of her room, she got out of her every-day skirt and waist and drew on a fresh chemise, new petticoats, and a pink silk dress. *Mama always likes me in fancy gowns. I think they make me look like a stick, but Mama calls it "slender."*

Jessie pulled her brush through her long brown hair and decided to wear it braided and up, in the old-fashioned way her mother liked. She could even pin on the dyed-to-match hair ribbons the dressmaker had sent. But leaning over to look in the glass above her dresser, she grimaced. *These ribbons and bows are for little girls.* Still, an exception to her usual ways did seem in order tonight.

She glanced at her hands, rough and tanned from playing tennis—nothing to do about that now. She could hear her parents' voices in the foyer and knew that she should hurry. Her mother always wanted everyone to be on time to the dining room. The Wainwrights seemed the perfect, cozy family, but weeks often passed without their being together except at the dinner table.

"I hope when Papa 'deals with' me, he'll at least see how hard I'm trying," Jessie said to her reflection in the mirror. Adjusting the soft folds of her dress, she opened her door softly and stepped out onto the landing. A pale light filtered red-and-blue through the stained-glass window above the staircase. Placing her hand on the smooth mahogany banister, Jessie let it rest there for a long moment.

Then, her heart racing, she took a deep breath and started down the stairs.

Two

HER FATHER, deep in conversation with Corey, gave Jessie a curt nod as she slipped into her seat at the table. Her mother and Mrs. O'Reilly stood at the sideboard, conferring in agitated whispers. "The nerve of that girl," she heard the cook say.

Jessie felt her stomach tighten as the cook hurried away. She glanced around, hoping for her usual smile from Patsy, the housemaid. But there was only Ching Lee, passing the soup plates—Ching Lee, who could do anything around the house but who never served at meals.

"Where's—?" she began, then thought better of it. Asking questions about the servants was considered unsuitable, and she mustn't risk angering her father twice in one day. "Good evening, Papa, Mama," she murmured.

Catherine Wainwright, taking her own seat, gave her daughter a slight smile. "You look lovely, dear." Dr. Wainwright went on listening to Corey tell about the automotive miracle he had witnessed that afternoon. Her brother's passion for the newfangled motorcars sorely tried Jessie's patience.

"Down at the Palace Hotel, Papa," he was saying, "two men bet their friends fifty dollars they can drive a Winton touring car clear to New York in only three months. A doctor and a bicycle mechanic, can you beat that? No one's *ever* done it. Why, there are hardly any paved roads! The car's a beauty, too. Cherry red, and it cost three thousand dollars, even without a top or glass windscreen."

Dr. Wainwright clapped him on the shoulder. "Well, bully for them if they want to waste their money that way. You'll make up the lost studying time tonight, I assume."

"Of course, Papa." Corey nodded solemnly. But the gleam in his eye told Jessie he would study as little tonight as he ever did.

People often admired the generous way Leonard Wainwright had adopted his wife's son by her first husband. It *was* admirable, but Jessie wished her father thought as much about her education as he did about her brother's.

Dr. Wainwright turned to his wife with a look of concern. "Is everything all right, my dear?" He raised his eyebrows as Mrs. O'Reilly returned to the dining room, carrying a platter of roast lamb.

"I'm afraid we have a domestic crisis on our hands, Leonard," Catherine replied. "I'm sorry, I know you dislike such matters, but—"

"It's mortifyin', just plain mortifyin'." Mrs. O'Reilly's hands shook so, she almost dropped the platter in front of Dr. Wainwright. "Beggin' your pardon, sir, for speakin' out. But I'll tan her hide, I will. She's got no notion of proper behavior."

"What's happened, Mama?" Jessie could stand it no longer.

Shooting her a stern look, her father asked, "Whose hide is to be tanned? And confound it, why isn't Patsy here to do the serving?"

Catherine looked anxiously at Jessie, then back to her husband. "That's just it. Right before dinner, Patsy put down her apron and . . . well, she's walked out on us."

"To run off with Jones, the ice-wagon driver, if you please," Mrs. O'Reilly said. "I'm so distressed, I don't know whether I'm comin' or goin'." Suddenly she was going, muttering to herself as she went back to her kitchen.

The ice-wagon driver! Jessie shuddered at the thought. Jones was a grump of a man, old enough to be Patsy's father. Now Patsy, barely sixteen, would be stuck with him forever.

"The girl did have a little mishap with the cream this afternoon," Catherine went on, trying to speak calmly. "I feel terrible for letting Mrs. O'Reilly be so hard on her about it."

Dr. Wainwright was unfazed. "The silly act of a simpleminded child is not your fault, my dear. It's entirely typical of the servant mentality."

Catherine frowned. "Well, it's a disaster, with the charity ball coming in two weeks. And with Mayor Schmitz invited as our guest of honor. Lee is wonderful, but he can't do everything alone, and you can hardly beg, borrow, or steal good help these days."

The doctor sipped at his wine. "This problem shall be solved," he said loftily. "I won't have you overworked, not with your delicate health. We'll place an advertisement and have a new girl in a few days. If we don't, why, Gene Schmitz and I will serve at your party ourselves."

"Heaven help us." His wife blanched. "I'll simply have to rely on Jessie's help to make the party a success."

Jessie's eyes widened. "I'm truly sorry for missing your tea, Mama. And for Patsy's leaving." Her resolve to be the model daughter all evening began to crumble. "But I'd really hoped I could spend that night at Hazel's."

"I'm afraid that won't be possible, dear," her mother said. "You have much to learn before you take your place in society. Helping me with the ball is one way for you to start. Besides, I've already ordered you a new dress, in pale persimmon taffeta. You'll look beautiful."

Suddenly Jessie felt hot and itchy. "I have lots of dresses," she said. "And I've never been fond of parties." At her mother's hurt look, she instantly regretted her words.

"You might show a little polite enthusiasm, Jessica," her father said sternly. "Don't make things worse for yourself than they already are."

There it was, after all. Jessie had half hoped that in the excitement over Patsy, her father might forget their afternoon encounter.

"I've spoken with your mother," he continued, "and we simply cannot understand why you feel you must ogle Huston's medical equipment as if it were a freak show."

"I'm just interested in medical things, that's all," she hedged. "You know I've always liked to help Wanda in your office."

"That's Nurse Shaw, to you. She does say you're good at rolling bandages and such, but that's not the subject here. It's your atrocious behavior in public. And today wasn't the first time."

Jessie went scarlet. It was true, he *had* caught her there a few months ago. That time, she told him she was just resting for a moment. A year before, when he found her reading medical books in his study, she'd given a flimsy excuse about researching a school project. But now she had no more excuses, and her father was impatiently drumming his fingers on the tabletop.

"Wait a minute." His eyes narrowed. "You're not imagining *you* could go into medicine? It's impossible for a woman, you do know that."

"It's *not* impossible." The words burst out before Jessie could stop them. Seeing her father's jaw drop, she swallowed hard, then rushed on. "There already are some women doctors, and I don't see—"

"Now, listen to me," he commanded, pointing a finger. "The feminine mind does not run along scientific lines. Medical training is far too rigorous."

"But Papa, Miss Susan B. Anthony says that men and women should be treated equally. So why wouldn't that mean women can be doctors, too?"

"That's absolute drivel!" he almost shouted. "Lord knows I keep the newspaper out of here so your mind won't be tainted. I repeat, the professions are not for women. Certainly not ones that would have them looking at men who are . . . well, without clothes on."

A blushing Catherine thought it best to intervene. "Your father does have your best interests at heart, Jessie." Her tone was milder than her husband's, but no less firm. "And he's right, a refined lady does not involve herself in a man's concerns. He gives you a beautiful home, and all the luxuries you could wish for. I think you need to count your blessings."

"Very well put," Dr. Wainwright agreed, with a nod. "If you feel you must work before marriage, I suppose you could teach school for a while. There were several women schoolteachers in our family tree, all the way back to Great-grandmother Cordwyn, in Pennsylvania."

"Yes, Papa, I know." Jessie had often watched Ching Lee dusting the gold-framed portraits of her Cordwyn and Wainwright ancestors that hung in the foyer. From pretty, English-born Jane Cordwyn to dapper Daniel Wainwright, who'd made a fortune in Nevada silver and become Papa's father, they all seemed pale, distant figures to her.

"Coming from a prominent family," her father was saying, "you have certain obligations that you are expected to fulfill. And we will fulfill ours by giving you a fine society wedding, and Corey a medical education."

At the mention of education, Jessie said, "I guess it's not a good time to ask if you'll sign for me to skip ahead and take biology next year?"

At this, Corey, who had been watching Jessie with amusement, almost choked with laughter. Ignoring him, their father barked, "Good heavens, I'll do no such thing. You'd best count your blessings, indeed. After this, I've a mind to take you out of school altogether."

Jessie's mother drew a sharp breath. "I know that children's education is their father's affair, dear, but she's too young yet to leave school."

"Well, we'll leave that discussion for another time," Dr. Wainwright said. "But no more talk of becoming a doctor. No more dawdling after school. And especially no dawdling at Huston's. Is that clear?"

Jessie nodded glumly. And this time, she wisely kept silent.

"Good," he said, glancing around the dining room. "Now, where's that delicious pie I've been smelling?"

———

As soon as dinner was over, Jessie escaped to her room. Corey bounded up the stairs after her. "Can't stay out of trouble, can you, Jess?" he said, his eyes dancing. "You know Papa's right. A girl would faint dead away the first time they made her dissect a frog in medical school."

"I didn't faint that time we found a dog that had been hit by a carriage," Jessie shot back. "I fixed him up pretty well, too."

"But we were just kids then, and now you're a delicate maiden," he said in a mocking tone. "How about nursing? Taking temperatures, emptying bedpans. You know, women's work."

"Oh, thanks a lot."

"Hey, you *should* thank me; I covered for you this afternoon. I told Mama you were with your friend whatever-her-name-is, planning the school dance."

"I doubt Mama believed *that*," Jessie said. "And her name is Hazel, as you very well know. But all right, thanks for that, at least."

She waved good night and closed her door.

Jessie threw herself across her four-poster, giving little thought to how lying on the bed would wrinkle her fine dress. She gazed at the ruffled canopy overhead. *If only I could learn to keep my mouth closed around Papa,* she thought. About her mother's tea parties, about fancy dresses, and about the idea that a woman could do a man's job. "Count your blessings" was all her mother would say. Just at the moment, it was hard to think of any. Still, it would be just like her father to ask her to recite them at breakfast tomorrow.

Well, our home is beautiful, she thought. Jessie had always loved its lofty turrets and cool, high-ceilinged rooms with their soft light. The cook, Mrs. O'Reilly, kept the house filled with delicious smells, even if she was bossy and a busybody. She had a soft spot for Jessie and always came through for her in a pinch. *Like making Papa that pie tonight.*

Best of all was Ching Lee. His title, "houseboy," didn't mean he was a boy. Though nimble as a cat, Lee had to be close to sixty. All her life, he had told Jessie enthralling tales of old China while he polished the silver or waxed the floor. He could make emperors, warlords, and fire-breathing dragons come alive. Her father looked down on him for being Chinese, but to Jessie, Ching Lee was a man of great wisdom and a loyal friend.

And we do live in exciting times, she had to admit. New marvels happened almost every day. Telephones had once been rare, and now Jessie's family had one of their own, in rich-toned wood and brass, hanging in their front hall. Corey's beloved motorcars sped along faster than any horse could run, even if they were a menace to everyone on the streets.

Of the luxuries her mother had mentioned, they had their share, maybe more. When Jessie wanted a new book to read, her mother would always order it for her from the bookseller. Most of her friends' mothers wouldn't let them read novels at all.

But there were only two possessions that Jessie truly treasured. One was a symbol of "our proud family name," as her father put it. The other was a token of her secret dream.

Jessie knelt before her dresser and opened a lower drawer stuffed with the scarves and gloves her mother was always reminding her to wear. Groping beneath the pile, she pulled out a carved wooden jewelry box and lifted its lid. There, in the satin-lined ring tray, lay a gold locket, handed down from her father's great-grandmother Jane. Jessie often thought how brave the young Jane must have been, sailing to America by herself, with a war about to start. Jessie had no interest in following her into teaching, but she felt proud to have Jane's name as part of her own: Jessica Jane Wainwright.

Nestled under the ring tray was her other precious treasure, a shiny stethoscope. She had saved up her own money for months, and one day, as if owning it would somehow make her dream come true, she had walked into Huston's and bought it. Mr. Huston had given her a curious look, but he sold it to her without asking a single question.

She slid her fingers along the gleaming metal surface. How simple life had seemed that day. If only things were half so simple with Papa. She knew he loved her, even though he didn't often show it. But he was so very determined that her future held a grand society life. And she was equally determined that it held a small black bag like the ones at Huston's, and all the tools of a medical career.

Three

"JESSIE, WAIT." Hazel Schelling raced out of class after the last school bell, long golden hair flying.

Jessie smiled. No one bothered Hazel about pinned-up hair or fancy dresses. But she always looked beautiful, just the same. "Where's your tennis racquet?" she asked when Hazel caught up. "Aren't we playing today?"

"My mother's going out on a drapery-hanging job, and I have to look after the monsters." This was Hazel's nickname for her younger sisters, but it never fooled Jessie. She knew Hazel was devoted to them. "Come with me this time," Hazel urged. "They're longing to see you."

"I'm supposed to go straight home, and Corey would love to tell my parents if I don't."

As they started walking, Hazel lifted her skirts and gave a waltzing twirl. "Speaking of Corey, has he said anything yet about the June dance?"

"About the what?" Jessie stared at her, puzzled. "Oh, that. He mentioned it last night, but not in the way you think. He was too busy laughing over the huge fight I had with my father."

"Again? What was it this time?"

"Like a dunce, I let it slip about becoming a doctor."

Hazel's eyes widened. "Jessie, no! You weren't going to tell anyone that. He must've hit the ceiling."

"He did, all right." Jessie frowned. "Hard enough to want to make me leave school. Or threaten to, anyway."

Now Hazel looked truly horrified. "I couldn't bear it if he made you do that. And it would ruin everything for you, all your plans."

"There's more." Jessie kicked at a loose cobblestone as they rounded a corner. "He insists that only *Corey* can be a doctor, because *he's* a boy."

"Ouch, I can see how you'd hate hearing that. But... 'Doctor Corey Trent Wainwright' does sound good, I have to say." Hazel went dreamy-eyed. "I wouldn't mind being sick if I had Doctor Corey to take care of me."

"Come on, Hazel, he'd be spending all his time chasing girls."

"He hasn't chased *me* yet." Hazel gave her a sly, sidelong glance. "Not that I'd run away if he did."

"Well, senior boys don't care about freshman girls."

"Oh, the age difference won't matter later on. When true love comes along..." Hazel sighed blissfully. "Nothing else counts. *Marrying* a doctor; that's what *I'm* going to do."

"You're hopeless," Jessie said, then laughed. "Last week in Debate Society you were going to marry a lawyer. And the week before, in athletics, it was an Olympic marathon runner."

"Pop talked me out of that last one." Hazel smiled. "He says a poor man's daughter has to find a wealthy husband. And I want to, so I can help look out for the girls later on, and my mother won't have to work so much."

Jessie nodded. "That *would* be perfect." For her, matters of money, in large or small amounts, had never been a worry. Her father had given her pocket money every week since she turned ten. But Hazel's father was a longshoreman on the San Francisco docks and couldn't afford any extravagance. Mrs. Schelling gave lessons in needlework to young girls to bring in extra income, and she hired out as a seamstress. She had worked for Mrs. Wainwright since their daughters Jessie and Hazel were a year old. Hazel had to watch other people's children to earn what little spending money she had.

The Schellings' small, plain home, only a few blocks from Jessie's, was a world apart from the Queen Anne–style mansion Grandfather Wainwright had built on fashionable Franklin Street. At Hazel's there were no charity teas, no fuss over dusting or scrubbing. Her home was a happy confusion of scattered toys, boisterous children, and friendly dogs. And Jessie had never forgotten how comforting that had been when the Schellings took her in during Amy's illness. The way she saw it, the Schellings, far from being poor, were rich in the things that really mattered.

They had reached Hazel's street, and Jessie started to say good-bye. But Hazel asked one more time, "Sure you won't come with me? There'll be two very disappointed little girls if you say no."

Jessie pondered a moment. "Well, I guess a few minutes couldn't hurt."

THE SCHELLINGS' PARLOR was the scene of more than the usual disorder that afternoon. Besides looking after six-year-old Claire and Ellie, Hazel would be watching three neighborhood children. They were already there, and Mrs. Schelling, eager to be off, gave Hazel and Jessie quick hugs, said she'd be back by suppertime, gathered up a bundle of draperies, and hurried away. The twins gave cries of welcome at the sight of Jessie, making her wish she could stay all afternoon.

Hazel's youngest charge was an overactive little boy. As Jessie watched him try to take apart Claire's doll, it struck her that in less skillful hands he could be a real problem. But Hazel had quickly started the other children on a game of Old Maid, then distracted the boy with an enticing invitation to play piano with her. She played a rousing march, with the little boy banging on the high keys, and Jessie led the other children in singing along, joining in with her clear soprano.

After playing two rounds of cards with the little girls, Jessie told them she would have to leave. The twins took turns protesting. "You just got here," Claire complained. "Eat supper with us," Ellie urged.

"Not this time, but soon," Jessie said. As Hazel walked her to the door, Jessie added, "You're amazing with children, you know. It's a gift, truly."

"Well, I spend enough time with them."

"It's more than that. My father said he'd let me be a teacher, but I know I'd be terrible at it. You're the one who'd be wonderful."

Hazel looked at her thoughtfully. "No, you have to love what you're doing in this world. I wouldn't sign up for a lifetime of dealing with unruly kids any more than you'd give up on medicine. I'm going to be the pampered wife of a prosperous doctor. Whose name I believe you already know."

At this, Jessie rolled her eyes. "Right, and I'll be the Queen of Sheba. See you tomorrow, foolish girl."

MINDFUL OF HER FATHER'S "no dawdling after school," Jessie truly meant to hurry directly home—that is, until his exact words came back to her. "No dawdling *at Huston's,*" he had said. Being innocent of that crime today, she decided she had time for one more quick stop. Veering off her usual route, she headed straight for the Wainwright Medical Clinic.

The office was quiet when she arrived, for that morning her father had unmistakably said he'd be at the hospital all afternoon. Jessie breathed in the clean, slightly medicinal smell she had always loved. Nurse Shaw—Wanda—was sitting right where Jessie hoped she'd be, at the front desk. For once, she was not racing around and too busy to talk.

Jessie guessed Wanda to be around thirty, though she seemed younger. Always ready to listen to Jessie, today she greeted her with a quick smile.

"Glad you're here. I could use some help filing these patient charts." She nodded at a pile of folders on a corner of her desk.

"Any interesting patients today?" Jessie picked up the charts and began to look through them. "I see Mr. Kelly came in. How's his hip?"

"Same as ever. He's slowly realizing that once arthritis sets in, it's pretty much forever."

"He should have some kind of therapy, don't you think?"

Wanda smiled. "That's not for us to say, Jessie, you know that."

Jessie began placing charts into the file cabinet. "I'm just trying to learn. You know, broaden my education."

Now Wanda's eyebrows lifted. "Speaking of education, I

hear you made quite a stir last night. Now Doc thinks *I'm* the one putting ideas about medical school into your head."

Seeing Jessie's embarrassed look, she quickly added, "Actually, I think it's a great idea, though I'd never tell him. But letting him know you've been reading about the Women's Rights Movement didn't help. Where on earth do you get all that?"

"From Papa's newspaper, of course. Ching Lee fishes it out of the dustbin for me every night."

Wanda had to laugh. "If Doc only knew!" Then her look turned sober. "Tell me honestly, Jessie. You haven't exactly been an overachiever at school. Have you any idea what medical school is like?"

"I *can* work hard, if that's what you mean. As hard as Corey, for sure."

Wanda began to sort a stack of patient bills. "How much do you know about Charles Trent, his natural father?"

"Only that he went off to South America on business when Corey was a baby, and died there of a tropical fever."

"Charming Charlie, they called him. Seems he liked get-rich-quick schemes better than holding a steady job. Good thing your mother had an inheritance, or she'd have starved when she was married to him."

Jessie's eyes widened. "And you think Corey will turn out like him?"

"I'm only saying that from what I know, I don't see him having the brains or the drive to go through the grind of medical school."

"Really! You haven't said that to my father?"

"Of course not, it would break his heart." Wanda leaned

across her desk. "I don't want to discourage you, but I spent a year in medical school myself once, and—"

"Wanda!" Jessie exclaimed. "You've never told me that."

Wanda shrugged. "Well, I'm telling you now. And it's a lot harder for women students than for men. The male students don't help you, they only sneer and call you strange. As it happened, I couldn't afford to continue my studies—but I hated it, anyway. Think you could handle that?"

"Maybe it's better now. Anyway, how will I know if I don't get to try?"

"Just keep in mind that most men are scared to death of females who want careers, or who have opinions of their own. When I was your age, my father thought marriage and a family were the only thing for me, too. It was around then that I first met Edgar." Wanda's gaze drifted to a small photograph, framed on her desk, of a young Mr. Shaw posing for a studio portrait.

Jessie remembered that her father and Wanda's father had known each other professionally when Wanda was a young girl. That was before she became a nurse, got married, and then lost her young husband in a train wreck.

"Make no mistake, Doc's been lovely to me," Wanda went on. "When he hired me right after Edgar died, he literally saved me from falling apart."

"He often says you're the best nurse he's ever met," Jessie said.

"I do try to be. Now, as for you, *I* think you've got what it takes for medical school. But you're going to have to prove that to Doc. First by racking up top grades in all your subjects. Then, after you graduate with honors, it'll be time to go back to him with your plan."

"When I graduate?" Jessie gulped. "That's *years* from now."

"They'll go by faster than you think." She pointed to the door. "Now, go on, it's getting late. Oh, and one more thing. You've got to stay on Doc's good side, starting today."

ALL THE WAY HOME, Wanda's words echoed in her head. There was a calmness about Wanda. She had a good sense about people, something Jessie wished she had.

She's right about me and school, Jessie had to admit. Her report cards usually said "Could try harder" or "Needs to concentrate." She could work on that. But staying on her father's good side?

That would be something else entirely.

Four

EARLY MORNING FOG blanketed the dining room windows two days later as Mrs. O'Reilly brought Jessie and her father their poached eggs and muffins. Catherine was still upstairs, feeling poorly, and Corey had left the table to get ready for school.

"That Lee is slower than molasses in the mornin'," Mrs. O'Reilly said as she refilled Dr. Wainwright's coffee cup. "Knows he's supposed to serve the coffee when I'm without a girl. I'll give him what-for when he shows up."

She had just returned to the kitchen when Ching Lee padded into the dining room, his long queue trailing down his back. "Much apology," he murmured with a low bow. "Important business today." He turned to someone hovering behind him, and a Chinese girl glided silently into the room. Lee put his arm around her shoulder as she stood beside him, eyes downcast. "This my niece," he said proudly to Dr. Wainwright. "Name Ching Mei-Li, mean 'beautiful one.' She hard worker. Be fine maid for Missus, sure."

The girl looked seventeen or so, Jessie judged. She had a delicate face and demure expression. But she was so thin, a breath of air could blow her away. Her dress was worn and shabby. Jessie knew it was rude to stare, but she couldn't help herself.

"Hello, Mei-Li," she said gently. She had long ago learned

from Lee that for the Chinese, the given name came last. "You have a lovely name. It sounds like our month of May."

The girl's dark eyes lifted. Jessie got a shy glance and a slight nod, then the eyes quickly dropped again. But in that instant Jessie glimpsed her fear. And her loneliness. "Papa, may I take Mei-Li upstairs to meet Mama?" Jessie asked eagerly. That way she could talk to the girl a little.

Her father shook his head. "You go on to school. First Lee is going to tell me what this is all about, and then I'll discuss it with your mother."

As Jessie rose from the table, she stole another look at Mei-Li. The girl returned her glance with sad, solemn eyes, which followed Jessie until she left the room.

JESSIE RUSHED HOME after school that day and found Ching Lee tinkering with the ancient grandfather clock in the foyer. "Grandfather tired," he explained. "But I fix. He run good soon."

"I know you will, Lee," Jessie said. "What's happened with Mei-Li?"

He shrugged, nodding toward the parlor, where Jessie heard her parents' voices. She slipped in and stood quietly, hoping not to be noticed. Mrs. O'Reilly hovered in the doorway, shamelessly eavesdropping.

"I did speak to the girl, Leonard," Catherine said. "She told me she's called simply 'Mei.' But she was so shy she could hardly say much else, and even Lee admits she has no experience in housekeeping."

"He also says she's only recently arrived," came the prompt reply. "And that she's a smart girl."

"Everyone knows you can't believe a word a Chink says," the cook muttered.

Dr. Wainwright scowled. "We can handle this matter without assistance, if you don't mind." Mrs. O'Reilly sniffed and withdrew.

"She'd certainly need to be smart," Catherine remarked. "Heaven knows she'd have a great many duties to master, and quickly."

Just then Corey sauntered in. "Hey, are we talking about the girl I saw Lee bringing in this morning?" he asked brightly. "What a doll!" He winked at his mother. "I'll be glad to teach her what she needs to know."

Jessie cringed at his remark, and her father huffed in exasperation. "Good lord, does everybody have to express an opinion?"

"And another thing," Catherine went on. "Lee's always told us he had no living relatives, yet now a niece appears. Isn't that strange?"

Dr. Wainwright was growing impatient. "See here, Kate, hordes of Chinese arrive in this city every day. Human smuggling is a thriving trade. They hide girls in crates marked 'dishware,' for god's sake, then sell them to so-called employers. If Lee vouches for her, I'm sure she'll be fine. I say let's be done with it."

Jessie stared at her father in surprise. So many times she'd heard him say scathingly about Lee, "He's the only Chinaman I've ever met who's even halfway honest." But when Lee's niece needed a job, and her mother needed a maid, he had shown himself to be a fair-minded man after all.

"You saw her, Jessie," her mother said. "Do you think she'd do?"

"Oh yes, I liked her. And I promise to help her get used to our ways."

Catherine nodded thoughtfully, then turned to her husband. "Very well, Leonard. We have no time to lose. Mei it shall be."

Still tinkering with the clock, Lee did not hear Jessie coming up behind him until she whispered in his ear, "She's hired."

He looked around, a thin smile creasing his usually solemn face.

"And tell her not to worry, I'll look out for her," Jessie added.

"That not proper, missee." He wagged his finger at her. "Look after servants not young lady's job."

"Now, Lee, you know I'd never do anything improper." With a grin, she turned and ran up the stairs.

Mei was soon outfitted with a crisp gray maid's uniform and the first leather shoes she had ever worn. But timid and unsure of herself, and overwhelmed by her elegant surroundings, she got off to a shaky start. Mrs. O'Reilly, who was not happy at having another "Chink" in the house, assigned her too many duties and criticized constantly. Catherine rarely had time for her. Jessie was glad when her father gave the new maid an encouraging smile now and then. She was not glad that Corey's idea of encouragement was to flirt with her, but she noticed with relief that Mei seemed more bewildered than charmed by him.

The first chance she got, Jessie invited Mei into her room for a chat. "So we can get acquainted," she said with a smile. "Please, sit down."

Mei looked shocked. "Oh no, Miss Jessie. I maid, I not sit."

"You needn't call me *Miss Jessie*. And in America, anyone can sit down if they're invited to." Taking Mei's arm, Jessie led her to a small armchair, then sat down at her desk. "Now, please, tell me about your life in China."

Mei sat stiffly on the edge of her seat. "What I say? Mother die when I am baby." Her face clouded. "Father work in British missionary school near Peking. They teach me little bit English. But he dead three year, in war."

"That's so sad, Mei. Is that why you came to America?"

"Yes. After war, school close. They say big ship go to Tie Fow. That mean San Francisco. I think maybe I find Uncle Lee. He only family I have. They give me money. I look for ship. Captain let me come."

"You did all that by yourself?"

Mei nodded. "Long, long time on boat. Hungry all the time. Finally, in Chinatown, captain help me find Uncle Lee. That all." Mei looked at Jessie as if for approval.

"Human smuggling is a thriving trade," Jessie had heard her father say. Mei was lucky that the captain had brought her straight to Ching Lee. "Your story's amazing." She gave Mei's hand a squeeze. "And what's Chinatown like?"

Mei made a sour face. "Much people, much noise, not like village in China. Not real America, I think. I want to be American."

Just then the booming voice of Mrs. O'Reilly echoed up the stairs. "Mei? Where've you gone to, girl?"

Mei shot to her feet. "Excuse, please. Cook call me, I must go."

The hurried smile Jessie gave her faded as Mei flew out of the room. *She wants to be American? She has no idea that the only thing most Americans will let her be is a good housemaid.*

MEI WAS A FAST LEARNER, and Jessie soon noticed how Mrs. O'Reilly came to rely on her quick competence with kitchen chores. And Mei began to display unexpected talents. One afternoon, Jessie found her putting the finishing touches on a dazzling arrangement of flowers. "How lovely, Mei," she said. "We've never had anyone who could do that."

"You like, Miss Jessie? Cook say I waste time."

"Then I'll remind her that a beautiful bouquet is Mama's favorite thing."

It irked Jessie that Mrs. O'Reilly's pride, and her dislike of the Chinese, kept her from appreciating Mei. One day she went down to the kitchen to press the matter. Pushing open the heavy swinging door, she was greeted by the delicious smell of Mrs. O'Reilly's cinnamon cookies. The kitchen was always the brightest room in the house, with sunlight pouring in through the high windows and onto the gleaming white walls. Mrs. O'Reilly stood at the marble-topped worktable, kneading bread dough. She nodded toward the cookie jar when Jessie appeared.

"Made Hazel's favorites today," Mrs. O'Reilly said. Hazel occupied a special place in her heart. When Jessie and Hazel visited Mrs. O'Reilly's kitchen to make cookies—or just to eat them—Hazel always took a serious interest in Mrs. O'Reilly's baking tips. And often put them to good use at her own house, Jessie was proud to observe.

Now Jessie helped herself to two from the cookie jar and got straight to her point. "Mrs. O'Reilly, don't you agree that Lee did us a big favor by bringing Mei here?"

Brushing flour off her hands, the cook stepped into her pantry, glancing over her shoulder at Jessie. "He says she's his niece, but if you ask me, she's more likely his concubine."

Jessie frowned. "What's that?"

"Never you mind, dearie." Suddenly Mrs. O'Reilly was preoccupied with the rows of fruit preserves and pickle jars that filled the pantry shelves. Carefully she rotated each jar away from the light so its contents would keep its bright colors. "Melodious is the closed mouth, my old ma used to say."

Jessie rushed to her father's study to consult his huge dictionary, and in two minutes she was back. Mrs. O'Reilly had set her bread dough to rise and begun cutting apples for a pie. "A concubine is a woman who lives with a man without being married to him," Jessie said. "Why do you call Mei that?"

"Sure'n that's what she is, I've no doubt. All the Chink menfolk have 'em. And I hear they like 'em young."

"That's an awful thing to say! You've seen how artistic Mei is. I'm sure she wasn't raised to be anyone's concubine."

With paring knife in midair, Mrs. O'Reilly frowned at Jessie. "Your mother would wash your mouth out with soap if she heard you say that word. And boot me out if she knew where you got it. Don't be sayin' it ever again."

"I won't say it if you don't," Jessie shot back. "And speaking of saying bad words, please stop calling Chinese people Chinks."

"I'll take that under advisement." Mrs. O'Reilly tossed Jessie an apple. "Now get out of my kitchen; you're in my way."

Jessie kept her part of the bargain, and as far as she knew, Mrs. O'Reilly kept hers. But it was a mystery to her how someone as naturally kindhearted as Mrs. O'Reilly could hold such unkind views.

EVEN MORE than Mei's artistic talent, Jessie appreciated the thoughtful ways Mei had of looking out for her. One day, Mei outdid herself.

Jessie often stole into her father's study at night and took a medical book for some secret bedtime reading. The night before, it had been *The Complete Medical Guide for Women*. But in her morning rush, she forgot to return it, leaving it instead on her desk. As school let out, she suddenly remembered that her father had said he'd be coming home for lunch that day. What if he glanced into her room? In a panic, she ran home, raced upstairs, then slumped in dismay. The book was gone.

"Miss Jessie?" Jessie spun around to find Mei standing in the doorway. "I hope I do the good thing this morning. I think you not want Doctor see his book here. Before he come for lunch, I take it to his study."

"Oh, Mei, thank you!" Jessie cried. "You did the right thing, exactly." Impulsively she pulled the startled maid into a hug. "In fact, you saved me."

"No, no. I just want you not get trouble," Mei said, pulling free. "You not tell Cook, please."

But her shy smile showed Jessie how pleased Mei was to have been of help.

Five

JESSIE'S DAYS SEEMED to be flying by—and seemed no longer to include Hazel. She felt bad about that and decided it was high time to make amends.

"Tomorrow's Saturday," she said as they walked home together on the last day of school. "Want to play a quick game of tennis in the morning?"

Hazel shook her head. "I have to help my mother hem a dress. And we leave on Sunday for a month in Monterey, where my aunt and uncle live."

"A whole month! I'll really miss you."

Hazel shot her an arched-eyebrow look. "You'll miss someone you've almost forgotten you ever knew?"

"I'm sorry, Hazel. I know we haven't seen each other much lately, but—"

"That's putting it mildly," Hazel said with a toss of her head.

"It's just that I've been so busy trying to help Mei settle in." At Hazel's puzzled look, she added, "Lee's niece, remember? Our new housemaid."

Hazel stopped abruptly. "You mean to say you've been spending all your time with a Chinese servant girl?"

"Don't sound like that." Jessie felt a stab of defensiveness. "Mei is a sweet, friendly person. You'd like her. Come home with me now and meet her."

Hazel thought about it for a moment. "Will Corey be there?"

"He went downtown to find out whether those men driving the Winton car made it out of Idaho. But I expect he'll be along later."

Hearing that, Hazel wavered, then finally said, "I'm supposed to be starting supper for my mother. I guess I'd better not."

"Are you saying that because Mei's a housemaid?" Jessie heard her tone growing heated, but she wasn't sure she cared. "Or because she's Chinese?"

Hazel stiffened. "I'm sorry, but I've never felt comfortable around Chinese people. They seem . . . strange to me."

"How can you say that? You've known Lee for years."

"Yes, but I'm not *friends* with him. Besides, I'm also supposed to be watching the twins—who keep asking when they'll see you again, by the way."

At the mention of Hazel's sisters, Jessie's temper cooled. It felt like ages since she'd seen them. "All right. As soon as you get back, let's take them to the new swings at the park." She smiled at Hazel's pleased look.

"You're on," Hazel agreed, and they set off again, the quarrel over as quickly as it had begun.

AFTER A WEEK of summer vacation, Jessie was counting the days until Hazel's return. She signed up to volunteer in the afternoons at the library, but that still left her with long Saturdays, when her parents called on friends. The prospect of three more weeks without Hazel seemed awfully bleak.

Arriving home one late afternoon, she found a card from Hazel on the letter tray in the foyer. And what Jessie had thought was a bleak prospect turned into a downright distressing one.

> *Dear Jessie,*
>
> *You'll never guess. I've gotten a job for the whole summer! A friend of my aunt's needed a girl to help with a children's group she runs. And she chose me! My favorite cousin, Sally, will be one of the kids. I'll earn real good money, and our family can sure use it. Be happy for me, and don't miss me too much. (Just joking about that last part.) See you in September.*
>
> *Love, Hazel*

Jessie lost no time in writing the most cheerful reply she could.

> *I'm truly happy for you, Hazel, it's just grand. Your aunt's friend couldn't have found anyone better, and the children will be lucky to have you. Give the twins a hug for me, and have lots of fun and a wonderful summer.*
>
> *Love, Jessie*

She went to her mother's secretary in the parlor, found an envelope and a two-cent stamp, and left the letter in the small tray, to go out.

THE FOLLOWING SATURDAY, preparations for the charity ball started early in the morning and would go on all day. Worried about how Mei might perform under pressure, Catherine whispered to the cook at breakfast, "Mrs. Arnold has offered us her kitchen maid for this evening. Should I accept, do you think?"

Mrs. O'Reilly shook her head. "No, madam, Mei's comin'

along fine. If she finishes her flower arrangin' in time to help me in the kitchen, sure'n we'll have things under control."

Jessie shot a look at Mei. Her eyes lowered modestly; she was busy with the silver tea service on the sideboard, but Jessie could almost see her glowing inside. To win even a grudging compliment from Mrs. O'Reilly was a special event for any housemaid. For Mei, it was a major achievement.

As it turned out, the party was a triumph. Beaming, Leonard introduced his handsome friend the mayor of the city to the gathering. Catherine chatted graciously with each of her guests, thanking them for donating to the Ladies' Aid. Corey was in his element, talking motorcars with the gentlemen and flirting with their daughters. Even Jessie had a good time, to her surprise. *Maybe it's because Mama's too busy to remind me to be charming,* she thought.

All evening, Jessie noticed, her mother kept an anxious eye on Mei. But there was no need. Mei was picture-perfect in evening black, with a starched white apron and cap. Her bouquets of carnations, iris, and delphiniums in the parlor were lavishly praised. "Wherever did you find her?" Any hostess would love to hear that about a servant, and Catherine heard it many times.

No one was more delighted than Jessie. Catching Mei alone for a moment, Jessie patted her on the back. "Congratulations, Mei. You're a success!"

"Much thanks, Miss Jessie," Mei said, smiling shyly. "You very kind."

Jessie beamed. Mei had proved herself, and the dreaded charity ball was finally behind them.

Maybe now their lives could get back to normal.

Six

Despite her pleasure at the party's success, Jessie's mother felt unwell for weeks afterward. Pleading fatigue and a constant stomachache, she often stayed in her room at mealtime, asking that Mei be sent up with a tray. Finally, one evening in midsummer, she announced, "The time Mei spends going to and from Chinatown could be better spent helping me." She wanted Mei to move into the house. "We have that attic room and water closet, Leonard, that your parents always gave to their house-maids. It would be perfect."

Willing to do anything that might lift his wife's spirits, he readily agreed.

"Good." Catherine smiled. "I'll speak to Mei about it tomorrow."

The next afternoon, when Jessie returned from the library, Mei greeted her in the foyer, jubilant at the news. But Jessie noticed that Lee did not seem to share Mei's enthusiasm. When Jessie went looking for him later to ask his opinion, she found him out in the toolshed, sharpening kitchen knives.

He frowned as he worked. "I tell Mei Chinese girl need to live in Chinatown, not here. But she not listen. And no one else care what old houseboy think."

"I care. Anyway, we're all her friends, Lee. Everyone here treats her well, don't you think?"

"Treat well one thing. Friend something else. *You* only friend here, missee. And take care of Mei *my* job, not other people."

Jessie patted his arm. "She'll be fine with us, you'll see."

He responded with a solemn nod. "If you say so, missee."

No matter what Ching Lee thought, it was the master's opinion that mattered. After a handyman had repainted the small attic room and Catherine had added gaily printed chintz curtains, Mei moved in. And overnight a change came over her. Timidity fell away and she became sunny and outgoing, even humming to herself as she worked. She took over caring for Jessie's usually messy room, keeping the bed made, the washstand neat, and the fire lit in the chilly mornings and evenings.

Sometimes Mei would gaze at the gold-framed photograph on Jessie's dresser of a much younger Jessie seated with Amy. "Uncle tell me about small sister," Mei said one afternoon. At Jessie's nod, she added softly, "She pretty, Miss Jessie, just like you." Mei picked up the picture and looked solemnly at Amy's image. Gently setting the photograph back in its place, she reached over and touched Jessie's hand, then slipped out of the room.

As often as she could, Jessie invited Mei into her room to talk while Mrs. O'Reilly napped. Mei's curiosity finally got the better of her shyness, and she was especially fascinated by the elegant dresses hanging mostly unworn in Jessie's armoire. "This one have nice jacket to match," she said one day, looking through the rows of gowns. "Why I not see you wear it?"

"Because dresses like that call for corsets, and corsets stop you from breathing. Women have even died from wearing them too tight."

Mei stared, wide-eyed. "But dresses so pretty." She sighed longingly.

"Why don't you pick one? We're the same height, and you're much thinner. You won't even need a corset."

"Oh, much thanks, but no. I maid, I wear maid dress."

"But you're not a maid on your days off." Jessie regarded her collection thoughtfully. "Here, this aqua one would look smashing with your black hair. You could wear it when you go out on Sundays."

"I not go out much. Maybe walk in park. I like in house best."

"And I like my plain everyday skirts best, they're more comfortable."

As Mei turned away from the armoire, clutching her new dress, Jessie waved toward her window seat. This time Mei sat down tentatively. "But Miss Jessie, young gentlemen not like plain skirts. You want to marry, yes?"

"I've told you, I'm Jessie, not *Miss* Jessie. And marriage isn't number one on my list. I want to do other things. Things a husband might not approve of." And suddenly, though Jessie had never intended to, it seemed natural to tell Mei about her ambitions.

Mei blinked in astonishment. "I not understand. Women not doctor."

"Sure they are. My father says they can't be, but he's wrong."

Now Mei was horrified. "In China, we respect elders, do as we are told. We never say they wrong."

"Well, my elders want me to be a fine lady, and that's just not enough for me."

"But you *should* marry nice young gentleman, be happy."

"Is that what would make you happy, Mei?"

"Oh yes." Mei's eyes shone. "I like to marry someday. Have nice house, babies. I want to be American, remember?"

"I remember," Jessie said uneasily. Should she discourage Mei's hopes? Or leave her with her fond dream? She was puzzling over the question when Lee appeared in her doorway, frowning disapproval at Mei.

"It's all right, Lee," Jessie said hastily. "I asked Mei to come in."

"She always want to be like American," he said to Jessie as Mei quickly excused herself and went out. "I say, why not Americans want to be like *her*?"

"That's a very good question," Jessie said with a laugh.

TRULY, JESSIE OFTEN THOUGHT, no one could accuse Lee of wanting to be "like American." He wore only traditional Chinese clothing—a black silk cap with a red button, an elaborately embroidered jacket, loose-fitting alpaca pants tied at the ankles, and black silk slippers with white corded soles. Every morning, he came to work with a basket of Chinese food, which he preferred to Mrs. O'Reilly's cooking. This she considered a deep insult. Like the cook, Lee had his own sitting room in the back part of the house, and often on Saturdays, when the cook had gone to the market, he would let Mei ask Jessie to join them for lunch there.

As the three sat together one day in late summer, Jessie again tried to draw Mei out about her life in China. "Do you miss your home village much?"

Mei smiled as she fell into a pensive mood. "Sometimes I take walk at end of day. Workers sing in rice fields. Flowers make color in gardens. Faraway hills, dark blue more than sky. I happy there, but I not miss it."

I believe you do, Jessie thought. But she only nodded and dipped her chopsticks into the fried almonds Lee offered. Just then, Mrs. O'Reilly appeared in Lee's doorway, arms full of grocery bags.

"Better not let your parents see you eatin' that Chinese grub," she snapped at Jessie. "You'll be makin' yourself sick."

"You don't know what you're missing," Jessie retorted. "It's good."

"Plenty here," Lee said pleasantly. "You like to try, maybe?"

"I'll do nothing of the sort!" The cook vanished in a huff.

Jessie shot an admiring look at Lee. "You do know how to deal with her."

His face wrinkled in a grin. "I tell Mei, do not be afraid of Dragon Lady. She hiss, but she not breathe fire. We get along fine."

MRS. O'REILLY WAS NOT ALONE in frowning on Jessie's friendship with a Chinese girl. One evening a few weeks later, Jessie was deep into *A Tale of Two Cities* when her mother stopped in at her doorway with an anxious look. Hastily Jessie closed her book. "Mama, are you all right?"

"Oh, I still feel some pain and weakness, but I'm sure it will pass." Catherine walked slowly to Jessie's small armchair and took a seat. "Jessie, I need to talk to you about all the time you've been spending with Mei. You did promise to help her adjust, I know. And she *is* a delightful girl. But she is also only a servant in this house."

Jessie felt her face flush. "But we get along so well, and with Hazel gone all summer, I like having her here. Is that so bad?"

"You know how strict your father is about correct behavior. He still hasn't gotten over the other ideas you've expressed on that subject."

"They're not just mine, Mama. They're a lot of people's. Changes are coming, and women *are* going to have more choices someday."

"I don't know about that. But I do want to help those who are poor and live in misery. That's why I work so hard for the Ladies' Aid." She smiled at Jessie's surprised look. "You mustn't think all we do is crochet doilies."

Jessie opened her mouth to speak, then closed it again, realizing that she had no idea what her mother, or her friends, thought about political matters. As a refined lady, Catherine never expressed her own opinions except where management of the household was concerned.

"We give to the hospital, of course," her mother continued. "But most of the money we raise goes to abandoned women and orphans. And to the noble efforts to curb the excesses of liquor in this country. Women in difficulty have no way to protect themselves."

Jessie's surprise grew. "Have you talked to Papa about all this?"

"Oh dear, no. Men are in charge of public affairs, he'd say. Such things are no concern of women. But even keeping to our proper place and performing our social duties, women can still do good in the world, Jessie."

"Of course, Mama. And everyone knows you do more than your share."

"I hope that's so, I try to do what I can. Now, back to Mei, dear. I'm not forbidding you to be friends with her. But you need to make sure to be very discreet. Good night, now."

Her mother rose, kissed her lightly on the forehead, and went out, leaving Jessie shaking her head in wonder.

Hazel looked concerned, but Jessie could tell her mind was elsewhere. "Imagine, Corey covered in grease. How adorable."

SEPTEMBER BROUGHT THE WARM and sunny days that Jessie's mother loved, but her pains only grew worse. For weeks she spent most of her days in bed, dutifully drinking the marigold-and-cider brew that Mrs. O'Reilly swore would cure any ailment.

Dr. Wainwright was unfailingly kind to her but, as far as Jessie could tell, would make no diagnosis. Nor would he prescribe anything, though Jessie knew he had a medicine chest full of treatments. Growing worried, she took to scouring his medical books and journals late at night, searching for answers. She read about bilious livers, appendicitis, ulcerated stomachs. She learned about patent elixirs, energy-giving potions, and every medicinal powder legally available. But none of the illnesses she read about matched her mother's symptoms; none of the treatments seemed appropriate.

Worried beyond endurance, Jessie finally worked up the courage to question her father. "Papa, people say that sepia powder can help for pain. Or perhaps it might help Mama to take some of those new aspirin tablets I've heard so much—"

"*You've* heard—how on earth?" He frowned. "Are you suggesting that I'm not competent to treat my own wife?"

"Of course not." Jessie tried to make her voice sound soothing. "It's just that she might be sicker than we realize, and I only thought—"

"Leave the thinking to me, if you please, Jessica. Your mother's ailments are all in her head. Women carry on this way, it's well-known."

Seven

HAZEL RETURNED at summer's end to report that "the kids in Monterey are no better behaved than the ones here."

"I'll bet you enjoyed every minute with them," Jessie said with a laugh.

"Well, maybe just a little. The girls got to play big sister to our cousin Sally, and they loved that. She's really smart for a three-year-old, kept them running the whole time. But the best part is my aunt's friend wants me back again next year."

"That's great! I'm glad for you."

It was the day before school started, and they were sitting in the park, watching Claire and Ellie pump high on the swings.

"What's been happening with you?" Hazel asked.

Jessie had expected this question—and had worried all summer how she would answer it. "Well, I spent a lot of time with—" She cut herself off. Somehow this didn't seem the right moment to tell Hazel how close she'd become with Mei. "With my books," she continued. "But Corey—he went out and got himself a real job." There was a safe topic.

"Really? Doing what?"

"Repairing motorcars. Came home covered with grease every day: upset my mother dreadfully. And she's not strong as it is, you know."

Desperate, but seeing that she would get nowhere with him, Jessie went to Wanda about Catherine's puzzling symptoms. Since Wanda had known Catherine for years, couldn't she pay a friendly call?

"I don't know about coming to your house," Wanda replied. "Your parents sometimes invite me to their charity events, and I always make a contribution. But you notice I don't attend."

"I know, and I don't see why not. You used to come to their parties sometimes, I remember."

Wanda considered her words carefully. "You know how I feel about Doc. And your mother's a lovely, gracious lady. But their high-society style is just so different from the life that suits me. I feel out of place there."

"But there wouldn't be any society people this time. And you'd only need to stay a few minutes. Please, Wanda. There's no one else I can ask for help." Finally Wanda agreed.

WHEN SHE ARRIVED, Jessie and her father were sitting in his study, he in his deep leather chair with the newspaper and she at the desk with her geography book. Dr. Wainwright seemed surprised to see his nurse but led her upstairs to visit his wife, then returned to the study. After a long, anxious half hour, Jessie heard Wanda coming back downstairs.

With a determined look in her eye, Wanda stood before her employer. "Please forgive me for speaking out, Doctor. But I believe Mrs. Wainwright should be seen by a gynecologist." Wanda never had been one to mince words.

Jessie froze, her book falling closed. Gynecologists, she knew, dealt with women's reproductive system. It was the way

Wanda boldly stated her opinion, and the way her father listened respectfully, then thanked her for it, that amazed her. As Wanda left, she flashed Jessie a small, secret smile.

If only something can actually come of this, Jessie thought.

THE GREAT FRONT HALL was unnaturally silent when she came in the next afternoon. Then her father appeared in his study doorway.

"Come in, Jessie, I have something to tell you," he said, his solemn tone giving her a chill. In the study he turned to face her. "This morning I asked a gynecologist colleague to examine your mother. He has recommended an operation, and I had her admitted to the hospital."

"My god!" Trembling, Jessie dropped into a chair. "She's gone before I even had a chance to see her?"

"You mustn't be alarmed, now. It's a simple operation, he'll do it tomorrow. She'll be home in a week or so."

"People die from operations, Papa." Her throat tightened in fear. "Does Corey know about this?"

"Not yet." He pulled his watch from his waistcoat pocket and scowled at it. "He must still be at school, studying."

Jessie knew Corey had gone to the bookshop, looking for the new bestselling book by Mr. Jack London—something about a dog. But she could see no good in letting her father hear that, not at a time like this.

"I can give him the details this evening," Dr. Wainwright added.

"Give them to *me,* now. I want to know exactly what's wrong with Mama."

"It's a minor female problem," he said, growing impatient. "Not a suitable topic for a young girl's ears."

Rising anger made Jessie reckless. "I hate it when you say that. Mama's been living in constant pain, while you've done nothing, said nothing." With shock she heard her own words, her accusing tone. He'd punish her this time, she knew. But she didn't care, not with her mother's life in danger.

He fixed his eyes on the floor as he groped for words. "She complains so often of what she calls the vapors. It's like the boy who cried wolf, you know? If it happens too many times, a person may not be taken seriously when something's *really* wrong."

"*I* took her seriously." Jessie could feel her fists clench.

But her father did not seem to hear. "I'm sorry, I guess I just wasn't paying enough attention," he said simply. "I hope you children can forgive me." He sat down heavily at his desk.

Hearing him apologize so unnerved Jessie that her anger evaporated. "You don't need our forgiveness, Papa. Only Mama's." She went to him, planted a light kiss on his cheek, then turned to leave. "And I'm sure she'll give it."

As she went upstairs, she carried with her a whole new image of her father as a doctor. For the first time, she reflected on something she'd known for years but never really thought about: He had never actually had any formal medical education. In his day, a young man interested in the profession simply apprenticed himself to an older physician, read all the books he could get his hands on, learned by doing, then set up a practice. That her father had risen from such a humble beginning to the high reputation he now enjoyed impressed Jessie immensely.

She could only imagine how much more she'd be able to learn in a real medical school. Relying on solid medical knowledge when treating patients would be so much better than having to waste time on guesswork.

Lingering with her longest, though, was the image of her father, the man, admitting a mistake. It was something she had never seen him do.

ALL EVENING Jessie's mind churned with fears about her mother's operation. Finally she gave up trying to concentrate on schoolwork and went looking for Mei. She found her in her attic bedroom, in tears.

"Oh, Miss Jessie, I so worried about Missus!"

Jessie sat down beside her and gave her a weak smile. "I know how you feel. But my father says she'll be fine."

"I hope so. Master is important doctor, yes?"

"Oh yes, he is." Jessie tried to sound confident, but her voice shook.

Mei wiped her eyes with a small handkerchief she was clutching. "I love your mother. She make me remember little bit mine, I think." She reached beneath the starched collar of her dress and brought out a thin gold chain. A small pendant of deep blue-green stone hung from its center. "Look, Miss Jessie. This all I bring from China. Father give me before he die, say my mother tell him to. When I look at jade stone, I know I am her daughter."

"It's beautiful," Jessie murmured. "It must be very special, and that's why she wanted you to have it." As Jessie thought of all Mei had lost, tears came to her own eyes. But Mei was not one to dwell on sadness. Silently, she handed Jessie her handkerchief. "For you dry tears," she whispered. Then she slipped her necklace back in place and was cheerful again.

KNOWING THAT HER FATHER would stay late at the hospital, Jessie headed straight to the clinic when school let out the next day. A sign on the door read: APPOINTMENTS CANCELLED TODAY. But Wanda was at her desk. "The operation went well," she said when Jessie walked in. "I was there. Doc will tell you all about it tonight."

"Thank heavens she's all right!" Jessie exclaimed in relief. "But he'll tell me nothing, same as always. *You* tell me."

"Well, they removed her uterus, to put it plainly."

"A hysterectomy—I was afraid of that. Now she can never—" She pressed her lips together and went silent.

Wanda looked surprised. "Oh, Jessie, were you still hoping your mother would have another baby?" Jessie nodded wordlessly. "I'm afraid that wasn't at all realistic, given her age," Wanda went on. "But she's going to feel *much* better after she recovers."

Jessie's mood brightened. "I do so want to be of help to her."

"You can. She'll need someone to look after her for a long time, and make sure she doesn't overdo. Doc can't be there all day, and Corey won't be around much. And you can't leave that sort of thing to servants, no matter how good they are. No, I'd say helping your mother recover will be pretty much up to you."

JESSIE TOOK WANDA'S WORDS to heart. Every day for a week, she made lists of things that needed doing and went over them all with Lee. She planned special menus with Mrs. O'Reilly. And she took Hazel with her to the fanciest ladies' shop and bought a tiny bottle of the perfume Catherine loved best, as a welcome-back present. Finally she conferred with Mei about fixing up Catherine's room. For at last her mother was coming home.

"She won't be able to walk in the garden for quite a while," she told Mei. "So we must make her room look lovely and smell divine." Corey was enlisted to carry in armloads of roses and daylilies, and Mei set to work.

The house was a beehive of activity all morning. When the carriage pulled up at eleven o'clock, an anxious Jessie, an eager Corey, and the servants were standing on the front steps to greet the convalescent. Hastily pinning up her hair, Jessie thought proudly of all she and the others had done to make things just perfect. And of all that she still had in mind to do.

Catherine was weak and pale but smiled bravely as she walked slowly into the foyer. "I'm so glad to be home," she said with a sigh, as Jessie and Mei helped her to her room. She stopped short at the sight of Mei's bouquets of flowers. "Oh my, these are lovely. Do I have Mei to thank for this?"

"Of course, Mama," Jessie said. "She's the artist around here."

"The roses are so fragrant. And daylilies are my favorite flower."

"Much thanks," Mei whispered, shy again. "Lily my favorite, too."

Catherine sank down on the edge of her bed. "Dear me, I can see how hard you've both worked to welcome me home. I'm going to try very hard not to be too much of a burden. So

I'm sure you'll be glad to hear my good news." She beamed. "Aunt Margaret is coming to help out. She'll take the train from Sacramento tomorrow and arrive in the late afternoon."

The "good news" hit Jessie like a thunderclap. "We don't—" *need any help,* she was about to say. But she stopped herself, trying for something more polite. "How nice," she mumbled.

"I know Margaret can be difficult at times, dear. But she's very efficient, and she does love us."

"She loves Papa, I know that."

"Well, after all, she practically raised your father, so of course he's her favorite. But she's like an older sister to me, too. You will try to be pleasant to her, won't you? For Papa's sake, and for mine?"

"I'll do my best," Jessie said dutifully. But unless Aunt Margaret had changed drastically, she doubted that her best would ever be good enough.

Eight

JESSIE RAN HOME through a pouring rain, arriving just minutes before the grand lady swept in like the storm raging outside. Already complaining about having to leave sunny Sacramento for damp, dreary San Francisco, Margaret greeted Leonard with a bear hug, then thrust her heavy woolen overcoat at Lee. When Lee didn't jump fast enough, she glared at him. "Don't just stand there, can't you see it's dripping?"

She looked Corey up and down like an army general inspecting the troops. "Have you no manners?" she demanded. "A gentleman always wears a tie." Having been prevailed upon to miss a motorcar demonstration for the occasion, Corey blinked in dismay. Then her aunt turned to Jessie. "You, my girl, look like a common dairy maid, with that ruddy face and those freckles. While I am here you will wash with horseradish water every night to eradicate them. A lady's complexion must be delicate and creamy white at all times."

With that she brushed everyone aside and headed upstairs, demanding, "Now where's the patient?" A minute later she stood at her sister-in-law's bedside and, without a word of greeting, frowned mightily upon her. "My word, Catherine, you look awful."

Jessie glanced at Corey, and the look that passed between

them told her that, for once, they were thinking exactly the same thing.

We're in for it now.

MARGARET LOST NO TIME in taking over the house, mostly ignoring her brother and noticing everyone else only to criticize. The first evening, at supper, she turned her eagle eye on Jessie's fingernails. "As I expected," she intoned. "Your nails are decidedly narrow, which indicates a quarrelsome nature. Leonard, I quite despair of your daughter." Seeing Jessie's irate expression, her father merely rolled his eyes, putting a finger to his lips.

On the second night, she pronounced Mrs. O'Reilly's cooking almost inedible. "There is altogether too much malodorous corned beef served in this house. And those rich pies are enough to give a longshoreman indigestion. While I am here, no sweets other than my own oatmeal custard will be brought to the table." Corey and his father exchanged pained looks at this news.

Then there was the matter of that cunning Chinaman, Lee. He was never around when needed, and forever in the way when he wasn't. "And that silly girl, Mei, constantly fussing over Catherine like a mother hen." Banishing Mei downstairs, Margaret herself hovered over the patient, ordering her to eat more and sleep less.

"I'm thinking of running away from home," Corey said to Jessie as they started for school the next morning. "Want to come along?"

She stopped in the middle of the sidewalk, as if to think seriously about the idea. "Definitely. Let's stow away on the next ship leaving for New York." Then, shaking her head, she added, "Come on, Corey, we've got to stick it out somehow, for Mama."

Corey nodded. "You're right. I guess it can't last forever."

"I suppose not. But it'll feel like it."

ON THE FOURTH EVENING, with her patient feeling well enough to come downstairs for dinner, Margaret made a startling announcement. "Leonard, I've decided that Catherine must come to Sacramento with me." Ignoring the shocked silence that fell over the group, she went on. "In my own home I can look after her properly, something that is quite impossible here."

"What can you mean?" Leonard scowled. "Seems to me she's doing fine."

"That may be true, medically speaking. But this house! In our father's day, you may remember, there were servants of quality here. But the idea that a foolish Chinese girl and your other slovenly servants can care for our patient—it's preposterous."

Foolish Chinese girl! Slovenly servants! Fuming, Jessie waited to hear her mother defend her loyal staff. But Catherine only sat looking at her plate. Jessie could not keep quiet. "Excuse me, Aunt Margaret, but our servants are neither foolish nor slovenly, they're—"

"If you please, I'm addressing your father." Margaret turned back to Leonard. "Just yesterday I tried to make a simple pot of burdock-root tea for Catherine in that dungeon you call a kitchen, and your ill-tempered cook had the gall to throw me out! The best restorative tea there is, and yet I am denied the very means to prepare it."

Jessie went on fuming. *Restorative tea! That foul-smelling bilge water does nothing but make people sicker.* But this time she forced herself to stay silent.

"Of course, Leonard," Margaret went on, "if Catherine should need medical attention, we do have perfectly competent doctors in Sacramento."

"I don't doubt that, Margaret, but—"

"Exactly so. What I'm offering is peace and quiet in a well-run household. And this Catherine has gratefully accepted."

She had *accepted*? Aghast, Jessie stared at her mother while her father earnestly inquired, "Is this true, my dear?"

"It would only be for a short time," Catherine said weakly. "Sacramento has quite a different climate, and—"

"One fit for human habitation," Margaret felt it necessary to add.

Jessie held her breath, waiting for her father's reaction. But he was strangely silent, a stricken look on his face. Finally he sighed. "Very well, then, if you're sure. We will miss you terribly, of course."

Jessie slumped, gazing blankly at her uneaten food. This was far, far beyond belief. She glanced across the table at Corey and, meeting his wide eyes, knew that his astonishment equaled her own.

"Good, that's settled," Margaret declared. "We leave first thing in the morning." She then launched into a rambling description of all the ways her invalid sister-in-law would be better off in the new arrangement.

But long before she finished, Jessie had stopped listening.

———

As October moved toward November, the days grew short and dark, and rain turned the streets into miniature rivers. But Jessie knew that it wasn't the weather that made the big house gloomy. Nor was it Margaret's departure—everyone had been glad to see her go. It was her mother's absence. And no one knew when she would return.

Jessie began to spend her afternoons at Hazel's, where she felt warm and welcome. Mrs. Schelling often invited her to stay for dinner, but she usually declined, feeling that she ought to be at home trying to lighten the mood. In the late afternoon, she would trudge up the front steps of her own darkened house. The cold days made her realize how much she missed her mother's patient reminders to wear her coat and gloves.

The dull mood in the house affected everyone. Dr. Wainwright immersed himself in his work, leaving early in the mornings and saying little to Jessie and Corey in the evenings. At supper, Jessie tried to get her brother to talk—about motorcars, or football, or anything. But Corey seemed to have run out of things to say, and her father hardly listened, anyway. More and more, suppertime passed in silence.

Jessie couldn't concentrate on homework, or even on reading a novel. She took to spending her evenings caring for a young goldfinch she'd found on the garden path, probably injured in a scuffle with a cat. She kept it in her room, in a tall birdcage she had dragged out of the basement. No one objected except Mrs. O'Reilly, who was horrified, but Jessie ignored her scolding. Mrs. O'Reilly snapped at everyone now, and most sharply at Lee. Lee, no longer so sure the Dragon Lady couldn't breathe fire, snapped right back.

But the most miserable of all, it seemed to Jessie, was Mei. Only Jessie's little bird brought a faint smile to her face. She seemed charmed by it. "He very sweet, Miss Jessie. You keep him, yes?"

"I'd like to, he does cheer me up. But he should have his freedom. I'm hoping he'll get strong enough to fly again."

Jessie had taken to spending even more time than usual with Mei. As much as she herself needed consoling, she felt that Mei needed it more.

"I much sad, Miss Jessie," Mei confessed one evening. "I maybe have to go back to Chinatown if Missus gone more time."

"No, Mei, she'll want you right here when she gets back."

"I hope so. Mr. Corey say same thing. He pinch my cheek and say he always want me here."

Alarms went off in Jessie's head. Corey flirting with Mei was nothing new. But, for the first time, Mei sounded as if she liked it. "Never mind Corey. My father makes the decisions around here. *He* hired you, and he wouldn't send you back to Chinatown for no reason. Ask him yourself, if you like. Some evening after supper, that's the best time."

The suggestion seemed to make Mei nervous. But when she stopped by Jessie's room the next evening, she was beaming. "I ask Doctor like you tell me, and he say I stay here long as I want."

"There, you see?" Jessie gave her a hug. "Everything's just fine."

That is, everything's fine as long as Corey behaves himself. She thought of Hazel. Good thing she didn't know that the latest object of Corey's affections was a pretty young housemaid, and a

Chinese one, at that. People were always saying that servants should know their place. Jessie only hoped that "Mr. Corey" knew his.

ONE NIGHT in early November a blustery rain started around midnight, pulling Jessie out of a restless sleep into dim wakefulness. She'd been dreaming of a little girl wearing a lacy white shawl—could that have been Amy? The shawl was familiar—it was just like the one her mother used to put on Amy every day.

She sat up, staring into the darkness as she tried to escape the eerie image of her little sister—but she tried to hang on to it, too. *Mama always told me to make sure Amy keeps warm.* The pounding of the rain drummed a doleful chant. *Mustn't let her take it off; don't let her take a chill.*

She lay back and closed her eyes. She had always loved the sound of rain at night. Now she counted on it to lull her back to sleep. Only when it began to soften did she become aware of another sound. Not steady like the rain; it was there one minute and gone the next, too faint to identify, but clearly coming from somewhere in the house. Whatever it might be, Jessie knew it was definitely not normal for that late hour.

Rousing herself and rising from her warm bed, she tiptoed to her door and eased it open. On the landing outside she held perfectly still so she could hear better. Nothing. Thinking she must have imagined the sound, she started to close the door. Then she heard it again. This time it was clear enough to identify as a muffled, giggling murmur. And it was drifting down the narrow stairs that led up to the attic. Up where Mei lived.

Creeping up the first few steps, Jessie stopped, listening to make sure. From where she stood she could see a thin strip of light shining beneath the door to Mei's room. And from inside came the secret sounds of whispering and soft movement—and a girlish voice, rising and falling. The lighthearted giggle belonged to Mei.

Fists clenched in shock and anger, Jessie could think only one thing: *Corey. It's Corey, and I'll kill him.* That is, she would confront him, accuse him, raise the roof if need be—whatever it took to convince him that taking advantage of a servant girl was utterly beyond the limits.

Turning back, she hurried the short distance down the hall to his room. She would wait inside and, when he returned, light into him with all her fury. But the moment she opened his door, she froze with her second shock.

Corey lay sprawled across his bed, sleeping the sleep of the innocent.

In a daze she groped her way back to her own room and sank into her bed. Her mind raced in a frantic search for an explanation. What if Mei had a secret lover and had let him into the house? No, it couldn't be. Mei knew practically no one, and she'd never do a thing like that. Maybe she was giggling in her sleep, dreaming of something in her past.

By now the rain had stopped. Jessie burrowed under her covers, desperate to get back to sleep. Instead, she lay staring at the ceiling. Then she heard tiny creakings on the upper stairs. If there had been someone with Mei, the person was creeping down from her room. Flinging back her covers, she rose and flew to her doorway just in time to catch a glimpse of her father disappearing into his bedroom. The door softly closed behind him.

A wave of nausea swept over her as she stumbled back to her bed and sat shivering in the cold. There would be no more sleep for her this night. Terrible knowledge was staring her in the face, knowledge about the father she loved and, despite their differences, had always admired.

Why do I have to know this? She buried her face in her pillow until it was soaked with tears. Her mind had become a muddle. She wished she had someone to talk things over with. Lee, her wise friend all her life—he could not hear about this. And Wanda—there had never been a problem she couldn't take to her. But not this one. The disgrace to her father's name would be utterly unthinkable.

No one could ever hear about this. Nobody, ever.

Nine

EACH WEEK a cheerful letter arrived from Catherine saying she was enjoying her stay with Margaret and was slowly regaining her health. Jessie knew her mother liked Margaret's husband, a quiet, modest man. But how could she enjoy being ordered around for weeks by her overbearing sister-in-law?

"This long rest is just what I needed," Catherine wrote toward the end of November. "I only hope nobody minds my being gone so long." Leonard passed the letter on to Jessie and Corey without comment, leaving Jessie to wonder if he really minded or not. For her part, she minded intensely.

Since that awful night, she had looked at her father with new eyes, disgusted eyes. Each day she grew more afraid of what might happen if her feelings began to show. Each night she lay awake for hours, listening for the telltale sounds she dreaded. Eventually, in the wee hours, she would hear the sounds again and cover her head with pillows, trying desperately to shut them out. When she didn't hear them, she lay awake, anyway.

She couldn't confront her father the way she would have confronted Corey. But she could avoid him. Most mornings she left a note saying "Going to Hazel's for dinner." She feared she might even wear out her welcome there. Still, she decided, it was better to lean a little too hard on her friends than to stay at home dreading the sight of her own father.

Meanwhile Mei's look of pure innocence had not changed. She went about her duties every day in the same serious, careful way. Was she the helpless victim of a man who held power over her? Or was she a willing partner? Many of Jessie's sleepless nights were spent turning over the question in her mind.

Finally, when she could no longer stand the wondering, she called Mei into her room and closed the door. "I haven't seen you much lately, Mei," she began after they were seated. "How have you been?"

"Fine, Miss Jessie. Sad Missus still away, but I fine."

At the mention of her mother, Jessie's hands tensed. In a tight voice she asked, "No problems on the job? Without a mistress in the house, I mean?"

"Problem?" Mei looked puzzled. "What kind of problem?"

"What if someone asked you to do something you didn't want to do, or—"

"Oh no," Mei replied earnestly. "Everyone here very nice; no one make problem."

Is she totally missing the point? Jessie thought. *Or just pretending?* "Are you sure? What about my father, who can take your job away any time he pleases? Suppose he wanted you to do something that was . . . not right?"

Mei's dark eyes fixed on Jessie in a long, grave stare. "Doctor very kind to me, teach me many things."

"Really!" This was unexpected. "What sort of things?"

"He talk to me, teach me new words. Show me new way to fix my hair. He give me extra money sometime. He make me feel, how you say? Important. He help me be American."

"Is *that* what he's been telling you?" Jessie struggled to remain calm.

"He not need to tell me. I know."

"How much do you *really* know?" Jessie leaned forward, trying with her penetrating gaze to see into Mei's mind.

Mei looked hurt. "I simple girl from Chinese village, Miss Jessie. But I not a child."

"Then why are you letting him teach you to lie?" Jessie could hear her voice rising but was powerless to stop it. "To be deceitful, and to betray my mother? Don't you know how much she loves you?"

"I love her, too, and all your family," Mei said in a trembling voice. "Everyone so kind, I want to be kind, too. I not want do anything wrong. I just want to be American."

Jessie felt a pang of guilt. Mei was no scheming "other woman." This was the sweet, naive Mei she knew so well, devoted to her employers. "I'm sorry, Mei." Jessie went to her, pulled her to her feet, and took her in a consoling hug. "I'm so sorry for you."

Mei wiped her eyes and pulled away. "Cook need me. Excuse, please." Before Jessie could say anything more, Mei hurried out.

AFTER THAT, Mei developed a sudden eagerness to do any afternoon errands for Mrs. O'Reilly that would take her away from the house. Jessie quickly realized that all she had accomplished with her questions was to make Mei avoid her, just as she tried to avoid her father. Her mother had always said, "Every bad experience holds the seeds of a new and better one." But the only seeds Jessie could see in this experience were bitter and hard.

Horrified curiosity and suppressed anger still kept her awake most nights, but she tried her best to close her ears to any sounds. Still, she couldn't help worrying about Mei. Of course she wasn't a child. But how much could she know about the ways of men and women? Jessie dared not speak to Mei again, for fear of making things even worse between the two of them.

And she worried about Lee. So firmly he had told her, "Take care of Mei my job, not other people." Could he possibly know what was going on? And if he did—what then? One Saturday morning she found him alone in his sitting room, sipping green tea.

He greeted her with a nod. "We not talk for long time, Missee. Come in, have some tea. Good for young and old."

"No, thanks, I only want to ask you something." She slipped into the chair opposite him. "Remember what you said about Mei's moving in here? Did you ever change your mind?"

"Not change. Bad idea then, bad idea now."

"Why didn't you take her back to Chinatown?"

"I try, many time. I tell her live here not right. Tell Doctor, too."

Jessie sat up straight, drawing in a sharp breath. "You spoke to my father? What did he say?"

"He say mind my own business."

With a long sigh, Jessie slumped in her chair. She could only hope that her mother would come home soon. Maybe then the nightmare would end.

TEN DAYS BEFORE CHRISTMAS, Catherine finally wrote that she was ready to return. Alone in the house when the letter arrived, Jessie let out a whoop at the news. Her father took the train to

Sacramento the next morning to escort his wife back. Late that afternoon, Jessie and Corey arrived home to find their mother seated in the parlor, with Lee poking at the wood fire in an open grate.

"Dearest ones, how lovely to see you!" Catherine cried, rising to wrap them in her arms. "What do you think—don't I look well?"

They were happy to agree that she had never looked better.

Just then Mei, returning from an errand, rushed in, clasping her hands ecstatically. "Oh, Missus, I so glad you back!"

Are you? Jessie wondered as she studied Mei's shining face. But she managed a smile as her mother stood chatting cheerfully with Mei while Lee, finished with the fire, hauled his mistress's baggage up the stairs.

CATHERINE HAD A GREAT many social obligations to catch up on, but her daughter's somber demeanor did not escape her attention. One evening soon after her return, she appeared at Jessie's doorway. "May I come in, dear?"

"Of course, Mama." Jessie rose from her desk, hastily cleared off her extra chair, and pulled it near.

As Catherine came in, she looked curiously at the birdcage that stood in the corner. Jessie had covered it for the night with a faded silk drape.

"Gracious, what's that old thing doing here?"

"It was Aunt Margaret's when she was young, Papa told me. I'm using it to take care of a baby bird I found." Jessie hoped against hope that her mother would say she approved. "Would you like to take a peek at him?" Gently she lifted a corner of the drape to show her mother the little bird, asleep on its perch.

Catherine glanced into the cage, wrinkling her nose. Then she stood back and looked thoughtfully at Jessie. "It's kind of you, dear, to care for sick animals. And I can see you're keeping things nice and neat. I suppose if Margaret kept a bird in this house forty years ago, you should be allowed to as well. But you must promise me that it's not for long."

A smile came to Jessie's face. "It won't be. I've known all along that as soon as he's strong enough, I'll let him go."

Catherine pulled her into a hug. "I'm glad to see you smiling again. You haven't seemed quite yourself since I returned. Are you all right?"

Startled, Jessie searched for a way to be truthful and still evade her mother's question. "Yes, I'm fine. But I missed you, and I guess it shows."

"Oh, I missed you, too. I missed everyone, dreadfully, and I'm sorry I stayed away so long. But Margaret was so very insistent..."

"Well, you're home now, and that's all that matters."

"Indeed I am. And I want you to know that this year we're going to have our merriest Christmas ever."

Jessie nodded. "That'll be nice."

"Good night, dear." Catherine rose, gave her daughter a kiss, then went out, her long skirt swishing, her perfume lingering in the air.

Jessie got up and went to her bay window to gaze out at pinpoints of light glittering like diamonds on the dark hills to the east.

Are you all right? her mother had asked. *No, Mama, I'm not,* she had wanted to reply. *I'm sick at heart, for reasons you must never know.*

LIFE DID SEEM to get back to normal. With quiet joy Jessie soon noticed her parents spending long evenings together before a crackling fire in the parlor, sitting side by side chatting and laughing. Often she saw that her father was holding her mother's hand.

She noticed, too, how Corey came back to life. He had begun a new suppertime campaign with their father—trying to convince him that the family should have a motorcar. "Ever since those two fellows made it across the country, everyone's buying them," he insisted. "Carriages are so old hat."

Catherine frowned. "They're perfectly satisfactory for me, thank you."

"Autos are still unreliable machines, in my opinion," Leonard remarked. "I seriously doubt they'll ever become anything more than a passing fad."

Whatever the topic of discussion, Jessie never minded their suppertime chatter. She just smiled and kept her eyes on her mother, back in her rightful place among them. Silently she gave thanks that the house was once again still at night, and the echoes of those furtive footsteps on the narrow attic stairs had faded into the past.

ONE DAY SOON AFTERWARD, she carried the birdcage out into the back garden, opened the tiny door, and watched the little goldfinch fly away. *Too bad you can't take my bad memories with you,* she thought as it vanished into a sunlit sky.

She knew the sounds she'd heard in the late-night darkness would never completely fade from her mind. But she had found that if she tried very hard, she could almost believe they had never happened.

Ten

TRUE TO HER WORD, Mrs. Wainwright threw the big house on Franklin Street into a flurry of Christmas festivities. Gifts for the whole family were stacked beneath the tall candle-lit tree in the parlor. There were envelopes for Mrs. O'Reilly, Lee, and Mei containing generous Christmas bonuses. By all outward appearances, the Wainwright household seemed happy and full of cheer. But Jessie knew there was more to reality than outward appearances. And now she knew that there was a great deal more to observe about people, if you kept your eyes open, than she had realized before.

Her father carried on as if nothing had changed. What went on inside his head, Jessie could not imagine. Someone else, too, seemed to Jessie to be trying hard to act like her old sunny self. But Mei had begun to look pale and drawn, and she moved about listlessly now. Several mornings in a row Jessie watched her make a half-dozen trips to the upstairs water closet in the space of an hour. Sometimes Mei smiled at her halfheartedly, but she rarely stopped to talk. Jessie was not sure whether to be hurt or worried.

Even before the joyful Christmas carols died away, Jessie's mother had turned her newfound energies to planning a lavish New Year's Eve banquet. The way Jessie looked at it, the amount of food Mrs. O'Reilly was preparing for the party would feed half the poor in San Francisco. She wished she knew of a way to give even part of the leftovers to those who could really use them.

In Catherine's view, the party would be another of those social experiences that were so important for her daughter's development. But Hazel had invited Jessie to celebrate with her family and stay the night, and Jessie begged to be allowed. Catherine liked Hazel, but she wanted Jessie to spend New Year's with her own family. Finally, on the day of the party, she relented.

As Jessie stood in the foyer pulling on her coat and gloves, she heard her mother in the parlor quietly asking Mei the same questions she had asked Jessie not long before. "Are you all right, Mei? You don't look well. I'm afraid we've been working you awfully hard lately."

Jessie leaned toward the parlor door just enough to see Mei's hands grip the back of a chair. "No need worry, Missus, please."

"Well, I'll make sure you have an extra day off soon," Catherine said.

Jessie stood rooted to her spot as they continued in low tones. *Mama has noticed, too.* Her mother might think Mei was tired from overwork. But Jessie had other ideas, other fears. Silently she stepped into her father's study. She wanted to double-check one particular fact, one more time.

There it was, plain as day in *Female Ailments and Remedies.* "A woman usually knows she is pregnant eight to ten weeks after conception." Anyone could understand that. But who could tell what Mei understood about any of it? With a shudder, Jessie realized she would have to talk to Mei again, and soon. She went looking for her, and found her in the dining room, polishing the table.

Mei glanced up, startled, when Jessie came in. "You wear your coat and gloves, Miss Jessie. You go away now?"

"Just to my friend's house, overnight. But tomorrow when I get back, we need to talk. I know you told Mama you're feeling fine, but I'm not so sure."

Mei put down her cloth and leaned against the table, gazing solemnly at Jessie. "I wish you happy for new year, Miss Jessie. I wish you—" She reached out and touched Jessie's hand. "I wish you happy for all your life."

Jessie was taken aback. Mei really did look pale, and her hand felt like ice. Still, Jessie responded brightly. "Why, thank you, Mei. I wish you a happy life, too."

Suddenly she wished they could have their talk that very minute. But Mei had duties to attend to, and it would upset everything for Jessie to take her away from them. Besides, Hazel was waiting. For the moment all she could do was pull Mei into a hug, smile into her eyes, and say, "Don't forget, tomorrow we talk." Then she hurried away.

THE WAINWRIGHTS' New Year's Eve would be all elegance, good taste, and perfect decorum. At Hazel's house everything was cheerful chaos.

To Jessie, Hazel's parents were a study in contrasts. Pop, as everyone including Jessie called Mr. Schelling, was a muscular, sandy-haired man, with merry blue eyes and a hearty laugh. Hazel's mother was serious and dark-haired, but with a warmth about her that made people take to her instantly. In that way, Jessie always thought, Hazel and her mother were very much alike.

At supper, Pop brought out a large bottle of red wine that had no label. "Made it myself," he told Jessie with a grin. "Just like they do back in the old country, only better." He filled four glasses, passing three of them to his wife, Hazel, and Jessie. Then he raised his own. "A toast!" he shouted. "May the new year bring good fortune to us all."

Jessie took one sip and her mouth puckered—it tasted like vinegar. She tried to smile, but Claire and Ellie, sitting on either side of her, weren't fooled. Claire leaned over and whispered, "One time Pop gave us some of that." And Ellie chimed in, "It tasted awful." Jessie and the two little girls exchanged smiles of secret agreement.

She watched, impressed, as Hazel sipped her wine, looking every inch the sophisticated young lady that Jessie herself was supposed to become. *My parents are the ones who should have a daughter like Hazel,* she thought. *And I should have sisters like Claire and Ellie.*

After the midnight bells rang, Jessie found a chance for a few private words with Hazel. Despite all the fun, she hadn't been able to shake the image of Mei, with her faint smile, reaching out to her. She wanted to talk to Hazel about it. Not tell the whole story, of course—no need for that.

"I know this might sound strange," she began as they climbed into Hazel's big feather bed. "But I'm worried about Mei."

"Why, what's wrong with her?"

"I don't know how you tell a sweet person like her that she's looking poorly, but she is. I certainly don't want to offend her."

"Well, your father's a doctor, he'd look after his own servants, wouldn't he?" Hazel yawned and rubbed her eyes.

"She'd never ask him. But I could. Or should I just keep quiet and hope for the best?"

She glanced at Hazel, eager to hear her advice. But Hazel was already drifting off to sleep. Jessie lay awake for a while longer, trying to decide what she would say to Mei the next day.

NEW YEAR'S DAY dawned clear but cold. Jessie could see her breath in the frosty air as she walked home late that morning. Just as she reached the front steps, Corey bounded out of the house. "Where're you going?" she asked.

"Motorcar show—the new models have come in. Papa slipped me the money for a ticket." He started past her, then turned and looked back. "Oh, and Jess, you'll never guess— Mei took off. Lee, too. The pair of 'em, gone, last night. Messed up Mama's party something terrible."

Jessie wasn't sure she had heard right. "What do you mean, 'gone'?"

"Vanished, disappeared. Mama's upstairs having one of her fits. I told her, servants come, servants go, but she won't hear it. Well, see you." He went on his way, whistling "Auld Lang Syne."

Speechless, Jessie stared after him. Mei wouldn't just leave, surely not before a big event. Neither would Lee. Hurrying inside, she headed straight for the kitchen. Mrs. O'Reilly always had the latest information.

Bustling about as usual, the cook barely glanced up when

Jessie entered. "Now here's another one wantin' breakfast," she muttered.

"I've already eaten, thank you. What's all this about Lee and Mei?"

The cook gave an angry snort. "Saints preserve us! I'm so busy gettin' things ready last night, I can't see straight. I need help—but where's Mei? Where's Lee? Can't be found, and no one's seen hide nor hair of 'em since!" She let out some of her anger by punching down a double batch of bread dough. "Like I always said, everyone knows you can't trust—"

Not waiting to hear more, Jessie wheeled around and headed up to her parents' room. From the top stair, she could see her mother sitting miserably at her dressing table. Her father, tight-lipped, stood gazing out the window.

"Lee's been with us forever!" Catherine was saying. "And Mei was so dependable. I just can't understand it."

"Probably got better jobs somewhere else," Leonard said, turning to face her. "But don't worry, we'll replace them, just as we replaced Patsy."

"But Mei's been looking so run-down lately. She might be unwell. Don't you think you ought to make an effort, at least, to—"

"I've told you, Kate, I will *not* go looking for them in that filthy Chinatown. It's much too dangerous, and full of rats carrying the plague, besides. And talk about a needle in a haystack! No, they chose to leave us. As far as I'm concerned, that's the end of it."

Jessie turned away and slowly climbed the attic stairs to Mei's room. She stood for a long time before the door. Then she forced herself to go in.

A chill passed over her as she gazed around the silent room, the same one her father had visited so often. Mei had left it so neat, it felt as if no one had ever lived there. Her mother's cheery curtains seemed sadly out of place now. Mei's pad and pencil lay next to the carefully made bed, along with the copy of *Little Women* she had borrowed from Jessie to practice her English reading. In the cupboard hung her two maid's uniforms with their stiff white collars. Her black shoes sat below, shined and ready. Next to the uniforms hung a set of her loose-fitting Chinese clothes. The other set was gone. And so was her only American-style dress, the aqua one Jessie had pressed on her as a gift. She had loved it too much to leave it behind.

Tears welled in Jessie's eyes. *Poor Mei—always trying to be American.*

JESSIE SPENT the rest of that day in a daze, trying frantically to convince herself there was a simple explanation. Something urgent had come up, but surely Lee and Mei would return soon.

Only when she turned down her bedcovers that night did she find the note. It was written in Mei's unsteady printing on a piece of the monogrammed stationery Catherine had given Jessie for Christmas.

> *Dear Jessie. Uncle Lee say I shamd. We must go. I sory. I leeve this gift please give to good person. Much thanks from your frend Mei.*

Carefully folded inside was Mei's most precious possession—her mother's jade pendant. And in leaving her gift of love, she had at last abandoned the formal *Miss Jessie*.

Feeling weak in the knees, Jessie sank down on her bed. The pieces were beginning to fall into place. If Mei had discovered she was in trouble and confessed all to Lee, he would have been outraged and taken her away. But who was the "good person" the pendant was meant for?

Tears brimmed as bitter regret came over her. If only she had taken the time to talk to Mei the day before. And she should have gotten her to a doctor, any doctor. "I wish you happy for all your life," Mei had said. *She was telling me good-bye, and like a fool I never realized it.*

Finally she dried her eyes and went to her window seat. She sat for a long time holding Chester, images of Mei swirling in her mind. Her frightened look that first morning when Lee brought her into the dining room. Her beaming smile when her mistress praised her flower arrangements. Her sad, tired eyes when she touched Jessie's hand, only the day before.

Gradually Jessie's tormented thoughts distilled into two simple ones: *Lee and Mei are my beloved friends,* and *I'm convinced that Mei is carrying my father's child.*

From those she came to a determined conclusion: *Sometime, somehow, I am going to find them.*

Eleven

FOR DAYS, Jessie watched and listened for the slightest sign that her father knew the real reason for Mei's leaving. But he steadfastly maintained that the problem was Lee. "Any servant can be lured away, anytime. All it takes is a better offer."

Catherine avoided the dreary task of finding new help, clinging to the hope that her favorites would return. Jessie, too, had found herself hurrying home those first few afternoons after school started, half hoping to find Lee sweeping the porch as usual. But deep down she knew it was not to be. As she brooded over the problem, an idea began to take shape in her mind. Soon it had grown into a bold and daring plan.

The only trouble was, she would have to get Hazel to agree.

"YOU'RE AWFULLY GLUM for someone who just scored top marks on a Latin exam," Hazel chided Jessie one afternoon near the end of January.

"I can't stop thinking about Mei. I'm sure she was—that she had some kind of health problem."

"I really am sorry about her leaving, Jessie. It must make things awfully hard for all of you, especially Mrs. O'Reilly. I'm glad *we* don't have servant problems."

"Lee and Mei were never a problem—that's the point. In a million years there will never be anyone else like them."

"I guess they were like family to you, in a way."

"That's just it. Lee gave me rides on his shoulders when I was a baby. I thought he was my uncle till I was almost five. And Mei was like a sister to me. That's why I've been wanting to tell you—we have to find them."

"What?" Hazel stared in amazement. "How? And what do you mean, 'we'?"

Breathlessly Jessie laid out her idea, and soon Hazel was shaking her head. "Jessie, you're plumb crazy."

"I have to try, at least once. Please, come with me on Saturday."

"I've got chores, you know. And I already told a friend of my mother's that I'd look after her children."

"There are other babysitters. And your parents always let you spread your chores over two days on weekends. I'll help you with them, on Sunday."

"But if we got caught going around the city on our own, I'd be locked up for a year."

"I'll make sure we don't get caught, I promise."

Hazel fell silent. As they reached her corner, she pulled Jessie to a stop and gave her a hard look. "You're actually serious about this?"

"I am, and I really, *really* want you to come along."

Hazel sighed in resignation. "I hope I'm not making a big mistake."

Jessie smiled. She had just succeeded with the first part of her plan.

SATURDAY MORNING was bright and sunny. *A good omen,* Jessie thought. Her father was at a medical seminar, and her mother had finally begun interviewing candidates to replace Lee and Mei. Jessie said only that she was going to Wanda's to help with her winter garden. She didn't like to lie, but in this case the truth just wouldn't do.

She and Hazel met at the Van Ness cable-car stop and boarded the big red car. First came the grinding climb up Nob Hill, where the city's richest dwelled in palatial mansions, then the breathtaking descent of the steep eastern slope. They had ridden the cable car before, but the deep hum of the underground cable that propelled it was always exciting. So was the clanging bell that announced its starts and stops. The ride this morning was especially thrilling.

They were on their way to Chinatown.

THE CABLE CAR deposited them in the heart of downtown, where they stood gazing in awe across bustling California Street. Over there lay a strange land where mysterious danger lurked, where "respectable" people, they had always been told, would never go.

Hazel was visibly nervous. "I've heard there are six thousand Chinese to every block, and half of them are thieves and murderers."

"That can't be. Lee always said that except for having very few women and children, Chinatown's like any other city. So let's go."

Lifting their skirts several inches, they threaded their way across the muddy cobblestones and entered the unknown.

For the first few minutes, Jessie almost forgot why they were there. All around them was a dazzling new world of exotic sights, sounds, and smells: curious Chinese buildings with their curved roofs turning up at the eaves, and narrow balconies, secluded behind intricate latticework. Huge wagon-horses clopped along the cobblestone street past shadowy, muddy alleys where colorful lanterns flickered and street cats roamed; tiny shops, their atmosphere heavy with strange incense, and cramped spaces filled with gorgeously patterned rugs and fabrics and beadwork, herbal cures, and trinkets of bronze and ivory. Everywhere there were tea rooms, offering varieties of Chinese cakes, candies, and other confections, along with teas of enticing aroma.

And the people! It felt like swimming upstream against a rushing torrent when they tried to push their way up Dupont Street, the busy main street Lee had often mentioned. Only once or twice did they see a non-Chinese face in the sea of humanity around them. They felt like aliens in a foreign land.

Up and down the streets they went, dodging horse-drawn carriages and peddlers' carts. In each shop, they asked if anyone knew an elderly man named Ching Lee, or a girl named Ching Mei-Li. They got blank looks, apologetic shakes of the head, curt shrugs, occasionally a mumbled, "Sorry, no English."

As they passed one shop, Jessie glimpsed a tiny child huddled in a doorway, clutching a crust of bread. She couldn't help staring at the child's pinched, hungry-looking face. She realized in horror that if she was right about Mei, that could be her own brother or sister in a couple of years, starving out on the street.

After two hours of tramping the streets with no results, they decided to find a bite to eat. They considered several places, and hesitantly chose one called the Heavenly Harmony

Tea Room. It was half full of customers, all of whom were Chinese. "No one will understand a word we say," Hazel whispered.

But the waiter on duty quickly proved her wrong. He was a Chinese boy, about sixteen, wearing an American-style shirt and trousers and with his hair cut short. "Welcome, ladies. This way, please." With a smile, he led them to a corner table and pulled out a chair for each one. "May I bring you a pot of jasmine tea? And let me recommend our almond cakes—the best in Chinatown."

"That would be nice, thank you," Jessie said. After he hurried away she whispered to Hazel, "Did you hear that? His English is excellent."

"He is different. Kind of seems like he's trying to be American."

Jessie winced at the painful reminder of someone else. The boy returned with their tea and cakes, and while he poured, Jessie described Lee and Mei.

He frowned thoughtfully as he repeated their names. "Let me ask my parents. They own this tea room and know a great many people here." He disappeared behind a beaded curtain at the rear of the shop, then returned, shaking his head. "Sorry. It's hard to find people in Chinatown, but I wish you luck." He gave a slight bow. "Enjoy your tea."

He went off to take care of other customers, but when Jessie and Hazel were ready to leave, he walked them to the door. "Please come again, ladies. I'll ask around, see if I can find out anything for you. My name is Henry Wong. I'm here most Saturdays."

Jessie was pleased. "Thanks, Henry, we'll stop by next

week." As they left she smiled at Hazel. "Henry! That's some Chinese name, isn't it?"

But Hazel was concerned about something else. "I thought you said you'd be coming here just once."

"Henry might get some information for us," Jessie said excitedly. "And we haven't even started asking in the smaller streets."

"I might have known." Hazel rolled her eyes. "Haven't you noticed how those alleyways stink of garbage?"

"I'm not scared of a little smell. And you don't give up on something just because it turns out to be hard."

"All right, one more time, then. Now let's get back to the cable car. I've still got those chores to do."

THEIR FOOTSTEPS were dragging by the time the cable car dropped them back at Van Ness Avenue. But instead of going home after waving good-bye to Hazel, Jessie headed straight for Wanda's. Winter and summer, Wanda spent most of her free time in her garden. And Jessie had a little matter of business to bring up with her trusted friend.

Sure enough, Wanda was outside, pruning her roses. And there was a man with her, someone Jessie had never seen. He sat in one of Wanda's lawn chairs, watching. As Jessie stood outside the gate wondering whether to go in, Wanda noticed her. "Jessie, good to see you! Come on in. I'd like you to meet Philip Nesbit. Philip, this is my friend Jessie Wainwright. She's Dr. Wainwright's daughter."

As he rose, Jessie contemplated his roundish face and immaculately tailored business suit. "I'm pleased to meet you, Mr. Nesbit."

He looked at her quizzically through pince-nez spectacles. "Likewise, I'm sure, Miss Wainwright." His voice was striking—a deep baritone.

"No need to stand on ceremony, you two," Wanda said, gathering up the stalks she had cut. "We go by first names around here."

"By all means," Mr. Nesbit seemed to agree. But the stiff way he said it made Jessie a bit uneasy.

"Let's all go inside," Wanda went on. "I'll make a pot of tea, and we can visit properly."

"Thank you, Wanda, but I must be on my way," Mr. Nesbit said. "I only stopped by to confirm our evening plans. Seven o'clock, then?"

"Seven o'clock it is."

He gave Wanda a courtly bow and turned to leave. Jessie wasn't sure whether to speak up with a polite good-bye or just fade into the background.

"Good-bye, sir," she finally said, trying to match his formal manner.

"Oh yes. Good day, miss," he replied, with a quick nod. Then he offered his arm to Wanda and started toward the street.

Wanda walked him out, calling over her shoulder, "You're welcome to go in, Jessie. I'll be there in a minute and we'll have that cup of tea."

Jessie was playing with Toby, Wanda's huge orange cat, when Wanda returned.

"That was odd," Wanda said, shaking her head as she put the kettle on. "Philip just asked me how I could possibly have a friend your age. I told him you're more interesting than most adults I know."

Jessie's smile at the compliment quickly faded. "Who *is* he, Wanda?"

Suddenly Wanda looked flustered. "He's just a friend— someone whose company I enjoy."

"You've never mentioned him before."

"Well, I don't tell you everything," Wanda said with a teasing smile. At Jessie's embarrassed look, she added, "Philip's the real-estate banker who handled the title documents when Edgar left me this house. He'd lost his wife not long before that, so he knew how it felt to be unexpectedly left alone. Not long ago I ran into him again, and he's invited me to dinner a few times since. I must say, it's lovely to have a gentleman friend to go out with."

Her words, though casually spoken, pierced Jessie's heart. "I'm sorry, Wanda. I never really thought about what it must've been like for you after—"

"Oh, never mind that—you needn't worry about such things." Wanda brought two steaming teacups to the table, then sat down. "Now, what have you been up to?"

"That's what I wanted to talk to you about." Toby was at her feet, looking for more attention, so Jessie pulled him into her lap. "Do you remember when our Chinese servants disappeared?"

"Your father was very put out about it, I remember that. And?"

"Well, I've been afraid they were in some kind of trouble. So I've started looking for them."

Wanda sat back in surprise. "How? Where could you possibly look?"

"I know some neighborhoods where they might be working," Jessie said. It was partly true, anyway. "And I have to find them."

"Your parents approve of this?"

"Not exactly. I sort of told Mama I was coming over here today." Jessie blushed at having to confess her fib.

Wanda frowned at this. "Oh, did you! And what if she had phoned here, looking for you? Don't expect me to lie to them, Jessie. Not after all your father's done for me."

"Couldn't you cover for me on Saturdays, even for a few hours?"

"It seems I already have," Wanda said dryly. "But on the next two weekends, I'm helping a friend move to a new house in the Western Addition."

"That's all right, I'll manage."

"In other words, you'll go, anyway. Really, Jessie, if you don't watch out, it'll be you who winds up in trouble."

Jessie sat tight-lipped, longing to tell Wanda about the suspicions that lay like a cold stone in her heart. "I don't expect any trouble," she said stiffly, rising. "Unless someone tells my parents what I'm doing."

"Hold on—I said I won't lie to them, not that I'm going to turn you in."

"Thanks, Wanda. That helps a lot."

As they walked outside, Jessie remembered Wanda's date with Mr. Nesbit that evening. "I hope you have a lovely time tonight."

"Thank you, I will. And tomorrow Philip wants to take me to Golden Gate Park, to see the Conservatory of Flowers. I surely never thought I'd meet a man who's willing to spend an afternoon looking at plants."

"I guess things are . . . getting serious." Jessie tried to sound cheery, but there was hesitation in her voice. Wanda gave her a shrewd look.

"What's the matter? Didn't you like Philip?"

"Yes, of course I did. It's just that—well, I got the feeling that he didn't like me."

"He's only just met you, give him time. He's a very sweet man, really. But he's never acted romantically toward me, if that's what you mean."

"Do you think you'd like him to?" Jessie ventured to ask.

"I just might, at that." Wanda's face went slightly pink. "Maybe soon I'll have a clearer answer to that. In the meantime, you must promise me—be very careful when you go wandering in strange neighborhoods looking for those servants."

"I will, that's a promise."

Weary as she was from hours on her feet, Jessie walked home feeling refreshed. *Wanda can be trusted,* she thought. *Now I can go full speed ahead.*

Twelve

JESSIE'S PARENTS finally filled the servant positions, settling on a middle-aged Irish couple, Patrick and Hilda Donegan. Mrs. O'Reilly had brought them in with high recommendations. Jessie and Corey were not to refer to Mr. Donegan as a house-boy, a term that would be insulting to anyone other than a Chinese man. He would be the butler and be called simply Donegan.

Jessie liked the Donegans all right, though she knew they would not replace Lee and Mei in her affections. Corey, who had never particularly cared for Lee, was delighted that Donegan knew motorcars. Catherine was delighted that her servant problem was finally solved.

WHEN SATURDAY rolled around, Jessie's mother and Mrs. O'Reilly were busy instructing the new servants in their duties, and her father was on his usual hospital rounds. With a quick wave Jessie slipped away, and soon she and Hazel were entering the noisy confusion of Dupont Street. Making their way past the countless sidewalk vendors hawking vegetables or fresh fish from heavily laden baskets, they headed straight for the Heavenly Harmony Tea Room.

Henry Wong seated them with a smile. "I have news," he

said excitedly. "The other day a customer told me he knows a gentleman named Ching Lee."

Though she had just sat down, Jessie leaped out of her chair, her heart pounding. "Can I see him?"

"I got the address, but you can't go there on your own. Haven't you seen the signs all over saying 'no whites allowed'? Most Chinese mistrust white people, I'm sorry to say. They even call them barbarians."

Seeing Jessie's look of frustration, he hastened to add, "My break is about to start. Come on, I'll take you there."

The three set off, Henry leading the way on what felt like an hour's walk to a shabby building many blocks away. "This is it," he said. They crept up rickety stairs and along a dimly lit hallway to a room stuffed with old books and yellowing news-papers. Jessie shot a nervous look at Hazel, who responded with a quick pat on her arm.

"Mr. Ching?" Henry called. "Is Mr. Ching Lee here?"

Out from behind a tall bookcase tottered a white-haired old man with a scraggly beard. "I Ching Lee-Ho, bookseller," he croaked. "You need book?"

Henry waited for Jessie to reply, but she was so taken aback, she almost couldn't manage it. "N-no, thank you, sir. We were looking for someone else. Sorry to disturb you."

Once back outside, Hazel and Henry burst out laughing. But they quickly turned sober, seeing the look on Jessie's face. "There must be thousands of Chings," Henry said. "Even Ching Lees."

"Thanks, anyway." Jessie cracked a thin smile.

"I really am sorry for wasting your time like this," Henry

said, "even if it is nice to have the company of two such charming ladies." Jessie had recovered enough to notice that Henry's warm smile was directed mainly at Hazel. "By the way," he added, "I don't know your names."

Jessie glanced at Hazel and knew they were thinking the same thing: There would be trouble at home if a Chinese boy came calling on them. Jessie hurriedly answered for both of them. "I'm Jessie, and this is Hazel. And we thank you again for trying to help. It's very kind of you."

Henry had gone thoughtful. "You know, Chinese girls aren't allowed to go to school, but an old teacher of mine gives lessons to some of them secretly. I could ask him if a new girl has shown up."

"Oh, I'm sure Mei would continue her schooling if she could."

"Well, I'll get back to work now. See you next week, I hope."

Jessie and Hazel roamed the streets for a long time after Henry left them, but they only got more negative responses. Finally even Jessie was ready to give up for the day.

"I don't know, Jessie," Hazel said as they boarded the cable car. "Henry pretty much said you're never going to find those people."

"He did not. He's trying to help, and I'll keep trying at least as long as he does. Even longer, if I have to."

But Jessie didn't blame Hazel for feeling skeptical. Lee and Mei could never mean as much to anyone else as they had to her.

IT CAME as no surprise the following Friday when Hazel announced she couldn't go to Chinatown the next day. "It has been kind of fun," she said, "but the twins' first piano recital is tomorrow afternoon. And they're counting on your being there."

But Jessie was resolute. "I'll try my best to get back in time for the recital. If you can't come with me, though, I'll just have to go alone."

At this, Hazel's tone turned icy. "Fine. I'll make up something to tell the twins. You can waste every Saturday for the rest of your life, if you like, trudging around that old Chinatown. Have fun!"

Jessie quickly tried to make amends. "Don't say that, Hazel, I only—"

But Hazel was already striding away.

THE NEXT MORNING, with clammy hands shoved into her pockets, Jessie told her mother she'd be spending the day with friends from school. But her mother was too distracted to notice Jessie's nervousness. "I'm having some ladies in for luncheon and handiwork today. I was so hoping you'd be here."

"Please, Mama. The ladies aren't coming to see *me*."

"Well... I suppose you'd at least be with girls your own age. I can't understand why you spend so much time at Wanda Shaw's. What in the world do you do there?"

"We work in her garden. It's beautiful, or would be if she had time to take care of it."

"You don't show any interest in *our* garden."

"We have a gardener. Wanda can't afford one."

"Well, do come home in time to join us for at least a few minutes."

"All right, Mama. I will."

———

So Jessie set out alone. It wasn't until she got off the cable car and stood facing the entrance to Chinatown that she began to feel shaky. When she reached the Heavenly Harmony, she peered in at the window. The tea room was almost empty, and to her relief, she saw Henry hurrying toward her.

"I asked my old teacher," he said, in response to her anxious look. "Turns out his oldest girl student is only ten."

Jessie tried to hide her disappointment with a smile. "Thanks, anyway. It was worth a try."

"But I do have something for you." Reaching into his pocket, he brought out a tightly folded note, sealed with a drop of red wax, and with Jessie's name printed on it. "Someone brought this in the other day and left it for you."

Jessie quickly opened the note, holding her breath as she scanned the few words of shaky writing.

Miss Jessie. Please you not look for me. I not want. Thank you.
Mei.

Trembling, she handed the note to Henry. "Nobody knows who brought it?"

"No, and I wasn't here. But this place is like a village. People know what's happening, and they don't like outsiders poking around." He glanced at the note, then gave it back. "It's plain to see your friend doesn't want to be found."

It was true, Jessie had to admit, that in Chinatown, people did look at her with suspicion. But how could Mei think of her that way? "I think it means I'm on the right track. Mei *is* here."

"Maybe she is—or was. Many Chinese go back home, you know, since American law forbids their families from joining them here. And those who do go back are never allowed to return."

"That's so awful. But I'm not giving up—not after this. I guess I'll just walk around for a while."

"I've got some time, let me go a little way with you." As they headed up Dupont, he asked, "Where's Hazel today?"

"She couldn't come, she . . . had other plans."

"That's too bad. I was looking forward to seeing her again. But she's probably tired of Chinatown by now. I don't blame her. So am I."

"But you *live* here, don't you?"

"Yes, I do, with my parents, in two small rooms behind the shop."

"Two rooms?" Jessie thought of her family's enormous home. "My, that sounds cramped." Then, hastily, "I'm sorry—that was rude."

"No, it *is* cramped. Some people live six or eight to a room, and these old buildings are flimsy as matchboxes. For years, the city's talked of tearing this place down, and I almost wish they would. It happened in Honolulu's Chinatown not long ago—they burned it to the ground."

"How terrible for the people who lived there," Jessie said.

"Oh, the Chinese are building it right back, same as they'd do here."

Now Jessie was intrigued. "You sound as if you're talking about some other people, not your own."

Henry shrugged. "My parents came from China, but I was born here. They gave me an American name and made me learn English. I'm glad, too, because I'm going to get out and make something of myself. I don't want to go through life being thought of as just another dumb Chinaman."

Jessie tried to ignore another sad reminder of Mei. "I don't think of you that way, Henry. To me you're a first-class fellow."

"Thanks, I appreciate that." As they reached a corner, he stopped and said, "Well, good-bye till next time. And tell Hazel I hope she comes along."

"I will. Thanks for the walk. And the talk, too."

She answered his wave with a bright smile as he hurried back to the tea room. But her smile faded quickly as she stood alone on the teeming sidewalk, clutching Mei's note. There was no denying it—venturing into Chinatown had brought her valuable things. A new friend, for one. And knowledge of another world, one harsher than she could ever have imagined. And now a sign from Mei, a clue. But it proved only what she'd known all along—that Lee always wanted Mei to stay in Chinatown. And now he had gotten his wish.

Well, if Mei is hiding, I won't find her strolling down a big street in broad daylight, she decided. With a sweeping look around, she tucked the note deep into her skirt pocket and turned off Dupont into a tiny alleyway.

The back alleys all looked so similar. Had she and Hazel already been there? No, she would remember the heavy oaken door covered with faded Chinese characters that faced her now. In small English letters near the bottom was printed the word BEADWORK. She recalled Lee had once told her that friends of his in Chinatown owned a bead shop. But this run-down place didn't appear to be a shop of any kind.

Suddenly the muffled giggle of a young girl floated out from behind the slightly open door. Jessie froze, her mind flashing back to the secretive giggling she had heard from the attic stairs that awful night months before. This sounded so much the same. . . . Almost overcome by the nausea she'd felt that night, for a long moment she fought the urge to turn and run. Instead, hardly daring to breathe, she stepped up to the door, knocked on it softly, then slowly pushed it open.

Once inside, she stood squinting into the darkness of a windowless chamber where thick, smoky air smelled sickeningly sweet. The giggling had ceased abruptly, and peering into the darkness, she could make out bleary eyes staring at her from the murky recesses. Uneasily she scanned the room. But there was no girl to be seen, only the ripple of a curtain at the rear of the room. And dozens of men with long pipes, lying about as if in a stupor.

This is not a place where I want to be, she told herself, turning to leave. But before she could take a step, a heavyset, fierce-eyed Chinaman lunged out of the shadows, silently blocking her way. "Why you here, girl?" he growled. "You look for someone?"

"Please excuse me for intruding," she said politely. "I was looking for a friend of mine. But I see she's not here, so I'll go now." She started to move past the man.

In an instant he had her arm in an iron grip. "No. You come where you not belong, you pay. You give me money now."

"I—I only have a few coins, for carfare," she stammered.

"You lie," he snarled, grabbing for her purse.

She tried to pull free. "Let go, you—"

Instantly two other shadowy figures came out of nowhere, and before she could react, the three had surrounded her, clutching and tearing at her clothes, pulling her by the arms, between them. She tried frantically to fight them off, until she staggered backward and hit the wall. Head throbbing, she sank to her knees, sure she was going to die. Then a sharp pain in her arm made her cry out. Her handbag had been ripped off her arm with a force that snapped its narrow strap. One of the men held the bag aloft with a triumphant shout—and as quickly as the assault had begun, it was over. The men ran shouting to the back of the room and disappeared through the curtain as Jessie sat on the floor, shaking with fear.

Then, realizing she was free, she scrambled to her feet and dashed for the outside—straight into the arms of another burly man.

"Whoa there, young lady. Where're you going?"

With sweet relief she saw that the man now holding her was a policeman. A second later the door behind her shut with a grinding thud, and its iron bolt shot closed.

"Officer!" Jessie cried. "Three men—in there—they stole my purse!"

"Not so fast. What were you doing in an opium den?"

Jessie stared at the scowling officer. "A what? I was only—"

"Surely the suppliers can't be sending young girls with the stuff now!"

"Officer, I was robbed! Can't you do something?"

"Ha! The city doesn't pay me enough to go in there. Those thugs are long gone by now, anyway. You were lucky to get out alive."

"But now I have no money to get home!"

"Don't worry, you're going to get a ride in a police wagon.

On the way, you're going to tell me exactly what you're doing here. And for your sake, I certainly hope you give me the truth."

Jessie sagged. She had told Wanda she expected no trouble. Now trouble had struck like lightning, and it was turning into a major storm.

Thirteen

CATHERINE WAS PLEASED that her guests had enjoyed the luncheon. But she was not pleased that Jessie had failed to put in an appearance as promised. How like her these days! She had excused the servants for their afternoon rest and was about to head upstairs herself when a knock sounded at the door. It was rare for the lady of the house to answer the door herself, but today she did—and almost fainted at the sight before her. There stood Jessie, looking like a grimy street urchin, and beside her, a burly policeman.

"Jessie! What in heaven's name—?"

"Afternoon, ma'am," the officer said. "Are you Mrs. Wainwright?" At Catherine's wide-eyed nod, he continued. "Can you identify this young lady for me? I found her outside an opium den in Chinatown and—"

"You found her *where?*" Catherine clutched at her throat. "Dear god!"

"She claims to have been attacked and robbed," the officer went on. "If that's true, it's a good thing I happened by. We don't normally police those disease-infested holes, you know."

Catherine had gone pale. "Is she under arrest, Officer?"

"Not exactly. I can release her into your custody this time, if I'm assured that she will be properly supervised in the future."

"You have my word. She'll never be seen in that dreadful place again."

"Thank you, ma'am. In that case, I'll say good day to you both." He shot a last disapproving look at Jessie, then headed back to his wagon.

Hanging her head, Jessie stepped inside. She had pleaded with the officer to drop her off at the corner, so her mother could be spared all this. *If she gets sick again,* Jessie thought, *it'll be all my fault.*

Catherine spoke in controlled calm. "Luckily for you, we're alone. Come into the parlor; you and I are going to have a serious talk."

Jessie knew it was confession time—but only up to a point. Perched on the edge of a chair, she gave her mother a sketchy version of her Chinatown search, making no mention of Hazel. "I'm sure Lee and Mei had some sort of problem. I wanted to help them if I could."

Sitting opposite her, Catherine sighed wearily. "God help us when your father hears about this. You know how dangerous Chinatown is."

"It's not that bad," Jessie declared. "I never had any problem until I stupidly wandered into that opium den. Anyway," she added heatedly, "it wasn't right for Papa to say Lee and Mei don't deserve to be looked for!"

"Temper, Jessie. You've disgraced yourself enough already. Here you are, almost fifteen and acting as if you're not old enough to be allowed out of the house. What's more, you lied to me. Spending the day with school friends, indeed! I trusted you, and look where it's gotten us!"

"I'm sorry, Mama. But can't this stay just between you and me?" Jessie waited tensely while her mother considered this.

"No, your father has a right to know about such a serious matter. Still, I wish we could somehow—"

But it was too late. The front door opened, then slammed shut, and heavy footsteps sounded across the foyer. There was her father, in the parlor doorway, glowering in barely controlled rage.

"How pleasant," he said in a biting tone, "to come home and find our neighbors gawking at a police wagon in front of our house. How delightful to have the officer tell me that my darling daughter was picked up in Chinatown, of all places!"

Jessie got to her feet. "Really, Papa, it's not what it sounds—"

"I do not wish to hear from you, Jessica," he barked. "You will go upstairs until you are summoned."

"And for heaven's sake, get out of those smelly, filthy clothes," her mother added. "We'll probably end up having to burn them."

Feeling two inches tall but holding her head high, Jessie walked past her outraged father and up the stairs.

AFTER A LONG BATH, she put on a fresh dress and sat at her desk, staring absently at Latin declensions and trying to ignore the appetizing aromas of Mrs. O'Reilly's cooking wafting up the stairs.

Suddenly Corey looked in. "Hey, Jess," he whispered. "I figure they'll send you upstairs without supper tonight." He tossed her a roll. "Fresh from the oven. Don't let Papa know, or I'm dead."

"Thanks. I won't say a word." Jessie eagerly bit into the roll.

"You really did it this time," he went on. "Mama's never been so upset, or Papa, either. They want you in the parlor right now."

Anxious to get through whatever was coming, she took another bite of the roll, laid the rest of it on her desk, and started downstairs. Before entering the parlor, she straightened her skirt and smoothed her hair. Then, feeling as if she were about to face a firing squad, she opened the door and went in.

Her mother sat on the sofa, twisting a handkerchief in her hands. Naturally she would let her husband do the talking. Standing in the middle of the room, Dr. Wainwright spoke in a tone of quiet deliberation.

"We have tried to be good parents to you, Jessica. We've given you far more freedom than most girls your age enjoy. Yet time and again you repay us with aggravation. And now, with deceit. The only solution I can see is to send you away to boarding school."

"You can't mean that!" Jessie cried in dismay.

"I most certainly can. Margaret has spoken to me about Miss Ida Kent's School for Girls in Sacramento, which—"

"But that's—"

"Do not interrupt." His tone hardened. "Miss Kent is said to be a strict disciplinarian, which is what we need to bring you into line, it seems."

Jessie turned desperate eyes to her mother. "Have you agreed to this?"

Catherine's hands fluttered in distress. "The idea grieves me terribly. I had so hoped we could find a less extreme solution."

"It is solely out of regard for your mother's feelings," her father continued, "that I have decided to allow you one more chance. But you are going to change your ways. You will remain at home all day on Saturdays and Sundays. And if you exhibit further defiance of any kind, you will be packed off to Miss Kent's in the blink of an eye. Take this as fair warning, Jessica." With a withering look at her, he strode out of the room.

Eyes glistening, Catherine rose, came to Jessie, and said softly, "I understand your feelings about Mei and Lee. You have a kind heart, and I love that in you. But what you did was foolish, and you must not do anything like it again. This truly is your last chance with him." Then she, too, went out.

Lost in despair, Jessie slumped into a chair and put her head in her hands. This was worse than trouble—it was disaster. Mei was there, she knew it. And Lee, too. But what else could she do? *I need help.* . . . Her thoughts led her to an inevitable conclusion. *I need to talk to Wanda.*

SATURDAY NIGHTS nearly always meant social engagements for Jessie's parents. That evening, they were invited to play bridge with Dr. and Mrs. Arnold. Corey would also be out, at a dance. Jessie would be home alone. That was nothing unusual, but this time her father was dubious. "Much as I'm tempted to, we cannot cancel on the Arnolds," Jessie heard him tell his wife in the foyer. "It would be unforgivably rude to ruin their evening."

"You laid down the law," Catherine said. "I believe she'll abide by it." Grumbling a reply Jessie could not hear, her father pulled on his coat and escorted his wife out the front door.

As soon as she heard her parents' carriage pull away, Jessie went to the foyer and eyed the telephone. She had rarely ever used it herself. When her father had it installed, he made it clear that it was there so that his patients could reach him if they had an urgent need, not for idle chatting. Now Jessie had an urgent need, so at eight thirty she telephoned, and again an hour later, without success. It was well after ten o'clock when she tried once more, and this time Wanda answered.

"Oh, Wanda, thank heavens you're finally home."

"Jessie, is that you? Are you all right?"

"I guess so. I mean, not really. I hope I'm not disturbing— is Mr. Nesbit there?"

"We went to a concert, but he's just left. What's happened?"

"A lot of things, all bad." It took a while for Jessie to tell the story of her venturing into Chinatown, and of that day's disaster.

"Chinatown—that's unbelievable!" Wanda exclaimed. "I can see why your parents are angry. What a crazy thing you did, Jessie."

"It would have been all right if I hadn't botched it. That's why I need . . . well, now I need you to help me in the search."

"*Me?* I can't find them. They're obviously gone for good, so you should just leave it at that. Unless there's something you're not telling me." A long silence followed. "Well? Is there?"

Leaning against the wall in the foyer, eyes closed, Jessie teetered on the brink of revealing the secret she had vowed to keep forever. Finally she pulled herself back. "No. There's nothing else."

"All right, then, forget all about this and get your mind back on your main goal. I'm afraid you've been losing sight of it. How have your grades been these past few weeks?"

"Pretty fair, I suppose."

"Pretty fair! That won't get you into medical school. Or have you given up that dream?"

"Of course I haven't." Jessie's voice was strong again. "And I'll put my mind on it again, I promise. Oh, I hear my father's carriage coming. I'd better say good night."

WHEN HER PARENTS came upstairs, Jessie was pretending to be asleep. Corey came in soon afterward, and she could hear movement in the house for a while longer. Then, gradually, the late-night stillness settled in.

But sleep was far from Jessie's whirling thoughts. An hour later she was still awake, huddled in the moonlight on her window seat, gazing out toward Chinatown. It seemed so far away now, and more mysterious than ever.

I've failed Lee and Mei, she thought sadly. She would never again think of Chinatown—even hear it mentioned—without feeling the pain of that. Yet Wanda's blunt words rang in her ears. And Henry's, too. If Lee and Mei had gone back to China, she would never see them again.

Moving cautiously in the dark, she went to her bed and pulled the blanket off, laid it along the crack under her door, then switched on her light. She brought out her jewelry box to look again at her mementos of Mei, the jade pendant and the heartbreaking farewell note. Alarm struck as she remembered Mei's second note. Rushing to her laundry hamper, she brought out her dirty skirt and thrust her hand into its pocket. To her deep relief, the note was still there. She unfolded it with care, laid it on her desk next to the first one, and studied them side by side.

They were different from each other—*much* too different. The printing in the first note was a large, childish scrawl, while in the second it was small and cramped. So often she had urged Mei to drop the *Miss,* and in the first note Mei finally had. But in the second, there it was again. The first note was full of mis-spelled words—that was typical of Mei. But the second note had none. And Mei never had known how to say *thank you* prop-erly—it was always *much thanks.* Just as in the first note, but not in today's.

Jessie was convinced—Mei had not written the second note. But now she had no way to go back and try to find out who had.

Slowly she folded the two notes, placed them in the jewelry box, and returned it to its hiding place. She turned out the light, retrieved the blanket, and crawled into bed. Tears soon dampened her pillow.

Lee and Mei were gone now, out of her reach. But that did not mean she would forget. To her, Lee would always be the dear old friend who had enchanted her with wonderful stories. And Mei would remain the innocent victim of a world she could never understand, trying so hard to be something she could never be. Jessie's memories of them, and her questions, would have to stay locked inside her heart.

From here on, the future would be everything.

Part Two

Fourteen

Saturday, March 17, 1906

My 17th birthday

Mama thinks I should rest because we'll be out late tonight. But I'm far too excited. It's going to be my first time going downtown to a real theater. She wanted to give me a big birthday party, but luckily I talked her out of that. Instead we're going with Mayor Schmitz and his family to see Mr. Oscar Wilde's play, <u>The Importance of Being Earnest</u>. Theatrical exhibitions are usually considered unhealthy for ladies, but Papa's making an exception.

I'll wear Mama's birthday gift to me, the most perfect spring hat. I've never had one like it—a glorious mix of silk flowers and birds' feathers. It even has pink roses on top. I love it! Much as I dislike fashionable dresses, I must say that lately I've become quite fond of beautiful hats.

I'll wear Corey's present, too—my lovely new charm bracelet. Hazel will envy me no end when she sees it. Papa thinks it's unsuitable for a girl to wear jewelry, but Mama can never resist buying me pretty baubles herself. She convinced him to make an exception for Corey's gift, just for tonight.

It was truly a surprise to see Corey today. He took the ferry home from the university for the occasion. I was so touched when he said that it's not every day his only little sister has a birthday. Those were his words, "only little sister." He never, ever mentions the little sister we lost, though I'm sure he thinks about her. He must have seen the look on my face when he said it. He started joking about the green birthday cake Mrs. O'Reilly made for me, with spun-sugar icing and candy shamrocks on top.

A bigger reason Corey's here, I think, is the young lady he telephoned this afternoon. To hear him tell it, he's got three or four pretty college girls after him all the time. I guess this one is free tonight, because he was supposed to go to the theater with us and now he's not. I don't know how much he studies, but he seems to do fine with the girls.

But most of all, I think he's here because of Papa's new motorcar.

When Papa came home last week with a brand-new, five-passenger Peerless, Mama was so upset. She sees autos as a threat to all living things. And the expense—he spent <u>four thousand dollars</u> on it! Mama almost passed out thinking of all the poor families such a sum would house and clothe. I guess Papa's finally facing what Corey's said for years—the city's most important people all have automobiles these days. And Papa does care about his reputation. His practice is so busy, he sometimes turns away patients. Maybe he feels he deserves a reward for his success. I only wish he'd chosen something less smelly and noisy. But he's as proud as a boy with a shiny new toy.

A sad thing happened this week—Miss Susan B. Anthony died. I read it in Papa's newspaper. "She envisioned a future holding grand possibilities for women," the article said. I only hope that turns out to come true.

AT THE SOUND of a soft knock on her door, Jessie hastily closed her journal and pulled down the rolltop of her desk. A grinning Corey stuck his head in with an unexpected proposition.

"Hey, Sis, it's gorgeous outside. Want to come with me for a spin in Papa's car? That is, if you've got the nerve."

"You know I do," Jessie retorted. "But he'd never let you drive it."

"On the contrary, he invited me to take it out. He's walked over to the clinic, and Mama's fallen fast asleep."

With a grin that matched her brother's, Jessie followed him downstairs. In a few minutes they were hurtling along Van Ness Avenue in a brisk wind. "She's got three forward speeds," Corey shouted, "and reverse. She'll do thirty miles an hour, easy. Papa sure did pick a beauty."

"It feels like we're flying," Jessie shouted back, one hand clutching at her hair as it whipped around her face. "I do see why you love it. Too bad there's no top, though."

Corey turned onto California Street, behind the cable car. "Let's see how a twenty-four-horsepower engine handles a really steep climb." The Peerless kept pace steadily up hill, hardly slowing until they neared the top. Then, as the cable car clanged its bell and sped down the other side, the car lurched to a halt.

Corey pulled over and climbed out. "Accelerator's quit. Something always breaks; that's the problem with these contraptions. Good thing Papa went out. He won't miss us, or the car."

"I thought you said he invited you to drive it!"

"That was to get you out here." Tossing her a wink, he thrust his head under the hood. "You need to know what motoring's like," his muffled voice continued. "And I was sure you aren't inclined to ride with him any more than Mama is."

Laughing, Jessie climbed out of the car. She loved the panoramic view from Nob Hill, and in the clear air, the city fairly sparkled. Her eyes swept from Rincon Hill, in the southeast, across downtown, past the Ferry Building, finally coming to rest on Chinatown.

It's still there, of course, she thought with a shiver. *And so is Mei. Even after all this time, she must be.* "I pray she's found happiness," she murmured.

"What's that you said?" Corey asked, still tinkering with the engine.

"Oh, nothing. Just thinking about an old friend."

"There's a lap robe in the back, if you're cold." Corey jiggled at a loose wire, shaking his head in exasperation. "Hey, while you wait, look over at the hills across the bay, behind the university."

Jessie turned back to the view, gazing out over the bay this time. "All I see is the Berkeley pier and a long road running through farms."

"Look closer—see the big *C* carved up there? It's for *California.* Sophomore class built it, along with some freshmen. Biggest project any class has ever done."

"But why do it at all?" Jessie asked. "It must've taken days."

"Weeks, actually. But it was a grand time, and I met some fine fellows, too. Good connections for when—well, I guess I can tell you. I've decided I'm going into business."

"*Business?* You're supposed to become a doctor!"

"That was Papa's idea, not mine. When I flunked biology last semester, even he could see that it was all over. Anyway, business is where the real opportunities are nowadays. The real money, too. Nope, medicine's out for me. Papa will just have to get used to it."

While she pondered this, Corey gave the car's crank two mighty turns and the Peerless was running again. They climbed into their seats and he turned the car around. As they plunged down the hill toward home, his blunt words echoed in Jessie's head. *Medicine's out for me.*

She watched her brother smile as he wrestled the car through the late-afternoon traffic of carriages and horses, motorcars and people. His infectious excitement, the light in his eyes, reminded Jessie of her father's expression the day he had first showed her and her mother the car. Then a surprising thought struck her—maybe her father had bought it so that he and Corey could share something new, now that the old dream was gone.

But what about her? Would he start noticing her honors in science and mathematics? She had been at the top of her class for three terms already, and her father had never said a word. Now, maybe. In time, perhaps he would even accept her plan to become a doctor.

AFTER THE PLAY and a stop at the Palace Hotel dining room for the latest novelty—ice-cream cones—Jessie got to bed around midnight. But she was too excited to sleep. Visions of actors floated before her eyes, speaking their witty lines. When finally she dozed off, still other faces drifted in and out of her mind . . . this time, the long-gone Amy and Hazel's new baby brother, Jonathan, and . . . someone else. The small, sad face of a young child floated in the misty scene. Boy or girl, she couldn't make out. But the eyes, two burning black beads, stared fixedly at her.

Wide-awake again, Jessie looked around, trembling, as if half expecting to see a ghost. She'd had this dream before, and each time it upset her more. *My little brother or sister would be walking and talking by now.* The words reverberated in her mind as if she had said them aloud. She lay back down and drew her blankets tight against the chill. But every time she closed her eyes, she saw the mysterious face again.

For two long years she had struggled to banish those old memories, and she thought she had mostly succeeded. But gradually she had realized that they could never be suppressed completely. Not of Mei, not of dear old Lee, and certainly not—she couldn't stop thinking it—of the child she felt sure Mei had. And she knew the torment wouldn't stop until she did something about it.

As she lay brooding, a sudden impulse made her rise, take out her jewelry box, lift the ring tray, and study the secret contents below—Mei's two notes and her jade pendant. She held up the pendant and let the green stone swing free. *My god,* she thought, *when Mei left this for me, she was about the same age as I am now.*

Moving to her mirror, she held the pendant up to her throat and stared, spellbound, at her reflection. After a moment she fastened the gold chain around her neck and dropped the stone beneath her nightgown collar, where it couldn't be seen. But even unseen, the image still held her enthralled.

The pendant had been the only valuable thing Mei owned, and the only thing she had from her mother. Lee once said that to the Chinese, jade was the most highly prized of all gemstones. Jessie couldn't stop asking herself, *Why did she give it to me?*

So many questions, so many memories. Why wouldn't they leave her in peace?

Fifteen

THREE WEEKS of wet weather passed before another sunny afternoon finally presented itself. It was the best kind of day for tennis, and Jessie eagerly raced to the court for her date with Hazel, only to find herself pacing outside the fence, waiting. Hazel had struck up a game with Ted, the boy she liked best in their class. He *was* the nicest, and the best-looking, Jessie had to admit. Besides, the last two times her afternoon plans with Hazel had fallen through, it had been her own fault. Because of her studies, to be exact. And Hazel hadn't been very happy about it.

You should send the same tough serve to Ted that you always send me, Jessie thought. But Hazel only tapped at the ball whenever boys were around, instead of hitting like the skillful player she really was.

Settling on a bench to watch, Jessie thought of how often these days she and Hazel wished they had more time to spend together. They could happily have devoted all their spare time to tennis alone. Hazel usually won their games, but winning wasn't the point for either of them. They had also started piecing a quilt. Watching Hazel expertly stitch together a great splash of gold in a blue field, called Sunburst, Jessie had become interested. On rainy afternoons, in Hazel's room they would lose all track of time, cutting small pieces and joining them with tiny stitches. Jessie designed a crazy quilt cut from scraps of velvet, a dazzling riot of color called Kaleidoscope.

But duties interfered all too often. Jessie was constantly called upon to attend her parents' social affairs. And Hazel was usually occupied with what she now called her "business," taking care of children all around her neighborhood for pay.

Racquet poised for a final shot, Hazel called to Jessie, "Almost done!" A few minutes later she ran over to where Jessie was waiting. "Isn't Ted divine? He's asked me to the dance this weekend."

"Oh, I'll be sorry to miss seeing you two lovebirds together," Jessie said, with a smile.

"You're not coming? Ted asked if my pretty friend might like to meet his cousin, who's visiting from San Jose. He meant you, Jessie."

"Sorry." Jessie shook her head. "I need the whole weekend to work on my anatomy report. It's due on Monday, and I want it to be a prizewinner."

"*You're* the prizewinner. A prizewinning bookworm! This is the biggest party of the year!"

"I'll let you enjoy it for both of us," Jessie replied. "And then tell me all about it."

WHEN SHE ARRIVED at school on Monday, everyone was talking about the party. "Ted's cousin was dreamy," Hazel said. "You really missed out."

"Maybe I'll meet him some other time," Jessie said absently. All she could think of was her anatomy paper and her hope that when the class met on Friday their teacher would show some appreciation of her work.

What happened on Friday left her feeling more embarrassed than pleased.

"Miss Wainwright's work describing the major organs is of the highest scientific excellence, and merits honors," the teacher told the class. "However——" His face reddened. "I must say I was startled by the very *explicit* drawings of——how shall I put it?—male and female anatomical features." The class dissolved into giggles and whispers. "One does not expect such details from a student," he added. "Especially a young lady."

Suddenly all the talk in school was about "Jessie's dirty pictures." Pleased as she was for Jessie that she had earned a high mark, Hazel got through the day only by sheer determination. "Those pictures *were* awful," she groaned as they walked home.

"I'm *so* sorry. But how could I discuss anatomy without illustrating what I was talking about?"

"Perhaps by finding a way that didn't make both of us laughingstocks? I just know Ted thinks I'm perfectly bizarre now, because I spend so much time with you."

"Oh, now you shouldn't be my friend because the school is full of clowns who snicker at every little thing?"

"I didn't say that. But it was you who *made* them snicker," Hazel shot back. "What's wrong with writing about horses, or dogs, or something? They have anatomies, too." At the hurt look on Jessie's face, Hazel softened. "I tell you what, you can make up for it. For once I have my whole Saturday free. Think up something new, something fun, for us to do tomorrow. Anything you want, as long as it doesn't involve books or school."

"Let me see . . ." Jessie grew thoughtful.

"Where did you get that stuff, anyway?" Hazel went on. "I know, your father's medical books. He'd never get over it if he— What's wrong?"

Jessie had abruptly stopped walking. She stood gazing off across the street, where a classmate was leading a small child by the hand.

"Jessie? Have you heard a word I've said?"

"I heard you," Jessie murmured. But she also heard a phantom whisper inside her head. *This is the chance you've been waiting for. Take it.*

She turned a bright smile on Hazel. "All right. I have an idea."

"Good. Let's hear it."

"You'll think I'm nuts."

"Oh, I already know you are. Come on, let's hear it."

Hazel might have thought she was ready for anything. But her mouth dropped open in astonishment when Jessie blurted it out.

"Let's go to Chinatown."

Hazel stared. "I said something *fun*. And you come up with *that*?"

"You enjoyed it last time, remember?"

"I remember a lot of dirty looks, horrible smells, and sore feet. Then you getting robbed, and your father practically putting you in jail."

Jessie waved this aside. "I'd never make that mistake twice. And you know we had fun. Remember Henry Wong? Wouldn't it be nice to see him again? I'll even treat you to tea and cakes at the Heavenly Harmony Tea Room."

Hazel's eyes narrowed. "This is about those servants, isn't it? We got nowhere looking for them before, and now it's two years later. Is it really worth—" Seeing Jessie's annoyed look, she stopped short.

"Never mind," Jessie said. "Forget I ever mentioned it." They had reached Hazel's corner, where they paused. "You're right, though, I do mean to start looking again. Tomorrow, instead of mathematics study group, I'm going to Chinatown."

THE NEXT MORNING, she bundled up her books, told her mother she was going to study group, and left the house. It was a fine April day, crisp and sunny. Not a good day to attend a study group, anyway, Jessie thought. After rounding the nearest corner, she circled around to the rear garden and deposited her book bag in the carriage-house wood box. Then, as hurriedly as a young lady could without attracting attention, she headed for the cable-car stop. A car was just leaving, but no matter, another would be along soon.

As the cable car pulled away, Jessie noticed a lone figure still standing at the stop. *Why did that person stay behind?* she wondered. As she drew nearer she was startled to see that it was Hazel.

"Don't look so shocked," Hazel remarked as Jessie came up to her. "I could see you were set on doing this. You didn't *really* think I'd let you go back to that terrible place alone?"

Jessie beamed as she threw her arms around her friend.

The next cable car soon clanged to a stop and they climbed aboard. As soon as they were under way, Jessie drew the chain with Mei's jade pendant out from beneath her collar and showed it to Hazel, who went wide-eyed.

"That's beautiful, Jessie! Where'd you get it?"

Jessie quickly told her its story. "Jade has great significance in Chinese culture," she said. "I'm pretty sure there was a gem-cutter's shop at the entrance to Chinatown, and if I'm right, we're going to find out more about it." Carefully she fastened the chain around her neck again.

A STRANGE SENSE of déjà vu came over Jessie as she and Hazel joined the teeming flow of people on Dupont Street. The memory of her nightmarish adventure in an opium den rushed back, and she gripped her handbag extra tightly. Luckily the gem-cutter's shop was right where she remembered it. The elderly proprietor promptly greeted them with a smile.

"Help you, ladies?"

"We won't take much of your time, sir," Jessie said. "I'd like to ask your opinion of this, if you please."

He gave the pendant a long, careful examination. "This much valuable," he said finally. "Chinese tradition say fine jade keep child safe from harm."

Jessie's mouth dropped open. She had never imagined that jade's importance might be directly connected to a child— Mei's child.

He held the pendant up to the light. "You like to sell, maybe?"

"Oh, no thank you. You've told me what I needed to know."

She acknowledged a slight bow from the old gentleman with one of her own, and a moment later she and Hazel were back out on the street, the chain once again around Jessie's neck, the pendant tucked safely beneath her collar.

"Next stop, the Heavenly Harmony," Jessie said, taking Hazel's arm and guiding her in that direction. "I sure hope Henry's there today."

On the way, a new thought burned in her mind. *Jade keep child safe from harm,* the gem-cutter had said. Mei must have known that. And now, if she had a child, she'd want that child to have the pendant.

It's up to me to find a way of getting it back to her.

Sixteen

IT WAS A JOLT when they arrived at the spot where Jessie remembered the tea room to have been. Instead they found a Chinese laundry.

"That's funny," Jessie said, frowning. "I'm sure this was the place."

As they entered, a stooped, gray-haired woman gazed blankly at them from behind the counter. "Excuse me," Jessie began, "do you know Mr. and Mrs. Wong? They ran a tea room here, called the Heavenly Harmony—"

"This not tea room," the woman said. "This laundry."

"I know, but it used to be a tea room, run by the Wong family."

The woman shook her head. "My name Chen. This laundry, no tea. Honest business, not want trouble."

Beaded curtains at the rear of the shop parted and a middle-aged man regarded Jessie warily. "Wongs close tea room, leave Chinatown. Go away, nobody know where. Gone."

Gone. The word had a mournful sound. "I see. Well, thank you."

As soon as they were outside again, Jessie's spirits sagged. "What rotten luck! Henry was our only friend in Chinatown."

"What do we do now?" Hazel asked.

"The only thing we can do. Start walking."

For a while it was like old times—Jessie asking shopkeep- ers about Lee and Mei and getting the usual nonanswers; Hazel examining the merchants' exotic wares. But as lunchtime neared, Jessie could tell that Hazel's interest was flagging. Fi- nally Hazel admitted it. "I'm no help, Jessie. I wouldn't know Mei if I saw her, and I doubt that I'd recognize Lee."

"But I love having you with me. Which reminds me, I prom- ised you tea and cakes. I saw another tea room back there, the Silver Moon."

"Fine. Let's try it. I'm ready for a rest."

In a few minutes they were seated next to a window at the Silver Moon, sipping tea and munching cakes. "These are very good," Hazel remarked.

"Not as good as the Heavenly Harmony's," Jessie said, glumly picking at her food. Losing track of Henry Wong, whose help she had heavily counted on, had her feeling so down she couldn't even try to look cheerful.

Hazel sensed Jessie's distress. "When we came here before, you were hoping for a miracle," she said. "This time we're both old enough to know better. And look—the fog's rolling in. You promised we could go home when I was ready, and I'm ready now."

It was true. The day had begun brightly, but now the sun had vanished behind a curtain of gray as dark as Jessie's mood.

The waiter brought their bill, and Jessie was counting out coins for payment when she heard Hazel gasp.

"Jessie!" Hazel was staring out the window. "I may be dreaming, but I think I just saw Lee."

Jessie spun around to look. "*What?* Where?"

"Just turning the corner, over there, across the street. It couldn't have been, though. This man had a little girl with him, and—"

That was as far as Hazel got. Jessie jumped up with a force that knocked over her chair, then flew out the door.

In seconds she was across the street and around the corner. There, fifty feet ahead, walked an elderly Chinese man leading a toddler by the hand. Could it be Lee? Or just someone who resembled him from behind?

Jessie cupped her hands and called, "Lee!" The man stopped and looked back. It was Lee. The little girl looked back, too. She had a doll-like face and distinctive copper-colored hair.

"Lee—it's me, Jessie!" Wild with excitement, she ran toward him—then stopped, stunned. Lee had snatched up the child and, with a terrified look, had darted into an alley. "Wait, Lee!" she screamed, and ran after him, reaching the spot where he had been standing, only to glimpse him disappearing around the next corner, the child dangling under his arm like a rag doll. Frantic, she raced on, turning into a narrow side street. Among its scattering of pedestrians, Lee was nowhere to be seen.

Unable to think straight, Jessie ran on, checking every doorway and passage, calling Lee's name. As if in a nightmare, she raced, bumping into people, almost knocking over street vendors, ignoring people's shocked looks, until finally she stumbled, slipped in a mud puddle, and went down.

When Hazel caught up with her, she was slumped against a wall, clutching a bruised knee, her skirt splattered with mud. Several Chinese people were offering to help, but they gave way when Hazel ran up and knelt beside her.

"Jessie, are you hurt? Come, there's a bench over here." Taking Jessie's arm, Hazel helped her up. Once they were seated, Hazel began to scold. "Honestly, have you gone berserk?" Then she saw the tears in Jessie's eyes. "Oh no, you *are* hurt." She fished in her purse for a handkerchief and handed it to Jessie. "What happened? Was that really Lee?"

Jessie nodded, barely able to speak. "It was Lee. He saw me, and he recognized me, I know he did. But he . . . he ran away."

"Why would he do that? And who's the little girl? Mei's daughter, maybe? She didn't look older than two or so. But wait a minute." Hazel frowned, calculating. "Back then, Mei was still living at your house. She wasn't married, was she?"

Jessie sat mute. Even in her misery she was aware that Hazel's thoughts were leading her into a danger zone.

"Do you suppose she got herself in trouble somehow?" Hazel went on. "That must be——" A look of horror came over her face. "Oh no! Not Corey—please don't tell me it was Corey!"

Now Jessie was trapped. Hazel had gotten within one step of the truth, only to go astray at the end. Jessie would have to let stand an unjust accusation against Corey, or reveal the secret she had vowed to keep forever.

She could see no choice. "It wasn't Corey, Hazel. The little girl is not my niece. She's——" Jessie shut her eyes and forced herself to say it. "She's my sister."

"You mean . . ." Hazel stared, thunderstruck. "It was . . . your *father*? My god! Why didn't you ever tell me?"

"I never meant anyone to find out, and I'm sorry that you did."

"Well, now I have. And now I see why you've been so set on finding Lee and Mei. But don't worry, I won't breathe a word to a living soul. Let's get home, and you can tell me all about it on the way. And I do mean *all*."

With Hazel's help, Jessie got unsteadily to her feet, took a step or two, then stopped, wincing. "My knee's already getting stiff. I'll have to ice it when we get home."

"It's pretty far to the cable-car stop, and a long walk back to your house. You'd better lean on me." They started off, Jessie leaning on Hazel's arm. "In fact, I think you'd better lean on me a lot from now on."

"You mean that?"

"Look, I still think this is a wild-goose chase. But, knowing you, I'm sure you'll keep it up forever, if you have to, so I might as well make up my mind to help."

"Thanks," Jessie murmured, squeezing Hazel's arm.

As they hobbled toward the cable-car stop, Jessie's mood began to brighten. It was really true—she had a little sister. That was the child Mei meant when she wrote "the good person"—except that she always mixed up *good* and *right*. *I'm not going to let this little sister disappear,* she promised herself. *Somehow, we're going to be together.*

Instead of hobbling, she suddenly felt as if she were floating.

BY THE TIME they reached the Van Ness stop on their return trip, Jessie had told Hazel the whole story in a whisper.

"Are you really sure about all this?" Hazel asked. "I mean, how well did you see the little girl?"

"Well enough. She was about the right age, and she had reddish hair."

"And you're absolutely certain the man was Lee?"

"Definitely. I've known him all my life. And I told you, he recognized me, too. Then he acts as if *I'm* to blame for Mei's troubles." Jessie was growing agitated. "I should just go to my father and tell him. After all, Mei's child is his child, too, and he has a moral obligation—"

"To do what? Not bring her into your family, Jessie. Whites and Chinese don't mix, you know that. It's just not done. And think what would happen if this ever got out. It would ruin your father's reputation."

"And devastate my mother. Besides, I'd be accusing Papa of something terrible with no real proof. He'd send me off to boarding school for sure, maybe worse. You're right, I'll have to keep quiet."

"Well, I'd better get on home," Hazel said as they reached the corner where they would go their separate ways. "But we need to talk more about this. In the meantime, promise me you won't do anything rash."

"I'll try not to. And thanks, Hazel. Thanks for coming with me today."

USING THE SERVANTS' ENTRANCE, Jessie managed to sneak into the house and slip her muddy skirt into the laundry unnoticed. It would come back showing no sign of her "unladylike" behavior. Soon she was upstairs, curled up on her window seat.

Learning to live with her new knowledge was going to be hard. Merely to suspect that the child existed had been one thing. Knowing for certain felt very different. A new resolve, even hope, rose within her. As soon as she could, and every chance she got, she would go back to where she'd seen Lee and the little girl. At last, she was sure they were really there. They couldn't elude her forever. And next time, Mei might be with them.

Now the question was, how soon would she get another chance? She had a week of exams coming up, and the following Saturday had long ago been promised to Hazel to help with the twins' birthday party. But her Wednesday mornings were free for study hall, and surely the monitor wouldn't mind if the best student in the senior class missed a session now and then.

Her decision was made. Wednesday after next, bright and early, she would head back to Chinatown—alone.

Seventeen

ON THE APPOINTED DAY Jessie awoke before dawn, as the milk wagon rattled its way up the street. Later, around six, Mrs. O'Reilly would come walking up the sidewalk, her arms loaded with fresh produce from the market. The Donegans would arrive at seven, and Hilda would come upstairs to light a fire in Jessie's room and tell her it was time to get up. Ordinarily Jessie would sleep until then. But not this morning. Whether from nerves or just plain excitement, she couldn't tell, but at the first sounds from the street, she was wide-awake, considering her plan.

With Corey away at college, the family rarely ate breakfast together anymore. Her mother often stayed in bed until after nine, while most mornings her father had already left the house long before that. But this morning, when Hilda came up to her room, she would find the bed empty and a note from Jessie saying she'd left early to meet Hazel before school to help her with quadratic equations. By that time, if all went well, Jessie would be in Chinatown. The cable cars started running at five, and she meant to catch an early one.

She swung her feet to the cold floor and tiptoed to peer out her window. Stars glittered overhead—perfect. That meant no fog, so she wouldn't freeze waiting for the cable car. Switching on the light, she glanced at her mantelpiece clock. It showed three minutes past five. Now, to get the note written, then throw on her warm clothes, slip down the back stairs, and vanish into the predawn darkness.

She sat down at her desk and was about to start the note when she heard the sound of running water in the bathroom. That presented a complication. This must be one of those days when her father made early rounds at the hospital—a possibility she had forgotten. Better lay low for a bit, until he had gone downstairs, had his quick cup of strong coffee, and left the house. Meanwhile she could go ahead and get dressed, then take her time about writing the note.

She finished dressing and had just reached for her hairbrush when she became dimly aware of a strange rumbling—curiously, not so much a sound as a movement. She raised her hand, and at that instant the house shook as if in the clutches of an angry giant. Her heart racing, she scrambled back toward her bed just as the floor started heaving from side to side. Then her feet flew out from under her and she went down, hitting her head on the bed frame. Paralyzed with fear, she felt the rumbling and shaking grow more violent. Beams creaked and groaned as the house rocked in the giant's grip. Great sections of plaster fell around her, and her washstand and basin toppled over, shattered fragments flying. Her massive armoire slid several feet and almost overturned.

Then came a lull, but only a brief one followed by another tremendous shock, even stronger than the first. Still lying where she had fallen, Jessie stared at the light fixture swinging crazily above her head. Her mantelpiece clock sailed past, narrowly missing her. She rolled once and grabbed the sturdy leg of her bed, afraid to try to get up, fighting against panic and desperately wondering, *How long can this go on?*

It seemed like an eternity before it finally ended. Holding on to the bedpost, Jessie pulled herself up and stood, unsteadily, listening. She had felt earthquakes before—the kind that rattled windows and broke an occasional dish. Her father had told her once about the frightful one that had struck the city when he was a boy, splitting streets open and knocking down walls. This one, she was sure, was much worse.

From her parents' bedroom, she could hear her mother's sobbing. It was the only sound in an almost eerie, sudden quiet. She was still standing there when her father pushed her door halfway open and appeared in the gloom. A cut on his cheek had made a bloodstain on his starched white collar.

"Jessie, are you all right?"

"Yes, but you're hurt, Papa. Let me get you a bandage."

"No time for that, I have to get to the clinic. I was shaving when it hit. Just lucky I didn't have the razor to my throat."

"Is Mama all right?"

"She's not hurt, just in a panic. I've told her to get dressed and be ready to leave the house if necessary, but she won't budge. I hate to do it, but there'll be people badly hurt in this thing, and I really have to go." He hurried back to his bedroom, and she heard him speak gently to Catherine. Then he headed downstairs. Jessie had often heard Wanda say, "Doc's at his best in an emergency." He would surely need to be now.

She tried to turn on her light again, but now it was dead. Groping her way past fallen objects, she went out into the hallway. Down in the foyer, her father had discovered that the telephone was still working.

"How soon can you come?" she heard him ask in an urgent tone. Then, "Thanks, Wanda. Try to reach Grace, too, will you? We'll need all the help we can get. Yes, we're fine. Kate's quite upset, but Jessie will look after her." He hung up and pulled on his coat.

So Wanda was all right. Jessie sighed with relief. And her father was lucky to have her, as well as Grace Edgerton, a part-time nurse he sometimes used. They, too, would be at their best at a time like this, Jessie knew. She yearned to go with her father to the clinic, to work alongside the professionals—to be at *her* best.

"I'll come and help, too, Papa," she called down to him as he worked to get the front door open. "I can be useful, I know I can."

"I'm leaving you in charge here," he said over his shoulder. "Take good care of your mother."

Just as he got the door open, the house was seized in a fresh outburst of severe shaking. Jessie crouched on the landing, clinging to the railing while the stained-glass skylight fell in splinters onto the foyer.

Out of the silence when the tremor stopped came her mother's terrified cry: "Jessie!"

"Coming, Mama!" she answered. Down below, her father hesitated in the doorway as if torn between his duties at home and those at his clinic.

"Go, Papa," she said to him. "I'll take care of things here."

He nodded, and she thought she saw a look of gratitude on his face as he turned to leave.

Now she hurried to her mother's side. Catherine lay clutching her pillow, her ashen face framed by her long brown hair. "God's punishing us for our city's excesses, Jessie. It's the end of us, I know it."

Jessie sat on the side of the bed and tried to speak soothingly. "It's not, Mama. We'll get through this." How true that might be, she had no idea, but the important thing was to sound reassuring. Even if she couldn't help care for the injured people who would come to her father's clinic, she could still be at her best—here at home. He was leaving her in charge, he'd said. That was important, too.

She sat holding her mother's hand until the light of dawn began to bring shapes into focus. Her parents' big bed was the only piece of furniture still sitting where it belonged. Her mother's dressing table had jumped across the room, with shards from its broken mirror strewn at crazy angles all around it. Drawers had been wrenched from the dressers, their contents spilled. The enormous armoire had fallen forward and lay flat on the floor.

"Maybe I should take a look downstairs," Jessie said, rising. "Keep calm, and I'll be right back." She picked her way toward the door.

The first thing she saw was a long, jagged crack splitting the wall above the stairs. Down in the foyer, the great mirror on the wall was reduced to splinters. Several large paintings had fallen, leaving deep gouges in the clear-heart redwood paneling her father loved so. Lightly she touched the portrait of Great-great-grandmother Jane, its heavy gold frame split into two jagged pieces. She moved cautiously into the parlor, where she stopped and looked around, amazed. Almost everything not fastened down lay smashed on the floor. Her mother's collection of Wedgwood figurines, all shattered. And the potted ferns had spilled dirt all over the rug. In her father's study, his massive oak desk had slid into the corner. Books and papers littered the floor. Going back into the foyer, she noticed one fragile thing that had come through unscathed—the ancient grandfather clock. It stood a foot away from its place against the wall, but its slumber was undisturbed. Other clocks had stopped with their hands stuck on times ranging from five twelve to five twenty. But the grandfather clock had been stuck on one forty-two for over a year, since Lee was no longer there to—

Jessie gasped, her hand flying to her cheek. Chinatown! What had happened there? That makeshift jumble of buildings was about as sturdy as cardboard. She tried to force her mind away from that horrifying thought. For that matter, the whole city could be in ruins. She knew Wanda was not hurt, but what about Hazel? What about Corey, in Berkeley? Mrs. O'Reilly, and the Donegans? She wanted to rush out of the house, sprout wings, and fly everywhere to make sure everybody she cared about was all right.

At least we've got the telephone, she thought. She was trying to coax some sound out of it when her mother called to her from the upstairs landing. She was sitting on the top step, clutching a bleeding foot.

"There's so much broken glass," Catherine groaned. "But never mind, keep telephoning. Try to reach Corey, I'm terribly worried about him."

"We can't, the line's dead." Jessie hung up and hurried to

her mother's side. "Let's see that foot." A quick examination revealed a long sliver of glass stuck in the broken skin. "That has to come out. Wait right here."

Making her way to the bathroom, she stepped over the spilled contents of the medicine cabinet to find the small bottle of alcohol that, luckily, had survived its fall. Her father kept tweezers, gauze, and adhesive tape in the drawer, she knew. In a few minutes, she had swabbed her mother's wound, extracted the glass, and bandaged the foot. "There, I think that'll do."

"Why, that's every bit as neat as your father would have done." Her mother looked at Jessie with new admiration. "Thank you, dear."

"Thank *you,* Mama." Jessie glowed at the compliment. At least she'd been able to help care for one injured person on this terrible day. That counted for something.

They sat together at the top of the stairs for several long minutes, trying to collect themselves. Jessie was sure her mother's foot must be throbbing with pain, but Catherine seemed not to notice, nor care.

At last her mother spoke, her voice weak and mournful. "Mrs. O'Reilly's dead, I'm sure of it. We'll never see her again. The Donegans, either."

"Don't, Mama," Jessie said gently. "Morbid thoughts won't do any good. I'm sure they're all scared stiff, but they'll come when they can." But she could see that her mother was not to be comforted.

Catherine gazed bleakly at all the chaos around them. Her hand was cold as she reached for Jessie's, and she heaved a despairing sigh. "Oh, Jessie, what are we going to do?"

For a moment Jessie, too, felt tempted to give way to despair. Then she remembered—she was in charge. That meant giving a practical answer to her mother's seemingly hopeless question. "For now, we can start cleaning up."

She went down to the kitchen, where she had to step over broken dishes and glassware. In the pantry she looked past overturned crocks of pickles, rice, flour, sugar, and honey, their spilled contents turning the floor into a pungent mess.

There, in the pantry corner, she found Mrs. O'Reilly's mops and brooms. She hauled them out and got to work.

Eighteen

CATHERINE FINALLY JOINED Jessie in the cleanup. It was an overwhelming job, and neither of them was experienced in the art of housekeeping. But they worked doggedly, interrupted only by another great aftershock at quarter past eight that sent more glassware crashing to the floor. By noon Catherine was ready to drop from exhaustion.

Jessie, too, was becoming weary. "I think we've done all we can on our own," she declared. "Do you mind if I go see what's happening outside?"

Catherine nodded her agreement. "I must rest for a while," she said, settling down on the parlor chaise. "Don't be long, now. And be careful."

Her father had found the front door stuck, and now Jessie had to give it a mighty pull to free it from its bent frame. Once outside, she couldn't shut it properly. *That's something else Lee would fix in a jiffy,* she thought with a pang of sadness. She did the best she could to close it securely, then went out the front gate, off its hinges now. She gazed in wonder at the destruction wrought by the awesome power of the quake. Gaps had opened in the street, wide enough to stop traffic, except that there was none to stop. No horses, no carriages, no automobiles clattered by. The cable cars over on Van Ness were silent.

She turned to look at her own house. Except for one toppled chimney in the rear, their property appeared amazingly undamaged. But at their nearest neighbor's, all the chimneys had fallen into piles of bricks, and the front door swung drunkenly into a darkened entryway.

She stood on the sidewalk, considering which way to go. Finally, anxiety pulled her toward Hazel's house. Hours had passed since the biggest shocks, and she still had no idea what had become of the Schellings. But after a few steps, an overpowering curiosity, a longing, came over her, making her stop short.

Visions of what must be going on at her father's clinic whirled in her head. At the very least, her father, Wanda, and Grace faced dozens of upset people with cuts, bruises, or far worse injuries. What if the clinic itself had been damaged and its precious supplies scattered all over the floor? Jessie shuddered to think of Wanda crawling around on the floor trying to salvage things while patients were demanding her attention.

I told Papa I wanted to help, she thought. *And the fact is, he never exactly said I couldn't.* He had left her in charge, and she had taken care of things so that her mother could rest. Her decision was made. She turned around and headed for the Wainwright Medical Clinic.

PUSHING HER WAY through the crowd with polite *excuse me*s, Jessie found Wanda in the waiting room, frantically trying to identify patients and their injuries.

"Tell me what I can do." Jessie had to speak almost directly into Wanda's ear in order to be heard.

Wanda blinked in surprise. "Goodness, how did you get here? If Doc comes out and sees you, he'll—"

"Let's just hope he's too busy to care. I know how things work around here, and I figured you could use another pair of hands."

"I can, indeed." Wanda handed Jessie her clipboard and pen. "Keep listing these people, would you? See which ones seem the worst off and pull them to the front. I'll go look for more gauze pads and tape in that mess of a storeroom. Doc and Grace are putting fifteen stitches in a man right now, and there are two more waiting, just as bad."

Jessie set to work, gently questioning each person in line and making them as comfortable as she could in the packed room. She had filled two sheets of paper with names and was searching in the desk for a third when she heard a commotion at the front door. A boy about her own age burst into the waiting room, carrying a small, screaming child.

"What's wrong?" Jessie dropped her list and ran to the boy's side.

"I'm George Dawson, and this here's my little brother." He gasped for breath. "Somethin's broke in him. We don't know what exactly, but a shelf fell on him in the shaking and he won't stop crying."

"Can he stand up?" Jessie asked. The older boy nodded, gingerly setting his brother down on his feet. He stood steadily enough, but his right arm stuck out crazily.

"Wait one minute." Jessie called to Wanda in the storeroom. "Wanda, can you call my father?"

"We can't interrupt him in the middle of a procedure." Wanda's voice was muffled. "Why?"

Before Jessie could reply, the little boy fell in a dead faint at his older brother's feet. She stared at him in shock. Then, as if instinctively, she realized that while he was unconscious, the time was right to help him. With both hands she took hold of his upper arm and gave a quick pull, a slight twist, then a push. A dull popping sound told her the boy's arm was back in his shoulder socket.

Emerging from the storeroom just as Jessie laid the boy's arm down by his side, Wanda stood watching in amazement. The boy gave a low moan but remained unconscious while Jessie pressed a cool hand to his forehead.

"Criminy!" George exclaimed. "I wouldn't have thought you were old enough to be a nurse."

"Oh, I'm not a nurse. I'm—" Jessie fumbled for words. "I'm only an assistant."

"Well, you're sure good at it. You took care of my brother just fine. Thanks a lot."

"I'd better see if the real nurse is available." But a quick look around told her that Wanda had been stopped by an elderly woman with a bleeding gash on her head and was trying to calm and examine the woman at the same time. Wanda waved to Jessie across the waiting room but shook her head "no" when Jessie beckoned.

With his little brother conscious now, George had set him upright. They stood waiting expectantly. Jessie looked into the injured child's eyes and saw that they were clear and focused on her. In response to her questions, he correctly gave his name and address.

"Can I take him home now?" George asked.

Jessie thought for a moment. "You might as well," she said finally. "My father—the doctor, that is—wouldn't be able to see you for hours, anyway. But bring him back right away if the pain gets worse."

By the time the two boys made their way to the door and left, Wanda had returned to her desk and collapsed into her chair. "My goodness, did you just do what I think you did? I can't believe it."

"It was nothing," Jessie said. "We should get back to work now."

This put Wanda in a quandary. "Wait, Jessie. Without a doubt, you saved that boy from winding up with a deformed arm. But you're not qualified to touch a patient."

"I know, but he was in such pain, and I was the only one—"

"I know, and you did a splendid job, believe me. I'm only saying you'd better go before Doc hears about this, or we'll both be in serious trouble."

"Well, *I* certainly won't tell him," Jessie replied. But she let Wanda give her a hug and lead her to the door. "Oh, Wanda— I almost forgot to ask—did you hear from Mr. Nesbit this morning?"

"He telephoned me right after your father did, but the line went dead while we were talking. He was all right, but his apartment is heavily damaged. When I have time, I'll go over and see if—"

"Wanda, I need you," Dr. Wainwright called from his examining room.

Like lightning, Jessie was out the clinic door, pushing through the crowd of people waiting to enter. Halfway down the block, she stopped and gazed back at the miserable group. *Too bad I couldn't do more to help them,* she thought.

Drawing a deep breath, she turned in the direction of Hazel's house. There should be enough time to check on the Schellings before heading back home to her mother.

As SHE REACHED Franklin Street, she saw Hazel hurrying toward her. They fell into each other's arms, thankful that the other was safe.

"I tried to telephone you, but they say the service will be out for ages," Hazel said breathlessly. "Your parents are all right, and Mrs. O'Reilly?" Her face fell when Jessie could not report on the cook.

At the Schellings, Hazel said, there were several cracked windows. "And that big lamp in our parlor crashed into a million pieces. Ellie was thrown out of bed—scared her half to death. But we're all fine, and lots of people have it much worse. Walk down to the end of Franklin with me, you'll see."

Farther down the block, electrical lines had snapped and lay across the buckled sidewalk. They were shocked to see many more ruined chimneys—one of which had crushed a backyard carriage house and the two horses inside. And an expensive motorcar had been destroyed by a fallen tree.

They saw families sitting, dazed, in front of their houses, afraid to go back inside. One little boy cried pitifully for his lost puppy. "That boy is in the twins' class," said Hazel. "I should see if I can help him."

Jessie waited while Hazel approached the boy. Soon she was leading him by the hand as they walked around calling and searching. As they neared the side yard of his house, she paused and peered beneath some broken-down steps. "Try under there," she whispered. In an instant the delighted child was on all fours, peering at the frightened dog, who ran to him and licked his nose.

"That's a good deed for today." Jessie smiled as they went on their way.

"Yes, but only one," Hazel said ruefully. "Imagine how many scared and injured cats and dogs there are, just like that one."

Jessie nodded soberly. Then a new worry struck her. "Should we go see about the school?"

They did but found it deserted, with a scribbled sign tacked on the gate reading: CLOSED UNTIL FURTHER NOTICE. Hazel put on a woeful face. "Oh, how terrible! Think you can live without school for a while?"

It was no joke to Jessie, but she forced a smile. "I'll try."

As they turned away, the ground suddenly heaved, almost knocking them over. "More aftershocks!" Hazel cried. For a full minute they clung to each other, hardly daring to move. When they were certain things were still, they hurried on back to Jessie's house.

Looking into the parlor, Jessie was relieved to see that her mother had not stirred. "She must have slept right through that last one," she whispered. In the kitchen they found some bread and cheese and took it up to Jessie's room, where they pushed aside her fallen belongings and settled on the window seat.

"Seems I've got a cracked window, too," Jessie observed. But it was what she saw in the distance, through the window, that made her sit up and look twice. Above the hills to the east, a column of black smoke coiled upward, mushrooming as it rose. "Wait a minute—what's that?"

Hazel turned to look. "Looks like fire—and lots of it."

Jessie gasped in sudden horror. "Hazel! You know what's over there?" She scrambled to her feet. "Chinatown!" With the astonished Hazel frantically following, she raced out the door and down the stairs.

THIS TIME she left the front door wide open as she ran toward Van Ness Avenue, where a crowd had gathered to stare at the smoke cloud towering over Nob Hill. Jessie was across the broad street and two blocks farther up the hill beyond, when a policeman blocked her path.

"Hold on, Miss, where d'ya think you're going?"

Jessie was panting hard. "I've got friends in Chinatown, and—"

"Not anymore, you don't. Word is it's burned to the ground, every stick. Folks ran outta there like rats off a sinking ship. Them that didn't go up in smoke, that is."

"Oh my god!" Jessie went pale. "Have many died?"

"Don't know. Nobody knows how many were there to begin with. From the thousands that came out, though, I reckon most of 'em made it."

"Where will they go?"

The policeman shrugged. "Maybe their Chinese gods know that, no one else does. Looks like all of downtown might burn. So you just turn around and go back where you came from."

Hazel had caught up in time to hear these words. "He's right, Jessie. For now, there's nothing more to do." Once again, Hazel led her defeated friend away.

———

Dr. Wainwright returned home long after nightfall, from what he declared was his most grueling day ever. Slumping in his chair at the candlelit dining room table, he was almost too weary to eat the simple supper his wife and daughter had managed to prepare. "The injured were hanging out the door," he reported. "I'd have been lost without Wanda and Grace."

Jessie gave him a long look but said nothing. *Maybe someday, a long, long time from now, you'll know that I was there, too.*

He had brought encouraging word about Corey. "I heard there's only minor damage in the East Bay. I'm sure we'll hear from him soon."

Catherine breathed a sigh of relief. "Thank heavens!"

"But all the other news is bad," he went on. "The fires downtown are spreading fast. Too many overturned stoves, broken electrical lines and gas pipes. Water pressure's gone, which leaves our firemen helpless while whole neighborhoods burn. They're setting up refugee camps at Fort Mason, the Presidio, and in the parks on the western edge of town. And I heard they might even start dynamiting buildings to make a firebreak."

Catherine was frightened all over again. "Are we in danger, Leonard?"

"Oh, I'm sure not. The fire's far from here. I think our greatest danger is panic. There are ridiculous rumors flying. A patient told me he'd heard that Seattle fell into the ocean! We'll take every reasonable precaution, of course. But it's most important to stay alert and keep calm."

Jessie waited through dessert and coffee, hoping her father would mention Chinatown. As badly as she wanted to, she didn't dare ask.

HUDDLED IN HER WINDOW SEAT late that night, she cringed at the small shocks that kept coming, while marveling at the fantastic orange glow in the eastern sky that threw Nob Hill into sharp silhouette. *How can something so terrible be so beautiful?* she wondered.

Spread out on her desk was a map of the city, which she had found in her father's study. She had circled two military reservations—Fort Mason and the Presidio. The refugee camps in those locations, and others, would have to be searched. But even if she could get away, how could she cover them all? There was no knowing, but it had to be done soon.

And *soon* had to be no later than tomorrow.

Nineteen

JESSIE OPENED HER EYES to a dark, yellowish light, with billowing black smoke filling the sky and blocking the sun. She was appalled—the fires must be much worse. Dressing hurriedly, she went into the hall and found her mother just coming out of her room. Catherine's cut foot seemed not to bother her anymore, but plenty of other things did.

"Still no word from Corey, or the servants," she said anxiously. "And your father's gone back to the clinic. How we'll manage I have no idea."

"Sure'n you'll manage, the same way you always do, madam." Mrs. O'Reilly's voice rang out from the bottom of the stairs.

Jessie and her mother rushed to welcome her with glad cries.

"Bless you, Mrs. O'Reilly," Catherine exclaimed. "You came back!"

"Humph! It'd take more'n a shaker to keep me away for long. Can't have you two messin' about in my kitchen." A minute later, after making a quick inspection of *her* kitchen, she added, "I will say, you've done a passable job of cleanin' it up." She set to work getting breakfast. "We won't be seein' a coal wagon around here today. Good thing we've still got the old stove and a pile of wood to burn in it."

As she bustled about, she told of the chaos in her own neighborhood, south of Market Street. "Slid clear off its foundation, my boardin'house did. Spent last night outside, on a mattress dragged into the front yard. Not fittin' behavior for civilized folk. Everyone cookin' in the street, too. When they started diggin' privies in the back garden—pardon the mention of it—that was my limit."

"My goodness!" Catherine blushed.

"Well, they've got to put them *somewhere*," Jessie said matter-of-factly. "I hope they throw in plenty of lime to prevent disease."

"I'm sure I don't know about such as that," Mrs. O'Reilly said with a sniff, nodding toward a suitcase in a corner. "If it's all right with you, madam, I'd like to move in here for a while."

"Of course, you'll stay as long as you need to. You can use Mei's old room, if you like."

The cook frowned at this suggestion. "Thank you kindly, madam. But if it's all the same to you, my sittin' room will do nicely."

"What about the Donegans, Mrs. O'Reilly?" Jessie asked. "Don't they live near you?"

"It's headin' straight back to Ireland they are, fast as they can get a train and a boat to carry 'em. Shows a lack of gumption, if you ask me. Oh well, mustn't speak ill of them that isn't here to defend themselves."

This time Catherine took the sudden loss of her servants in stride. "No, I suppose we can't blame them, after all that's happened."

Before long Mrs. O'Reilly had toast, jam, and hot tea on the table. Then the three of them spent another hour cleaning up. As

Catherine and the cook sat at the kitchen table discussing how to ration their remaining supplies, it seemed to Jessie that this was the moment her mother finally realized that they had survived.

Catherine was too distracted to mind when Jessie said she wanted to go check on Hazel. "Give my best to her mother. I do hope they're all right. And don't be late coming home."

That was all Jessie needed to hear. In an instant, she had grabbed her coat and hat, and gone.

WORN DOWN from trying to calm her frightened sisters and brother, Hazel was in a dark mood. She cheered up a little at Jessie's news of Mrs. O'Reilly and reluctantly agreed to go with Jessie to Fort Mason. "Since it's not that far, all right. But we mustn't stay long."

Neither of them was prepared for what they saw at the hastily set up refugee camp. As they entered the grounds, they were surrounded by the sad evidence of uprooted lives. Tents had been pitched, and people had dragged tables and chairs from their ruined houses, but such meager furnishings were far from adequate. At a booth in one corner, Red Cross ladies ladled soup from a kettle to bedraggled refugees standing in a long line. Here and there children played, but mainly the camp was a picture of despair.

"We've been so lucky," Jessie whispered.

Steeling themselves, they threaded their way up and down rows of empty-eyed people clutching the few belongings that were now their only earthly possessions. About half of the refugees were Chinese, but to Jessie's question about the Chings, they got the familiar negative answers.

Suddenly Jessie stopped and stared. A young Chinese man, the driver of a Red Cross truck parked near a soup kitchen up ahead, was unloading stacks of blankets. She grabbed Hazel's arm. "That looks like Henry Wong over there!"

She walked up to the man, and it was Henry, but his glance contained no recognition. "Sorry, miss, I can't give out blankets. You'll have to ask the Red Cross ladies."

"I don't need one," she said. "Henry, it's me, Jessie. Remember?"

As he looked at her more closely, surprise came over his face. "Of course! I always wondered what became of you, but I never even knew your full name. Is your friend here, too?"

"She is, and this time we'll introduce ourselves properly. I'm Jessie Wainwright and . . ." She looked around for Hazel and pulled her forward. "Here's Hazel. Hazel Schelling, that is."

At the sight of Hazel, Henry positively beamed. "It's great to see you again, both of you," he said, pulling his hat off with a polite nod. "I'll just be a minute, and then we can talk." He accepted their offer to help, and in a few minutes the job was done. Henry conferred briefly with the Red Cross ladies, then rejoined Jessie and Hazel. "Now, let's see," he said, frowning in thought. "I remember you were looking for some people. What was the name?"

"Ching," Jessie said. "We finally saw Lee a couple of weeks ago, but we couldn't catch up with him. He had a little girl with him."

"And you think they're among the refugees. Where've you looked?"

"Just here, but no luck so far. We want to try the parks next."

"The Presidio camp's much bigger and has the most Chinese. That's my next stop, if you want to come along."

Jessie was ecstatic, but Hazel hung back. "We should get home, Jessie."

"But this could be my only chance to get there," Jessie pleaded. "The Presidio's much too far to walk."

"Well, if Henry's offering us a ride. I guess we could try."

They climbed into Henry's truck and were on their way. On the twenty-minute drive to the Presidio military base, he brought them up to date on himself. His parents had moved across the bay the year before, he told them. He now lived in nearby North Beach and worked in a print shop, hoping to save enough money to go to the university in the fall. He'd be one of only a handful of Chinese there, but that didn't bother him.

"When the quake hit, I knew Chinatown would go up in flames," he told them. "My father always said people shouldn't bottle themselves up in that place. I guess Mother Nature agreed with him—she's destroyed it." Wanting to help somehow, Henry had gone to the Red Cross. "They asked me to deliver supplies to the camps."

He grew solemn as they drove onto the vast Presidio military base. "Brace yourselves, ladies. Fort Mason's a picnic compared to this place."

They soon saw what he meant. Before them lay a broad field of human suffering. Army tents dotted the trampled ground, but here, too, there was clearly far less shelter available than there were people who needed it. And they needed it badly, for the camp was near the ocean and often swept by biting winds and thick fog. The refugees, among them many Chinese, sat huddled in forlorn groups, or wandered aimlessly. A few soldiers patrolled the camp to keep order, but they had little to do. An air of dull acceptance of their fate lay over the helpless victims.

Henry spoke in a hushed tone. "Most of these people escaped with only the clothes on their backs. Some don't even have that."

Nature's upheaval had made little distinction between rich and poor. Jessie noticed that among the refugees there were many for whom "the clothes on their backs" included fur coats and other expensive belongings. But in this frightful place, everyone was reduced to the same misery. Far more than at Fort Mason, she felt like an intruder.

Hazel echoed her thoughts. "It doesn't seem right for us to walk around staring at these people. Besides, we'd need days to search this huge place."

"Maybe you won't need to," Henry said. "Let's see if we can find Dr. Lundgren." He led them across the field, past piles of trash and the empty stares of somber, silent refugees, toward a large tent with a sign reading INFIRMARY. "The sign says 'U.S. Army Medical Corps,' but Alan Lundgren's the only doctor I've seen the few times I've been here. He seems to know the place inside out."

If Lee or Mei were there, surely the camp doctor would know where they might be. *But I mustn't hope for too much,* Jessie thought, as they stepped past smoldering cookstoves.

Halfway across the field, Henry pulled up short. "There he is." He headed toward a group of refugees. "Dr. Lundgren, got a minute?"

Jessie thought she and Hazel must look like half-wits, gaping at the young man who walked toward them. Slim and tanned, with green eyes and unruly blond hair, he wore a blue denim work shirt and jeans. This was a *doctor*? He looked more like a college student, and a handsome one at that. To Jessie the word *doctor* had always meant someone mature and dignified. Someone like her father.

Smiling, the young man shook Henry's hand. "If you keep calling me Dr. Lundgren, my friend, I'm going to have to start calling you Mr. Wong."

Henry laughed. "Dr. Lundgren—Alan, that is—I'd like you to meet Jessie Wainwright and Hazel Schelling."

His friendly smile still in place, the young doctor shook Jessie's hand, then Hazel's. "If you've come for the charity ladies' tour, I'm afraid they passed through an hour ago. There'll be another one tomorrow morning."

Before Jessie could correct this impression, Henry explained her purpose. "Jessie's looking for some Chinese people who used to work in her home. They may have ended up here, so I thought you might be able to help."

The doctor's reply made Jessie's heart sink. "Sorry, but we don't even know the names of most of the Chinese people here. Very few of them speak English." A nurse came up wanting to speak to him. "Please excuse me," he said, and started to turn away.

"If I could just tell you about them," Jessie blurted, surprising herself at her boldness as she tugged at his sleeve. After describing Lee, Mei, and the little girl, she waited in suspense while he thought it over.

"There *is* an old man in the infirmary," he said finally. "Seems he was run over by a horse and wagon in the stampede out of Chinatown. He's out of his head most of the time, muttering in Chinese. But he had a little girl with him. I know, I had to pull the poor thing out of his arms."

Jessie swallowed hard, going weak in the knees. "Was she hurt?"

"Didn't seem to be. Not physically, anyway. But she's in deep shock. She's over in the orphanage tent with the other unclaimed children."

Unclaimed children. Jessie blanched at the expression. "Please, Dr. Lundgren, may I see them?"

"Sure. Give me a minute, and I'll be glad to take you there." After stepping aside to speak to the waiting nurse, he gestured to the visitors and led them toward the infirmary tent.

As they walked, Jessie felt herself being stared at by the refugees. *Don't worry about that now,* she told herself, thinking she should be terribly excited to have this chance.

But all she could feel was a bewildering mixture of anticipation and chilling dread.

Twenty

IT SEEMED TO JESSIE that the tent was large enough to hold a three-ring circus. Now it served as a grim field hospital. The injured lay like wounded soldiers on long rows of army cots. A few nurses, with several Red Cross ladies assisting them, were busily in attendance. Moans came from some of the more seriously injured, and the air was heavy with a dank, musty smell. Partly medicinal, partly—what? *The smell of death?* Jessie wondered. It was too much for Hazel. She went pale and whispered that she would wait outside, and Henry was glad to keep her company.

"The old man is over here." Dr. Lundgren led Jessie to a far corner. "We think he's got broken ribs, and maybe internal injuries. With no examining equipment, we can't really tell." He pointed to a narrow cot, then turned away when another nurse came up to him.

Hardly daring to breathe, Jessie moved closer and stared down at the shrunken form lying there. Then she recoiled in horror. At first she hadn't recognized him, but now she knew— it was Ching Lee. Eyes closed, he lay still as death, looking like a picture she had once seen of an Egyptian mummy.

Kneeling beside his cot, she murmured, "Lee? Can you hear me?" After a few seconds his eyes fluttered open. He turned his head slightly and stared at her with no hint of recognition. "It's Jessie. Don't you know me, Lee?"

"Young missee," he mumbled, but his expression remained blank.

"I saw you in Chinatown, with a little girl. Is she Mei's daughter?"

His answer, a feeble croak, was slow in coming. "Lily. Where Lily?"

A dim memory floated into Jessie's mind. *Lily—Mei's favorite flower.* At least she finally knew her name. "The doctors are taking good care of her, don't worry. But where's Mei?"

For a long moment he seemed far away, and the cold dread that Jessie had felt overtook her again. "Please, Lee. What's happened to Mei?"

At last he spoke, with deep, labored breaths. "Mei have white man's child, disgraced in Chinatown. Neighbor man want to marry her, take back to China. But he not want child. She weep many tears but say she always know she have to lose Lily. She tell her she come back someday, then kiss her good-bye. Lily year old then."

"Oh, Lee." Jessie squirmed in distress. "How could you let her go?"

"I cannot stop her. She pray to the gods, she decide. Once she love America. Then she learn to hate it."

"Where is she now?"

His one-word reply, softly spoken, tolled like a funeral bell. "Dead."

"Dead?" Jessie felt as though the breath had been knocked out of her.

"Long time later, letter come," Lee went on. "Mei took sick. Died."

Jessie bowed her head. But there was no time to mourn now. Forcing herself to go on, she leaned closer to Lee, who was mumbling to himself, watery eyes wandering. "Lee, why did you run away from me in Chinatown?"

It was as if an electric charge had rushed through his wasted frame. Wild fury burned in his eyes as he raised his head and glared at Jessie. "You want to give Lily to Doctor!" he shouted hoarsely. "He evil man, bring shame on us. I take Mei away from that house; he not get Lily!"

"No, Lee, I wasn't going to do that! He doesn't even know she exists. All I wanted was to help you if I could."

But she could see that Lee wasn't hearing her. His meager energy spent, he fell back, eyes shut tight, breathing hard, his face turned to the wall.

Dr. Lundgren had returned. He stepped closer to adjust Lee's covers, then helped Jessie to her feet. "Come away, Miss Wainwright. Maybe he'll be stronger tomorrow."

She was grateful that he held her gently by the arm and led her out.

ONE LOOK AT HER told Hazel and Henry that she had found the person she was looking for. "It's Lee," Jessie told them simply. "And Mei's dead."

"Oh, Jessie..." Hazel wrapped her in a hug. "But at least your long search is over. What about the little girl?"

Jessie tried to keep her voice steady. "Her name is Lily." She turned to Dr. Lundgren. "Please, could we go to the orphanage tent now?"

At this, Hazel objected. "We've done enough for today.

Look, the fires are getting worse." She pointed to the southeast, where the roiling smoke clouds had risen to a colossal, churning mass. "Henry says he'll drive us back, and we really should go."

Jessie shook her head firmly. "I have to see Lily first."

Dr. Lundgren gave a grim half smile. "I'm afraid Miss Schelling is right about the fires," he told her. "Perhaps if you could come back tomorrow..." Seeing the stricken look on Jessie's face, he stopped to reconsider. "Tell you what, Henry— why don't you and Miss Schelling go on, and I'll drive Miss Wainwright home later."

Left with no choice, Hazel had to accept the idea. Promising to meet Jessie in the morning, she gave her another hug. Then Hazel and Henry left, and the doctor walked a shaky but determined Jessie across the camp to the orphanage tent.

"I'm very sorry to put you out like this, Dr. Lundgren," she said on the way. "I know you have more important things to do. And I apologize for being rude before, interrupting when the nurse needed to talk to you."

"Don't worry about that. It is unusual, though, for a visitor to ask after a Chinese patient. Most of the ladies who come here speak only of 'those miserable Chinese'—if they speak of them at all." His tone was bitter, and Jessie felt uncertain about replying. She was relieved when they reached the orphanage tent. But as she stepped up to the tent flap, she was seized by a wave of panic. What could she say to Lily? And how would the child react? One thing she was sure of—it wouldn't do to get all weepy here.

Dr. Lundgren had pulled back the tent flap. "After you." Jessie gathered her courage and stepped inside.

It was a much smaller tent than the infirmary. In its dimly lit interior, Jessie saw perhaps two dozen children, most of them Chinese, ranging from babies to adolescents. Some played idly, some wandered about, some were obviously too sick or frightened to do more than lie on mattresses scattered across the canvas floor. At the rear of the tent, a woman wearing a Bureau of Adoptions badge sorted papers at a small table. She looked up, nodded to the doctor, then went on with her work.

"That's Nurse Cowell. She's in charge here," he whispered to Jessie.

Scanning the pathetic scene, Jessie noticed a tiny girl huddled in a corner, apart from the others. She sat motionless on a mat, with only a tin cup of water by her side. Her eyes were black pools with no expression, no flicker of life. And she had the distinctive copper-colored hair, now dirty and matted. But it was her delicate face that held Jessie mesmerized. She knew at once that this was Lily—the child bore an uncanny resemblance to Mei. And in a certain way, Jessie thought, to herself.

"I see you've spotted her," Dr. Lundgren said. "Mrs. Cowell says she seems bright enough, but she hasn't uttered a single word. Good luck."

Jessie took a deep breath, went over to the little girl, and knelt beside her. "Hello, Lily," she said softly. The child paid no attention. Jessie leaned closer and tried again. "My name's Jessie, and I've come to visit you." Still no response. "Please, may I be your friend?"

At last she was rewarded with a look, but it was a cold stare. Jessie noticed that Lily's dress was little more than a rag, a piece from some worn-out dress cut down to size. One of its sleeves was torn, exposing a small cut on her arm. And she badly needed a bath.

"Well, Lily," Jessie went on cheerfully, beaming a bright smile at her, "I'm sure we'll get along wonderfully. Let's see what happened to your arm, shall we?" Still Lily returned nothing but an empty stare, making Jessie wonder if she understood a word of English. Knowing better than to touch the child, she leaned closer and saw that the cut had not been cleaned and was already scabbing over.

Mrs. Cowell came and stood over her. "Excuse me, young lady, it's almost time for the children's rest period."

"Yes, ma'am, I won't be long. But I see that Lily's hurt. May I have some tincture of iodine and a bit of gauze?"

The nurse peered down at Lily, then frowned at Jessie. "We have no such supplies here. And it would be against regulations to put them in the hands of untrained personnel if we did. So many of the children are badly hurt, we'll get to her when we can." She turned and walked away.

"A little scratch can become just as infected as a major wound," Jessie said to Nurse Cowell's retreating back. "And this scratch is going to be cleaned and bandaged," she added in a whisper.

She tore a strip of ruffle off her own white petticoat and dipped one end into Lily's cup of water. Looking into Lily's eyes, she held up the moistened cloth and said, "This will feel cool, but it won't hurt." Then, holding her breath in case Lily screamed, she dabbed gently at the skin around the cut. At first Lily shrank from her touch. But as if realizing that this stranger was trying to help her, she finally permitted it and sat quietly while Jessie cleaned the wound as best she could.

Jessie talked softly to her as she reversed the strip of cloth, then wrapped it gently around Lily's arm to cover the cut. "Guess what, Lily," Jessie said. "Before I came to visit you, I saw your uncle. You know, your uncle Lee?"

The effect was startling. Lily's eyes grew wide and a thin little voice exclaimed, "Uncle!" Searching Jessie's face, she repeated the word in a questioning tone, "Uncle?"

"That's right." Jessie sat back, the bandaging complete. "I've just talked with him. You remember, he was hurt when the earthquake came, but—"

"Earth dragon," Lily said fearfully. "Earth dragon angry!"

"It's all right, Lily, that's over now. And the doctor's taking care of Uncle Lee, so I'm sure he'll be fine soon. Don't worry, all right?" Jessie reached out to smooth the child's tangled hair. "Can you give me a little smile?" Jessie coaxed. But that was too much to ask. Lily lowered her eyes and picked at a loose thread in her tattered dress.

Now Mrs. Cowell was back, again speaking sharply. "It's the children's rest period, young lady. And we maintain a strict schedule here."

"I'm just leaving," Jessie said. "I'll be back tomorrow," she told Lily, "I promise. Remember, I'm Jessie. And I'm your friend." She touched Lily's cheek, then rose and went back to the tent entrance, where Dr. Lundgren was waiting. There she paused for a last look.

Lily was staring at her again. And in her tiny piping voice, she had one more word to say: "Jessie." Though barely audible, it went straight to Jessie's heart. It was all she could do to hold back tears as she blew Lily a kiss and gave her the cheeriest smile she could muster.

She hurried out while Dr. Lundgren stayed behind to speak to Mrs. Cowell. When he joined her, Jessie was hastily wiping away tears. He stood silent for a moment, then said gently, "I must say, you did remarkably well with that child. Got a couple of words out of her, at least. Had you met her before?"

"It's a long story." Jessie frowned. "I can't really explain. But I can tell you this——" She struggled to speak without a tremor in her voice. "I'm not just a visiting charity lady."

"Sorry about that—I can see you're not. Well, I've got a break now. Let me get you home." His touch was gentle as he took her arm and led her away.

Her head was spinning with too many emotions to sort out. Happy ones and distressing ones.

Yes, her long search was over. She had wanted it to be, so desperately, and yet she'd given no real thought to what she'd do if it ever was.

Now she wondered, *What do I do next?* She had no idea. All she knew for certain was that she had only just begun.

Twenty-one

FEELING NUMB, Jessie brooded in silence while Dr. Lundgren coaxed his little Ford into sputtering life. Then he helped her into the passenger seat. A moment later the car lurched forward, and they were on their way.

"I got this ornery machine my last year in medical school," he told her. "I could afford it only because of a small inheritance from my grandfather. But I have to say, it's been mighty useful. Especially at a time like this."

Jessie managed a weak smile. "It's awfully generous of you to devote your time to those poor refugees."

"God knows they get very little help. Doctors, nurses, food, medical supplies—everything's in short supply."

"It's so sad. And those children in the orphanage tent—that's the saddest thing of all."

"Which reminds me, how *did* you get that little girl to talk?"

"Lee once told me that most Chinese children call men other than their own fathers *Uncle*. I thought it might be an English word she'd know."

"That was really clever."

As they drove out of the Presidio grounds, Jessie gazed in alarm at the towering smoke clouds covering the sky to the east like a sinister black shroud. "Gosh, it looks awful over there."

"And I hear the firemen's hoses are completely dry now. I'm

sure you're anxious to get home. Where am I taking you? Nowhere near downtown, I hope?"

Jessie gave him the address on Franklin Street.

He nodded. "Good, this side of Nob Hill. I'm sure that's out of the danger zone."

"I wish my mother could hear you say that, Dr. Lundgren. She'll be in another panic."

"Please, call me Alan. I'm only an intern, a year out of medical school. I'm not used to being called Dr. Lundgren."

"All right. And you should call me Jessie." Instantly—confusingly—she felt color rising in her cheeks.

"Good. Now, if I'm not being too nosy, may I ask you about the young woman you were looking for? Would that be Lily's mother?"

"Yes, Mei was Lee's niece, and yes, she was Lily's mother. She worked for us for a while, but she got in trouble with—" Jessie stopped herself just in time. "Anyway, she got in trouble. Now she's dead, and Lee is all Lily has left. That poor child, alone and terrified!" She was in danger of losing control again. "It just breaks my heart."

"Believe me, I sympathize," Alan said, then hesitated. "She needs her uncle, that's plain to see. I hope she doesn't lose him, too."

Jessie looked at him in alarm. "You think Lee might die?"

"I'm only saying that we don't know how serious his injuries are. You saw what we're up against. No facilities, no supplies, no way to treat patients properly. If I could get him into a well-equipped hospital like Pacific General—"

"Oh, could you?"

"An old Chinaman? Homeless and probably penniless? Not

when there are wealthy white patients waiting in line and able to pay handsomely. The senior physicians who run the hospital care as much about getting rich as they do about their patients. I wish people could be served according to their needs, not according to their race or ability to pay."

"That would be wonderful. But I doubt my father would agree with you about Pacific General. That's where he takes his patients."

Alan blinked. "Wait a minute—is your father Dr. Leonard Wainwright?"

"Yes. You know him?"

"Not personally. But everyone knows who he is. And what I just said about the older doctors doesn't apply to him. He's highly respected there."

Everyone there doesn't know him as well as I do, Jessie thought.

"At any rate, I'll do all I can for Mr. Ching," Alan went on. "But you need to be prepared, Jessie. He may not make it. And if he doesn't, little Lily will be just another one of those unclaimed children who—"

"Unclaimed! She's not lost baggage at the railway station!"

"I'm sorry, I know it sounds heartless. But it's what they call them. And like the others, she'll be sent to some overcrowded orphanage."

"No!" Jessie cried fiercely. "I will not let that happen."

"I'm afraid I don't see how you can stop it."

"I don't either, right now. But I'll find a way."

For the second time since they met, Alan's eyes crinkled in a smile. "You know, I'll bet you will."

The smoke had grown thicker as they drove, and by the time they drew near Jessie's neighborhood, it was stinging their eyes. Alan had to maneuver around debris in the streets and a snarl of horse-drawn wagons and motorcars. Jessie gasped at the sight of a team of horses fallen in the road, possibly struck by an auto. The owner struggled to get them back on their feet as people hurried past him toward safety, farther west.

"Alan, stop!" Jessie cried. "There must be some way we can help."

But Alan shook his head, his hands gripping the steering wheel. "He'll get them going all right. We've got to keep moving—this is getting bad," Alan muttered.

Ashes and embers, driven by a stiff wind, rained down around them as they approached Franklin Street, and the great black cloud loomed directly overhead. Suddenly an explosion shook the car so violently that Alan had to work hard to keep control while Jessie held on in terror. Just ahead, firemen and soldiers were erecting a barrier across the street.

Alan grimaced, pulling the car to a stop by the curb. "Roadblock, damn it!" Then, with a glance at his passenger, "Sorry, Jessie."

An army lieutenant came over to them and fixed a hard look on Alan. "Sir, civilian vehicles are being confiscated for official use during the emergency. Therefore I command you to turn this auto over to me."

Alan held up a U.S. Army identification badge for the lieutenant's inspection. "I'm a doctor at the Presidio refugee camp. I'm just driving this young lady home, but I've got to get right back there."

The lieutenant studied the badge, noted Alan's white coat, then glanced over at Jessie. "All right, we make exceptions for doctors. But the young lady goes the rest of the way on foot.

Nob Hill's burning, and the fire's coming down this side. We're dynamiting east of here, trying for another firebreak. This whole area could be evacuated any minute."

"My god!" Jessie cried, clambering out of the car.

"Wait, I'll walk you the rest of the way," Alan offered.

"No, you needn't, it's only two more blocks." Just then another explosion rocked them. "Good-bye, Dr. Lundgren," she said hastily. "Alan, I mean. And thank you for everything."

"See you again soon, I hope," he called after her. But she was already running for home.

Before she had gone half a block amid the acrid smoke and falling ash, weariness overtook her. Her feet felt like lead—she could barely drag herself along. It had truly been a long day. And it was far from over.

THE FIRST THING she noticed when she came near the house was a big touring car parked in front. *Who could that belong to?* she wondered as she went up the steps. Visible through the parlor windows was the flickering of candlelight. Chased by the roiling smoke clouds, daylight had long since faded, and the electricity, which had gone on and off several times since the quake, was evidently off again. With a good shove, she got the sticking front door open and stepped inside. There she paused, listening.

Agitated voices came from the parlor. One was her father's. The threat of evacuation must have forced him to come home early. But it was another voice, its raspy, quarrelsome tone unmistakable, that stopped her in her tracks. Suddenly she knew who owned the touring car....

She groaned softly, took a deep breath, and went inside.

Twenty-two

HER FATHER PACED the parlor, looking grim, while her mother perched nervously on the edge of a chair. Corey was there, too, having somehow made his way home from Berkeley. The first to see Jessie come in, he winked at her, then nodded toward the person holding forth in the center of the room.

"I've always said this dreary fog-bound peninsula is unfit for human habitation. And now that I've been proven right, perhaps—" Just then she caught sight of Jessie. "Well, look who's honoring us with her presence."

Jessie managed a thin smile. "Aunt Margaret, how nice to see you."

Her father stopped his pacing to turn and glower at her. "Where the *devil* have you been?"

Her mother rose to add her tearful reproach. "How could you, Jessie? Worrying us half to death, when we're about to lose everything!"

"Oh, Mama, surely that's not—"

"Jessica." Her father's voice was hoarse with anger. "In case you haven't noticed, this city is in flames. The fires are so hot they make their own draft, which only creates more fires. Downtown is wiped out, and on top of that, our fire chief has died in the blaze. That is the state of things. Now answer my question. Where have you been?"

She had a wild impulse to tell him. It would be so easy. *I've been to see Ching Lee, Papa. And a little girl named Lily, who happens to be your daughter.* But that wouldn't do. "I'm sorry to have upset anyone. I was with Hazel, and we sort of lost track of time."

He huffed in exasperation. "Meanwhile the authorities bickered so long about the firebreaks, they had to settle on Van Ness as the final one. If it doesn't hold, this house could go up in flames by tomorrow. I had to close the clinic, and Margaret barely made it past the roadblocks. They let her keep her car only because she's from out of town and will be leaving again soon. Does all this begin to sound serious to you?"

"The fact is, Jessica"—Margaret could not resist taking over—"I've come to rescue you and Catherine from imminent peril. You will come with me to Sacramento, where you'll be safe until—"

"Oh no!" Jessie fought against rising panic. "I can't do that."

Margaret's mouth dropped open. "I beg your pardon?"

Her father stepped closer. "What do you mean, you *'can't'*?"

Because Lily has lost her mother, Jessie wanted to say. *And if she loses Lee, too, she'll have no one at all.* "I—I can't explain, Papa. But I have good reasons."

Her mother came over to her. "Are you worried about school? We're told it will be closed for quite some time."

"No, Mama, it's not that. I just...I can't go away right now."

"I'll handle this, Kate." Leonard spoke in a low voice. "Look here, Jessica. Mrs. O'Reilly is going to her relatives in San Mateo, and Corey is returning to Berkeley. I'm moving to the physicians' residence at the hospital, and you and your mother are going with Margaret. The house is being closed, do you understand? Everybody's leaving, and that includes you."

From deep inside Jessie rose something she didn't know she had—the courage to defy her father to his face. "No, Papa, I'm not," she said firmly. "I can stay at Hazel's. They're west of here, where it's safe."

"But they already have a full house," Catherine pointed out.

"I'll sleep in Hazel's room. I do it all the time." A cold knot formed in Jessie's stomach as she waited for her father's response.

"You should let her stay, if you ask me," Corey volunteered. "She's a big girl now, she'll be all right."

"I didn't ask you," Leonard snapped. "And I'm not *asking* Jessie. She will go with your mother and Margaret, and that's final."

Dead silence filled the room. Jessie had never been physically afraid of her father, but as he stepped toward her with his jaw clenched in anger, she decided it might be a good idea to withdraw. "I'm very tired," she said. "If you'll excuse me, I'd like to go upstairs now."

"Yes, go," her father said. "And get yourself packed and ready."

Just then Mrs. O'Reilly looked in from the dining room. "Jessie, I'm about to serve supper, such as it is."

"Thank you, Mrs. O'Reilly, but I'm not hungry," Jessie called over her shoulder, and fled into the foyer. Her unexpected show of defiance had amazed her as much as anyone, but she knew she had accomplished nothing. Even if she went to the Schellings, they still might decide to leave the city. She needed a better plan.

She stole over to the front door, quietly tugged it open, and sneaked away.

IN LESS THAN half an hour she was back, tiptoeing in the front door. The hum of voices from the dining room told her that the family was still at dinner. Silently she dashed upstairs to her room, where she pulled off her shoes, unpinned her hat, and threw herself on her bed, her heart pounding. So far, so good.

Luckily Wanda had just returned from seeing Mr. Nesbit off to Los Angeles. He had real-estate prospects in Southern California that he needed to check on, and a contractor friend of his had agreed to repair the damage to his apartment while he was away. Wanda seemed distressed that he'd gone, but Jessie felt guilty relief when she heard the news, for Wanda had readily agreed that, if "Doc" permitted it, Jessie could stay with her.

But what if he refused? Maybe she should simply leave a note and sneak down the back stairs. *I could be back at Wanda's before they finish dessert.* But she knew these were thoughts of wild desperation.

An explosion a few blocks away rattled her windows and made her jump. *"This house could go up in flames tomorrow"*... She shuddered as her father's frightful words sank in for the first time. Rising, she lit a candle, then dragged a valise out from under her bed. Now, what to pack? First, a quick trip down-stairs to her father's study to find a couple of his best medical books. Other favorite books—the Jane Austen, Dickens, Mark Twain, and her beloved *Jane Eyre*. And her journal, of course; mustn't forget that. Nor the picture of herself and Amy, half hidden in the jumble atop her dresser. The valise and the book bag were both filling rapidly.

A knock at her open door made her spin around. It was Corey. "Jess, Mrs. O'Reilly left a plate for you in the icebox. She didn't believe all that about you not being hungry."

"Oh, bless her! Thanks, I'll get it later."

He eyed the valise. "So, you're going after all?"

"I'm going, but not with Aunt Margaret. How'd she get here, anyway, with the ferries not running?"

"She'd just bought that fancy new Oldsmobile, so she drove it all the way around the bay by herself. Can't you just picture that?"

"I'd rather not picture her at all, thank you very much."

"Amen to that!" he agreed with a chuckle.

"And what about you? How'd you get here?"

"I caught the last private boat out of Oakland. It was weird out there on the water—totally silent, but with a bright red sky. They say you can see the smoke a hundred miles from here." He crossed the room and draped himself across her window seat. "Now that Mama's seen I'm all right, I can't wait to get back. But before I go, out with it, Jess. Who's the fellow?"

She gave him a blank stare. "What fellow?"

"The one you're so madly in love with, you two can't bear to be apart."

"I have no idea what you're talking about, Corey."

"Come on, I know how girls are. You can't fool me. Fess up."

"There's no fellow, Corey, really."

"All right, have it your—" Just then an especially loud explosion rocked the house. "I heard they're going to use army cannons on Van Ness tonight," he continued when the noise died away. "This is like being in the middle of a war. Good luck getting Papa to let you stay."

"Thanks. I'm sure I'll need it." She reached past Corey to grab Chester and Mademoiselle from the window seat.

He got to his feet. "Well, I guess I'll go watch the blasting. It's a real show, bigger than the Fourth of July. Want to come?"

She was shocked. "Corey! People are losing their homes and all their possessions—and you call it a *show*?"

"It's bad, I admit," he said sheepishly. "Still, if it has to happen, it's quite a spectacle. See you later." He gave her a wave and went out.

IT WAS LATE and the house was quiet by the time Jessie finished packing. Two valises, a hatbox, her book bag, and her pocketbook were spread across the window seat. One more thing not to be left behind was her jewelry box, with her mementos of Mei. She dug it out and pushed it into the book bag.

The job done, she snuffed out her candle and, once more, looked out her bay window into darkness streaked with terrible orange-red light. Up on the hills, great mansions, lofty as castles, stood in stark relief against the flaming sky. Over the crest the fire advanced like a conquering army, destroying all before it. Again and again, violent explosions seemed to shake the very earth. But in the midst of the awful sights and sounds, and the feeling of impending doom, a deep calm descended upon her.

Tomorrow I may lose my home, she thought, *but today I found my sister.*

Twenty-three

FOR HOURS Jessie lay awake that night, half expecting to hear soldiers banging on the door, with orders to evacuate. When she finally dozed off, images of Lee and Lily, Dr. Lundgren and Mrs. Cowell, herself and Hazel, all swirled in her head. Then she felt a hand on her shoulder and awoke to find her mother standing over her. They had made it through the night—almost.

"It's four thirty," Catherine said. "A fireman just told us the fire's crossed Van Ness south of here. We must leave as soon as possible. Get dressed and grab your things, quickly now."

Shivering from cold and fear, Jessie dressed hurriedly, pulling on an extra skirt and two blouses that wouldn't fit into her valise. She was still not sure how to approach her father. With the clinic closed, he wouldn't be needing Wanda. But would he be reasonable and allow Jessie to stay with her?

DOWNSTAIRS SHE FOUND her mother and Aunt Margaret in the foyer. Catherine looked worried and Margaret was fuming.

"Is something wrong?" Jessie asked. "Besides the fires, I mean?"

"In this house something's always wrong," Margaret muttered.

Catherine explained. "When Margaret went to crank up her

motorcar, it wouldn't start. Corey's out there now, trying to fix it. But even if he does, he says he'll need to drive us to Sacramento himself, in case there's more trouble. He'll take the train back to Berkeley."

Jessie pondered, trying to decide whether this was good news or bad.

"Unfortunately, however," Catherine went on, "with all our luggage and the family heirlooms we can't bear to leave behind, there's room for only three of us. This is a problem, and I'm not sure how we can..."

Jessie stifled a delighted gasp. "Oh, don't worry about me, Mama," she said. "I've had a whole new idea. I'll go to Wanda Shaw's. She's told me I'm welcome, and she lives farther west than Hazel. It'll be perfectly safe."

"Oh dear!" Her mother looked uneasy. "We'll have to see what your father says. He'll be down in a minute."

Just then Corey came in, pulling off greasy work gloves. "The auto's running," he announced. "For now, anyway. So what's the decision? Do we unload some of the stuff, or does Jessie stay behind?"

It was Margaret who settled the question. "Unload nothing. Jessica says she can go to this Wanda person. And quite frankly, if a person doesn't want my hospitality, I certainly don't need that person in my home."

For once Jessie was grateful for her aunt's bossiness. "Aunt Margaret, any other time I'd love to visit you," she said as politely as she could. "I'm sorry if I gave the wrong impression."

Margaret responded with a withering glare. "Young lady, I hope you'll eventually focus your attention on some worthwhile endeavor. Lord knows you're willful enough to succeed at anything you undertake."

Jessie smiled. "Thank you, Aunt Margaret. I take that as a compliment."

"Now what's keeping Leonard?" Margaret had already dismissed her. "For heaven's sake, we really must be off!"

When told of the decision his sister had already handed down, Leonard meekly agreed. "You're sure it's all right with Wanda?" he asked Jessie.

"Absolutely, Papa. I just spoke to her. Luckily, the telephone's working again for the moment."

"Well, if it becomes inconvenient for her to have you there, contact me at the hospital's physicians' residence and we'll make other arrangements."

JESSIE AND HER MOTHER were last to leave the house. As they took a final look around, Jessie's eyes fell on the grandfather clock. "Too bad you can't take that heirloom, too."

"Margaret doesn't think so. She called it an ugly old thing." Catherine smiled sadly. "I know it was hard for you to apologize to her, dear. She may not appreciate it, but I do."

"Anything to make this a little easier for you, Mama."

Amid the smoke and haze of the early morning light, they gathered at Margaret's car to exchange good-byes. Catherine climbed into the rear seat, next to the luggage, and while Margaret spoke briefly to Leonard, Jessie went around to the driver's side for a quick parting word with Corey.

"How'd you fix it?" she asked.

"It was nothing much, really. But it's no wonder Margaret

couldn't make it start." Pulling a broken matchstick out of his pocket, he gave Jessie a quick glimpse, then whisked it away again. "The smallest thing stuck in a motorcar's throttle can disable it completely. Amazing, don't you think?"

She stared at him. "Corey! You mean——"

"Shhh! Let's just say you owe me one." He grinned as he revved up the motor. "See you later, Jess. Oh, and give my regards to the fellow."

Jessie could only smile and shake her head as Margaret got into the front passenger seat and the car coughed, sputtered, and pulled away.

She and her father waved until the car was out of sight, then he turned to her. "Well, Jessie——" She was Jessie again, his anger spent. "Take a good look at the house. It may be your last. They're dynamiting on Franklin now, several blocks down." With a mournful expression, he, too, took a long look. "This house was my parents' pride and joy. If it's going to be reduced to ashes, I'm only thankful they're not here to see it."

A wave of sadness came over Jessie as she gazed at him. "Papa, I'm sorry about making a scene in front of Aunt Margaret yesterday."

"Oh, never mind that. But something's going on with you, and sooner or later I'm going to find out what it is." He paused to consult his pocketwatch. "Now I've got to run. Shall I drop you at Wanda's?"

"No, thanks. She's coming over to help me with my things."

"Please tell her we appreciate her taking you in."

"I will." *Should I hug him?* she wondered. But he had already picked up his bag and started away.

WEARING HER BEST HAT, she was sitting on the front steps when Wanda arrived. Her two heavy valises were piled into Corey's old play wagon, rescued from the carriage house and pressed into service.

"You look awfully forlorn, sitting there," Wanda remarked.

"That's just how I feel. But thanks to you, and to Corey, at least I've escaped exile." She was explaining the part Corey had played, when another explosion split the air around them, making them both cringe.

"I may never see this house again," Jessie said bleakly. "And people all around have lost theirs already. It's all so awful."

"We'd best not dwell on it, Jessie. Come, let's get away from here."

They took up the bags and started off, Jessie pulling the little wagon. After a few steps she stopped to look back at the house— her bay window set in its corner turret, the graceful gables and finely carved trim adorning the windows and roofline—"ginger-bread decoration," in Margaret's disdainful view.

"When I was little," Jessie said, "Lee used to take me for walks, and I'd stop right here and say, 'Bye, door. Bye, front steps. Bye, my room, Bye, house.' Then he'd say, 'Come along, missee, the house will still be here when you get back.' But even if he were here, he couldn't promise that now."

Wanda took her by the arm and gently coaxed her on.

Twenty-four

In somber silence they made their way through streets littered with possessions people had tried to drag with them but had to leave behind.

A sofa stood in the middle of the sidewalk, an upright piano graced someone's front yard. As they turned west on Lombard Street, heading for Wanda's house, a series of great blasts made them turn and look back. A three-story building had exploded in a shower of wood, bricks, mortar, and glass. When the smoke cleared, a pile of rubble and dust was all that remained.

Jessie was thankful when they finally reached their destination. Though completely different from the spacious home she was used to, Wanda's cozy bungalow felt like a calm, safe haven.

"Drop your bags in the back bedroom," Wanda said, "and take off some of those layers while I make us some cocoa. We've got lots to talk about."

We surely do, Jessie thought as she carried her bags into her temporary room, for she had made a difficult decision. Telling Wanda the shocking truth about her deeply respected "Doc" would hurt her dreadfully. But it could no longer be avoided—it was time for her to know.

Still, even after they were both seated in the kitchen, Jessie hardly knew how to begin. "Wanda, do you remember that time

a policeman brought me home after I'd been robbed in Chinatown? When I telephoned you that night, you asked if there was
something I hadn't told you."

Wanda regarded her young friend with narrowed eyes. "I
remember. And why do I get the feeling that I'm about to find
out there was?"

Jessie took her time folding and unfolding her napkin, and
stirring her cocoa. "I didn't know it for sure back then. But I do
now. And it's the reason I couldn't go away with my mother and
Aunt Margaret."

Wanda settled back in her chair. "All right, let's hear it."

Once she had started, Jessie spilled it all out in a rush.
Wanda gave it her usual careful attention, and when Jessie had
finished, they sat for a long moment staring at each other.

"Well," Wanda said at last. "Well, well, well." For once, it
seemed, she was practically speechless.

"I just couldn't forget what my father did, you see. And because of it, an innocent child sits in that horrible camp, while
he—"

"Jessie, stop right there." Wanda's sharp tone was startling.
"It's my turn to talk now. I agree that what you say Doc did was
a shameful thing. But from what you've told me before, those
people *wanted* to disappear when they went back to Chinatown.
You have to leave this alone. Put it straight out of your mind and
never mention it again."

"But Lily's my sister, Wanda. Don't you think I'd want to
know her?"

"You may well *want* to. But even though you've managed to
find her, believe me, you'll be better off not knowing her."

Jessie sat in glum silence for a moment. "I was hoping you'd be on my side. Anyway," she went on, rising, "I told Lee and Lily I'd go back and see them today."

"I hate to see you tormenting yourself like this. Especially when there's absolutely nothing you can do for them."

"I made a promise," Jessie said simply. "But first I have to find a way to get there. Maybe Hazel made a plan with Henry." She started to leave, then hesitated. "But you said we had lots to talk about. Was there something you wanted to tell me, too?"

"Oh . . . no, it'll keep. Now you've made me terribly worried about you and that child. Are you sure you won't—"

"I'll be right back." Before Wanda could say more, Jessie was gone.

HALF AN HOUR LATER she returned. "The Schellings are all right, but Hazel's forbidden to go out," she reported. "And not just for coming home late yesterday. Her parents saw her drive up with a Chinese fellow, and that was it. They blame *me* for leading her astray."

"That *is* a shame, all of it."

"But there's good news, too. Henry said he'd pick us up at noon today, on the corner near her house. I'll be there, and please come along, Wanda. Once you see Lily, you'll understand."

"I'll think about it. But first let's get you unpacked."

Wanda was amazed at what came out of Jessie's bags. "Good grief, you've brought almost no clothes, but a ton of books. Even medical books of Doc's."

"I might want to look up some things," Jessie explained. "Especially now that there's Lily to worry about."

Wanda let that pass. "And what are these?" she exclaimed. "A doll and a stuffed bear. Aren't you a little old for those?"

"That bear is Chester, and I've had him forever," Jessie said. "He's a little worn, but he's still very sweet, and now he's going to be Lily's friend. I've got a feeling she could use one."

"I'm sure that's true," Wanda said softly. And from the look in her eyes at that moment, Jessie knew that despite her misgivings, Wanda would come with her to the camp.

WHEN HENRY DROVE UP at the corner, Jessie introduced Wanda, and he greeted her with his friendly smile. He nodded when Jessie explained Hazel's absence. She left out the part about Hazel's arriving home with a Chinese boy, but from the way Henry lowered his eyes, she suspected that he guessed. At the Presidio camp he let them out near the entrance, saying he would pick them up in an hour.

Jessie had told Wanda about Dr. Lundgren and the grim conditions he labored under. But experienced nurse though she was, Wanda cringed at the sight of so many sick and injured crowded into the infirmary tent. "My god, Jessie, this is like a field hospital after a major battle."

Jessie scanned the scene. "I don't see Alan anywhere. But we'll find him later. I'd better check on Lee."

"I'll stay back," Wanda told her. "It'll be better if you're alone."

Jessie started across the tent. But as soon as she saw Lee, she recoiled in dismay. Racked with chills and fever, he lay with eyes tightly shut, shivering and sweating heavily. Placing a hand on his burning forehead, she spoke softly. "Lee? It's me, Jessie. Can you hear me?"

Roused either by the sound of her voice or by her cooling

touch, he opened his eyes, blinked rapidly several times, then squinted at her.

She smiled. "Hello, Lee. How are you today?" It was a foolish question, she knew, but perhaps it would get him to talking.

At first he only stared. When he finally answered, his hoarse croak was weaker than ever. "Missee, you come for Lily?"

"Oh no, I'm only visiting her. Both of you, really."

"No, not visit." He grew agitated. "You take, missee. She your sister. Before Mei go . . ." He had to pause for breath. "She want to tell you. I say no. I send you message not go to Chinatown."

"*You* sent that note?"

He nodded slightly, lifting his bony hand to grip Jessie's arm. "All change now. Time you take Lily." He sputtered, choking, unable to go on.

"Try to stay calm, Lee," she said helplessly. "We can talk about all this later, when you're—"

"No!" A fierce light shone in his bloodshot eyes as his grip on her arm tightened. "I go soon, leave Lily alone. Promise, missee, you take . . . take care . . . Lily. . . ." His voice faded, his hand fell limp. His ebbing strength gone, he lay staring up at the tent ceiling.

Frightened now, Jessie leaned close and murmured, "I promise, Lee. If it comes to that, I'll take care of her." But she couldn't tell if he heard her or not. "Lee, can you hear me?" But he was drifting away, the light in his staring eyes fading. His frail body shuddered, then went still. Frantic, Jessie kept calling his name, lightly slapping his cheek, pleading with him to hold on. It was no good. His eyes went on staring upward, but now they stared at nothing.

She was holding his hand, still talking to him as if she thought it could bring him back, when Alan gently helped her to her feet. "He's gone," she told him in a flat voice.

In only a few seconds he'd seen for himself, then summoned one of the nurses to handle the procedures used when a death occurred. It all appeared dreadfully routine to Jessie. Then Wanda was at her side. "I'm so sorry, Jessie. I saw what was happening, but before I could take five steps to get here, it was too late. He did go peacefully."

"I'm sorry, too," Alan said. "And sorry I wasn't here when you arrived. But I couldn't have helped. There was nothing anyone could do."

Jessie nodded, feeling numb as they led her away. But once she was outside, her tears broke free, streaming down her cheeks. Wanda offered a handkerchief, which she gratefully accepted.

Alan pointed across the way. "There's a canteen tent over there. Would you like a cup of tea to steady your nerves a bit?"

"No, thank you, I'm all right." Clearly, she was anything but. Floating in her mind were soft, golden-hued memories of happier times, when Lee stood tall in her child-eyes, as her friend, her teacher, her fountain of wisdom. But she could not allow herself to give way to grief. She tried to look composed, then turned to Alan. "May I see Lily now?"

"Of course. But I wouldn't tell her about her uncle if I were you."

"Oh no, I wouldn't do that. Not now."

Wanda handed her the bag they had brought containing Chester and an orange Wanda had contributed. Clutching it tightly, as if to gather courage from it, Jessie headed for the orphanage tent.

Twenty-five

AT THE SIGHT OF LILY huddled in the same corner, staring into space in the same expressionless way, Jessie stopped short. Someone had wrapped a tattered white shawl around the little girl, and it had slipped off one shoulder. *Your sister mustn't take a chill.* The words flew into Jessie's head like a cold wind.

She went to Lily, knelt beside her, and put on the brightest smile she could. Surely smiles were understood in all languages. "Hello, Lily," she murmured. "I'm Jessie, remember me?" If Lily did, she gave no hint of it. "I said I'd come back today, and here I am. How's your arm?" Jessie sighed when she got no response. At least the bandage was still there, so she needn't tangle with Nurse Cowell again.

She was about to open the bag containing the gifts, when the sharp-eyed nurse strode over with a stern look on her face. "You're back, I see. May I ask why you pay so much attention to this one child, when there are so many other poor orphans?"

"Oh, I don't know. Because she's so sad, I suppose."

"They all are. Thank heavens we'll soon be rid of the un-claimed ones."

Unclaimed—that hateful word again! "Where will they go?"

"To orphanages, church groups of various kinds, some as far away as China. I'll be especially glad to see the last of *this* one."

"Why do you say that?"

"She's quite impossible. Won't speak, won't obey even the simplest instruction. Frankly, I think she's mentally retarded."

Mrs. Cowell moved on, leaving Jessie fuming. Lily must not be sent away, and she most certainly was *not* mentally retarded! She brushed aside the interruption and put her smile back on. "Look, Lily, I've brought you something." Opening the bag, she brought out first the orange. "You like these, don't you? Shall I peel it for you?"

Lily looked as if she had no idea what it was.

"Well, maybe you'll like this little fellow." Now came the plump brown bear. "His name is Chester. He used to belong to another little girl, and now he can be yours. Would you like to hold him?"

Obviously not. Her wide-eyed stare was as uncomprehending as ever.

"That's too bad. Chester's very nice, and he wants to be your—"

"Just a minute, what's all this?" Mrs. Cowell was back, this time scolding as if Jessie were a naughty child. "You can't bring such things in here. It creates unacceptable clutter and confusion."

"An orange and a stuffed toy create confusion?"

"Please don't argue, young lady. Remove those objects at once. You seem to have a knack for making a nuisance of yourself, but it will not do here." With a warning glare, Mrs. Cowell again moved away.

Never mind her, Jessie thought. Lily hadn't cared about the presents, anyway. One more time, she tried. "So, Lily, I hope you're feeling fine today?"

Now Lily's stare was fixed on Jessie. And finally, she chose to speak. "Uncle," she mumbled.

That was the one subject Jessie had hoped to avoid. "Lily, your uncle Lee is . . . well, he's sick and can't come to see you right now, but——" *But what?* she wondered. *What should I say?*

It was Lily, a kind of wistful pleading in her stare, who gave her the answer. "Home," she said in her tiny voice. "Jessie, home."

Her words touched Jessie in a way she could not have imagined. Her own little sister was asking to be taken away from all the horror and pain. Surely Lily sensed that awful woman's dislike of her, heard her disdainful tone. What misery she must feel——it seemed to flow from Lily into Jessie, and as it did, all rational thought flew out of her head.

A glance around told her that Mrs. Cowell was busy on the farside of the tent. And a phantom whisper inside her head told her something else.

You can save her from this place, right now. Do it.

Sweeping Lily up in her arms, she raced for the door.

IT WAS LIKE A NIGHTMARE, as if she were outside watching herself bolt in headlong flight, Lily clinging to her for dear life. On she ran with no idea where she was going, desperate to remove her sister from this dreadful prison, knowing only that one unclaimed child had just been claimed.

She never saw Alan until he stepped in her way. "Jessie, stop!" His distant voice pierced through the ringing in her ears. "What are you doing?"

"I'm rescuing Lily!" she cried, trying to push past him.

He caught her arm, bringing her to a halt. "You can't do that."

"Let me go!" She shook herself free, only to run into Wanda.

"For god's sake, Jessie, have you lost your mind?"

Mrs. Cowell came running up behind her, shouting, "You insane girl! Give me that child this instant!" She clutched at Lily, but Jessie batted her hands away. Lily, frightened by all the commotion, shrieked in protest.

Alan pulled Lily from Jessie's arms and handed her over to her official keeper. "Please excuse this incident, Mrs. Cowell. I'll see that this young lady makes no further trouble."

Just then a military policeman appeared. "What's going on here?"

Mrs. Cowell pointed at Jessie. "Arrest this girl immediately!"

"It's all right, Sergeant," Alan told him. "Everything's under control."

"If you say so, Doc." Satisfied, the policeman walked away.

Alan turned to Mrs. Cowell. "You may take the child back inside now. I give you my word, nothing like this will happen again."

"It had better not," she snapped. With a last angry glare at Jessie, she carried the now-bawling Lily back into the tent.

Seething, Jessie turned on Alan. "Why did you have to stop me? Lee's gone, and I'm all Lily has."

"What are you talking about, Jessie? With no known relatives, she's legally the ward of the Bureau of Adoptions, so—"

"That's not true! She *has* a known relative. She's—" In her agitation, Jessie rushed ahead without stopping to think. "She's my *sister!*"

"I see," he said quietly. "Well, that's quite a different matter. Care to tell me about it?"

Jessie shot a horrified look at Wanda, standing by. Wanda gave a slight nod, as if to say, *You can't take words back once you've said them. Go on.* So she told Alan the story she had thought she'd keep hidden away forever.

Alan spent a moment in thoughtful silence after she had finished. "If Lily is your father's child, and he doesn't know about her, who else does?"

"Only Hazel. And Wanda. Oh dear, I should introduce—"

"We took care of that ourselves, while you were with Lily," Alan said.

"Jessie, it's almost time for us to meet Henry," Wanda said gently. "We really should go."

Alan offered to walk a little way with them, and they started off.

"What am I going to do about her?" Jessie said fretfully.

"I don't know," Alan said. "But kidnapping isn't the answer. How would it help Lily for you to wind up in jail? Only your father can legally claim her now. What if you simply told him? After all, he's got a right to know."

Anger flared up in Jessie again. "I don't think he deserves rights. He drove Lee and Mei away from us. Besides, he'd only deny everything. Still, I have to make it up to Mei somehow, and to Lily, for the wrong he did."

"I don't see why you feel responsible," Alan remarked. "But I do understand your distress. Whatever you do, I'm sorry to say, you'll have to stay away from here from now on."

"What?" Jessie stared at him in dismay. "And not see Lily again?"

"I'll keep an eye on her for you."

"But I need to—will you watch that cut on her arm?"

"Yes, and don't worry, they're not going to move those children out anytime soon. They can't get organized that quickly. But Nurse Cowell is one tough lady, as you found out. If she sees you near the orphanage tent again, she'll have you arrested, you can count on it."

"That witch," Jessie muttered. "I offered Lily an orange and a little bear, and she——" A hand flew to her cheek. "Oh no—I left Chester back there!"

"I take it Chester's the bear," Alan said. "Well, you can't go back for him now."

"I know." Again Jessie found herself fighting back tears. "Alan, you won't tell anyone about . . . Lily and everything, will you?"

"Absolutely not, I promise."

"I'm really sorry I've been such a troublemaker."

"Well . . . at least you're a charming troublemaker." With a smile he reached for her hand and gave it a slight squeeze. Surprised, she looked at him and saw kindness and understanding in his smiling eyes. A warm feeling came over her.

As they drew near the camp entrance, he stopped. "I've got to get back to work, so I'll leave you here." He turned to Wanda. "You'll consider what we talked about, won't you? I'll see you both in the morning." With a last smile for Jessie, he hurried away.

"Why did he say that?" Jessie asked, as she and Wanda continued walking.

"We got to talking while you were with Lily, and when I told him I'm a nurse, he asked me to volunteer here at the camp. He's going to stop by tomorrow to hear my decision."

"That's a wonderful idea! You said you would, didn't you?"

"I said I'd think it over. There's Doc to consider. He'll want me back as soon as he can reopen the clinic. Not to mention, you're with me now."

"He won't be able to reopen for ages, with so many repairs to do. And you needn't worry about me, I'll be fine."

But Wanda shook her head. "The thing is, I've also got Philip to consider."

Jessie was taken aback. "Didn't you say he'd be away for weeks?"

"I did, but . . . oh, Jessie, I didn't want to tell you this way. Not here. But right before he left, Philip asked me to marry him."

Jessie stopped short. "Wanda! Why haven't you said anything?"

"In the middle of all this horror?" Wanda turned to face her. "I can't even think about it, much less talk about it."

"Well, what did you tell him?"

"That I'd need time to think about it. He said that was fine, but I don't know how long he'll be willing to wait."

"Do you . . . love him?"

"I know I'm fond of him. But where to go from there—oh, I've just got to put it all out of my mind for now and hope he'll be patient with me."

As they walked on again, Jessie returned to the previous subject. "If you did come to work here, even for a short time, you'd be helping these poor people. And you could also watch over Lily."

"I'm aware of that, believe me. I didn't exactly meet her, but after getting that little glimpse, I see what you mean about her. And I must say, I'm very impressed with Dr. Lundgren."

"So am I." Jessie could still feel his squeeze of her hand, how understanding he had been, even when he had to intervene to keep her out of trouble. But as they neared the spot where they were to meet Henry, dark thoughts once again filled her mind.

"Aftershocks," she murmured. "They're all bad, but today's was the worst." Pausing, she looked back at the infirmary, thinking of the sad scene burned into her memory. "Lee knew he was dying. And knowing it, he thought only of Lily. He begged me to take care of her, and I said I would. I don't know if he heard me or not." She turned tearful eyes on Wanda. "But I gave him my word, and I'm going to keep it."

Wanda shook her head. "I just wish I knew what you can do."

Jessie had only one answer to that. "Whatever has to be done."

Twenty-six

IN SPITE of a deep yearning to collapse in exhaustion at Wanda's house, Jessie knew she would not rest until she learned whether her home was still there. Wanda went with her—to hold her up, if need be.

Even from a distance they could see that the area around Van Ness Avenue looked like a war zone, where the invading force of the firestorm had been met by a defensive one—the army's dynamite, and ordinary citizens wielding wet blankets and rags. The stench of charred ruins hung in the air as people stood staring, some silent, some weeping, at the mountains of smoking rubble that had been their homes.

But on Franklin Street, her house was just as Lee had always said it would be—still there, standing proudly. Never mind that inside the wrought iron fence, her mother's garden was a trampled ruin, that several windows had been shattered by the nearby explosions, and that flying embers had so scarred the delicate cornices that the whole house would need repainting. The important thing was that it had survived. Jessie wept tears of gratitude for their good fortune—and tears of pity for those who had lost so much.

"CHESTER AND I bid you good morning." Alan Lundgren smiled at Jessie as he handed her the stuffed bear when she opened the door to his knock the next morning. "Mrs. Cowell had thrown him in the trash, but I found him before it went to the incinerator."

"Oh, Alan, thank you!" She held the bear close. "Come in, Wanda's—"

"Right here," Wanda said, suddenly appearing. "And ready to go."

His face lit up. "You're coming? That's great!"

"Couldn't I come, too, Alan?" Jessie put in hastily. "Ask Wanda, she'll tell you I'm not entirely ignorant of medical procedures."

"It's true," Wanda said. "Every word of it."

But Alan was frowning. "Sorry, Jessie, I wish you could. But Mrs. Cowell often comes to the infirmary, and if she were to see you—"

"I understand," Jessie said, swallowing her disappointment.

"So, shall we be off?" he said to Wanda.

She cast an anxious glance at Jessie. "You sure you'll be all right?"

"Of course I will. I'm looking forward to a nice restful day."

But she felt a twinge of envy as she waved to them when they drove off a moment later. *How nice it must feel to know where you're going,* she thought. *And to know what you'll be doing when you get there.*

She wandered into the parlor, where Wanda's cat reclined in majestic serenity on the windowsill. "You're awfully lucky to be safe and happy here, Toby. What do you think of that?" Jessie scratched his head, and he gave back a contented purr, blinking sleepily. "Oh, I forgot. You're the mighty lion, lord of the African plains. You don't need to think."

Soon she put on her hat and coat and went out. Maybe she'd walk over to Franklin Street and take another look around. She might find some first-aid things in the medicine cabinet there that Wanda could take to the camp.

Or maybe . . . maybe I just need to see one more time that our house is really still there.

THE SILENT HOUSE seemed strangely unfamiliar when she pushed open the stubborn front door. Every room was coated with fine gray ash. And this time there was no Mrs. O'Reilly to organize a cleanup, to light the stove, to fill the house with the aroma of cinnamon cookies and all the good things of a normal life. She sorely missed the faithful, reliable cook.

Upstairs she went into the bathroom, found two rolls of gauze and the vial of alcohol, and put them in her skirt pocket. Then, venturing into her room, she stared at the mess she had left behind. She had walked away from so many things she loved, even knowing she might never see them again. It struck her that the love of possessions was a rather shallow form of love.

Straightening up her desk a little, she discovered at the back of a drawer an envelope containing some of her pocket money. That would buy even more supplies for the camp. She turned to her dressing table, but soon gave up the effort to clean it. It all seemed meaningless somehow. Going over to her bay window, she looked out at the hills to the east. Where once a prosperous city rose to glorious heights, desolation stretched as far as the eye could see. *I wonder when the view from this window will be a pleasant one again.*

Turning away, she curled up on her bed to rest for a minute. Despite the cozy comfort of Wanda's guest room, she had slept poorly the night before. Nightmarish thoughts had tumbled through her mind—thoughts of an old friend, found one day, lost the next; another gone from the earth at a tragically young age; and a small, bewildered orphan, left all alone. But Lily *wasn't* an orphan—her father was alive and well. Shouldn't he be told?

If only I could sort this out as easily as I decided on what belongings to pack! She snuggled down, her heavy eyelids drooping closed. *Oh, to be like Toby, with a life so simple . . .*

THE SOUND of the front door slamming startled her awake. She rose, hurried to the landing, and peered down from the top of the stairs. It was her father, and he was coming up. Wanda's question came back to her: *"What can you do?"* And her reply had been: *"Whatever has to be done."* At last, as she watched her father coming closer, she knew what that meant.

His eyes lowered, he did not see her until she spoke. "Hello, Papa."

"Jessie! Good god, what are you doing here?"

"I came to see if the house was all right."

"Well, as you can see, it survived. We can thank Providence for that." Reaching the top of the stairs, he added, "I'm here for clean clothes, then I've got to rush back to the hospital. It's an absolute madhouse there."

Jessie followed him into his bedroom, where he opened a bureau drawer and began taking out shirts. "Papa, the other day you said you expected to find out what's going on with me. Well, I've decided it's time you did."

He stopped, turned to fix a curious look on her, then lowered himself into a chair. "In that case, you have my full attention."

Steeling herself, she stepped closer. "I've been looking for Lee and Mei. And yesterday I found Lee, lying injured in the Presidio refugee camp."

His answer came just as she expected. "Damnation! In the middle of this crisis, you've been traipsing around looking for those ingrates again? Now I suppose you have the gall to ask me to help him."

"No, it's too late for that. Lee's dead. And so is Mei."

His jaw dropped. "Dead?" he echoed feebly.

"Mei had a child, a little girl. Naturally, Mei was disgraced. Someone took her back to China, where she died. Of a broken heart, I imagine."

Her father sat mute, his stare burning into her. She forced herself to go on. "She had to leave her child with Lee, you see. But he died yesterday. I was with him, and I saw the little girl. Now they mean to send her off to some horrible orphanage, far away."

"Well, that's . . ." He groped for words. "That's sad, of course. But it doesn't justify your inexcusable behavior yesterday. And it certainly does not concern me." He stood and went back to collecting his shirts.

She hurried on before the knot in her stomach could climb into her throat. "Oh, but it *does* concern you, Papa. The little girl's name is Lily. She's a beautiful child, and—" Jessie swallowed hard. "She is your daughter."

The silence was deafening. Slowly he turned, his face flaming with fury, and crossed the room to tower over her. "You wicked girl! You dare to call some stranger's child mine? I've had only one other daughter besides you, and she was cruelly taken from me years ago!"

She took a step back but continued to hold steel-firm. "Lily is *not* some stranger's child. She's your own flesh and blood, just as I am, just as Amy was. And I *don't* want to lose her, too."

"Exactly why do you think this child is mine?"

"Lee made that very clear to me before he died."

"Well, it's a vicious lie. Coming from that cunning Chinaman, I might expect it. But from *you*—this is beyond belief!"

Calm was deserting her now. "Lee spoke the truth, Papa. But I already knew it. At first I thought it must be Corey up there with Mei. But it was you—I saw you. How could you do such a thing?" She took a step back, unsure what he might do.

"You presume to judge me? I do not answer to you for my conduct!"

"Rage at me if you wish, Papa. But what I've said is true. And you know as well as I do that Lily is your responsibility."

What came over him now seemed less like anger than a desperate attempt to avoid panic. Sinking into his chair, he wilted before her eyes. "How could this happen? You, who have received from me only the tenderest care and affection, are bent on destroying everything I hold dear. My career, my marriage, our family name—"

"No, I'm not! All you need to say is that you came across this poor neglected child and thought of all the room we have in this house—"

"Never!" He leaped to his feet in a fresh outburst, the veins in his neck throbbing, his eyes pinpoints of flaming rage. "I'll hear no more! And I warn you, Jessica, if you ever mention this evil fantasy again, I'll..."

Strangely, her calm returned. "All right, Papa," she said quietly. "I won't speak of Lily again. But she's not a fantasy, she is *real*. I won't forget her. And now that you know she exists, neither will you."

She turned to leave, then paused in the doorway. "I'm going now. And I'll stay gone. Deny your other daughter, and you can deny me, too."

The last look she saw on his face was one of speechless, slack-jawed astonishment. Then she turned her back on him.

I WILL NOT CRY, she told herself as she left the house. *He made a coward's choice and should hang his head in shame. I can hold mine high.*

All the way back to Wanda's she consoled herself with this thought. And all the way, her eyes were so clouded with tears that she could barely see where she was going.

Twenty-seven

WHEN ALAN brought Wanda home from the camp that afternoon, he walked in with a large carton and deposited it on the table. "Bandage supplies," he said to Jessie, with a smile. "Wanda noticed we were running short, and says she knows someone who's great at rolling bandages."

"I've done quite a bit of that," Jessie admitted.

"We need small, medium, and large. I hope it's not imposing on you?"

"Not a bit, I'm happy to do it. In the meantime, anything new with Lily today?"

Alan gave an apologetic shrug, and Wanda said, "No, she still sits in her corner, always alone. And that awful Mrs. Cowell watching me all the time only makes it harder to get near her. I'll try again tomorrow."

What did I expect? Jessie asked herself. *Progress, already?*

AT WANDA'S INVITATION, Alan stayed for supper that evening. There was so little food available to buy that it had to be a simple meal, but no one minded. Electricity was back on, which helped lighten the mood.

Jessie had intended to stay quiet about her painful confrontation with her father. But when Alan asked her how her day had gone, it all came pouring out. "I know, Wanda," she said when she finished. "Go ahead and say 'I told you so,' anytime you like."

"Well, did you imagine he would take it gracefully?" Wanda said sharply. "Now you've spoiled things between the two of you, maybe forever."

"But he had to be given the chance to choose about Lily, and he did. If she's sent to an orphanage, or who-knows-where, it'll be his fault."

"Seems to me you're both right," Alan said. "He had to be told, and it was bound to be a disaster. So I guess you won't be needing these." He pulled a sheaf of papers out of his pocket and laid them on the table.

"What's that?" Jessie asked.

"An application from the County Bureau of Adoptions. I picked it up in case you decided to approach your father some-day. Even if he did acknowledge Lily, they'd still want him to submit one."

"Obviously that's not going to happen," Wanda declared. She rose and began to clear away the dishes. "Anyone for coffee?"

"I could use some," Alan said. "Let me help you."

Jessie always made a point of helping Wanda serve and clean up, but three were too many in Wanda's tiny kitchen, so she stayed in her seat. Idly she picked up the application forms and began to look them over. "Legally she's a ward of the Adoptions Bureau," Alan had said. That meant Lily would never escape un-less someone adopted her.

As she stared at the papers, an idea came to her that was so wild, she had to suppress a smile. How easy it would be to fill in the information required and send in the application!

Child's name: *Lily Ching.* Needless to say, Wainwright wouldn't appear.

Applicants. Husband's name: *Edgar Shaw.* Age: *Forty.* No, that seems old. Thirty-five would be better.

Occupation: *West Coast representative for a New Jersey pharmaceutical company.* Wanda would know the name of it.

Wife's name: *Wanda Kirkland Shaw.* Age: *Thirty-two.*

Wife's occupation (if any): *Registered nurse.* That sounded good.

Place of occupation: *Self-employed* would have to do. She couldn't list the clinic, they'd go ask her father.

Jessie heaved a discouraged sigh. What was the use? Mr. Shaw had been dead for years, and that made all of it pointless.

Wanda and Alan were back. "What are you doing, Jessie?" Wanda asked.

"Nothing. Just wishing there were some way this application could actually be used." She laid it aside.

Alan picked it up and put it back in his pocket. "Well, since it can't, let's say no more about it."

They had their coffee, Alan and Wanda chatting about patients at the camp. Only half listening, Jessie sat glumly contemplating Lily's fate.

When Alan was ready to leave, he thanked Wanda for dinner and told her he'd pick her up again the next morning. Then he turned to Jessie and asked, "Walk out with me?"

"Of course." She hadn't expected to have a chance to talk with Alan alone. It seemed oddly appealing.

When they reached his car, she dared to bring up the question on her mind. "Could I ask you . . ." She hesitated, almost embarrassed to go on. "You'll think I'm a fool, but—"

"No, I won't. What is it?"

"I was wondering . . . if a single person wanted to adopt a child on their own—someone like Wanda, for instance—do you think there's the slightest possibility that the Adoptions Bureau would allow it?"

Alan frowned at the question. "You know Wanda much better than I do. But the idea of her, or any woman alone, trying to adopt seems pretty far-fetched to me."

"You're right, I know. But I also know I'm getting desperate over what's going to happen to Lily."

"I understand, I really do. Maybe you're worrying too much, though, and too soon. Try to be patient, and let's see if we can think of a more practical solution." He paused, smiling. "It's funny, but I feel a part of all this. I want to help in any way I can."

Jessie smiled weakly in return. "Thank you, Alan. That makes me feel better." They said good night, and she waved as he drove off.

BACK INSIDE, Wanda was still sitting at the kitchen table. Jessie slid into a chair across from her, and for a long moment neither spoke.

"Alan says he wants to help with the Lily problem," Jessie said finally. "He doesn't know how yet, of course, but . . ."

"That's nice of him. Well, heaven knows you'll need all the help you can get. I must say, you astonish me, Jessie. I'm still trying to make myself believe you actually confronted your father that way."

"No one in this world can make things right except him. What else could I do?"

"I can't imagine. But when you think of something that might work, please, let me be the first to know."

Jessie looked away. What would Wanda say to the wild idea she had thought up just a little while ago?

Wearily, Wanda pulled herself to her feet. "Well, it's been a long day, and I'm exhausted. I'll see you in the morning."

JESSIE SAT MOTIONLESS at the table for a long time after Wanda had gone to bed, thinking back over a day that felt like the longest of her life. She, too, felt exhausted, but wide awake at the same time. And her mind kept returning to what Alan had said.

"Let's see if we can think of a practical solution." We—that was the word he'd used. Was it just a slip of the tongue? It certainly had sounded reassuring. And, *"I feel a part of all this . . . I want to help."*

Did he mean that? *You don't know him well enough to judge,* Jessie reminded herself. But she would pin her hopes on it. At the moment it seemed the only ray of hope she had.

Twenty-eight

ALAN WAS SURPRISED to find three stacks of bandages, neatly rolled and stacked, ready for him the next morning. Quickly inspecting them, he smiled in approval. "Nice work, Jessie, thanks. I hope I can call on you again?"

"Anytime. It's a blessing to have something useful to do."

But now what? she wondered bleakly after he and Wanda had left. So it felt like another blessing when an hour later Hazel appeared at the door, just as a rainshower began. "Hazel, you're free again!" Jessie cried. "It seems forever since I've seen you."

"Pop's in a good mood because he found some lumber to cover our broken windows. '*Now* it rains,' he says, '*after* we needed it.' Anyway, he only let me out on the promise of good behavior. What's happening with you?"

"I wish I had good news to tell," Jessie said, a shadow coming over her face. "That first day you had to stay home, Lee died."

"Oh, I'm so sorry. What about the little girl?"

"She's still at the camp. And badly in need of a home." Hazel's sympathetic nod encouraged Jessie to go a step further. "You don't suppose your parents would like to adopt an orphan?"

Hazel looked stricken. "You're not serious, Jessie! I couldn't even tell them about a half-breed child, much less suggest they adopt one. Besides, little Jonathan's enough for them to handle."

You knew how she'd react, Jessie told herself. With a sigh she went to the hat stand in the front hall and picked up two umbrellas. "Let's go look in the shops. Wanda's put me in charge of provisions, and we're out of almost everything. And I want to see if Huston's Medical Supply is open."

As they walked near Van Ness, they were struck to see so many people already at work clearing away mountains of rubble. On one street corner, a large hand-lettered sign had been nailed to a post.

VOLUNTEERS WANTED

TO HELP IN THE MONUMENTAL TASK
OF CLEANING UP OUR STRICKEN CITY.
SOME WERE VICTIMS OF THE RECENT
CATASTROPHE, SOME WERE NOT.
BUT THE WORK OF RECOVERY IS
EVERYBODY'S JOB.

Hazel gave Jessie a questioning look. "Do you think we should join in?"

Jessie's reply came instantly. "The rain's cleared up. Why not?"

AT FIRST they felt unwelcome. The cleanup crews consisted mostly of tough-looking laborers, toiling under the weight of fallen roof beams or pushing wheelbarrows filled with bricks and chunks of concrete. "Go on home, girls," one of them said with open scorn. "You'll just be in the way here."

Hazel surprised Jessie by firing back a heated retort. "Excuse me, sir. The sign says recovery is *everybody's* job."

The foreman walked over and settled the matter. "Over here, young ladies; see this pile of lighter stuff? It's full of people's personal belongings. You can sort through it for us, salvage what you can. The rest goes into the trash bins yonder. Glad to have you with us."

Even coping with the so-called lighter stuff was backbreaking work. And trying to fish out broken furniture, kitchen utensils, mangled and muddy clothing, shattered toys, the remnants of once-peaceful living now in wreckage, almost broke their hearts. Hazel gasped when she uncovered a tattered and bloodstained baby carriage. "This is horrid," she cried. "I wish we'd never come here."

Gently but firmly, Jessie urged her on. "I know, but we've got to do this. We're helping the people who lived here to get on with their lives."

It was the hardest physical labor either of them had ever engaged in. Every morning they went to Van Ness Avenue and toiled alongside other volunteers, some of them women. They became so well acquainted with a few that they almost seemed like old friends. Every afternoon when the foreman blew his whistle for quitting time, they limped home with stiff, aching muscles, glad to have made themselves useful.

They were glad, too, when they were able to find fresh fruit or a few vegetables at an open-air market or grocer's store. Often they stood in long lines for small rations of bread or canned meat, and milk was almost impossible to come by.

Arriving back at Wanda's each evening, Jessie peeled off the old dress Wanda had lent her for the dusty cleanup work. Then she stared into her tiny closet, trying to decide between her blue poplin and the plaid skirt and waist she had brought from home. Next she would try to put together some kind of supper for herself and Wanda, using her minimal cooking skills. All the while, she wondered when Wanda would arrive, what news she would bring about Lily—and whether Alan might stop in when he drove her home.

But Wanda usually arrived late and with the same discouraging news: Lily was still silent and withdrawn. And equally distressing, after dropping Wanda off, Alan usually drove away without coming in. Once he brought in another box of supplies for bandage rolling. But in reply to Jessie's anxious question, he still had no ideas for solving the Lily problem. With a sigh, she pushed up her sleeves to start shelling peas.

In her frustration she began to wonder whether there really was anything Alan could do to help, even if he wanted to. After all, short of somehow changing her father's mind, what could *anyone* do?

ONE EVENING near the end of her second week of work on the salvage effort, Jessie settled on the sofa with Toby for some reading while Wanda went to draw herself a bath. When a knock sounded at the door, Jessie opened it—and had to stare at the visitor for a moment before she recognized him. "Oh, Mr. Nesbit, hello! Won't you come in?"

He frowned in puzzlement. "Have we met, miss?"

"I'm Jessie Wainwright. I've been staying with Wanda during the emergency. Let me tell her you're here."

By the time he stepped inside, Wanda had rushed to greet

him. "Philip, you're back. How wonderful!" Jessie averted her eyes, thinking it impolite to watch the ardent kiss that followed.

"Just pulled in this afternoon," Mr. Nesbit said. "Please forgive my barging in unannounced, but I had to see you."

"I'm so glad you came. Would you like something to drink?"

"No, thank you. But I need to speak with you about, shall we say, a private matter. May we go for a drive?" He glanced nervously at Jessie.

Wanda looked uncertain, but Jessie insisted, "Please, don't mind me. I have work to do, anyway."

A minute later she was watching them climb into Nesbit's four-seater. She turned away from the window and tried to go back to her reading. Even with all the turmoil, and no school, she was determined to keep up with her studying. Each night she read in her biology book, or in one of the medical books she had brought with her. But this time, her mind kept wandering. *You're just bothered because he didn't remember you,* she told herself. *And because you've always disliked him. And . . .* slumping, she let her book fall shut. *Because Wanda might say yes to him.*

She couldn't get past the frightening thought.

TWO HOURS LATER she was still at it, sitting up in bed now, staring at a full-page illustration of the cardiovascular system. She heard Wanda come in and gently close the front door behind her. Soon Wanda looked into Jessie's room. "May I visit a minute?"

"Sure, come in." Jessie laid her book aside, and Wanda came to sit on the edge of the bed. But then she seemed to have nothing to say.

Finally Jessie said, "Mr. Nesbit seemed surprised to see me here."

"He was, a little. But I explained about your parents' house being closed up. I think he understood."

"Did you have a nice drive?"

Wanda nodded wordlessly, then drew a deep breath. "He still wants me to marry him, Jessie. More than ever, he says."

Even though she had expected this, Jessie went pale.

"He's got a new project going," Wanda went on, "building houses in a new community near Los Angeles. Hollywood, I think it's called. And there's a beautiful hospital where I could work. After we're married, he wants to move there permanently."

Jessie sucked in her breath. "Oh, Wanda—what did you say?"

"I didn't say yes, and I didn't say no. I mean, there's so much to consider. Disaster and all, I love it here. And in a funny way, I've come to like living alone. Still, do I want to live alone for the rest of my life?" Jessie could only watch, wide-eyed, as Wanda went on debating with herself. "Philip does very well financially, and he treats me like a queen. I could do worse, you know."

"So could he—a whole lot worse. But I just can't imagine your not being here. Are you very much in love with him?"

"Oh, Jessie! I was in love with Edgar, and I never thought that could happen to me again. Philip can be socially awkward, I know, but he's always been kind and generous to me. I know I should do what's best for me in the long run. The only problem is, I have no idea what that is."

It was Jessie's turn to sigh. "I don't know what to say, Wanda."

"Well, fortunately I have a while longer to think about it. Philip will be in Los Angeles most of the next few weeks. He says he won't try to rush me. So that's where things stand."

They said their good nights, and Wanda went out. But Jessie knew she couldn't possibly read anymore. Closing her book and turning off her light, she tried to imagine Wanda married to Mr. Nesbit. There surely were things to consider. To tell Wanda that she disliked Philip would be unspeakably mean. Especially since she'd only seen him a couple of times.

Suddenly she sat up in bed. The idea of Wanda's having a husband had struck her in a new light. That would make it easy for Wanda to adopt a child! Even if they lived far away, at least Lily would have a home.

Just as suddenly, she fell back onto her pillows. No matter how desperate she felt about Lily, she would not deserve to be called Wanda's friend if she urged her to marry Mr. Nesbit when it might not be the right thing for her.

The rest of the night she spent tossing and turning. Worries piled upon worries! Would there ever be an end to them?

Twenty-nine

JESSIE HEARD ALAN come in with Wanda the next evening just as she pulled a fallen soufflé from the oven. "Of all days!" she gasped, shoving the hot dish onto a shelf in the pantry. *What was that trick of Mrs. O'Reilly's for beating egg whites?* She had been thrilled to find fresh eggs at the market that afternoon, but they had been costly, and now they were wasted. Flustered, she smoothed her skirt and stepped into the front room to greet them. And one look at their faces told her something had changed.

"There's news, Jessie," Wanda began. "When I was checking on Lily this morning, two women from the Bureau of Adoptions came in. Mrs. Cowell's an absolute angel compared to those shrews, I tell you. They poked at the children as if they were cattle. Some of them cried, but not Lily. I wish she had, it would have been normal behavior. Then I heard one of the women say they'll be moving the children out soon."

Jessie shot a frantic look at Alan. "You said that wouldn't happen for a long time."

"I never thought they could make plans that fast," he said. "But there's more. Mrs. Cowell is leaving day after tomorrow, to take care of her invalid mother. That means you can come back to the camp."

"Oh, I will, gladly," Jessie said. "Maybe I can cheer Lily up. But now we really must find someone to take her before she disappears."

"How about a Chinese family?" Alan said. "Why don't you see what Henry thinks? He'll be along in a few minutes, actually. I hope you don't mind that I invited him. He said he'd bring dinner, by the way."

"Mind? Goodness no, it'll be nice to see him again," Wanda said. Jessie quickly agreed, and thinking of her ruined attempt at a meal, gave silent thanks, too.

WHEN HENRY ARRIVED, he presented Wanda with a large paper bag. "Chinese specialties, from a merchant I know at the waterfront. There's fresh shark-fin meat, pickled seaweed, and steamed rice. But if anybody doesn't like it, I won't be offended."

"You may be sure, we'll like it," Wanda declared. "Thank you, Henry."

Jessie thought of the Chinese food she used to enjoy with Lee and Mei in happier times. *The littlest things bring back sad memories . . .*

Soon they were relishing the food, which was unanimously declared to be excellent. Henry was impressed to see how expertly Jessie used the chopsticks he had brought. Then, as Wanda poured drinks, Alan and Henry got into a spirited discussion of the refugee-aid effort. Jessie listened quietly as they roundly criticized her father's friend Mayor Schmitz.

"First that crook posts a notice saying the army can shoot to kill anytime they want," Henry complained. "Then the soldiers turn around and steal the same supplies they're supposed to be guarding. I've had them grab things right off my truck. The Red Cross people don't want to give the city any more supplies. They're sure Schmitz will seize it all, sell it for top dollar, and pocket the money."

Alan laughed derisively. "And considering that he was on the way to jail for corruption the same day the quake happened, I think they're right."

"That's hard to believe," Jessie declared. "My family has known Mr. Schmitz for years. He's always seemed a perfect gentleman to me."

Alan and Henry exchanged looks of embarrassment. "Sorry, Jessie," Alan said. "We didn't mean to offend."

Jessie responded with a faint smile. She wouldn't argue with them about her father's old friend. After all, there could easily be things she'd never known about his life as mayor. Besides, she was far more interested in another subject. She turned to Henry and said, "Could I ask you something?"

"Sure, what?"

"Do you think any Chinese family might be willing to adopt Lily, so she wouldn't have to go to an orphanage?"

He frowned at the question. "I seriously doubt it. To Chinese parents, a daughter is only another mouth to feed until she marries and moves into someone else's household. And the Chinese won't accept mixed-race children. Whites won't either, I'm sure."

At Jessie's glum look, Alan tried to soften Henry's answer. "Jessie, how about if I ask the Adoptions people which orphanages they're considering? If they'll tell me, maybe you can at least keep track of her."

Jessie nodded morosely. "Thanks. And maybe you could—" A knock at the door interrupted her. "I'll go," she said, then opened the door to a surprise. "Corey, what on earth?"

"Hello, Sis. Does that little beauty belong to your fellow?" He pointed to Alan's motorcar, parked at the curb.

"It belongs to a *friend*," Jessie said. She stepped onto Wanda's front porch and pulled the door shut behind her. "What are you doing here?"

"Papa wanted me to tell you that he's going up to Aunt Margaret's to fetch Mama. Don't know why he didn't telephone you directly, come to think of it."

Jessie gazed at him impassively. *He and I know why,* she thought. *And no one else needs to.*

"Anyway, they'll be back tomorrow night," Corey continued. "He's sent for Mrs. O'Reilly, too, even though it'll be Saturday. Says he wants to get the house up and running again as soon as possible."

"That'll be nice. Will you be there?"

"Can't. I take off early in the morning for Saratoga to spend the weekend with my new girl at her family's country estate."

"Another one?" Jessie rolled her eyes. "Nobody I know, I guess."

"No, but you must've heard of Fielding's Department Store, downtown." Impatient to get back inside, Jessie only nodded. "Ken Fielding's a fraternity brother of mine," Corey went on. "And his kid sister Eleanor is a real peach! But hey, even if she weren't, with that kind of money behind her, how could a fellow go wrong?"

"A fellow could," Jessie said wryly. "But enjoy your weekend."

WHEN JESSIE RETURNED to the dining room, Alan and Henry had already cleared the dishes and taken them to the kitchen. "That was my brother," she told Wanda.

"Why didn't you invite him in?" Wanda asked.

"Oh, he wouldn't have wanted to. He just kept going on about his 'peach' of a girlfriend, who's got tons of money. Good thing Hazel isn't here. She's had a hopeless crush on Corey for years, and—"

She stopped short as Henry came back into the dining room, but he had heard every word—and looked as if he'd been slapped. "I'm sorry, Henry," Jessie said. "I know you care for Hazel."

Henry shook his head. "Really, it's not a problem." But the sadness in his voice told Jessie something different. "Where is she, anyway?" Henry asked. "I was hoping she'd be here tonight."

Now Jessie would have to give him more bad news. Searching for the right words, she finally said, "The thing is, Hazel's family is anti-Chinese. She was quite upset when she found out the truth about Lily..."

Now Henry looked puzzled. "The truth about Lily? What do you mean?"

She answered, with an apologetic smile. "You've been such a good friend, it's not fair that you're the only one here who... You see, I not only have a brother, I have a sister, too."

So Henry became one more who knew Lily's story. "I see what you're up against." He shook his head. "And Lily's being half Chinese only makes it worse. I'm sorry to hear about Hazel, though. I hope she'll change her mind about Lily."

"Well, everyone, I've got to be going," Alan said. "And

Wanda, I'm sorry, but I can't drive you tomorrow. Every fourth Saturday they have an all-day conference at the hospital. Tomorrow's the day, and I have to be there. At least the camp's clearing out pretty fast now. The railroads are giving free passes to the refugees for anywhere they want to go."

Jessie gasped in alarm. "If neither of you is there tomorrow, who'll look out for Lily?"

"I can drive Wanda," Henry offered. "I'm taking a load of supplies."

"Thanks, Henry, that's kind of you," Wanda said.

"Then on Sunday, I can go, can't I, Alan?" Jessie shot a look of appeal to him. "You said Mrs. Cowell wouldn't be there after Saturday, so——"

"That's right, you could," he told her. "I'm going over on Sunday afternoon, so I'll pick you both up here about two."

"Pick Jessie up," Wanda suggested. "As long as she's going, maybe I'll treat myself to a rare day off. Not much to do there now, anyway."

So it was settled. A few minutes later, Henry said good night and headed out to his truck.

"It's too bad about Henry, isn't it, Jessie?" Alan mused. "The way he pines after Hazel, I mean, while she pines after your brother. That's the merry-go-round of love for you. It'll spin you around till you're dizzy."

How odd for you to say that, Jessie thought. *And how interesting.* But she made no reply.

WHEN SHE WALKED OUT to his car with him later, she had a question. "Truthfully, Alan, do you think they'd tell you where Lily might be taken?"

"I surely hope so. You do have to be prepared for disappointment, but you can be prepared for successes, too."

"That sounds a little optimistic, at least. I am grateful for all your help, truly. Why you're giving it is what I don't understand."

"Maybe because I grew up a loner, never really close with anyone. Oregon apple country, where I'm from, is beautiful, but it's got more trees than people. Seeing how devoted you are to Lily made a big impression on me." Jessie was about to thank him, but before she could speak, he went on. "There's something else that impresses me, too. I hope you don't mind, but Wanda told me you're planning to go into medicine."

"I'd like to. It's been my dream since I was little."

"That's very intriguing. I was delighted to hear it."

"But it probably won't happen, because my father insists that a girl couldn't do such a thing. And one from a refined family shouldn't want to."

"He really thinks that?" Alan couldn't resist a chuckle. "I've only known you a couple of weeks, but even I could tell him you're never going to be just a society lady, sipping tea all day."

"Like my mother, you mean?"

Suddenly he was flustered. "I'm sorry. I didn't mean it that way."

"That's all right. My mother is a society lady, but she's a lot more than that. She's also a lovely person who does worthwhile things."

"I'm sure she is. What I meant was, of course you can be a doctor. You have the brains for it, and the determination, too. I admire those things in you. I admire you, period."

"Not half as much as I admire you," she said, blushing to hear herself say it. *Oh dear, that sounded so forward!* "I hope sometime you'll tell me more about growing up in Oregon," she hastened to add.

"It'll be my pleasure." He bowed low, his green eyes smiling.

She smiled back. "Thanks again, Alan. See you on Sunday."

They lingered another moment in saying good night, then he drove away.

So people spin around on—what did he call it? A merry-go-round of love. Whatever that is, it'll make you dizzy, he had said, too.

With a slight feeling of—could it be dizziness?—she turned and walked slowly back to the house.

Thirty

AFTER STEWING about it all night, Jessie packed her bags the next morning, and when Henry came to pick up Wanda, she asked him to drop her at home. Her vow to stay gone would have to be abandoned. It would be too unfair to her unsuspecting mother.

Back on Franklin Street, she found teams of workers repainting the house in shades of soft gray and replanting the garden with camellias and roses. In the kitchen, Mrs. O'Reilly hummed as she scrubbed every inch of her worktable. After taking her things to her room, Jessie astonished the cook by offering to help prepare a special dinner to celebrate the reopening of the house. For Jessie it would be a private celebration, as well, because tomorrow, with Mrs. Cowell leaving the camp, she would see Lily again.

With some time to herself before Mrs. O'Reilly would need her, she decided to walk over to Van Ness and put in an hour or so on the cleanup job. But the people she and Hazel had worked with were no longer there. The cleanup foreman explained why.

"All the volunteers have been sent home, miss. Strictly a hired crew now. Mostly bulldozer work, as you can see. But you and the other young lady were a big help. Thank you kindly."

Just as Jessie started to leave, glad to get away from the noise and dust, a motorcar careened around a corner and into the work area. Its driver blasted the horn as he screeched to a stop near the foreman.

"You there!" the driver shouted. "I want a word, now!"

Jessie stopped abruptly. She would know that deep voice anywhere.

"Yes, sir, Mr. Nesbit." The foreman whipped off his cap as he went over to the car. Other workers dropped their tools and gathered around, and Jessie edged close enough to listen, while keeping well out of sight.

Nesbit continued in an angry, booming tone. "This area was supposed to be cleared days ago. You know the time pressure we're under."

Between two workmen, Jessie could see the foreman nervously twisting his cap. "Well, sir, we've had some rain, and—"

"Damn it, man, I need results, not excuses! I've only got a few days to close my deal with the city for this land at a rock-bottom price, and the bank won't co-sign unless the place is cleared. If the losers who own these lots start thinking they want to hang on and rebuild, it'll be too late."

"But, sir, we're almost—"

"No *buts*! This is costing me a pretty penny, and I won't have you ruining the deal by lying down on the job. You finish up by tomorrow night or you're all out on your ear, without pay!"

With that, Nesbit gunned his car's engine and roared away, leaving the workers muttering and the foreman thoroughly shaken.

Her head in a spin, Jessie hurried toward home. *His deal with*

the city? That must mean more payoffs to Mayor Schmitz! No wonder
Alan said the mayor was corrupt. And no wonder Mr. Nesbit
did so well in real estate. He didn't just invest in property, he
stole it! The thought repelled her.

And worst of all was the thought that Wanda might marry
this man.

WHEN LEONARD AND CATHERINE arrived in early evening, they
were met by a beaming Mrs. O'Reilly and a worn-out Jessie.
"'Tis a fine feast we'll be havin' tonight, madam," the cook said.
"Yesterday the crews dug out a warehouse full of beef, still
packed in ice, and the butcher saved me a lovely roast. Our
girl's been tendin' it in the oven for me. Cut up the beans and
potatoes, too, she did."

"You can't mean my Jessie!" Her mother laughed. Jessie
threw her arms around her, then greeted her father stiffly, not
meeting his eyes.

"How thankful I am that our house survived," Catherine
said, as Jessie accompanied her upstairs. "And how glad I am to
see you, dear. I've felt so guilty about leaving you here in this
dangerous place, all alone."

"I wasn't alone, Mama. I was with Wanda, and we were fine."

"Well, I kept telling myself that you did choose to stay, although I'll never understand why. Anyway, we're all together
now, thank God. Tomorrow I'll contact our friends and start
putting our lives back in order."

IT WAS NOT UNTIL late that night that Jessie went to her father's
study, thinking he had already gone to bed. But he was working

at his desk, by the thin light of a gas lamp. He frowned when she came in.

"If you're here to bring up unpleasant topics again—"

"No, Papa. I'm just returning a couple of your books." She laid his medical reference book and medical dictionary on a corner of the desk.

He looked mystified. "Why did you have them in the first place?"

"When we thought the house might burn, I took them with me to Wanda's."

He studied her for a moment, his frown deepening. "Of all things to choose, you lugged those heavy books to safety? Is it possible that, once again, you're hankering after a medical career?"

"Not again. I've never stopped hankering after it."

"Good lord." More frowning. Then he seemed to reach a decision. "Sit down, Jessie."

Taken aback, she sat on the edge of the big armchair.

"I'm glad you decided to come home," he began after a pause.

"I only did it because of Mama," she said coolly.

"Exactly. You wouldn't want her to be hurt, and neither would I. That's what I want to talk to you about. You see, it has occurred to me that your bizarre ideas—groundless though they are—if they ever reached her ears . . ." He seemed unsure how to proceed. "Let's just say that if you promised me that would never happen, I'd be very grateful. Grateful enough, perhaps, to view your medical ambitions in a more favorable light."

Jessie's eyes widened. "Let me see if I have this right. I promise not to tell Mama the shameful truth about you and

Mei, and you'll change your mind about my going to medical school?"

She saw his hands close tight around the arms of his chair. But his tone remained controlled. "Don't misunderstand, I'll never actually approve of your going. And it does seem insane to reward you for not telling lies about me. However, I am saying that I might agree to such an arrangement."

Jessie hesitated. "I'm trying to think—is bribery the name for this, or is it blackmail?"

He reacted with a scowl. "Come now, there's no need for such ugly words. I'm simply proposing a mutually beneficial agreement."

After a moment of tense silence, she rose and looked down on him as if from a great height. "Don't worry, I'll never breathe a word to Mama. And here are two more things I won't do. I'll never blackmail you, and I'll never accept a bribe. Thanks just the same, but I'll get where I'm going without that kind of help. Good night."

Once again she turned her back on him. Shaking, she ran upstairs to sink down on her window seat. She had expected her father to ignore her as much as possible. But to see him— he who had once stood so sturdy and strong— reduced to such wretched weakness made her heart ache with grief.

And what about me? she wondered, her mind in turmoil. Should she feel proud that she'd taken the high road? Or disgusted with herself for throwing away a once-in-a-lifetime chance at medical school? Tears stinging her eyes, she looked toward the stars in search of wisdom. But in the blackness of a fog-shrouded night, there were no stars, no wisdom to be found.

Upset by the scene with her father, troubled by thoughts of the unscrupulous Mr. Nesbit, and anxious over how she might find Lily the next day, she slept badly. The house was still when she woke up late the next morning and went to the kitchen in search of breakfast.

"They've both gone out," Mrs. O'Reilly said, pouring her a cup of coffee. "The doctor sent the workers to the clinic this morning. The damage over there ain't fixin' itself, you know. Your mother's gone callin' on the Arnolds. Their telephone's still out, even though ours is workin' again, thank the Lord. She's invitin' them for Sunday dinner. Said to tell you we'll be servin' at two o'clock sharp."

Jessie's hand flew to her mouth. She'd hardly paid attention until Mrs. O'Reilly said the words *two o'clock*. Exactly when she was supposed to meet Alan at Wanda's house.

"Oh, and Hazel came by," the cook went on. "They're goin' to Monterey for a week. Her mother's plumb worn out from all the troubles."

Jessie thanked her and, coffee cup in hand, headed back upstairs. The last thing she would have expected was for her mother to ask people in on her first day back.

Now she'd have to find a way to get out of the house.

She was still mulling over the problem when Dr. and Mrs. Arnold arrived at one twenty with their thirteen-year-old son, Frank. *Mama and Papa won't know what to do with him,* Jessie thought. Mr. Gregory Hayes, her father's longtime attorney, was another guest. A confirmed bachelor with eccentric taste in clothes, he had the bushiest eyebrows she had ever seen. She liked him best of all her parents' friends.

Talk was lively in the parlor as Dr. Wainwright poured a round of champagne from the only bottle in his wine cellar that had survived the quake. Mr. Hayes told the group about the lawsuits arising from the earthquake and fires. Many of the ruined downtown buildings had been found to contain inferior mortar and poor foundations. The buildings' owners, convinced their losses were caused by the mayor's taking bribes from local builders, wanted Mr. Hayes to help them sue the city. Jessie expected her father to leap to the defense of the mayor, but he only grumbled, "Bad time to talk politics."

Out of the corner of her eye, Jessie watched the parlor clock tick toward one forty-five as she tried her best to chat with shy, tongue-tied Frank Arnold. She tried to signal to her mother that she felt ill and needed to bow out. But she couldn't catch her eye. And when Mrs. O'Reilly announced, "Dinner is served," she was hopelessly trapped.

As everyone rose, she felt her father's hand on her arm. "You'll sit next to Frank, of course," he said.

"I'm not feeling very well, Papa. I'd like to be excused."

"Oh, come now, I'm sure it's nothing Mrs. O'Reilly's fine cooking won't fix." He led her into the dining room and pulled her chair out for her.

Feeling all eyes upon her as she took her seat, she gave the group a weak smile through gritted teeth. Alan would be waiting for her, and she'd be stuck sipping consommé!

The guests were enjoying their first course when the telephone rang in the foyer. All morning, calls from Leonard's patients had been incessant. A moment later Mrs. O'Reilly appeared in the doorway, but instead of summoning the doctor, she beckoned to Jessie. "It's a young man askin' for you, miss."

Jessie's heart skipped a beat. She had never been telephoned by a young man. Uncomfortably aware of her parents' frowns at this irritating interruption, she rose and murmured, "Pardon me," and tried to walk sedately as she went to the foyer. There she hurried to the phone.

Alan's voice came crackling over the wire. "Jessie, you've got to come right away. I'm at Wanda's, but she's not here." He sounded almost panicked. "I need your help with Lily."

"Lily's *there?*" Jessie almost dropped the receiver. "What happened?"

"I'll tell you when you get here, but please—"

"I'm on my way," she said, and hung up.

Mrs. O'Reilly, always touchy about mealtime etiquette, watched in horror from the dining room doorway as Jessie shockingly breached it. "Where d'you think you're goin'?"

"To Mrs. Shaw's house," Jessie called over her shoulder. "Back later."

"Heavens, girl, what's got into you?" But this time there was no reply. Jessie was already out the door.

Thirty-one

ALAN LOOKED THOROUGHLY FRAZZLED when Jessie arrived. "At last she's asleep," he whispered. "She's like a scared rabbit. I didn't know what to do for her."

"I don't understand. Why is . . ."

Taking her hand, he led her into the guest room that had so recently been hers. There, small and still, in the middle of the bed, lay Lily. As if in a trance, Jessie gazed at the porcelain-smooth face and listened to the soft, gentle breathing. *It's a miracle,* she thought. *However this happened, it's a miracle.* Just then Lily pushed her blankets away with a whimper. Catching her breath, Jessie quickly pulled the covering around her again—*she mustn't take a chill.* She stood for a long time just watching Lily sleep. Finally she stole away to join Alan, who had returned to the parlor when he heard Wanda come in.

"I was just explaining to Wanda why there are intruders in her house," he said. "And why you and I didn't go to the camp today."

"I'd better sit down," Wanda said, sinking into a chair. "Go on, Alan. And while you're at it, explain to me how on earth you got in. Jessie has a key to the house, but since she wasn't here and neither was I—"

"Lucky for me, your back-door latch is broken. I'll ask

Henry to fix it, he's a whiz at things mechanical. But it was a lifesaver today. After what I did at the camp, I felt like a criminal on the run."

"What do you mean?" Jessie asked, taking a seat. "What did you do?"

He sat down beside her. "Around noon I got a message at the hospital that I was needed at the orphanage tent. The Bureau of Adoptions ladies were getting the Chinese children ready to send to a missionary group somewhere in the Far East. They needed a doctor to sign off on each child's physical condition, and quickly. When I got there, they had them lined up outside—Lily, too, of course. I don't think they cared a bit about their condition, as long as I signed the papers. The older ones were scared to death. Some of the little ones were crying. Not Lily, she was quiet as a mouse."

"That's Lily, all right," Wanda said.

"I examined the older kids first," Alan continued. "Two of them had such severe tonsillitis that Mrs. Cowell should have sent them to the infirmary days ago. I'd have spoken sharply to her about that if I'd known. One girl knew enough English to tell me she'd recently seen her aunt. So I said she had to stay back, in case the aunt came looking for her."

"And still Lily wasn't talking?" Jessie asked.

"No, she just watched me the whole time. When I put my stethoscope to her chest, she wrapped her little hand around my finger. That's when I told the ladies—well, I'm afraid I told them she has pneumonia. Then the funniest thing happened— it was as if Lily knew what the word meant. As soon as I said it, she gave a great big sneeze."

Jessie started to laugh, but then a troubling thought struck her. "Gosh, maybe she *is* sick. I'd better go and see if she feels feverish."

Alan put out a hand to stop her. "She's fine, Jessie, I promise. I really did listen to her chest. Sleeping's the best thing for her."

"So you lied about a patient," Wanda said. "You feel guilty about that?"

"That's right. I broke professional rules." A worried look came to Alan's face. "I just kept thinking about Hippocrates— you know, that phrase of his they teach in medical school. 'First, do no harm.' Lily *is* very fragile. I told myself, it *would* do her harm for me to send her away with them. But now I don't know what I think."

"Nothing could be more right than what you did," Jessie declared. Then she added soberly, "But what about the Adoptions workers?"

"When I told them Lily would be properly taken care of, they took the other children and left. She's on their list, though. 'Two-year-old female, reddish-black hair, denied.' And they'll be back." Alan frowned as he cupped his chin in his hands. "The older ones gave me such dirty looks as they were marched off . . . I think they knew Lily had gotten special treatment. The minute they left, I carried Lily to my car and drove straight here."

"You kidnapped her," Jessie said, a twinkle in her eye. "Just what you wouldn't let me do. But, of course, this is different."

"The worst part of it is, I've put a huge burden on *you*, Wanda—bringing Lily to you without asking. I apologize deeply for that."

Jessie held her breath, waiting for Wanda's response. Surely she'd agree that for Lily to be safe, and with them, was all that mattered.

Finally Wanda spoke. "After seeing Lily and the other orphans, and meeting those awful women, I understand why you did it, Alan." She was choosing her words carefully. "And I see that you had nowhere else to take her." Then she rose and turned away, gazing out the window. "But quite frankly, I'm afraid I don't see what we are to do now."

Alan still had rounds to finish at the infirmary, and regretfully had to leave, but promised to return as soon as he could. "Tonight we can talk about the next few days, at least. Is that all right, Wanda?"

Never one to be at a loss for long, Wanda was already coming to grips with the situation. "That's fine. And if the volunteer supervisor asks about me, tell her I had to go back to my job. It'll be true soon enough, anyway."

After Alan had left, Wanda turned to Jessie with a question. "What's going on at your school?"

"All I know is they're working on the building. Why?"

"If Lily's going to be our responsibility for a while, you'll need to be here. We have to get the right foods for her, and clothes. Tomorrow, when the shops open, we'll need to stock up." Neither of them had any idea what Lily might be willing to eat. Meanwhile Wanda would find an old nightgown and fashion it into a dress for Lily. "Those rags she's been wearing are going straight into the trash," she declared.

Just then the telephone rang and Wanda answered with a crisp "Hello?" Then her tone softened. "Oh, hello, Philip. How lovely to hear your voice."

Jessie stiffened and started to edge out of the room. Even after what she'd seen of Mr. Nesbit, she reminded herself every day that his business dealings were just that—his own business.

And that Wanda must know what she was doing. Still, it made her feel queasy to hear Wanda speaking to him.

"I'm so sorry, Philip," Wanda continued. "I'll have to cancel tonight. Something's come up and——" She listened for a moment, shooting a patient look at Jessie, lingering in the doorway. "I can't explain right now, but I'll phone you tomorrow, I promise. Bye."

"Alan's worried about the burden he's put on you," Jessie said after Wanda hung up. "And he doesn't even know about Mr. Nesbit. Or does he?"

"No, and don't say anything to him. He feels bad enough as it is. Now, where were we?"

"Maybe we should see what's in your kitchen that Lily might like when she wakes up. But first let's take another look at her."

They tiptoed into the bedroom and gazed down at the sleeping child.

"Sad little thing," Wanda whispered. "Anyone would feel sorry for her."

Except Papa, Jessie told herself. She said only, "We'll need Henry, too. If Lily talks, it'll be in Chinese, not English."

At that moment, Lily opened her eyes. Blinking in the semidarkness, she looked from Jessie to Wanda, finally fixing her eyes on Jessie.

"Hello, Lily," Jessie murmured, smiling. "We're so glad you're here."

Is that a ghost of a smile on her face? she wondered as Lily stared back. In fact, it was merely the beginning of a great yawn, just before Lily turned over and went back to sleep.

———

Around dinnertime, Lily awoke and took a long look at the banana Jessie offered her. Then she refused it and pushed away bread as well. When Alan arrived a few minutes later, she had fallen asleep once more. After looking in on her, he joined Jessie and Wanda in the parlor.

"I spoke to the lead Adoptions lady about Lily while I was at the camp," he said. "She said that if I verify that Lily's in an approved foster-care facility, it's all right—for now."

"'Facility.'" Jessie repeated the word anxiously. "Can you declare this a facility? Or does someone else have to do that?"

"I stuck to my pneumonia story, then told the lady I'd taken Lily to a registered nurse. I think that'll do it, and it's true besides." He sat back, beaming. It was the first smile Jessie had seen from him that day.

On that encouraging note, the telephone rang again. Jessie winced when Wanda said, "Oh, hello, Mrs. Wainwright. Yes, she's still here." A pause. "Nothing's wrong, no." Another pause. "Really? Yes, I'll tell her. Not at all. Good-bye."

She hung up and turned to Jessie, smiling. "It seems you ran out this afternoon with guests in the house. They want you back there, *now*."

Jessie sprang to her feet, promising Wanda she would see her first thing in the morning. Alan volunteered to drive her home.

"I must say I'm glad that Lily's out of that camp," he said as they got under way. "Especially since tomorrow's my last day there."

Jessie stared at him. "Is it really?"

"Yesterday I got word that the board of directors expects me to return to the hospital full-time next week. I go to the camp one more time to tie up loose ends, and that's that."

"I hate to think what would have happened if you hadn't gone today!"

"I know, but the fact remains, I acted unprofessionally."

"Oh, Alan, you had every right to tell them Lily was too ill to be carted off like that. And if anybody ever tries to take her away again, they'll have me to reckon with." With a soft smile, she stole a look at Alan. "I can't imagine what this day has been like for you."

He replied with a shrug. "We still don't have a solution."

"But we'll find one. We've got to. In the meantime, I'm going to help Wanda as much as I can while Lily's with her."

"Count me in for that. And this means we'll see a lot more of each other. That's something else I'm glad about, because—" He hesitated, then finished softly. "Because I've discovered that you're a very special person."

Before she could think how to reply, they had turned onto her street. "We're here," she said, then felt like kicking herself. *Goodness, how are you supposed to answer when a young man says you're special?* she thought frantically, as he parked in front of her house.

Alan came around to help her out of the car. Awkwardly, she held out her hand to shake his. Instead, he took her hand and held it. It seemed he still had one more thing to say. "I'm really glad I met you, Jessie." Lifting her hand to his lips, he gave it a feather-light kiss, then climbed back into his motorcar and drove off.

THE HOUSE WAS QUIET when she let herself in. Upstairs she tapped softly on her parents' bedroom door. "I'm home."

"About time," her father said, sounding more annoyed than angry.

In her room she fell onto the bed, a mixture of hope, worry, and a mysterious excitement swirling in her head: Hope, because with Lily finally out of that awful camp, she could spend time with the frightened child, perhaps calm her fears a little. Worry, because it might be only for a short time—and worry for some other reason she couldn't quite pinpoint. *Maybe because of what Alan did today. Was I properly grateful?* She tried to remember every word she'd said to him, but her mind kept wandering to memories of another kind. The way it sounded when he'd said, "We're going to be seeing a lot more of each other." The way he'd taken her hand and held it. The tingly feeling of his fleeting kiss on that hand. From those memories, that feeling, grew the excitement she felt; she knew that now. That mysterious, wonderful excitement came from *Alan,* not from what had happened, or what he had done. It came from who he *was,* and from how she felt when she was with him.

Rising, she went to her mirror and took a long look at herself, as if for the first time. Her large dark eyes gazed back at her. She'd rarely thought about it, but . . . maybe they were a little bit pretty. Her waist was slim, corsets or no. *And I suppose I have filled out nicely on top,* she thought. Pulling the pins from her hair, she let it fall to her waist. From now on, one hundred strokes a night. She reached for her brush, suddenly wanting desperately for her hair, for all of herself, to shine.

As she brushed, a sweet serenity overcame her. Hope, she decided—and excitement—were bound to prevail.

Thirty-two

HER MOTHER WOULD RISE late in the morning, Jessie felt certain. With a quick "See you tonight," to Mrs. O'Reilly, she managed to get away before the cook started breakfast.

"Lily's still asleep," Wanda told her when she arrived. "I'm sure she'll be up soon, but I need to do some errands. Will you stay with her?"

"Of course. That's what I'm here for. Take your time."

So began Jessie's first day caring for her little sister. And trouble was not long in coming. Lily seemed to have made up for weeks of very little sleep, but when a thunderstorm rumbled overhead mid-morning, it was as if another aftershock had hit. *"Ai-yah, ai-yah!"* she screamed. "Earth dragon!"

Hurrying in, Jessie found her out of bed and hiding in a corner. Pulling her close, she spoke soothingly, telling Lily there was no Earth Dragon, she was safe, and there was nothing to be afraid of. Not sure she understood a word, Jessie tried to think of some way to distract her. Chester—this might finally be his big chance. She retrieved him from the drawer where she had stowed him, then offered him to Lily.

Lily took one look and screamed louder than before, pushing him away. *She's never had a stuffed animal,* Jessie thought. To Lily the bear was just another thing to be afraid of.

"Go away, Chester," Jessie said, tossing him aside. At that Lily began to calm down, but fear seized her again when Jessie carried her into the parlor. Seeing Toby reclining in his usual perch on the windowsill, Lily instantly made it clear that she saw him as another danger.

"Cat!" she cried, squirming in Jessie's arms. "Cat hurt, cat hurt!"

"No, Lily, Toby's nice, he won't hurt you," Jessie assured her. By then the startled Toby had jumped down and fled.

Sure that Lily must be hungry by now, Jessie took her into the kitchen. But Lily shook her head vigorously at every tempting morsel she offered. Jessie carried her around the house, speaking in low tones. "It's all right, Lily, you're safe here." She got back only stony silence. Instead of making progress, Jessie began to feel she was moving backward.

From that unpromising beginning, things continued to go downhill. Lily remained stubbornly silent, but tense and jumpy, afraid of every sound. To make matters worse, Wanda was distressed when she returned home around noon.

"I ran into your father on the street," she said. "He's got the office fixed up enough for us to open it again, and he wanted me there day after tomorrow. I said I couldn't come and suggested he call Grace Edgerton instead. I'm afraid he got awfully upset with me."

Learning of Jessie's lack of success with Lily only made Wanda feel worse. She tried to interest her in some toys she had bought. Lily refused to touch them.

"I don't think she knows what toys are," Jessie said.

When Wanda took a turn offering several kinds of food,

Lily expressed her lack of interest by turning her back. She rarely looked directly at Wanda, and when she did it was with undisguised fear in her eyes.

Again Jessie tried to think of an explanation. "After that horrible time in the orphanage tent, maybe she sees you as another Nurse Cowell."

"Nonsense!" Wanda snapped. "I don't look anything like her."

Meanwhile Toby continued to be a problem. Even a glimpse of him made Lily scream and hide in her room. Hard-pressed, Wanda tried shutting Toby into her own room, but she had to give it up when the cat, accustomed to roaming the house, yowled in protest and scratched at the door. That set Lily to screaming even louder. Toby was as frightened of the strange new creature in the house as Lily was of him, and the cat quickly learned to stay out of the child's way.

"We'll just have to keep talking to her, help her feel at home," Jessie said. She and Wanda both tried, using their most soothing tones. Lily's only response was a stone-faced stare.

"If only Henry were here," Wanda exclaimed.

Her wish soon came true when Henry stopped by. "Alan told me about Lily. He can't make it till later, but I thought I'd better not wait."

Sure enough, the moment he spoke to Lily in Chinese, things improved. He pulled a banana out of a sack, peeled it, and handed it to her, and this time she grabbed it, took a big bite, and kept eating. His next offering, a rice cake, was eagerly devoured as well. Jessie and Wanda breathed sighs of delighted relief. At last Lily's hunger strike was over.

Henry easily explained Lily's fear of Toby. "Chinatown was full of wild cats, some of them pretty fierce. She must have had some bad experiences. I'll tell her your cat's not like that." Though she said nothing herself, Lily was a good listener. She paid rapt attention whenever Henry spoke to her, and after he finished, her eyes followed him everywhere.

Lily's day was as exhausting for her as it was for everyone else, and by late afternoon she was willing to take a nap. Henry had to leave, but promised to return the next day. Wanda and Jessie heaped thanks upon him for coming to the rescue, and after he had gone, Wanda collapsed on the sofa. "Alan said she'll only be here a few days, thank goodness. I wonder what arrangements he's made for her."

"Tomorrow will be better, Wanda, you'll see." Jessie tried to sound cheerful. If only she felt sure of that. She couldn't bear to think of sending Lily to some unknown foster home—or worse, back to the camp.

Alan never did make it to Wanda's that day, and his absence troubled Jessie. Several times when she should have been helping Wanda, she caught herself daydreaming about the tender look she'd seen on his face when he took her in to see Lily the day before.

THE NEXT MORNING, she was relieved to see Alan's car already parked in front of Wanda's house when she arrived. As she walked up the steps, she heard him just inside the half-open front door, telling Wanda, "I know I promised to find her another place, but with the city in such a mess, it's taking longer than I thought. She can stay here if an Adoptions officer certifies this as a foster home. They like your nursing qualifications, but they're insisting on a home visit tomorrow morning at ten."

"Tomorrow!" Wanda's voice was shrill in alarm. "I thought she'd be *leaving* by tomorrow. She's too much for me to handle, or Jessie, bless her heart. I'm about to lose my job, besides."

"I understand. I can always take her back to the camp if need be."

Shocked into action, Jessie pushed open the door and went in. "Alan, please, don't do that!"

They both looked at her in surprise. "Ah," Alan said. "Jessie's here."

"I didn't mean to eavesdrop, but I heard what you said." She turned anxious eyes on Wanda. "We can handle being inspected, Wanda, you know we can. You'll do it, won't you?"

"What's the use? Even if they approved a single woman as a foster parent, which I seriously doubt, it would only delay the inevitable."

"But delay is just what we need, to give Alan more time. We can manage that, can't we?"

Wanda looked resigned. "Well, when you put it that way . . . get ready for some hard work, then. Besides taking care of Lily, we're going to spend the whole day straightening up this house."

"I brought you a few groceries," Alan said. "I'll bring them in, then I can stay and help for a while."

EVEN WITH ALAN there that morning, Lily did only slightly better. Alan gave her a colorful rubber ball, but she showed no more interest in it than she had in Wanda's toys or poor, rejected Chester. But when Henry arrived around noon, Lily watched him as closely as she had the day before. Soon after he arrived, she went to him and gazed earnestly into his face. Then the child who had kept silent for so long let out a stream of Chinese. Jessie caught only one English word, the first one she'd heard Lily say: *uncle.*

Henry looked around at the others. "She says she wants her uncle," he told them. "And she wants to go home now."

Jessie swallowed hard as a deep silence fell on the room.

"Uncle," Lily said again. Her pleading eyes now sweeping the group, she called forth one more word from her limited command of English. "See Uncle."

"She has to be told," Alan said quietly but with conviction.

Jessie knew he was right. "Henry, please, as gently as you can."

Henry bent close and began to speak softly to Lily in their common language. Her little face slowly twisted in distress as he spoke, and when he finished, she dropped to the floor, shaking with sobs.

Jessie knelt on the floor before her, stroking Lily's hair. "We're all so sorry, Lily," she murmured. "I loved your uncle, too. And I love you, and so does everybody here. We all want to keep you safe and happy."

Once again Jessie had no idea how much of what she said Lily understood, if any. But perhaps it didn't matter. In the face of inconsolable sorrow, even the kindest words fall flat.

Thirty-three

WHEN JESSIE CAME in that evening, she slipped into her father's study, took his copy of *Diseases of Infancy and Childhood* from the shelf, and crept upstairs to her room. She dropped the book on the bed and was taking off her coat when her father spoke to her from her doorway.

"Spent the day at Wanda's again, I suppose?"

Jessie barely had time to toss her coat over the book before spinning around. "Yes, I did, Papa. Sorry to be so late."

He came in and sat down at her desk. "I'm reopening the clinic in a few days, as you may know. I've informed Wanda, but it seems she's chosen this highly inconvenient time to desert me. And I was so sure she liked her job."

"Oh, she loves it, you needn't doubt that."

"How can she afford to quit? You two have been tight as glue lately. I thought you might know something about it. Does this have anything to do with that banker she was seeing before the earthquake?"

"He's in real estate, Papa, and he's——" The urge to tell her father about Mr. Nesbit was almost overpowering, but she forced herself to resist. "Wanda and I are good friends, it's true. But she doesn't discuss her finances with me, or her personal life."

"Well, I find it all very strange." He sat frowning thoughtfully for a long moment. "I'll ask her again soon," he said, then got up and went out.

Jessie lay down on her bed and opened the medical book. Although Lily's distrust and hostility were understandable given all she had been through, Jessie hoped to find something that might throw additional light on the matter. But she only stared at the pages without seeing the print.

She wished she hadn't needed to lie. *But when Papa washed his hands of Lily, he made his choice. He'll get no information from me.*

JESSIE RUSHED through breakfast the next morning, then pulled her hair into a smooth chignon, and rifled through the two dozen dresses hanging in her armoire. On this day, she needed one in particular—the ugliest one, in fact. It was a plain brown woolen Aunt Margaret had once sent, with a high neck and a stiff white collar. Jessie had come up with an idea she would put into action the moment the Bureau of Adoptions officer knocked at Wanda's door.

EVEN AFTER all they had done to tidy up the house the day before, Wanda was still not satisfied, and a restless Lily had kept her up half the night. Now she took advantage of Lily's sleeping late to embark on a final cleaning binge. When Jessie arrived at eight thirty, Wanda was already in a nervous state. She regarded Jessie's getup with a puzzled frown.

"We want the gentleman to think you're a prosperous, respectable lady, don't we?" Jessie asked.

"Why, yes, I suppose we do. But how does that—?"

"Well, a respectable lady has a maid," Jessie said with a grin. "Now, if you please, ma'am, let's put the finishing touches on this place."

She was dusting in the parlor and Wanda had just finished scrubbing the kitchen floor when a sharp rap sounded at the door. It was nine fifteen.

Wanda gasped. "He's so early. Look at me—I'm a mess!"

"Go on. I'll take care of him," Jessie whispered, pushing Wanda into her bedroom. Then, patting at her hair, she walked with artificial calm to the front door and opened it. Before her stood a tall man with a hawklike face and piercing gaze. Her heart sank at his stern appearance.

"Gilmore, Bureau of Adoptions," he announced curtly.

She forced a smile. "My mistress is expecting you, sir." She took his hat and coat, then ushered him into the parlor. In a moment Wanda sailed into the room in her Sunday-best dress, the very picture of a gracious lady.

"Mr. Gilmore to see you, madam," Jessie announced in a prim voice.

Wanda gave her visitor a charming smile. "So glad to meet you, sir. Won't you sit down? And Jessie, will you bring us some coffee, please?"

Gilmore declined both offers. "Thank you, ma'am, but I'm pressed for time. We'll need to talk for a few minutes, but first I'd like to inspect the premises, if I may."

"Of course. Lily's still asleep, but you're welcome to look in on her. This way, please."

It took only a few minutes to tour the small house. Mr. Gilmore followed Wanda through the rooms, his sharp eyes taking in every detail. They went to Lily's room last, and Wanda softly opened the door.

But Lily was not sleeping at all. She was not even in her bed.

Puzzled, Gilmore looked around. "Do you mean to tell me the child doesn't have a proper crib? Where is she, anyway?"

Jessie, peering over his shoulder from the hallway, noticed the closet door cracked open. Wanda also saw it, went to the door, and looked in.

"Lily, will you come out, please?"

Lily would not come out. Mr. Gilmore poked his head inside. Jessie could just imagine Lily peering up at him, deathly afraid.

Mr. Gilmore scowled down at her, then turned away with a snort. "Most peculiar," he said to Wanda. Leaving Lily in her hiding place, he returned to the parlor, this time accepting Wanda's invitation to sit down. Jessie slipped into the kitchen to listen.

"I must say, Mrs. Shaw, you keep a neat, orderly house."

"Thank you, sir," said Wanda. "I do think that's important."

Then he spotted Toby dozing on the windowsill. "I'm sorry to see you have a cat. I don't believe cats and small children mix well."

"Oh, Toby's very gentle," Wanda told him earnestly. "Lily loves him," she fibbed sweetly.

"Just the same, I'd keep him away from her. Cats often carry fleas. And their claws are sharp; he might scratch her."

"I'm being very careful about that."

Mr. Gilmore pulled from his pocket the foster-care application Alan had turned in for Wanda, and spent a moment studying it. Then he gave her a curious look. "You have no children of your own, Mrs. Shaw?"

"I'm sorry to say, Mr. Shaw and I have not been blessed in that way."

"Well, I must ask why you want to take in a child of—how shall I say it?—impure race, when there are so many white children in need of homes. We normally frown on that sort of thing."

"Lily is a child in greater difficulty than most, sir. I can't imagine any better reason for foster parents."

But Mr. Gilmore evidently did not agree. His next question was a harsh one. "That habit of skulking in the closet—does she do that often?"

Wanda laughed it off. "Oh no, that's just a little game she plays."

"Well, it's inappropriate and shouldn't be allowed." Then came the question Jessie dreaded most. "Why hasn't Mr. Shaw signed the application?"

Wanda's response was smooth as honey. "Unfortunately he's away just now, on an extended business trip in the East."

"You mean to say this form was submitted without his knowledge?" Peeking into the room, Jessie saw the visitor shaking his head firmly. "A formal application requires the signatures of both husband and wife. And I'll need to interview him. His attitude toward children is very important."

"Oh, my husband *loves* children. And he's eager to help during this emergency. I assure you, he's the kindest, most loving man imaginable."

"That may be. Still, I'll need to meet him." Mr. Gilmore got to his feet. "I appreciate your time, ma'am. Let me know when he's back in town."

Wanda rose, smiling pleasantly. "Thank you for coming, Mr. Gilmore."

Jessie glided into the room with the visitor's hat and coat.

"Step outside with me for a moment, will you please, miss?" he asked. Jessie was startled but did as she was asked.

He turned his penetrating gaze on her once they were safely out of Wanda's earshot. "Tell me, how long have you been working for the Shaws?"

"Not long, sir, but I've known them both for years."

"What sort of man is Mr. Shaw? A good employer?"

"Oh yes, he's the ideal employer, a wonderful man. Really, you must approve them. It may be irregular and all, but that poor child needs their care, she's so sad and lonely—"

"I did not ask for advice on how to do my job," he said sharply.

"No, sir. Sorry, sir."

"That'll be all, thank you." Abruptly dismissing her, he departed.

WANDA WAS SITTING at the kitchen table, reading a letter, when Jessie came back inside. She looked up quickly, folding the letter into her pocket.

"Is something wrong?" Jessie asked.

"Oh no. It's just a nice note from Philip, reminding me of the wonderful life he's offering me in Southern California. He'll be heading down there again in the next few days."

"I see." Jessie tried hard for an entirely neutral tone.

"Well, what did Mr. Gilmore say to you?"

"Oh, he asked me what I thought of Mr. Shaw," Jessie said.

"I tried to say nice things about him, but he didn't let me get very far."

Wanda sighed. "It doesn't matter. He's got his job to do, and he's going to do it. You mustn't get your hopes up about all this."

"My hopes aren't up. At least, not all the way up. They're just not all the way down. And they're not going to be." Jessie went over to the windowsill and scratched Toby under the chin. "Not till ol' Toby says he won't be nice to Lily while she's here."

Toby's only response was to rise, stretch languidly, jump down, and stroll out of the room.

Thirty-four

Mrs. O'Reilly had cinnamon cookies waiting for Jessie when she got home that afternoon. "Oh, and Miss Hazel came by. Seems your school's startin' again on Monday. She's desperately wantin' to talk to you."

Jessie knew she had been neglecting Hazel. "I'd better go right now," she said.

"In that case you'll be takin' her these." Mrs. O'Reilly thrust a packet of cookies at Jessie. "They weren't done bakin' before, and I don't want her to miss out."

Hazel bombarded her with questions. "Where were you? The Jessie I know would be at home, hitting the books. Are you still going to that horrible camp every day?"

Jessie was torn between wanting to tell Hazel everything and fearing her reaction if she did. *She'll find out soon enough,* she told herself. *There'll be nothing to find out if Wanda can't keep Lily,* she argued back.

"Oh, all right, it's Lily," Jessie finally burst out. "She's living at Wanda's for a while. That's where I've been every day."

"How did *that* happen?" Hazel cried.

"It was Alan. He sort of . . . convinced her to do it."

"That doctor from the camp? But Jessie, people will talk behind Wanda's back if they see her with a half-breed."

"Please don't call Lily that. She's a full-blooded human child, who means everything to me. And you know very well why."

At this Hazel's tone softened. "Yes, I know. But you *are* coming back to school, aren't you?"

"Of course. And I'll be with Lily every afternoon, for as long as we're able to keep her. Come with me one day, Hazel. You've never even met her."

"Jessie, I never imagined things could go this far. I'll have to think about it."

They agreed to meet at school on Monday, and Jessie hurried home, arriving in time to slip into the dining room just ahead of her parents. She was already wondering whether pressuring Hazel to meet Lily was such a good idea. Maybe she should leave that subject alone.

LILY SHOWED INTERESTING SIGNS of change during the next three days, and Jessie was eager for Alan to see her. For the first time, Lily had wandered about the house alone, pushing open doors, exploring. *Curiosity,* Jessie thought. *That has to be good, doesn't it?* But not hearing from Alan for so long dampened Jessie's hopes. *He's a busy doctor,* she kept telling herself. *He doesn't account to you for his time.* Still, she felt a strange loneliness as the days went by.

One afternoon Jessie arrived to find Wanda lying on her parlor sofa. "Just snatching a few minutes' rest while Lily's napping," Wanda said.

"You sound kind of down," Jessie remarked. "How's it been going?"

Wanda gave a discouraged sigh. "Philip stopped by on his

way to catch the train. He knows I worked with orphans at the camp, and I told him she's only with me temporarily, but he was put off to see Lily here."

"I hope she didn't make a bad impression?"

"Well, it didn't help when she gave him her icy stare. Then, when he took a step toward her, she screeched like a banshee and ran into her room. He told me I must be out of my mind, and then left right after that. He's the soul of good manners, so it was clear he's displeased with me."

If he hates Lily's being here for a few days, Jessie thought with alarm, *how will he react if she stays much longer?* "Does this mean you'll withdraw the foster-care application, even if it's approved?"

"Let's hope it doesn't come to that. But this is another complication on top of an already complicated situation." Wanda got to her feet. "Well, I'd better go check on Lily."

But if it does come to that, Jessie wondered, *what then?*

WHEN ALAN FINALLY APPEARED, he was full of apologies—and sporting a big black eye. "Sorry I disappeared. Got into a little skirmish the other day."

Jessie's eyes widened. "You were in a *fight?*"

"I caught a couple of soldiers who were . . . let's just say they were trying to liberate some medicines from Henry's truck outside the camp. I tried to run 'em off, and it wound up costing me a night in jail."

"Alan, the police shoot people on sight for much less! You could have been killed!" Jessie felt herself go cold at the thought.

But he shrugged it off. "Tell me about Gilmore. How did the inspection go?" As Lily sat at their feet, examining Alan's hat,

Jessie and Wanda told their story. His reaction surprised Jessie. "Mr. Shaw or no Mr. Shaw, Gilmore's so overloaded I'll bet he hardly knows his own name anymore."

"He knows Edgar hasn't signed that application," Wanda observed.

"And he's not the only one who's overworked. I haven't been questioned anymore about Lily, and I'm sure it's because the Bureau ladies are too busy trying to close the place down to think anymore about her. There's been a consolidation—orphans from the various outlying refugee camps are being brought to them. They've got more children on their hands now than they did at the beginning." Alan paused, growing thoughtful. "Today I heard that a factory owner in New York has said that some of the older children can go work for him, for room and board. Thank heavens Lily's too young for that. But one way or another, they're all going to be provided for. What it comes down to, Wanda, is that it's still up to you. The Bureau ladies will be around for a few more days. It's not too late for me to take Lily back, if that's what you want."

Jessie bit her lip so hard it almost bled. Wanda must be thinking about Mr. Nesbit. *If he had his way, he'd ruin everything,* Jessie thought. *But this is her decision. I won't say a word.*

"Not yet," Wanda said tersely. "Though how we'll manage when Jessie goes back to school, I don't know."

Jessie's eyes met Alan's, and she saw that his look of relief matched her own. Could it be only one week since he had said those surprising words to her about the merry-go-round of love and how it could make you dizzy? The mysterious, excited feeling stirred inside her once again, and she found herself wondering, *Does he know?*

Soon Alan had to leave, and Jessie walked outside with him. *This is becoming a pleasant habit,* she thought. For a moment she considered telling him about Mr. Nesbit, then rejected the idea. It would be gossiping, and Alan wouldn't appreciate it. "If you can't say anything nice..." The old adage echoed in her head.

"So your school's reopening," Alan was saying. "Are you glad?"

"Yes, but I'll miss spending time with Lily. And I don't suppose I'll wind up with grades high enough to convince my father that women can be doctors. Let alone that *I'm* capable of being one."

"I still can't believe he's not pleased and proud that you want to follow in his footsteps."

"Oh, but that's not my reason at all." Her tone was somber. "You see, when I was little, I had a baby sister who became very ill. Nobody could help her—not my father, with all his expert knowledge. Not my mother or our cook, with their quinine-and-hot-pepper cures, or their extract of ginger."

Alan grimaced. "Worthless household remedies, all of them."

"Well, I was no help, either. They always told me to make sure she kept her wraps on, but sometimes I forgot." All of a sudden Jessie felt her face flush and her throat grow tight. "She must have caught a chill. Then she was sleepy, so sleepy. And then she was dead. I've always been sure that I—"

"Stop, Jessie, stop right there," he said firmly. "I'm very sorry to hear about this. But you cannot blame yourself for your sister's death."

"I never thought I was doing that. But in some way, maybe I was. Anyway, soon after that I started searching through my father's medical books, trying to figure out why she'd died, what

I could have done. I never did find out, though. And no one ever told me."

"You mentioned unusual sleepiness. Were there other symptoms?"

"I suppose so, but all I remember is my father shining a light into Amy's ears and throat, and saying she was very, very sick. Then they sent me to stay at Hazel's."

"Undue sleepiness. A sore throat. And then quarantine. That adds up to diphtheria, Jessie, which can cause sudden death. Chill or no chill, believe me, what happened to your sister wasn't the least bit your fault."

His words stunned Jessie. "*Diphtheria!* I've read that it spreads through tainted milk or contaminated water, but I never thought . . . and after all these years, I—" She bowed her head in gratitude and relief.

"I'm starting to see why you've been so single-minded about Lily."

"It was when Amy got sick that I made up my mind about being a doctor."

"But with your father so dead set against it . . . yes, I can see what a serious obstacle you face there."

Jessie nodded. "What's funny is that not long ago, he *did* offer me his support." She told him about her father's attempt to bribe her into silence about Lily. "I'd never dream of letting Mama find out about her, but I turned him down flat, anyway. I still wonder if that was foolish of me."

"Not at all. You kept your self-respect, and you'll never own anything more valuable. Believe me, I've been there. My father tried something like that with me, too."

Jessie had wondered about his family but never dared to ask. "You mean he didn't want you to go into medicine?"

"It wasn't that, exactly. But if you think a prosperous apple grower wants his only son to leave the farm, think again. He said he'd disown me if I chose college over the farm. But here I am, in spite of it."

She gazed at him for a moment. "I'm sorry I haven't confided in you before," she said softly. "I should have known you'd understand."

His eyes crinkled in that now familiar smile. "Well, I'm glad you've told me. And I can tell you this—you *are* going to make it."

She had to laugh. "You sound so sure."

"That's because I am." He lifted her chin and looked deep into her eyes. "You'll get there, I know it."

You know nothing of the kind, she thought, *but you can say that anytime.*

Thirty-five

Two weeks after Jessie returned to school, stunning news came to her family. Abandoning his floundering college career, Corey had dropped out and eloped with Eleanor Fielding. With no prior business experience, he would become a junior executive at Fielding's Department Store. Catherine felt humiliated, in part because her social set was deprived of what could have been a magnificent, stylish wedding. But she consoled herself that Corey had settled down, found a respectable place for himself in the world, and had married into a prominent family besides. Leonard shrugged off the whole affair, declaring that he had given up on the boy long ago.

Hazel was crushed. "No one could make him a better wife than I would have. He's made a terrible mistake."

With no way of knowing whether that was true or not, Jessie decided it was useless to say anything at all.

Left mostly on her own, Wanda was having still more trouble with Lily. Jessie tried to help out as much as she could. One afternoon she discovered Wanda in the kitchen hard at work—and unusually upset.

"Thank God you're here, Jessie. Lily's in her room, after making all the mischief she could think of today. Won't let me dress her, gets furious at every little thing. She eats all right, but throws more food on the floor than she puts in her mouth."

"Isn't that normal for small children?"

"To chase Toby, pull his tail, then cry when he hisses at her? She hardly ever says a word, and when she does, it's in Chinese."

"I'm sorry she's making so much trouble."

"It's as if she's being naughty on purpose. Today when I had to scold her, she shouted at me as if *I'd* misbehaved, then ran and hid in her room."

"You scolded her?"

"I had to, when she broke a crystal vase. I thought I'd put it out of reach, but let me tell you, she can climb like a monkey."

Jessie went looking for Lily, and in her room saw the closet door once again open just a sliver. Lily was crouched inside, her eyes gleaming in the shadows. "Bad," she mumbled. "Lily bad girl."

Jessie knelt and took her into her arms. "You're not bad, Lily. You're just having a rough time."

"Lily bad girl," Lily repeated gloomily. "Jessie good girl."

Jessie's heart melted. "So are you, Lily. We're both good girls. After all, we're—" She stopped herself just in time. "We're good friends, that's what we are," she murmured, gently rocking Lily.

When Jessie returned to the kitchen, Wanda was madly peeling carrots. "She's calmed down now," Jessie said. "Maybe she'll take a nap."

"I hope so, and a long one, too. The only time there's any peace around here is when she's asleep."

Jessie felt a wave of guilt. "I wonder if it's the horrible news we had to give her about Lee. That had to be a blow."

"Maybe. But meanwhile I have problems of my own. Your father wants me back at work, to name one. And I don't think I'm cut out for this life."

"I just keep hoping things will improve."

"That's easy for you to say. You don't deal with it all day long."

Her words struck Jessie like a blow. But they were true. The weight of Lily's care had fallen on Wanda, and Jessie didn't know what more she could do to help. The responsibilities she was juggling—to Wanda, to her mother, in school—were becoming too much. *I wish I were triplets,* she thought bleakly.

"And besides," Wanda added grimly, "a letter's come from Mr. Gilmore."

Jessie felt her pulse quicken. "What does it say?"

"That I'm provisionally approved as a foster parent, although he would still need to meet Mr. Shaw. But he has what he calls a better solution to offer. A church group in Colorado is taking several of the orphans, and he'd like to send Lily along with them next week. They'll eventually live and work on a cattle ranch."

Numb, Jessie watched Wanda's pile of peeled carrots growing. She realized it was time for the hard truth. "Even when Alan brought Lily to us, he told us she might have to be sent away. We all knew it. And you'd just as soon have her go, wouldn't you?"

Wanda's simmering anger exploded. "I most certainly would not! That's very unfair, Jessie. Just because I'm upset about the vase—"

"Wanda, this isn't about a vase. It's about an enormous mistake that I have made. I've been so frantic to save Lily, I never thought what it would mean for you to have her here. I'm truly sorry for that. Please, tell Mr. Gilmore that she can go."

"Oh sure! If I did that you'd hate me forever."

"No, I wouldn't. I'd know you tried your best, and that's all anyone can ask. Just please, make Gilmore promise to tell you where she ends up. Colorado's not the end of the world." She stopped, dismayed to see tears brimming in Wanda's eyes. The unaccustomed sight made her feel even worse.

"Wait, there's one more thing," Wanda began. Then something startled her, and she looked down. Neither of them had seen Lily slip into the kitchen, clutching Chester. But suddenly she was there, gripping Wanda's skirt and gazing up at her.

"*Tai-tai.*" She pointed to Wanda. Then, "Lily," pointing to herself.

"What's she saying?" Wanda wondered. "What's *tai-tai?*"

"It's a word Lee used, I think, when he spoke Chinese to Mei, talking about my mother. I'm pretty sure it means 'mistress.' Mistress of the house."

Lily put Chester down and held out her arms, reaching for Wanda to hold her. Stunned, Wanda put down her paring knife and scooped her up. Lily snuggled in Wanda's arms, a contented look on her face. "Well, I never!" Wanda exclaimed.

Jessie had to blink hard to hold back her own tears. Then she glanced down at Wanda's huge pile of peeled carrots and laughed. "Goodness, you've got enough carrots here to feed an army."

"That's all right. I like to keep a good supply on hand. Lily loves them, you know." Wanda leaned down so Lily could pick one up, and when she turned to Jessie again it was with glistening eyes and a confident smile. "As I was about to say before I was so pleasantly interrupted—I don't want this child to wind up on a cattle ranch, in a factory, or wasting away in some orphanage. So the other day I asked Alan if he still had that adoption application. He did. I filled it out and sent it in, with a note telling Gilmore to cancel the foster-parent application, I'm filing for adoption."

Jessie stared at her, almost unable to speak. "But . . . what did you put down for name of husband?"

"Why, Edgar Shaw, of course. Alan keeps saying Gilmore must be terribly overworked and eager to get rid of those children. Maybe he'll sign off on the application without meeting my husband or having his signature."

"Heaven help us! You know that has to be illegal!"

"Desperate problems sometimes require desperate solutions, Jessie."

"But what about Mr. Nesbit?"

"Well, that's the other thing." While Lily munched on her carrot, Wanda continued in a calm, even tone. "Philip came by again and said he wanted an answer, his patience had run out. Lily was playing in her room, but just then she made a big noise. Philip snapped at me that he couldn't believe that strange little creature was still here. Suddenly I knew exactly what to tell him. I said, 'I'm going to keep her if I can,' and when he said, 'Don't expect me to be involved,' I told him we might as well part company right now."

Jessie gasped. "You sent him packing?"

"It would never have worked, Jessie. I'd have spent the rest of my life comparing him to Edgar and finding that he didn't measure up. I'm just lucky that Lily came along to make me realize that."

Jessie was breathless. "Oh, Wanda, I . . . I can't believe . . ." Ecstatic, she clapped her hands, and Lily, having polished off her carrot, clapped, too, looking from one to the other with wide eyes.

"Let's not get too excited," Wanda cautioned. "Mr. Gilmore's the one who'll decide about Lily. We have to wait and see what he says. In the meantime, here you go." She handed Lily over to Jessie. "It's time for this young lady to have her bath, while I finish up in the kitchen."

Taking Lily in one arm, Jessie slid the other around Wanda in a tight hug. Their tears flowed freely, and though Jessie knew that they could turn to tears of bitter disappointment any day, today they were tears of joy.

Thirty-six

In mid-July, three months after the earthquake had sent them fleeing in terror, the Donegans reappeared at the Wainwright house. They had made it as far as New York, where they worked to save money for their passage to Ireland. But glowing newspaper accounts of San Francisco's rapid revival, and fond memories of their employers' kindness, made them change their minds and return. Catherine gave them a good reprimand for running off, but took them back, thankful that her domestic staff was once again complete.

The most visible evidence of the quake remaining in the big house was the long crack in the wall above the staircase. Catherine had decided she wished to leave it there as a silent reminder that, no matter how safe and secure life seemed to be, it was always at risk. Leonard disliked the idea, but to humor his wife he permitted it to stay.

The school board had extended the disrupted spring term, which meant that Jessie graduated with the grades she had hoped for, more or less. She sent her application to Berkeley and looked for a summer job that would help pay for college while leaving her time to spend at Wanda's.

For Hazel the end of school meant the beginning of working life. She still had her part-time babysitting business and would be spending July with her relatives, caring for her younger cousin and teaching her beginning needlework. But what had her truly excited was that she'd enrolled in a secretarial training course. It would start the day after she got back.

For both Hazel and Jessie, leaving high school meant parting with teachers and friends. And, in a way, with each other.

"I guess it'll be harder for us to get together from now on," Jessie remarked sadly as they walked home from school for the last time.

"Seems that way," Hazel agreed. "My course will go from eight o'clock every morning till the end of the day. I'm lucky, though—they're going to let me learn the typewriting machine."

"I'm at Wanda's in the afternoons," Jessie said hopefully. "Couldn't you stop by sometime? I still want you to meet Lily."

"Well, I'll be awfully busy. Maybe one day, I might try."

"Sure." Jessie sighed. *And maybe one day it'll be too late, depending on Mr. Clarence Gilmore's decision.*

He never had responded to Wanda's adoption application. Some days Jessie felt that must be a good thing. But then she'd remember how Mrs. O'Reilly always said "a thing's never done until it's done properly." Even though the cook was talking about cakes and pies at the time, Jessie knew that the words applied to all that was important in life.

It bothered her to hear strangers in the shops, on street corners, almost everywhere she went, complaining about the city's handling of "the Chinese problem." And every day, it seemed, the newspapers urged the mayor to force the Bureau of Adoptions to accept all outside offers to take the orphan children away. That would relieve San Francisco of the burden of feeding, housing, and educating them. Jessie heard her mother's friends speak of the matter often, and worries about it nagged at her day and night.

THE SUMMER JOB Jessie landed was as a sales clerk at Huston's. She worked mornings and had her afternoons free. Mr. Huston, who had been forced to move his shop to a new, more structurally sound building, was glad to have the help of someone so interested in the merchandise—almost too interested, he sometimes thought.

"Try not to handle the delicate instruments so much," he said with a smile. "You're like a kid in a candy shop."

Jessie was delighted about her new job, but her parents were not. One evening they called her into the parlor to discuss it.

"I've a mind to telephone Huston," her father grumbled. "The idea of his letting you hang around there—I won't have it."

Jessie was quick to protest. "Papa, setting up the new store has Mr. Huston almost worn out. He wants me there, and I'm glad of it. It wasn't easy to find a summer job."

"Well, it's ridiculous," her father grumbled, but said no more.

Her mother was mystified. "What I don't see is why on earth you'd even *want* to be there. I hate to think what our friends will say."

"I doubt your friends will ever notice, Mama."

"Speaking of friends, we saw the Arnolds the other night," her mother went on. A vague uneasiness gripped Jessie when she saw her father bury his head in his newspaper as her mother continued. "Mrs. Arnold said she'd heard that Wanda Shaw has a child living with her. A little girl, part Chinese and part white. I found that very hard to believe. Is it true, Jessie?"

Jessie went rigid. She glanced at her father, but he was pretending to be absorbed in his reading. Still, she knew he would listen to every word she said. "Yes, it's true. Wanda found her in one of those refugee camps after the fire destroyed Chinatown. Her name is Lily, and she's quite delightful." She noticed that her father's head remained buried in his newspaper.

"Well, if that isn't the most amazing thing," her mother exclaimed. "A widow like Wanda, taking in a child! And a mixed-race one, at that. Leonard, do you suppose you ought to look into it?"

"I should say not!" He glared at his wife. "Wanda refused to return to my clinic, giving me some poppycock about spending more time in her garden. Her private life was not my concern before, and it's certainly of no interest to me now." He rose, flinging his paper aside. "Excuse me, but I have better things to do than engage in idle gossip." Without looking in Jessie's direction, he strode out of the room.

Taken aback, his wife stared after him. "Why is he so bothered? I was just curious. It's really not important."

"No, it really isn't," Jessie agreed.

ALAN CONGRATULATED HER on the summer job the next time they saw each other at Wanda's. "And your parents know you've applied to college?"

Jessie nodded. "My father still wants to send me to a finishing school so they can turn me into a proper lady." Then, with a saucy glance at Alan, she added, "I told him Berkeley would be a better place for me to find a suitable husband. That brought him around."

She saw his eyebrows shoot up, but he looked pleased. "Well, it sounds like you've got everything under control."

Jessie didn't see it that way. Not only did Mr. Gilmore remain unheard from, there was still the worrisome matter of Lily herself. True, she was less tense now. She had even learned to enjoy being read to, and the reading duties usually fell to Jessie. They could never start until Lily had gone to find her little bear. Although she was still wary of Toby, she seemed finally to have decided that Chester could be trusted.

But still she spoke only rarely and looked frightened most of the time. Never did a smile cross her solemn face, and that worried Jessie most of all. Sometimes Lily awakened from a nap crying from a bad dream—the terrible earth dragon, or some other nameless, menacing thing, still lurked in the shadowy recesses of her mind. Jessie wished she could get inside her dreams and chase the demons away. All she could do was comfort her and rock her back to sleep. Jessie knew Wanda had spent many a night doing just that.

As she walked out with Alan one evening, she confessed her fears. "Lily can be trying, and Wanda's nerves are always frayed. Now I have to tell her that people are talking—my parents know Lily's here. Wanda will hate that."

"She must have known it was bound to happen. But I can tell what you're leading up to. You feel responsible for Wanda's problems, so you feel you have to help her take care of Lily."

"Of course I do. And if Lily stays with her, Wanda *will* need help. Besides, Lily needs me, and—" Jessie had to pause to control a tremor in her voice. "I admit, I need her, too. I might feel better if I saw her make some real progress by the end of summer."

"You just have to make yourself believe you will. Anyway, that's weeks away, she can still make progress if we keep working at it. I promise you, we'll see this through."

She smiled. "Thanks for staying so optimistic. It means a lot to me." *And there's that "we" again.* Just the sound of it made her warm inside.

Thirty-seven

OFTEN ON SUNNY AFTERNOONS Jessie took Lily to a nearby park to feed the ducks living on a small pond there. Usually Lily resisted leaving the house and would scream if Wanda tried to take her out on errands. But she loved the ducks, and it seemed a stroke of good luck when Jessie discovered that the promise of an excursion was the one sure way to get her outdoors. Jessie especially enjoyed the times when Alan had an hour or two of free time and could join them. He and Jessie would sit in the shade of a tree nearby and watch Lily at work.

"Lily feed ducks," she would announce, throwing out bits of bread from a sack. She always called herself Lily now, and she went about feeding the ducks as she did everything else—with intense concentration. "Ducks hungry!" she would call as the noisy quackers greedily gobbled up her offerings.

It struck Jessie that these were the only times she and Alan had been together without being in the midst of some crisis or with other people around. For her these private moments were rare and special pleasures.

"How are things at the hospital?" she asked him one day.

"Fine, thanks. My internship's ending, so I've applied for a position as staff physician. I think I've got a good chance. How's your job going?"

"I'm really only a shop clerk, but I love every minute of it."

Another time she asked, "When did you decide you wanted to be a doctor?"

"When I was about twelve. And it was all because of Dr. Mac—Dr. Horace MacElvain, but everybody called him Dr. Mac. He was the one doctor in the little town in Oregon where I grew up. He used to let me drive his buggy while he made house calls, and he'd talk to me about his patients."

Alan's thoughts moved back in time. "One of them was a friend of mine named Tim Kelso. One day he cut his leg terribly, sawing lumber. Everyone thought he'd be a cripple, but Dr. Mac said a surgeon he knew in Portland could fix him up. Trouble was, Tim's folks were poor as church mice. Soon after, Dr. Mac put out a sign: GONE FOR TWO WEEKS. Funny thing, Tim's family went away at the same time. Two weeks later they were all back, Tim saying he'd had two operations in Portland. Soon it came out that Dr. Mac had taken a big loan from the bank. Unexpected expenses, he said. Tim wound up walking with only a slight limp. And nobody doubted that his operations were Dr. Mac's unexpected expenses." Alan smiled at the memory. "Dr. Mac never got rich, but he was beloved in our valley. He taught me that medicine can be a noble profession—and made me want to be the kind of doctor he was." Now his smile was apologetic. "Anyway, sorry for rambling on like that."

"Oh, but I'm glad I heard about Dr. Mac. It tells me a lot about you."

IN THE MIDST of duck feeding one day, Lily came running up from the pond to where Jessie and Alan were sitting under their usual tree. "Uncle die," she informed them. "And Mama go to China. But she come back soon." After delivering this message, she ran back to the ducks.

"There you are," Alan said quietly. "Not only is her language growing by leaps and bounds, but she's coming to terms with her uncle's death."

"But what about her mother?" Jessie wondered. "Lee must have told her Mei would come back soon. I wish I thought that letter he got saying she'd died could have been wrong."

"But as we know, people who return to China are forbidden to come back."

Jessie couldn't think of anything hopeful to say to that. As she pensively watched Lily, Alan pulled an official-looking document from his pocket. "I brought you a declaration of U.S. citizenship form for her," he said, handing it to Jessie. "With all the records destroyed in the fires, hundreds of Chinese are getting their citizenship claims approved every day because there's no way to tell if they're valid or not. Being native born, Lily *is* a citizen, of course, but this is a good time to make it official."

"Even though Wanda's never heard another word from Mr. Gilmore?"

"We can do this regardless of him. The form asks only for the usual information. I've already signed as a witness. Have Wanda sign as Lily's guardian, then send it in. Oh, and you'll need a birth date."

"Wanda and I were talking about that the other day. I figure Lily was born two years ago in August. We decided on August eighth. Two eights—maybe that'll be her lucky number."

"That's coming right up," Alan said. "How about if I round up Henry and we give her a little party?"

"Good idea!" Jessie exclaimed. *How sweet of you to think of that,* she wanted to say. "Let's try to make it a happy day for her. After all, it may be the only birthday we'll ever——"

"Don't say that, Jessie. I'll bet this party will be the start of a long tradition. If not, at least we can make this birthday a memorable one."

Jessie's brooding about this was interrupted a moment later by the sight of Hazel coming toward them. "Hazel!" Scrambling to her feet, she gave her friend an enthusiastic hug. "I didn't know you were back from Monterey."

"Got back yesterday, started my secretarial class this morning."

"Well, I'm so glad to see you. How'd you find me?"

"My class let out early today, so I stopped by Wanda's——figured you'd be there. She told me you were over here with a friend. I thought she meant the little girl, but..." She cast a glance at Alan, who was now on his feet. "I hope I'm not interrupting anything."

"Not at all," Alan said with a smile, stepping forward to shake hands. "I'm Alan Lundgren. We met at the Presidio camp, remember?"

"Of course. Nice to see you again, Dr. Lundgren."

"Alan, would you fetch Lily for a moment?" Jessie asked excitedly. "Tell her there's someone here I'd like her to meet."

Hazel's eyes followed him as he went off to the pond. "Goodness, he's more handsome than I remembered," she whispered. "And a doctor. Lucky you."

Jessie went scarlet. "Hazel, *shhh!* We can talk about that later. Now, Lily's a little shy with strangers. Please don't be hurt if—"

"I know how little children are, Jessie," Hazel reminded her.

Lily looked as if she'd much rather be feeding her ducks when Alan led her back by the hand. Jessie beamed a reassuring smile at her. "Lily, I'd like you to meet a dear friend of mine. This is Hazel."

For a long moment they stared at each other. It was Lily who spoke first. Holding up her sack of bread crumbs, she asked, "Feed ducks?"

Hazel blinked in surprise, then leaned down close. "Why, thank you, Lily, I'd love to. But I'm sorry, I can't today. Maybe some other time."

Gazing fascinated at Hazel's long blond hair, Lily hesitantly put a tiny hand up and touched it. "Pretty," she said. Then she turned away from the astonished group and ran back to her impatient ducks.

"Shy with strangers, you say?" Hazel remarked dryly.

Jessie and Alan exchanged amused glances. "Feel honored, Hazel," Jessie said. "She's never said that to me. Come to Wanda's soon, won't you, and get to know her better?"

Hazel hesitated. "It'll be hard for me to get used to her. But yes, I'll come, because it's probably the only way to see you." To Jessie's delight, she agreed to make a real visit soon. After shaking hands with Alan again, she said good-bye quickly and hurried away.

"Poor Hazel," Jessie said, looking after her. "She's put up with a lot, being my friend."

"She should realize that being your friend is the best thing that could happen to her," Alan remarked.

Jessie smiled at his gallant words. Now it was time to get Lily home, and time for Alan to get to the hospital to start his evening shift. There would be no more talking for them that day. But altogether, she decided, it had been a wonderful day just the same.

WHEN HAZEL FINALLY VISITED at Wanda's a few days later, she took a dim view of Lily's aimless wandering around the house.

"She has so many toys," Wanda told her. "But except for Chester, she pays them no attention."

"Toys aren't always as interesting as *things*," Hazel remarked. "Do you have some teaspoons I could use?"

Wanda looked puzzled but went to the kitchen and returned with a handful of spoons. Hazel sat on the floor and arranged them in squares and triangles. In a few seconds Lily was standing over her, watching. Inside of a minute she had taken over the game, focusing intently on creating her own intricate shapes. Hazel rose and joined Wanda and Jessie at the dining room table, where they sat marveling at Lily's sudden new interest.

"I had no idea how to keep her happy like that," Wanda said. "Thank you, Hazel. Jessie's told me you're a marvel with children, and she's so right."

Jessie cast a sly look at Hazel. "Our friend Henry will wish he'd been here, too. He's crazy about you, you know."

Hazel frowned, perplexed. "What can you mean?"

"Are you blind?" Jessie laughed. "He was smitten with you the first day we met him in Chinatown. And he still is."

"Oh, really. Well, look who's calling people blind! If anyone is smitten, it's Alan Lundgren, with *you*. I could see that in an instant, the other day at the park."

"He was there for the same reason that he comes here to Wanda's—because of Lily. After all, he's the one who saved her from that awful camp."

"Yes, but as a doctor he's cared for lots of pitiful children. I'm sure he doesn't go visiting them at their homes afterward. He comes around here because of *you*. Isn't that right, Wanda?"

Wanda smiled but, seeing Jessie's puzzled expression, turned serious. "Hazel has a point. It's clear to me that he cares for you, Jessie."

Hazel tossed her head. "There. As long as we've known each other, you've never even noticed a male member of the species. Then, when one starts to notice you, you have no idea what's going on."

Jessie felt herself blush to the roots of her hair.

By then Lily had grown tired of the spoon game and was looking expectantly at Hazel. "She's wondering what else you have up your sleeve," Wanda said. "If you know a way to get her outdoors without going to the duck pond, I'll be eternally grateful."

Hazel thought about it briefly, then stood up and announced, "I think I'll go out to your garden, Wanda, and look for four-leaf clovers. Anyone want to come?" Getting a blank look from Lily, she told her. "Clover is a special kind of grass. Mostly it has three leaves, but if you find one with four, it brings you good luck. Maybe we can find one."

"I'll come," Jessie said. She and Hazel went out to the back-

yard, and as Wanda watched in delight, Lily followed right behind. For a long time the three crawled around on the grass.

"No four-leaf clovers today," Hazel reported when they finally returned. "But Lily found some other treasures."

Lily opened her hand and proudly displayed three colorful
pebbles and a marble, which Wanda admired with *ooh*s and *ah*s.

Soon Hazel had to go. "Bye, Lily," she said to the little girl.
"I had fun playing with you."

"Hazel come back," Lily said. She opened her arms to hug
her new friend. A surprised Hazel smilingly accepted the hug.

"Well!" exclaimed Jessie as she walked Hazel out. "Lily
plainly adored you. That was quite amazing."

"I was just trying to be helpful. Taking care of little children
for so long has to count for something."

"It counts for everything. Couldn't you bring the girls with
you sometime, or Jonathan? Lily should play with other kids,
don't you think?"

"Sure, that would be good for her. But I couldn't bring the
kids, my parents would die if they found out. You know how it
is, Jessie. Chinese children aren't even allowed to go to school
with whites in this city. And I'm sure that includes children of
mixed blood."

"But *you'll* come back, won't you?" Jessie asked anxiously.
"You can promise Lily I will."

"And don't forget the birthday party. August eighth, at three
o'clock."

"I wouldn't miss it."

Jessie smiled as she waved good-bye. It had been another
good day. If only the days like this could go on and on.

Thirty-eight

ON THE DAY of the birthday party, Lily was tucked in early for her afternoon nap, leaving a nervous Jessie just enough time to get everything ready. Wanda had gone out looking for one more present for Lily. Henry, who had already moved to Berkeley to start college in the fall, was crossing the bay for the occasion. And Hazel had promised to come by after her class. Alan, taking a few hours off from the hospital, had volunteered to stop by the bakery and pick up the small cake Wanda had ordered.

As she finished washing the morning's dishes, Jessie saw Alan coming up the walk. Quickly she made sure that Lily was sound asleep, then opened the front door and signaled for him to come in.

"This is going to be the world's best party," he said, setting the cake on the table. Then he saw Jessie's tense look. "Are you worrying again? You have to put on a happy face for Lily, you know."

"I know, and I will," she assured him.

He gazed at her intently, with a melancholy expression she had not seen before. "I hope someday I'll see genuine happiness on your face, Jessie."

She forced a weak smile. "You could, if you waved a magic wand and made Mr. Gilmore disappear." Her turbulent feelings threatened to erupt. "If he comes back and tries to take Lily, I swear I'll run away with her. I messed it up before, but next time I'll get it right, and—"

"Stop, Jessie, calm down." Taking her hands in his, he pulled her close. "Good things do come to the good people who deserve them. I truly believe that. And you must believe it, too."

She pulled back and looked into his eyes. "You're such an optimist, Alan. You're just saying what you know I want to hear."

"Believe, Jessie, believe." He kissed her on one cheek, then the other, then on the lips. His kisses were soft and sweet, and he held her close all the while.

Her head was swimming—she had lost all sense of time, knowing only that the merry-go-round was turning. Taking her where, she dared not guess, but maybe—just maybe—to a place she wanted to be. And if this was dizziness, she liked the feeling.

Just then Lily's light voice piped up from her room, singing "Ring Around the Rosy" to Chester. Jessie stepped back, trying to collect herself. "Everyone will be here soon." She smiled brightly at Alan. "Do I look happy enough?"

"Barely," he said, smiling back. "But you sure look plenty beautiful."

She felt herself turning pink as she went into Lily's room.

LILY HAD BEEN TOLD that today was her birthday, and she was going to have a party. But the words *birthday* and *party* meant nothing to her. Even after being dressed in a fancy new outfit, complete with shiny shoes and a red ribbon in her hair, she seemed more bewildered than excited when Jessie led her into the parlor.

In the doorway she stopped and stared, transfixed by the spectacle before her. Both parlor and dining room were decorated with colorful balloons and paper streamers. The sofa was piled high with gaily wrapped presents. On the dining room table stood the cake, with white icing gleaming beneath the flickering flames of two tiny candles. Around them was written: HAPPY BIRTHDAY, LILY. Five smiling faces beamed at her, and five voices delivered a slightly off-key rendition of the "Happy Birthday" song.

Lily reacted to the strange goings-on with wide-eyed alarm. Jessie took her hand again and led her to the dining room table, lifted her onto a chair, and pointed at the cake. "Blow out the candles, Lily." She showed Lily by pretending to do it. "You make a wish, and then you blow them out."

Lily looked at the candles, then at everyone gathered around, then back at the candles. There was no knowing if a wish was made, but finally she leaned forward, took a deep breath, and blew out both candles with one mighty puff. Her audience laughed, clapped, and called out, "Happy birthday, Lily."

At that moment, understanding dawned. Even with no clear idea what a birthday party was, Lily knew the word *happy*. And she began to realize that all the fuss was for her. "Happy birth-day!" she cried. "Happy Lily, happy birth-day!" Then came the sight Jessie had yearned so long to see. Like the sun breaking through on a dark day, a radiant smile illuminated Lily's face.

"Shall we have cake now?" Wanda asked the little guest of honor. "Or would you like to open presents first?"

"Presents!" Lily shouted. Seeing the pretty packages, she finally understood that word, too. Soon she was tearing open the gifts and examining each one with squeals of delight. Jessie could have danced with joy—until something happened that was not part of her plan.

Chancing to glance out the front window, she saw a man approaching the house—and her blood ran cold. It was Mr. Gilmore. Her eyes darted to find Alan, who was on the floor, admiring Lily's presents. When the knock sounded, he looked up, distracted. "Are we expecting someone else?" Seeing Jessie's panicked expression, he got up hurriedly and went to open the door.

"Gilmore, Bureau of Adoptions," came the clipped greeting.

Alan was slow to respond, but when he did, his tone was cordial. He shook Gilmore's hand, saying, "Hello, sir. Come in. Please excuse the mess, we're having a little birthday party for Lily."

Briefcase in hand, Gilmore stepped inside. "I realized it's been some time since I stopped by here." He fixed an inquiring look on Alan. "And you are?..."

Alan swallowed hard and then answered firmly, "I'm Edgar Shaw, sir, very glad to meet you."

At his words, Jessie drew a sharp breath. Alan threw a glance in her direction but kept on talking. "A birthday's very special for a child, don't you agree? Thank heavens I could be in town for it. By the way, I apologize for being so slow to contact you. But I'll be traveling much less from now on. And since I have the most capable wife in the world—" Now he shot a look at a dumbfounded Wanda. "Lily is safe and happy here." He went to Wanda, wrapped an arm around her waist, and planted a kiss on her cheek.

If Mr. Gilmore noticed that "Mr. Shaw" looked somewhat younger than his "wife," he did not show it. Nor did he seem to observe that Wanda very nearly fainted when "Mr. Shaw" kissed her. But he did notice Jessie. "You're out of uniform, miss—I forget the name."

Seeing that Jessie was too deeply shocked to speak, Alan answered for her. "That's Jessie, our maid. It's her day off, but she's so fond of Lily that she wanted to come to the party, anyway."

"I see." Gilmore frowned as his eye next fell on Henry. "And who's the Chinaman? If he's a relative of the child, that could complicate things."

"No, he works for my company as a driver," Alan said. "We hire him to come to the house and help out now and then. He also helps with translating for Lily. So . . ." He looked around. "Let's find a quiet place to talk, shall we? I assume you have our adoption application with you?"

Gilmore tapped his briefcase. "Right here. But there are certain details that still need to be worked out."

"Of course. Will you join us, my dear?"

By now Wanda had gathered her wits. "Certainly, Edgar," she said smoothly. "We can use Lily's room. This way, Mr. Gilmore."

Jessie stared in astonishment as the three went through the parlor and into Lily's room. A look at Henry and Hazel told her they were equally amazed. Lily, always wary of strangers, had retreated to the farthest corner of the room, taking several of her presents with her. Trying to stay calm, Jessie busied herself by picking up the wrapping paper the birthday girl had strewn about.

The meeting behind Lily's closed door lasted only a few minutes, but to Jessie it seemed like hours before the three emerged.

"May we offer you a piece of birthday cake, Mr. Gilmore?" Wanda asked him as they came back into the parlor.

"No, thank you, I must be going. Several more stops to make today. But I do wish the little one a happy birthday."

The little one shot a suspicious look at him, then turned back to her presents. "Mr. and Mrs. Shaw" saw their visitor to the door, shook his hand, thanked him profusely for his visit, and waved as he went on his way.

Jessie was trying to recover her senses when Alan came over and, with a sly smile, held up the adoption application in front of her.

There it was—"Final Approval"—written in a strong, clear hand, and signed by Clarence A. Gilmore, San Francisco County Bureau of Adoptions.

While Jessie stood dazed, Lily rushed up to Alan, clutching a tawny stuffed lion, her present from Hazel. "Look! Chester have a friend!"

Alan bent down to say hello to Chester's new friend as Hazel beamed at the child she had thought would be so hard to get used to. Henry and Wanda excitedly discussed the sudden turn of events. It was all too much for Jessie. She slipped unnoticed out of the room.

Following her a minute later, Alan found her sitting in the kitchen, her cheeks streaked with the tears she could no longer hold back. "I'm sorry, I—"

"You don't need to apologize," he said gently, taking her hands and coaxing her to her feet. "But Wanda's about to cut the cake, so please come back to the party." He took out a handkerchief and patted her damp cheeks dry. "It doesn't mean a thing without you there."

As THE FESTIVITIES wound down, Lily fell asleep on the sofa, her new lion clutched in one arm, Chester in the other. Everyone stood for a moment smiling down at her.

"She has no idea what just happened here," Wanda mused. "But someday she'll know this was one of the most important days of her life."

Alan carefully scooped Lily up, stuffed animals and all, and carried her off to bed. The others gathered at the dining room table for a light supper. And when Alan rejoined the group, he found himself the object of four pairs of curious eyes as they awaited his explanation.

"I know, that was a bold and reckless thing to do," he began. "But when I saw Jessie's face at the sound of Gilmore's knock, I knew who it had to be. And I knew I had to convince him somehow that this case had gone on far too long." He gave Wanda an apologetic look. "Sorry to pull that on you, Wanda— hope you weren't offended. But there was no time to think, no time to do anything except just wade right in."

"I was not offended," Wanda said with a smile. "I was impressed. You were such a good actor, I almost believed you were Edgar myself."

"You caught on fast, too. But even if I hadn't convinced him, I'd have hounded the man's footsteps until he gave in. It's fitting, though, that it happened today—a special birthday present for Lily."

"The most special present she could ever have," Wanda declared fervently. "And someday she'll thank you for it."

Hazel and Henry took turns exclaiming over Alan's daring action. But his eyes were now fixed on Jessie, who so far had said nothing.

"It's a miracle," she murmured at last. "You really did wave a magic wand and make Mr. Gilmore disappear. But it scares me, Alan. That was an awfully dangerous thing for you to do."

"Don't forget what I told you once, Jessie," Wanda said. "Desperate problems sometimes require desperate solutions."

"And besides," Alan added, "it's by no means certain that we fooled Gilmore for one second. I suspect he was just as eager to have this matter settled as we were. Beyond that, all I can say is that any risks involved were more than worth it."

Jessie shook her head. "I don't know how we can ever thank you enough. How I can . . ." *Still, you must know how much I want to,* she thought. *How badly I want to come around the table, smother you with kisses, and be wrapped in your embrace.*

But for the moment, the solemn gaze that held their eyes together, the clasp of their hands across the table, would have to do.

Thirty-nine

As the unforgettable afternoon drew to a quiet close, Henry and Hazel left first—Henry to walk Hazel home. He would stop short of her house, so her parents wouldn't see him. Alan had night shift at the hospital, starting at nine o'clock, and offered to take Jessie home. As they drove, he brought up the question she'd been dreading to hear him ask.

"By the way," he began, "what became of your application to the university?"

"Oh, they admitted me for the fall," she said evenly.

"That's wonderful, congratulations!"

But Jessie wasn't finished. "I wrote back and asked them to put my application on hold for a year."

Alan's face fell. "Oh no, Jessie, that's not smart at all."

"I still don't feel right about leaving, when Wanda needs me. Besides, even if I became a star student at college, without a scholarship I couldn't go to medical school. And I'm never crawling back to my father for support."

"Wanda's got things well in hand," Alan said with a frown. "And you have to get on with your life. We'll worry about medical school *after* your two years of college. Please say you'll go this fall. I'd like to know that's settled, before I—"

His troubled look gave her a chill. "Before you what? Is something wrong?"

"I didn't want to say anything at Lily's party, but—remember when I applied to be a staff physician at Pacific General? Well, I didn't get it. Seems the board of directors weren't too happy when they learned about my arrest record."

"Your *what?*"

"During the emergency, remember? When I spent that night in jail for fighting with those thugs? Never mind that I was only trying to prevent a robbery, the board only wants you if you're squeaky clean. We won't even guess what they'd say about my impersonation act."

Jessie's mind was in a fog. "My god! So that means . . ."

"It means I'm out of a job. But only temporarily. One of my medical school professors wants me to come and work with him. He's chief of surgery at the best hospital in Portland. It's a real honor, I'd be crazy not to go."

"Yes, I suppose. Well, I guess it's my turn to congratulate you."

"Thanks. He's offering a fellowship, actually, named for his old mentor. Mine, too, years later. Dr. Horace MacElvain, the doctor in our valley when I was a boy."

Feeling numb, Jessie was barely aware of it when Alan pulled the car up in front of her house and shut off the motor.

"Portland," she murmured glumly. *Try to sound cheerful,* she ordered herself. "That's in Oregon, so you'll be near your family."

"Yes. Not that I'll be seeing that much of them. My sister, maybe. She's years older than I am, but we always got along pretty well."

"What about—" Jessie hardly dared ask, but finally she gave in to the impulse. "You had a sweetheart there, I imagine?"

He nodded, gazing pensively down the street. "Charlotte, daughter of the local bank president. Everybody agreed she was the most beautiful girl in the valley. But you know . . . things get complicated sometimes."

Suddenly Jessie wished she hadn't asked. "Well, I should probably go in," she said softly.

"I'm sorry about the bad timing," he said, as she gathered her things. "The fellowship with Carlini—that's my old professor—starts in two weeks, and I have a pile of work to finish before I go. I don't know when we'll see each other again."

Jessie felt shaky now. "This is my second big surprise today. And I have to say, I liked the first one much better." It was all she could do to keep her composure while Alan came around to help her out. They stood for a long moment, gazing at each other as if neither was quite sure what should happen next. *An hour ago this was the best day ever,* Jessie thought despairingly. *And now we're saying good-bye?*

"I'm going to miss you," she finally said. "More than you know."

"I'll miss you, too. But I'll write often, and I hope you'll do the same. And hug Lily for me sometimes. I wouldn't want her to forget me."

"She never would. Neither would I, even if I never saw you again."

"Oh, I'll be back. I couldn't stay away. You mean too much to me for that." He cast a quick glance toward her house. "Oh, what's another broken rule? Nobody's looking." Before she knew it, he had pulled her close for a tender kiss. "You're still my favorite charity lady. Now please, reopen your application, go to the university this fall. And by all means—*believe.*"

"In what?" She clung to him a moment longer. "I don't dare believe in any more miracles."

"In yourself, Jessie. Believe in *yourself.*"

HER PARENTS WERE OUT for the evening, so the house was quiet when Jessie went up to her room and collapsed onto the window seat. The day had been like a carnival ride, lifting her to dazzling heights one minute, plunging her back to earth the next. How wonderful to know Lily was safe at last. But Alan, gone? Even though the idea was awful to contemplate, she supposed she might as well start trying to get used to his not being around. Still, she knew that every time she closed her eyes, day or night, she would see his smiling face, the look in his kind eyes, would remember the feel of his arms around her and the way he had kissed her in that last moment together.

Am I on that dizzying merry-go-round, the most dangerous carnival ride of all, with someone who's on his way out of my life?

Even Mademoiselle, reclining in a corner, seemed to look sad. "He promised he'd be back," Jessie said, thinking out loud. "I must remember that. And I must remember something else he said: 'Believe in yourself.'"

I'll hold on to that, Alan, come what may.

Part Three

Forty

Sunday, March 17, 1907

St. Patrick's Day (My birthday)

My life was so different on my last birthday. Between chemistry lab reports and the essay that's due in freshman English, I've hardly had time to notice this one. I hadn't planned to mention it to anyone here at the boardinghouse. Mrs. Benton's other college girls are nice enough, but we hardly see one another except standing in line for the WC in the mornings. But someone must have put a bug in Mrs. Benton's ear. When she served supper tonight, she put a beautiful daffodil at my place.

One of the senior girls knocked at my door earlier to say I had a telephone call. My heart jumped; I thought it might be Alan. But then she told me it was my mother. It was sweet of Mama to think of telephoning. She said Hazel had dropped off a big package for me to open on my next weekend at home. Then, as a surprise, Mama put Mrs. O'Reilly on the line. She shouted into the telephone, "Mighty lonesome it is without you hangin' about, my girl." All at once, I felt so homesick.

I noticed Papa didn't come on the line. I guess he's still unhappy with me over that last argument we had. I only asked why poor people and laborers are still living in shantytowns almost a year after the disaster, while rich bankers and railroad barons are having their Nob Hill palaces rebuilt by those same workers. It was a sensible question, I thought. But he just scowled and retreated to his study.

There was a fancy card from Corey, which I noticed Eleanor did not sign. It's almost as if we hardly know her. And I had a lovely note from

Wanda, with a picture from Lily showing her and me, and a big sun in the corner. It's heartbreaking to hear Lily say, "Don't go, Jessie," whenever I visit.

For a long time I wondered if I was right to leave Wanda and Lily and come to Berkeley last fall. After Wanda decided she'd rather be Lily's mother than Mr. Nesbit's wife, I worried that she might have made a terrible mistake. But I've never seen her so happy. She's a wonderful mother, and Lily has truly blossomed. For now, she has the income from Mr. Shaw's insurance, and when Lily is older, she plans to go back to work.

Luckily for me, the university let me change my mind about coming. It was Wanda who finally convinced me to do it. She was hurt to think that I would set aside my goals and turn myself into a child's nanny instead—those were her words. I miss Lily terribly, but the last thing I'd ever do is hurt Wanda after all she's done for both of us.

I confess that when Henry and I walked out of class on Friday, I told him about today. He stopped right in the middle of the sidewalk and sang "Happy Birthday"! I really couldn't have a better friend here, or anywhere. Chinese are not forbidden to go to the university, but they're not exactly encouraged to, either. Henry gets dirty looks from whites, same as I'll surely get from male students if I go to medical school. But he's undaunted. He's all excited about engineering now, and full of the most amazing ideas. He says that someday there will be <u>talking</u> in the moving pictures at the nickelodeon show. That ordinary people will travel from city to city on those new airplanes. And that we won't need the ferry because there will be a bridge across the bay! His fantastic predictions always make me laugh.

But even he couldn't make me smile when he mentioned the last time we sang "Happy Birthday" together—last summer, with Lily, Wanda, and Hazel . . . and Alan. Sometimes Henry comes with me to visit Lily, and Hazel joins us, too. Then it almost seems like old times—except for Alan's empty chair. His fellowship with Dr. Carlini was supposed to be over months ago, but he still has not returned.

I think of him all the time—the way he'd say "we," the way he laughed. And his kisses. At first he wrote often, sometimes even short letters to Lily for Wanda to read to her. For Christmas he sent me a lovely woolen scarf, and a windup music box for Lily that plays a cheerful tune. She loves it, and plays it endlessly. But it doesn't make up for Alan's being "gone-gone," as she says. His last letter said he'd be delayed in returning—some problem had come up in his family. He promised to write again, but that was in January, and I've heard nothing since. With more confidence than I've got, Wanda tells Lily he'll be back soon. Lily says her mama will come back soon, too, then adds, "But soon is a long time."

Soon is becoming a very long time for me, too. The worst part is, I can't stop thinking of the beautiful Charlotte.

It's not fair that a lady always has to wait for the man to speak first. So the other day I sat down and wrote him a letter. I said that I'm certain now that I fell in love with him last year. That I wouldn't want to burden him, but I need to know if he could ever feel the same way about me. I must say it was an exquisite letter. I put it in a scented pink envelope and addressed it in my finest hand to Dr. Alan Lundgren, at the last address he gave me, in his hometown of Hood River, Oregon.

Then I tore it up.

I just couldn't send it, not after so long has passed without word. I'll just have to be patient and wait to see what happens, if anything ever does. I should be good at that. I've had plenty of practice.

JESSIE SLID HER JOURNAL into the middle drawer of her desk. It was late, and she still had her essay to write. She glanced at the topic: "Friendship in Shakespeare's Plays." If she thought about Hazel while she wrote, it would be easy. She took out a new sheet of paper, dipped her pen in the inkwell, and set to work.

She didn't often see Hazel now, since they lived a ferry trip and two streetcar rides apart. And Hazel had landed a job as secretary in a law office. She could operate the typewriting machine faster than anyone else in her office—thirty-five words per minute—so her employer often asked her to work extra hours. In her free time, she loved to go shopping downtown, and Jessie would sometimes go along. She rarely bought anything for herself, but she always enjoyed watching Hazel do what she enjoyed doing.

THE FOLLOWING SATURDAY, Jessie and Hazel had planned to finish their Easter shopping. But Hazel, it turned out, had another idea as well.

"Let's go to Fielding's," she said when she met Jessie at the ferry. "It's my favorite store, and we can stop in and say hello to Corey."

Jessie groaned. "He's a married man now, remember?"

"You can't spare a minute to say hello to your own brother?"

I should have seen this coming, Jessie thought. But there was no way to avoid it now.

Corey's office was in the fifth-floor executive suite, behind a door marked VICE PRESIDENT FOR MARKETING STRATEGY. An elderly, tight-faced secretary ushered them into a spacious office, where Corey leaped up from behind an enormous desk to greet them.

"Jess, how nice to see you! And this is—wait, don't tell me. It's Hazel . . . Simmons, right?"

"Schelling," Hazel said with a smile. "Nice to see you, Corey."

"Nice to see *you,* Hazel. Very nice, indeed."

"Your office is beautiful." Hazel gazed at the fine furnishings and the panoramic view. "Truly magnificent."

Soon they were seated across from Corey, who grinned at them from behind his desk. "Easter shopping at Fielding's, are you? Before you go I'll give you some gift certificates, my compliments."

"Why, thank you!" Hazel gushed. "Imagine, vice president of marketing strategy. That sounds so important. What exactly *is* it?"

"Tell you a little secret," he replied, his grin widening. "I have no idea." He waited while Hazel rewarded his little joke with a ripple of laughter, then went on. "I have assistants who take care of the tedious details. My job is just to make sure everything runs smoothly."

"I see, you being an executive and all," Hazel said breathlessly.

An executive who got his job because his father-in-law owns the store, Jessie thought wryly. *Hazel is far too easily impressed.*

Corey was impressed, too. "For heaven's sake, Jess, why didn't you tell me your friend had turned into such a doll?"

She glared at him. "Gosh, Corey, I didn't know I was supposed to."

Rising, he came around his desk, pulled up a chair next to Hazel's, and leaned close. "Tell me all about yourself, won't you?"

She blushed at the unexpected attention. "Not much to tell, really. I live at home, I work as a secretary, I——"

"Really! Say, how would you like to work at Fielding's?"

Jessie cringed as Hazel uttered a soft gasp and said, "Are you serious?"

"Absolutely. I need a personal secretary." Corey winked, adding, "I can teach you things you never learned in secretarial school."

Hazel stared at him. "But don't you already have one?"

"That schoolmarm? She can be reassigned. I need someone young and pretty." He reached out and took her hand. "And you'd be perfect."

She drew back from his touch. "How would your wife feel about that?"

"Oh, Eleanor never comes around here. Tell you another little secret—she shops in much fancier places than this."

He laughed, but this time Hazel was not amused. "We mustn't keep you, Corey," she said, rising. "If you'll excuse us—"

"Yes, we ought to be going," Jessie said, instantly on her feet.

Corey accompanied them to the door. "When you're ready to start work, let me know," he said to Hazel. "Meanwhile, I'm glad you came by."

"So am I," she replied coldly. "Good-bye." She walked away without looking back.

Puzzled, Corey turned to Jessie. "What's wrong? I was only being friendly."

"Guess you don't know as much about girls as you thought you did." She gave him a playful pat on the cheek and followed Hazel down the hall.

They were back on the street before either spoke. "Oh, gracious me!" Jessie exclaimed in mock alarm with a sideways glance at Hazel. "He forgot to give us the gift certificates."

"Who cares?" Hazel muttered. "I'd never shop there, anyway."

Jessie smiled. Only thirty minutes before, Fielding's had

been the finest store in town. "Congratulations, I think you're a very smart shopper."

BACK IN BERKELEY, she told Henry about Hazel's encounter with Corey. "You still like her, don't you, even after all this time?"

"Sure, I'm fond of her," he admitted. "Always have been."

"Well, now that she's over her crush on Corey, why not make a move?"

He shook his head. "She's never seemed to care for me the way I do for her. And even if she did, you know it's illegal for Asians to marry whites."

"I'm sure that stupid law is what's kept Hazel from thinking about you in that way," Jessie declared.

"We'll never know, I guess. Anyway, defying American customs would only turn both our families against us. I couldn't do that to her. We'll always be friends, I hope, but that's all we can be."

"Well, I think some of our customs are just ridiculous."

"I agree," Henry said with a patient smile. "But Chinese teaching says you take what life hands you, and keep moving on."

"Yes." Jessie sighed, suddenly thinking of Alan. "Keep moving on."

Forty-one

JESSIE KEPT HER TRIPS across the bay to a minimum for the rest of her spring term, except for spending Easter with Lily. The demands of her studies weighed on her. But in May, her mother telephoned to say that the San Francisco Medical Association's annual spring ball would take place soon at the newly opened Fairmont Hotel. Would Jessie join them?

"You mustn't study all the time, dear," Catherine said. "It's important for you to be seen socially once in a while, among the city's finer people."

Jessie was reluctant but agreed. "As long as I can get back early the next morning," she replied.

IN A GRAND BALLROOM festooned with colorful decorations, a small orchestra played on a bandstand. A few couples danced, but most of the guests milled around, greeting friends and chatting.

Why did I agree to this? Jessie asked herself, feeling awkward and plain in a mauve silk borrowed from Hazel. Mauve had always struck her as a sickly color. But there had not been time for her mother's new modiste to make her a gown, and these days her own wardrobe included nothing suitable.

Absently she watched her parents mingle. *Papa's lucky,* she thought. *He has the ideal wife for a professional man.* Her mother clearly enjoyed the important role she played, and like the other doctors' wives there, played it to polished perfection.

As she wandered at the fringes of the crowd, she noticed three tittering young ladies gather around an important-looking gentleman and heard one of them call him "Dr. Carlini." Unable to resist listening, she hovered nearby.

"Smart move I made, taking Lundgren to Portland," Carlini said. "He's a fine doctor, with a bright future. I'll introduce you when he gets here."

In a daze, Jessie sank into a chair at the edge of the dance floor, staring blindly at the elegant couples waltzing to "The Blue Danube." *Alan's back, and he didn't let me know?* She sat motionless, her mind whirling as fast as the dancers. Suddenly the lighthearted merrymaking was unbearable to watch. She rose, pasted on a tense smile, and headed for the exit.

THE LAST NOTES of a waltz were followed by the sound of couples politely applauding as she reached the hotel lobby. There she stopped short and sucked in her breath when she saw Alan coming toward her.

"Dr. Lundgren," she said frostily. "How nice that you could make it."

"Jessie! I never thought I'd see *you* here. You look lovely." He went up to her and waited expectantly. "Don't I get a smile of welcome?"

She had thought that anger was all she would feel when she set eyes on him. She hadn't imagined how her heart would race. "You'll find Dr. Carlini inside," she said curtly. "No doubt the attractive ladies he's with will have plenty of smiles for you."

Alan was clearly abashed. "I need to explain, Jessie, I know that. I'm sorry it's been such a long time. My train just got in this morning; I haven't even unpacked yet. I wanted to surprise you, and——"

"Oh, you surprised me, all right. But you owe me no explanations."

"I have to say hello to some people, but then——"

"Indeed, you'd better. I won't take up any more of your time."

"Please." He put a hand on her arm as she started to move past him. "I want to talk to you. In just a few minutes, all right?"

Saying no was harder than she thought it would be. "Well . . . until my parents are ready to leave, I'll be in the lobby."

As Alan entered the noisy crowd, Jessie lingered near the door. Dr. Carlini welcomed his favorite colleague with a hearty handshake. Jessie saw the young ladies taking note of the tilt of Alan's head, his slightly tousled blond hair. All aglitter in their finery, they offered their hands to the man of whom Dr. Carlini had spoken so highly. And he beamed right back. He was in his element, laying the groundwork for a brilliant career. *It makes a pretty picture,* Jessie thought. *And I don't fit into it at all.*

THE SPEECHES honoring distinguished officials and guests seemed endless, but Alan finally emerged. He found Jessie sitting in the quietest, farthest corner of the lobby. Sitting down beside her, he studied her solemn face. "You look wonderful, Jessie. And different, somehow."

"Well, it *has* been the better part of a year." It took effort for her to sound polite but nonchalant.

"I never meant to stay away so long. Or to be silent for so long, either. Please let me explain."

She lowered her eyes. "Truly, you don't need to—"

"Jessie, I do." He leaned forward and began. "Working with Carlini was great. But going home after that was—well, difficult doesn't begin to describe it. My father has aged greatly, and he's not well. He'd decided to sell his orchards, for a quarter of their value. My sister and her husband were arguing with him all the time. They don't care about the farm, but they want her inheritance. And they wanted me to straighten out the mess."

"I thought you said he'd disowned you long ago."

"He had, but he seemed willing to talk to me. Maybe *because* I'm not in his will, I don't know. Anyway, we finally got him to cancel the sale, but it was a real struggle. One day he got so angry that he picked up a footstool and threw it at me."

"It does sound like a difficult time."

"That wasn't all. There were other reasons I had to go back there."

Jessie felt a chill. *Here it comes.* "Charlotte," she said softly.

"She was there, yes. Lovely as ever, and queen of Hood River society with at least a dozen suitors after her. We reminisced about the old days, when she wanted me to come back and start a medical practice there."

Now it was hard to sound polite—or unconcerned. "Maybe you should."

"It's true that if we'd married, her parents would have built me a new medical office with all the best equipment. And she *is* delightful to be with. My sister thought I made a big mistake to walk away from all that." Alan sat back in his chair and stared into the distance.

Would the blow ever fall? Jessie steeled herself. "And was it?"

"I suppose I've always wondered a little. But going back

there showed me that it's not where I belong. It was nice seeing Charlotte again, but except for some pleasant memories, we realized we have nothing in common."

As he paused, Jessie felt a wave of sweet relief.

"All that is a poor excuse for not writing, after I'd said I would," he continued. "But I just couldn't manage a sensible letter. And now I've got a new reason to lose sleep at night."

"What do you mean?"

"Dr. Carlini's been put in charge of the whole hospital in Portland, starting next January. He wants me at Pacific General with him until he leaves, then I would go back to Oregon and join his permanent staff. It's an excellent hospital, and with Carlini boosting me, I could rise to the top there in practically no time. It's a dream begging to come true."

"I see." Jessie forced herself to remain properly upright while her spirits plunged. "Too good to turn down, in other words."

"Extremely appealing, certainly. Luckily, Carlini's giving me until November first to think it over."

While you're thinking, remember the people here who love you. Lily. Wanda. Me. Especially me. "I'm sure you'll make the right decision," she said lifelessly. "And whatever it is, I'll wish you well."

Alan gazed at her for a long moment. "Thank you, Jessie. I'd better say good night now. I start back at the hospital at five tomorrow morning."

"Will you make sure to visit Lily? She asks about you all the time."

"Of course. I'm anxious to see her and Wanda. How's Lily doing?"

"She's fine, but my studies keep me so busy I don't see her enough."

"And school's going well for you?"

"Very well, if I may say so myself." Jessie tried not to sound boastful.

"There, you see?" He got to his feet. "I always knew you'd get where you want to be."

She had to smile at this. "I thought that's what you'd say."

"Will you be coming home for the summer?" At Jessie's nod, he smiled broadly. "That's good. And I'll come to Wanda's as often as I can. After all, we need to get Lily back out to her ducks, don't we?"

"Yes, she'd love that." *And I hope that's a promise you really mean to keep.* Jessie rose and held out her hand. "I guess I'll say welcome back, after all." She shook his hand briefly but warmly, then turned and, head high, walked back into the ballroom.

"Who was that young man you were talking to, Jessie?" Catherine asked.

"A doctor who used to be an intern at Pacific General."

"Does your father know him? Probably not, he wouldn't notice an intern. I must say, the young man looked a little windblown. He's not anyone you're interested in, is he?"

"Don't even dream of it, Mama. I don't know what my future holds, but I'm certain I'll never be a doctor's wife."

"Goodness, what a strange thing to say. Well, I see your father's ready to leave. Just let me say good-bye to the Arnolds."

As she faced the bracing wind on the ferry deck the next morning, watching the city recede into the distance, Jessie tortured herself with questions. Going to Portland was a dream begging to come true, was it? Would the beautiful Charlotte be nearby, waiting with open arms?

"Don't worry about it," she could almost hear Hazel say. "He said they had nothing in common, remember?"

"Yes, but did he mean it?" she would reply. "Or will he be thinking of her this summer every time he looks at me?"

A blast of the ferry's horn jolted her to attention. The vessel bumped to a stop at the Oakland dock, and her hands gripped the railing as she awaited the signal to disembark. She'd spent enough time grappling with questions that had no answers, she decided. *Just remember that Lily's doing fine and your work is going well,* she told herself firmly. What would come after that . . . well, that was one more unanswerable question.

Forty-two

JESSIE NEEDN'T have worried about Alan's making time for Lily. Within days of his return, he had visited Wanda's, where he was welcomed by Lily with jumping-up-and-down joy. "You not go away anymore," the little girl commanded. "Lily not like it."

Little does she know, Jessie thought sadly, when Wanda wrote to her of Alan's visit.

As the summer got under way, Jessie returned home, working mornings at Huston's and spending her afternoons with Lily. Alan's new job at Pacific General kept him even busier than he had been as an intern. But he sometimes joined Lily's expeditions to the park, carrying sacks of breadcrumbs and supplying Lily as she fed the ducks. He also joined Jessie and Wanda in taking Lily on outings to the seashore. The first time Lily gazed out over the sun-dappled ocean stretching away almost to infinity, she was awestruck.

"Look!" she cried. "See big water!"

Through all these pleasant times, Alan talked endlessly to Jessie, asking her about the courses she had taken last year, or telling of his new interests in surgery and internal medicine. But he never spoke of Dr. Carlini, nor of Oregon, nor of the delightful-to-be-with Charlotte. Jessie knew these things must be on his mind, but she dared not question him. She wasn't sure she wanted to hear the answers. Meanwhile, if he still had any romantic feelings toward her, she could not detect them.

Wanda and Hazel took a different view. They felt sure that despite Alan's silence on personal matters, he did have feelings for her. Alan paid rapt attention to Jessie, they pointed out. And he watched her admiringly through long, quiet moments. These things, they assured Jessie, must speak as loudly as words. But Jessie was not convinced. Much as she valued the time she had with Alan, and treasured their friendship, the feeling never left her that both fell far short of what she longed for. Still, a young lady could not wear her heart on her sleeve. She kept silent.

WITH AUGUST CAME Lily's third-birthday party. Henry had to work, but Hazel came, as did Alan, and this time, two other children from the neighborhood, who had become Lily's playmates. Eating birthday cake with her little guests, Lily made them laugh by slipping dabs of whipped cream under the table to the eagerly waiting Toby. She had long since made friends with the cat, who now slept at the foot of her bed almost every night.

Keeping pace with Lily's expanding horizons was her rapidly growing curiosity. And in a certain way, this presented Jessie with a problem.

"Where do you live, Jessie?" Lily would often ask. And when Jessie was leaving to go home, "Why I can't go with you? I want to see your house."

How to reply? Jessie was at a loss. "Not now, Lily," she would say. "Someday, maybe, but not now." It was an unsatisfactory answer, but the best she could do.

———

ALL TOO SOON it was time for Jessie to go back across the bay for her second year at the university. Alan joined them at Wanda's for a brief farewell gathering that day, and afterward drove her to the ferry terminal.

On the way he chatted about an elderly patient of his who had a rare heart ailment. And all the while Jessie wondered if they were about to say a final good-bye or if this would be only a temporary parting. If good-bye, she had no idea how she would handle it.

"Good medicine's not just science, you know," he was saying as they drove down Market Street. "It's also the art of communication: knowing how to talk to your patients in a way that gives them confidence in you, and the will to help themselves."

"Oh . . . yes, I'm sure that's true. Especially if your patients are children."

"My point, exactly. And a sick child couldn't have a warmer, more confidence-inspiring doctor than you're going to be. I hope you'll specialize in pediatrics when you go to medical school."

"If I go, Alan. Not when. But yes, *if* I go, I will do just that."

"Well, I prefer *when*. If you were an ordinary girl, I might have doubts about your making it. But you're not, you're someone very special."

She smiled ruefully, doubting now that when he said "someone very special," it meant what she'd once hoped it did.

At the ferry terminal he helped her out of the car with a smile that revealed nothing one way or the other. "Have a great term, Jessie," he said brightly. "And I'll remind you—believe in yourself, and you *will* get there."

She thanked him and waved as he drove off. He'd been a wonderful friend all summer. But what had happened to his tender touch, his kisses? *Where is your heart?* she thought. And with November not far off, where was his fateful decision?

At least her own plans were firmly in place. She would apply herself even more diligently during this second year of college but set aside all foolish dreams of the future. If that meant getting on with life without Alan, or without any reasonable hope of becoming a doctor, she could face that. She felt strong and determined, her resolve rock-solid.

And it stayed that way until one rainy day in October, when her father wrecked his car.

Forty-three

HER MOTHER'S VOICE came shrilly over the telephone. "Oh, Jessie, you've got to come right away!"

"Mama, what's happened?"

"The fog was so thick this morning your father couldn't see five feet ahead, but he insisted on driving off. When he got down to Van Ness, the car wouldn't stop, and he sailed across and slammed into a lamppost. Oh, how I hate that machine!"

"Was he hurt?"

"Dr. Arnold thinks he may have a concussion. He's keeping him in the hospital a few days."

"I'll go see him, then come home as fast as I can. In the meantime, Mama, try to stay calm."

It was difficult to stay calm herself. She rang Wanda and gave her the news, then rushed upstairs, threw a few things into a valise, and ran to catch the streetcar that would take her to the ferry dock.

ACCUSTOMED TO SEEING PATIENTS at Pacific General, Leonard was not happy about being confined there himself. He greeted Jessie with a scowl. "What are you doing here?"

"I heard about your accident, Papa. How are you feeling?"

"I'd be fine if my confounded brakes hadn't failed. My mechanic will hear about *that,* I can tell you. Then that busybody

Arnold stuck me in here so the nurses can drive me crazy. And the food is terrible. They could learn a thing or two from—what's her name?—our cook."

The question startled Jessie. "Mrs. O'Reilly, Papa, you know that."

"Whatever her name is. And a cheeky young doctor came nosing around. Name of Lundberg, Lundquist—something like that. Said he knows you. I told him to get out. There's no end to the aggravation, I tell you."

"That would have been Dr. Alan Lundgren."

"Well, how the devil would he know you?" Jessie was glad he didn't wait for an answer. "And why are you here, anyway? You'd better get on back to—where is it you're living now?"

Now Jessie was shocked. "Berkeley, Papa. I go to the university."

"Yes, well, go on back there. I appreciate your concern, but there's no need to come running just because I got a bump on the head."

She stayed only a few minutes longer, then gave him a light kiss on the forehead, promised to see him again soon, and hurried out.

SHE WAS GRATEFUL to find Alan waiting for her downstairs.

"I heard you were here," he said. "How did he seem?"

"He was acting very strangely, Alan. It scared me. He didn't even remember that I go to the university."

"A concussion can have that effect. But Dr. Arnold will keep a close watch, and so will I."

"I'd best go home, then, and look after my mother."

"Try not to worry, Jessie. It'll be all right."

She thanked him for his hopeful words. But she felt only a little comforted.

AT HOME SHE TRIED to sound hopeful herself. "Papa's doing fine, Mama. I'm sure we'll be able to bring him home in a day or two."

Her mother, deep in distress, was not reassured. Nor was she reassured when Dr. Arnold called later to tell her there was no change in Leonard's condition. With a biology experiment under way, Jessie was anxious to get back to Berkeley, but now that would be impossible. Sitting with her mother that evening brought back memories of the earthquake, when Catherine was like a dependent child.

THE NEXT DAY they went to the hospital together, but her father was worse than ever—calm and sensible one minute, incoherent the next. Alan was on emergency duty and unavailable. But Corey was there briefly, and before leaving he drew Jessie aside for a private word.

"I've been to the garage where Papa's car was taken, Jess. Talked to the mechanic and looked at it myself. Fact is, there was nothing wrong with the brakes. Papa just didn't use them."

Jessie went tight-lipped, absorbing one more blow. "Thank you, Corey, for telling me."

SHE PACED THE FLOOR restlessly that evening, longing to talk to Alan. To her relief, he finally telephoned from the hospital just after nine o'clock. "Sorry to be out of touch. They kept me in emergency all day."

"It's much worse, Alan. And wait till I tell you what my brother found out this morning about his car."

After hearing what Corey had reported, Alan said, "Oddly enough, that makes sense. Dr. Arnold told me earlier that your father's been ranting and raving. At one point he turned on Arnold and demanded to know who he was."

"What's causing this do you think?" Jessie asked anxiously. "Could he have had a small stroke?"

"Possibly. But Arnold's afraid it's something worse."

"Something worse, like what?"

Alan hesitated before replying. "I hate to say it, but Arnold is inclined to suspect a brain tumor."

"Oh dear lord!"

"Arnold's arranging for him to be seen by Dr. Emerson, the chief surgeon. Emerson's away right now, but he'll get right on it as soon as he's back. He's tops in his field, he'll know what needs to be done."

"Let's hope so." Jessie had to take a long breath before she could go on. "Anyway, it's nice of you to take such an interest in someone who was so rude to you the other day. I do appreciate it."

"That wasn't his fault. A brain tumor's a serious thing. And he happens to be the father of someone I care very much about."

Jessie paused for a moment, taken aback at his words—and at the warmth with which he'd said them. "Well, it's a comfort to know you're there," she said unsteadily.

"I'm glad to do what I can. I'll call again if I learn anything more. Hope for the best, Jessie."

"Yes, I will." *And be prepared for the worst,* she thought.

———

LONG AFTER her mother had fallen into a fitful sleep, Jessie stayed curled up in her window seat, still the best place she knew to think things through. Finally she crept downstairs to the phone. She had decided what had to be done.

"I hope I'm not calling too late," she said when Wanda answered. In low tones she repeated what Alan had told her earlier.

"Oh, Jessie, I'm so sorry. Is there anything I can do?"

"Well, I was wondering—could I borrow Lily for a little while tomorrow afternoon?"

"Of course. What do you have in mind?"

"I think it's time my father met his other daughter."

Forty-four

LATE-AFTERNOON SUNLIGHT filtered in at the window as Dr. Wainwright sat dozing in an armchair in his hospital room. Earlier Jessie and her mother had been happy to hear that he was having a good day, no irrational outbursts so far. Still, Jessie knew it was a dangerous thing she was doing.

"Papa?" She touched his arm lightly.

Barely opening his eyes, he squinted up at her. "That you, Jessie?"

"Yes, Papa. I'm sorry to disturb you. But Dr. Arnold said I could come in after hours because I've brought a special friend to visit you."

"Arnold." He snorted the name in scalding contempt. "Claims to be my doctor, but I don't need him. *I'm* a doctor, I can look after myself."

"Of course you can. Now, may I introduce your visitor?"

"All right, but make it brief. I'm a busy man, don't forget."

He hadn't noticed the child standing a few steps behind Jessie. Now he watched, half annoyed, half puzzled, as Jessie beckoned to the little girl, whispered something in her ear, then led her forward.

"Papa, I'd like you to meet Lily."

The few seconds of silence that followed felt like an eternity.

Jessie held her breath while Lily stared at the glowering man and he stared back at her. At last he turned his stare on Jessie.

"Who is this child?" he demanded. "I don't know anyone called Lily."

"You've heard me speak of her, Papa. She's Wanda Shaw's adopted daughter." Drawing her closer, Jessie murmured, "Lily, can you say hello?"

Frightened of the strange man, she managed a small "H'lo."

Another long silence. *Speak to her,* Jessie pleaded silently. *Be angry with me later, but for god's sake, speak to her.*

At last he mumbled a grudging reply. "Hello, Lily."

Jessie breathed a thankful sigh. Then, seeing them go back to staring at each other, she quietly prompted Lily again. "Your present, Lily."

Lily was clutching a sheet of paper. "I made you a picture," she said, and offered it to the stern man in the armchair.

He took it, but appeared baffled by its mass of colorful blotches.

"Maybe you should explain it," Jessie suggested to the young artist.

Lily took a step closer. "This is the lake," she said, pointing to a blue patch in the center. "The green is grass, and these are ducks. I feed them. They get very hungry."

He nodded. "Yes, I'm sure they do. Very good. Thank you." He laid the artwork aside, then went back to staring at Lily.

Jessie's nails dug into her palms as she waited for what might come next. Finally her father thought of something else to say. This time, to her delight, he adopted a conversational tone. "How old are you, Lily?"

"This many." Lily held up three fingers.

"Three, eh? Well, you're a big girl, then."

"No, I'm not big," Lily told him. "Big girls go to school."

"You'll go to school soon enough. That'll be fun, won't it?"

"Maybe. I don't know. It might be too hard."

"Oh no. Not for a smart little girl like you."

"How do you know I'm smart?"

"How do I know?" He seemed surprised by the question, but faintly amused as well. "I just do, that's all. I know about these things."

Jessie's hopes rose. Lily's natural charm was beginning to work.

Growing bolder, Lily stepped up closer to his chair. "Are you really sick?" she asked.

"Me, sick? Where'd you get that idea? I'm not sick."

"Then, why you're in the hospital?"

"Because there are some silly people around here who think I am."

"Silly people." Lily giggled, then turned serious. "Toby got sick once. That's our cat. But the animal doctor made him well. You'll get well, too."

"You think so?"

"Oh yes," she said casually. "I know about these things."

Almost before it appeared, Jessie saw the smile crack her father's rigid features. "Very well, if you say so, Dr. Lily."

"I'm not a doctor," Lily told him. "But Jessie's going to be one."

Jessie cringed and steeled herself for an angry explosion. Her father's jaw dropped. "Is she, now!"

"Oh yes. Then if I get sick, she can take care of me."

He looked at Jessie, and as their eyes met, volumes seemed to be spoken between them. Whatever he was thinking, she saw no anger in his eyes. Then he turned back to Lily. "I suppose you like Jessie a lot, do you?"

"Sure I do. We're best friends."

"Well, you couldn't have a better one." Jessie's spirits soared as he picked up Lily's drawing and examined it again, this time more closely. "This really is quite beautiful, Lily. Thank you for bringing it to me."

A bright idea popped into her head. "I know. You can come feed the ducks with me sometime. You like to feed ducks?"

His answer came without hesitation. "With you, Lily, I'd love to."

That's enough, Jessie thought, rising. She had promised Dr. Arnold she wouldn't stay long. "We'd better go, Papa. But I'll come see you again in a few days." She leaned down to give him a kiss, then took Lily's hand. "Say good-bye now, Lily."

But Lily had another idea. Studying the man with whom she had so quickly made friends, she said, "Maybe a hug would make you feel better."

At first he looked startled, but after a brief hesitation, he nodded in agreement. "Maybe it would. Let's try it."

The hug was long and tight, and afterward he held on to her a moment longer and smiled into her eyes. "You were right— I feel better already! Good-bye, Lily. And don't forget—we have a date to feed the ducks."

"Okay." She reached for Jessie's hand, and they started away.

They were just going out the door when he called softly, "Jessie?"

She turned. "Yes, Papa?"

"I, uh . . ." He struggled for words. "Well, just . . . thank you."

"You're welcome." She managed a quick smile, then hurried out.

Lily sauntered ahead, innocently unaware that anything of particular importance had happened. Jessie followed, half blinded by brimming tears, proud in the feeling that, at great risk, she had done a good thing.

Forty-five

THE CONSULTATION with Dr. Emerson had been set for two days later, on Friday afternoon. Jessie planned to spend that morning studying, skip her afternoon class, and go home in time to spend the weekend with her mother.

She was in the library, taking notes out of her chemistry book, when someone slipped into the chair beside her. She looked up and blinked in surprise as Alan covered her hand with his and spoke in a low voice. "Jessie, I'm very sorry to bring you sad news."

She felt as if her heart had stopped. "He's dead," she heard herself say. "My father's dead." Barely able to put two thoughts together, she fidgeted with her pencil. "What happened?"

He moved closer and began. "I had just come on duty this morning when the alarm sounded on his floor. When I got there, he was standing in the corridor, yelling at the nurse. I tried to tell him Dr. Emerson was coming, but he shouted, 'He's a fraud! We're all frauds! The entire medical profession is witchcraft!' I told the nurse to call Dr. Arnold, but then we heard him fall. We got him back into bed, but he'd apparently had a severe stroke. He lay there talking for a while, as if to himself, then gradually went quiet. By the time Dr. Arnold arrived, it was too late."

Jessie put down her pencil, lowered her head, and gripped her temples, her mind paralyzed.

"I went to your boardinghouse," Alan went on. "Your landlady said you might be here. I'm so sorry to have to tell you like this."

Dry-eyed and numb, she raised her head and stared sightlessly across the library's huge reading room. "My father has died," she murmured. It was as if by saying it, she might better absorb the fact. "Just when it seemed we might—" She turned to Alan with a question she knew he could not answer. "Shouldn't I cry at a time like this?"

He rose and held out his hand. "Maybe we should go out and get some fresh air."

Taking a deep breath, she forced her mind to work on a practical level. "I guess I'd better ask you to take me home," she said at last.

They gathered up her things and, with Jessie leaning on Alan's arm, walked out into the bright autumn morning.

HER MOTHER was sitting quietly in the parlor when they arrived. *Is she thinking back over her years with Papa?* Jessie wondered. To be widowed twice seemed an especially hard fate. Jessie sat on the sofa beside Catherine and wordlessly took her in a consoling embrace.

"Thank heavens you've come," her mother said dully. "Corey was here for a little while. He'll be back this evening."

"There's someone with me, Mama," Jessie said. "Dr. Alan Lundgren. You saw me talking to him at the ball last spring, remember?"

"Yes, Dr. Arnold mentioned him this morning." Catherine smiled wanly at Alan and extended her hand. Even in grief, her social instincts were perfectly in place. "So nice to meet you, Dr. Lundgren."

"Please accept my most sincere sympathy, Mrs. Wainwright."

"Thank you, that's very kind. I understand you were with my husband when he—at the time of his passing."

Alan glanced at Jessie before replying. "I was, ma'am. And I can tell you that it was completely serene and free of pain. We might all hope to depart this world with such admirable grace and dignity."

Catherine's eyes shone with pride. "Grace and dignity. Of course, that would be his way. That's a great comfort, Dr. Lundgren. Thank you."

What a kind, considerate liar you are, Jessie wanted to say, hoping the secretive smile she gave him showed how grateful she was. Her mother would receive countless expressions of condolence in the coming days, but none could mean more than the words of this gentle young man. Then, in an instant, her fond thoughts were wiped out by a horrifying one. The first of November was just two weeks away—and Dr. Carlini was waiting.

THE DRAGGING HOURS before the funeral on Sunday were the dreariest Jessie had ever spent. Her mother wandered through the house, trying to come to terms with her sudden loss. She wanted Jessie close by but seemed to take little comfort from her presence. Margaret arrived on Saturday, commanding her sister-in-law to pull herself together, without noticing that she was actually holding up remarkably well. Margaret's presence provided a sense of order for Catherine that Jessie quickly came to appreciate.

Meanwhile the phone rang constantly with sympathy calls. Jessie knew her father had been a prominent, highly respected man, but how prominent, how respected, she had never fully realized.

Mrs. O'Reilly mourned as deeply as anyone. Her face a picture of gloom, she talked only of what a fine man "the doctor" was. Many a time he had snapped at the faithful old servant, but all that was forgotten now.

Every chance she got, Jessie retreated to her window seat, thinking of Alan and of how she wished he were with her. Thinking of the last time she had seen her father and the way he'd talked with Lily. And wondering why it was that, in her sorrow, she could not find the merciful release of tears.

BEFORE IT WAS TIME to go to the funeral, Jessie went to Wanda's for a short visit with Lily. Hazel was expected later, to stay with Lily while Wanda attended the service with Jessie.

"I told Lily what happened," Wanda said, meeting her at the door with a warm hug. "She didn't say anything, just went on with what she was doing. She's outside waiting for you."

On her hands and knees in the back garden, Lily jumped up and ran to meet Jessie when she came out. "Jessie, I found a four-leaf clover for you," she cried. "Now you can be lucky."

"Oh, thank you, Lily." Jessie sat down in a lawn chair and admired the offering. "It's beautiful. And I can use some luck right about now."

"Are you sad because your papa died?"

"Yes, I am. Very sad."

"Me, too. Now he can't feed the ducks with me." Lily's brow creased in thought. "I sad when Uncle died, too. But he wasn't my papa. I don't have a papa." This was a fresh stab of pain for Jessie. Then, still in her thoughtful mood, Lily delivered another. "Uncle Lee said my mama will come back soon." Her little face clouded. "But it's not soon anymore."

Unable to think of anything comforting to say, Jessie pulled her close for a moment, then was glad when Lily scampered off to continue searching for lucky clovers. Lily had never stopped hoping for a joyous reunion with her absent mother, but she had finally given up the word *soon*. Slowly, the dream was dying.

WITH ITS MOUNTAINS OF FLOWERS and multitude of mourners, the funeral was strangely unmoving to Jessie. There was nothing of her father in the solemn ceremony, nothing but ceremony itself. The bereaved widow, wrapped in black, sat still and quiet throughout. Afterward she stood between her son and daughter to accept condolences from people who filed by in a long line. Jessie noticed that her mother's thanks were delivered graciously but mechanically, with no distinction between one person and the next. Even to Wanda, whom Catherine had known for so many years, she displayed no sign of recognition. She endured it all as if in a trance.

Jessie simply endured.

Forty-six

THE REST OF THE AFTERNOON afforded no more time for brooding. The house was to be closed again, and Catherine would go for a long stay with Margaret. But first, Mr. Gregory Hayes, her parents' old friend and attorney, would come for the reading of Dr. Wainwright's will. The family gathered in the parlor, Mr. Hayes standing before them. He took a document out of his briefcase, cleared his throat, and began.

"Dr. Wainwright's will is dated June 23rd, 1887, shortly after he and Mrs. Wainwright were married. It begins, 'I, Leonard Cordwyn Wainwright, being of sound mind and body, do hereby bequeath...'" The paragraph of legal language that followed amounted to the fact that the doctor was leaving all his worldly goods to his wife, Catherine.

"We could have guessed that," Margaret snapped. "May we go now?"

"Remain seated, please," Mr. Hayes said. "Dr. Wainwright recently added three codicils to the will. Last Thursday, to be exact."

Corey, slouching in his chair, now sat up sharply. "Thursday—that's the day before he died. Why would he add codicils at that late date?"

"All I can say is that he sent for me that morning and said it was his wish to do so," the attorney replied. "So, codicil one: 'The financial assets listed in Appendix A shall be deposited in the First National Bank of San Francisco in the name of my daughter, Jessica Jane Wainwright, as her sole property. This shall include the proceeds from the sale of my medical practice, as well as of the building housing it. Jessica has the character and resourcefulness to achieve all her goals, and this bequest is to offer the support she so clearly deserves. I regret that it was so slow in coming.'"

Jessie was stunned. Her father, after all these years, encouraging her with kind words and financial help? It was almost beyond belief.

"I don't begrudge Jessie, of course," Corey said with a frown. "But it's supposed to be Mama's money now, to do with as she sees fit."

A low chuckle came from Margaret. "I wonder if you'll change your tune if the next generous bequest comes *your* way, dear boy."

"I happen to be married to a Fielding, Aunt Margaret," he said coldly. "I don't need anything for myself, I'm concerned only for Mama."

"Where *is* that fancy wife of yours, anyway?" Margaret demanded.

"Traveling with her parents in Europe, if you must know."

"To continue," Mr. Hayes said firmly. "Codicil two: 'The holdings listed in Appendix B shall be deposited in the same manner, and held in trust for the child Lily, adopted daughter of Wanda Kirkland Shaw.'"

"*What?*" Margaret fairly shouted.

Corey was on his feet. "What's going on here?"

"Wanda's child!" Catherine went pale. "Gregory, what does this mean?"

"These were your husband's last wishes," the attorney said patiently. "It is my duty to make them known to you."

Catherine turned to the only other person in the room who might be able to offer an explanation. "What do you make of this, dear?"

Jessie was too far away to answer. Pulled into a whirlwind of feelings that seemed to carry her aloft, she sent a silent, heartfelt message into the vastness of eternity. *Thank you, Papa. Thank you, thank you . . .*

Mr. Hayes completed his reading of the second codicil, which ended in the same way as the first, except that Lily was to receive the funds on her eighteenth birthday. Codicil three bequeathed similar holdings to Wanda Kirkland Shaw, adoptive mother of the aforementioned Lily. "These funds, available to Mrs. Shaw immediately," Mr. Hayes read, "are in recognition of her kind generosity in providing a home, loving care, and the opportunity for a productive life to a parentless child." He succeeded in finishing without further objections only because those inclined to object were now speechless.

Margaret was the first to find her voice. "This is outrageous!" she cried. "Are you telling us, sir, that you allowed my brother to add these codicils, even though you knew he was not in his right mind?"

The attorney could only shrug. "He seemed perfectly normal to me."

"You call it *normal* when a man suddenly gives away a huge

piece of his life's savings for no good reason? Please, be so kind as to tell us the value of these holdings he so cavalierly bestowed upon others?"

"They're mostly Southern Pacific and other railroad stocks, with good growth potential. Each is worth about twenty thousand now, but eventually they may bring a good deal more."

"That's much more than our father spent building this entire house!" Livid, Margaret turned to Catherine. "A fortune in *Wainwright* money going to a child we've never seen, and a woman who worked in Leonard's clinic! Catherine, are you sure things between those two were strictly professional?"

This brought Jessie quickly back to earth, and to her feet. "That is the most vile, disgusting thing I've ever heard anyone say, Aunt Margaret!"

Margaret fixed her in a ferocious glare. "How dare you! You've always been insolent, but this is too much!" Fire in her eyes, she advanced on Jessie. "Your mother asked you a question. What do you know about this?"

"I know that there's no more honest, virtuous person in the entire world than Wanda Shaw!" Jessie declared hotly.

"Hold on, everybody." Corey stepped forward with an air of forced calm. "Jess, we all know you and Wanda have been thick as thieves for years, so—"

"Thieves!" Margaret barked. "That's it, exactly." She turned her glare on Catherine. "You can break this will, Catherine. Any number of people will testify in court that Leonard was not in his right mind when he did this!"

"Come on, Jess," Corey went on grimly. "Tell us what you know."

In the sudden quiet that descended, all eyes fell on Jessie. She looked to her mother and was dismayed to see her quietly weeping. Much as she wished she could comfort her, she was overcome with a need to get away from there, away from Margaret. Going to her mother, she knelt and took her hand. "I have to leave now, Mama, but—"

"Wait, Jessie." Catherine clutched at her. "Not yet, please."

"I must, I'm so far behind—" Impulsively, Jessie reached out and hugged her mother. "I'm truly sorry, Mama. Sorry about Papa, sorry I can't answer your questions, sorry I've never been the kind of daughter you wanted—"

"No, don't say that! You're the best daughter a mother could wish for. It's just that I see for the first time how far from me your life has taken you." Dabbing at her eyes, she gave a weak smile. "See you soon, I hope?"

"Of course. Have a nice rest at Aunt Margaret's, and I'll see you when you get back."

Jessie kissed her mother on the cheek, then rose and turned to the attorney. "May I speak with you in private, Mr. Hayes?" Without a backward glance, she strode out of the room, picked up her valise waiting by the front door, and left the house. Mr. Hayes followed, and when they reached the front sidewalk she turned to face him. "Did my father tell you why he wanted to add those last two codicils?"

"Only that he admired Mrs. Shaw's humanitarian spirit and wanted to help her and the child. Essentially what he asked me to write down."

"I see. Well, if it will make things easier for my mother, I'll decline Papa's bequest to me. But if Aunt Margaret convinces her to challenge the other two, please, move heaven and earth to stop her. It would be a mistake she'd spend the rest of her life regretting."

The attorney gave this solemn consideration. "I think the world of your mother, Jessie. That being so, I take what you've said very seriously. Don't decline your bequest, that would contradict your father's wishes. If there's any more talk of challenging the other two, I'll do all I can to discourage it. You and I both know that certain questions are better left unanswered."

He knows, Jessie thought. *Or he's made a very good guess.* "Thank you, Mr. Hayes. I appreciate your understanding."

"Not at all. Before you rush off, it's funny you asked me to step outside. I was going to ask *you* to do the same thing. I have something for you."

As he led her the short distance to his car, he explained further. "Your father sent me out for something the day I saw him in the hospital, and when I left, he asked me to take it along. If by chance he didn't see you again, he wanted me to give it to you—in private."

Reaching into his car, he brought out a bulky package wrapped in brown paper and handed it to Jessie with a kindly smile. She tore open the package, then stared, entranced, at a shiny black leather doctor's bag just like the ones she admired in Huston's window so long ago. She swallowed hard and tried to speak. But no sound came.

"I deem it an honor to perform this last service for an old friend," Mr. Hayes added. "I believe you'll find a note from him in the bag. And allow me to add my good wishes to his."

Jessie finally managed a few words. "Mr. Hayes, I just—I can't tell you what this means to me. Thank you, again. Goodbye." Afraid she might lose her composure, she turned and hurried away. In one hand she carried her valise. In the other, her new treasure, the medical bag. In her heart, an aching mixture of joy and sorrow.

To THE LONELY SOUND of foghorns, the ferry pulled away from the dock and chugged toward the eastern shore. Only then did Jessie open the bag, to find two pieces of paper inside. One was the note from her father. The other was Lily's crayon rendition of the duck pond.

> *My dear Jessie,*
>
> *I return Lily's picture, asking that you preserve this loveliest of gifts that has brightened what may be my final hours. The bag I offer as an early present for your graduation from medical school. May it serve you well for years to come. I know you will make me proud.*
>
> *With my enduring love, Papa*

Standing at the ferry railing, Jessie stared down at the churning water, thinking over all that had passed between herself and her father. Only now, at the end of his life, had they begun to make peace, but too late, too late. At last her locked-up tears broke through and streamed in blessed relief.

But before the ferry docked, she had dried her eyes and filled her mind with brighter, more hopeful thoughts. Perhaps it wasn't too late, after all. In the end, her father had accepted her goal, even supported it. And he had done it, as Alan might say, with admirable grace and dignity.

This, I vow, Papa, will forever be my most treasured memory of you.

Forty-seven

It had been hard to get back to work, so now Jessie felt like having a lazy day. Perhaps she would stay in bed and reread *Jane Eyre*. A visit with the brave governess and the moody Mr. Rochester might be restful. But first, time to write another letter to Alan. And this one, she would mail.

> *Dear Alan,*
>
> *It's another Sunday afternoon, one week after the day of my father's funeral. It seems so distant, somehow, yet I can't stop thinking about it.*
>
> *Henry dropped by the other day to make sure I was all right. He asked if you've decided yet about Dr. Carlini's offer. I told him I supposed you were packing to leave. If that's so, please don't bother with good-byes. I don't think they serve any useful purpose. Just know that you'll be remembered, and that I'm keeping my promise to wish you well. You might like to know, too, that, just as you predicted, I <u>will</u> be able to go to medical school, because my father left me a sizable*

"Jessie?" Her landlady called to her from the bottom of the stairs. "That young man is here again, the one who came looking for you when your father died."

Jessie's hand flew to her throat. Alan! Had he made his decision and come to say good-bye? Once again a letter to him, this one unfinished, was tossed in the fire. And she was still in her dressing gown! Frantically she grabbed the first dress she saw in her armoire and pulled it over her head. *No time to put on a corset—let's hope he doesn't notice.* Twisting her hair into a lumpy knot, she shoved her bare toes into her high boots and tied the tops without bothering to lace up, then raced out of the room.

Downstairs she paused outside the parlor to run a hand over her hair. Peeking inside, she saw Alan standing by the fireplace, waiting for her. Trying to assume a ladylike calm, she went in. "Good morning."

He turned to her with a smile. "Jessie, hello. I phoned Wanda, and she said you wouldn't be visiting today. So I jumped on the auto ferry, hoping to find you here."

"You brought your car?"

"Sure did. It's parked right outside. And I heard about a beautiful spot not far from here. Feel like taking a drive?"

To hear the dreaded news, she thought. She smiled and said, "Love to."

"Come on, sweetie, you can do it." Alan was talking to his Ford as it labored up a steep climb in the hills behind the university campus.

"This is new to me," Jessie said. "I've never been up here before."

The car proved up to the task, eventually arriving at a small clearing beside the road. From there a short path led them to a vista point.

"Oh my, this is spectacular," Jessie declared, admiring the view.

"And we have it all to ourselves," Alan added.

Soon she was seated on a flat rock, he sprawled on the ground beside her. Below lay an immense panorama—the university grounds and surrounding town, the harbor at Oakland, the bay beyond, shimmering in the afternoon light, the hazy outlines of San Francisco visible in the distance.

The afternoon sun was strong, and as she waited for Alan to speak, Jessie began to feel hot and itchy in her dress. Only then did she realize that she had snatched her heaviest winter wool from the armoire. *But that'll probably be the least of my troubles today,* she thought.

After a moment Alan turned to her with a look of calm resolution. She held her breath as he said, "I've sent Carlini my answer, Jessie."

"Oh?" She fixed her eyes on the horizon and waited. The sun seemed to grow cold in the sky, and her hands and feet turned to ice.

"I told him I deeply appreciated his offer, that it's a great honor. And that with all due respect, I've decided to decline."

She almost fainted as a wave of relief swept over her. "But you said it was—how did you put it?—a dream begging to come true."

"And it is—for someone else. Remember my telling you about Dr. Mac?"

"Yes, very clearly. The doctor who inspired you when you were a boy."

"I got to thinking about the kind of doctor he was, the kind I wanted to be. And I suddenly realized that I was in danger of losing sight of all he had taught me. No, I told myself, I'm not going to let that happen."

"So . . . what will you do?"

"See that city over there?" He waved an arm toward San Francisco. "We saw so many poor, destitute people in that refugee camp. Plain people, who live hard lives and when they're sick have no one to turn to. We saved Lily, but there are thousands like her. They need doctors like Dr. Mac. And in me they'll have one, when I open my own clinic right over there."

Fighting the urge to throw her arms around him and shout with joy, Jessie said softly, "I can't tell you how happy I am to hear that."

He got up and came to sit beside her. "Wait, there's more. When you finish this year at the university, it'll be time for medical school." He held up a hand to discourage interruption. "I know you're doing well, so don't tell me you can't do it. I know you can. Why am I so sure? Simple. I'm prepared to finance it myself."

Jessie blinked in amazement. "You're prepared to *what?*"

"Now please don't say you won't accept. It could be a loan, if you like. Or even better, an investment in our future."

"*Our* future?" Her amazement grew. "Now I *am* confused."

"My *dream* for our future, I should say. I figure you'll finish school about the same time I've built up a practice at my clinic. And then I'd like you to join me as a partner. Would you, Jessie?"

"Alan, I—" She could hardly think straight. "That's a long time from now. How do you know you'll still want me as a partner by then?"

"Because I know *you.*" He reached for her hand and held it tightly.

She could find no words to reply. Seeing her stunned look, he hurried to add, "I'm sorry for mentioning this so soon after your father's passing. But I've been so happy to have you back in my life these past few months, I decided it's high time I spoke up."

She finally managed a single word. "Truly?"

"I'm clumsy in matters of the heart, I admit," he went on. "But in my slow way I've realized how important you are to me. Once I thought I was in love with Charlotte. But I had no idea what love really feels like. When I'm with you, I do, and when I realized that, the idea of our becoming partners seemed like pure inspiration. I'd be general practice, and you'd be in pediatrics —assuming that's still your interest."

"Yes, it is, but—"

"Perfect. Then, I'd like to think that the sign on our clinic could read, 'Alan Lundgren, MD, General Practice, and Jessica Wainwright Lundgren, MD, Pediatrics.' How does that sound?"

She stared at him. "Alan, are you—what are you saying?"

"That I'm not just talking about being partners in a medical practice. I want us to be partners in every way, for the rest of our lives. And I'd like you to have this, to show you I mean it." Shyly he pulled a tiny square of black velvet from his pocket and unfolded it. "I hope you like it."

Jessie looked down at a delicate gold ring, with a sapphire in the center, flanked by two small diamonds. *It's beautiful,* she wanted to say, but the power of speech had temporarily deserted her.

"I think I've loved you since that first day in the camp. Took me a while to figure it out, but I finally did. And now in my awkward way, I'm asking you to be my wife. Will you?"

As she gazed at him in wordless wonder, he took her in his arms and kissed her, then drew back and gave her a searching look. "Well, my dearest charity lady, do you think you could love me, too?"

Her head was spinning, but when she found her voice it was firm and steady. "Alan, I've loved you for a long time. And a partnership sounds wonderful. But marriage..." She rose and moved a few steps away. He followed, perplexed and anxious. After a moment she turned to him.

"There's just one thing..." A faint smile played on her lips. "That sign on our clinic? I'd like my name to come first."

It took him a few seconds to comprehend. Then, "You've got it!" he shouted exultantly, wrapping her in his arms again. "So, future Dr. Wainwright," he murmured in her ear, "may I take that as a yes?"

"You may. Yes, I love you, yes, I'll marry you. Yes to our clinic. Yes to everything. And I was only joking about the name."

"But you can have it that way. You can have it any way you like, as long as we're together." He took her hand, slipped the ring on her finger, and a moment later, holding her again, so tightly she could barely breathe, came another kiss, this one hard and lingering.

At last she pulled back and said shakily, "It's true what you once told me. The merry-go-round of love surely can make you dizzy."

He smiled, then turned serious as he searched her eyes. "Did you really accept me? Are we engaged? Or was I dreaming?"

"I did, Alan, and we are. I should tell you, though, you won't be paying my way through medical school. I'll be doing that myself."

"I don't understand. How is that possible?"

"I'll tell you all about it later. For now, let's just sit here quietly so all this can sink in. It's a perfect day, let's enjoy it to the fullest."

He put his arm around her waist as they sat on the flat rock for a long time, gazing at the view. Gradually, afternoon fog gathered on the horizon.

But in Jessie's eyes all the world seemed aglow in a rosy light.

Epilogue
Sunday, April 19, 1908

It's hard to believe it's been two years and a day since the earthquake and fire turned everything upside down. Since I found Lily, and met my beloved Alan. I'd never have imagined that we would be planning our June wedding already. Or that my own little sister would be my flower girl.

Hazel will be my maid of honor, of course, and Henry will be Alan's best man. It will be a simple ceremony in Wanda's parlor. Wanda was thrilled when we asked if we could have it there. She and her new beau—the doctor she's keeping company with—are planning to decorate her parlor to perfection. Lily's already so excited she can hardly stand it, and she hasn't even seen the "wedding-day dress" she'll be wearing. Hazel went with me to choose a special silk for it. And I felt like crying, right there in the shop, when she told me she's going to sew every stitch of Lily's dress herself, to match her own.

I hope Mama won't feel uncomfortable around Lily. Watching her own little girl get married will be hard for her, too. But I hear she's been happily telling all her friends about her brilliant future son-in-law.

She never did challenge Papa's will. Over Aunt Margaret's strong objections, she stood up for her choice to live only for the future, and I'm so pleased. Corey wasn't, but he didn't kick up much fuss. He's had other things on his mind, what with Eleanor asking for a divorce. It seems she wants to live with another man—in Italy. Corey looked truly shaken when he told me Mr. Fielding is "paying me off to disappear." But I know he'll be all right. He's moving to Los Angeles to open a motor-car dealership. I can't imagine why he chose that remote town, but he's sure he can make a fortune there.

It was nice to see that Hazel didn't care when she heard that Eleanor was out of Corey's life. After a year of doing well in secretarial work, she's begun to think maybe it isn't her true calling. She's taking a night course now to prepare for a career in teaching. Her pop's not too happy about it, since teachers earn so little. But I couldn't be more pleased. I've always known she'd be a wonderful teacher.

Today Alan and I did the most exciting thing—we paid a deposit on a set of rooms, where we'll live after the wedding. I know we won't have much time together after I start medical school. Probably only enough to kiss each other good morning and good-bye at the same time, as one of us rushes out the door while the other is just dragging home. Just the same, we'll be together in all the ways that matter, in mind, body, and spirit. He makes me feel safe and fulfilled and whole.

I hope I look half as beautiful at my wedding as Mama did when she married Mr. Hayes. She was truly radiant, dressed all in ivory. And I think Alan liked me in my pale gold and my long white gloves. His eyes never left me when I walked into the parlor ahead of the bride.

I grieve that Papa won't be there to give me away. But I'll ask Mr. Hayes—Gregory—now that he's my stepfather. He and Mama make such a lovely couple and bring out the best in each other. Mama's gradually giving him a new sense of style, one as modern as his progressive ideas. And he's encouraging her to widen her activities beyond the Ladies' Aid. She's just joined an organization that's fighting for the vote for women. Gregory insists it will come, and he's proud to have Mama work openly for it.

I do worry about Lily, growing up in this city. Not that she isn't doing wonderfully well. She is, and Wanda's the world's greatest mother. But already other children call her names like "Chink" and "slant eyes." I thank God for our president, Mr. Theodore Roosevelt. Last fall, he ordered Mayor Schmitz to let Chinese and Japanese children go to the same schools as the whites. Mayor Schmitz was forced to obey, especially since he's already been sentenced to five years behind bars for the bribery scandals. Gregory says that endless court appeals are all that's keeping him out of prison. In spite of everything he did, or what people say, I feel sorry for Mr. Schmitz.

Mama gave me upsetting news yesterday. She and Gregory leave next week on a delayed honeymoon to Europe. But that wasn't the distressing part. It's that they're moving into a new house when they return. Franklin Street is no longer fashionable, she says, and nearby Van Ness has become a nightmare of commercial establishments. Privately, I think she fears that Gregory could never think of the famous Wainwright mansion as his home. He's too considerate to say so, but I expect she's right.

Tomorrow she's putting the house up for sale.

So IT WAS that on a bright afternoon in May, Jessie went "home" for the last time. Her mother and Mr. Hayes had moved into their fine new house in Pacific Heights, taking Mrs. O'Reilly with them. Mr. Hayes already had a cook, but Catherine could not bear to be parted from Mrs. O'Reilly. She would be a part-time cook and full-time head housekeeper, with her own small apartment at the rear of the house. The Donegans had been discharged with good references for a new position. The house was now empty, but since the new owners would not take possession for another week, Jessie had arranged with her mother to go there for one last look around.

With her that day was Lily, who had always wanted to see "Jessie's house." Almost four now, she looked upon the outing as great fun. In a way, Jessie dreaded it and the onrush of memories that were bound to tug at her heart.

The memories began the moment she walked in. Without its furnishings the great house smelled musty and felt strangely unfamiliar. Yet still standing in the foyer was the long-dead grandfather clock. Jessie could almost see Lee tinkering with it. Scrawled in chalk across its glass face were instructions that it was to go to her mother's new house, to be stored there for Jessie. The old portrait of Great-grandmother Jane sat next to it, tagged with the same instructions. Jessie smiled. *How thoughtful of Mama to remember that I'd want these.*

On the floor of her father's study, she found another surprise—his medical books, packed and labeled for her, too. "My father used to read these books in here," she told Lily. *So did I. Only he never knew it.*

Next, the dining room, sadly bare without its Persian rug, brocaded draperies, and expansive table. "I sat right there," she told Lily, pointing at the approximate spot. She remembered the morning Lee brought Mei in as their new maid. *I wanted us to be friends, and we were. And it was here that we saw each other for the last time, only I didn't know it then.*

Leading Lily to the kitchen, she told her about Mrs. O'Reilly. "She called this *her* kitchen, and nobody dared dispute her. Someday I'll take you to meet her." *She wouldn't have understood about you, but people do change. Who knows, she might even come to like you.*

Going upstairs, she took Lily into her parents' bedroom and pointed out where their giant bed had stood. But her memories of that room were mostly unpleasant. Her mother, cowering in terror after the earthquake. Her father, turning on her in red-faced fury.

As they went on down the hall, she paused for a moment and gazed into Amy's old room. After keeping it closed up for years, her mother had turned it into a sewing room, the only reminder of its earlier use being a tiny cradle. Now it too was gone, no trace left behind.

She moved on to show Lily her brother's room. "I wasn't allowed in here very often," she said with a smile. *But late one night I rushed in, only to find him fast asleep.* How strange it seemed to her now, to have been so horrified to learn that Corey was innocent.

Jessie was glad that Lily didn't notice the narrow stairs leading up to Mei's room. No need to go into that.

Finally the last stop. "Here's my room, Lily." She perched in her window seat. "And this was my favorite place. I would sit here and pretend I was a princess and this was my castle." She reached for Mademoiselle, still sitting in the corner of the window seat, her golden hair as bright as ever.

"Is she yours, Jessie?" Lily's small hand gently touched the doll.

"She is, and someday maybe she'll be yours, too."

But Lily's attention had already fallen on something else. "Look, somebody left these here." She held up two small, flat packages wrapped in brown paper. "And this one has my name on it. See?"

"So it does. And the other one's for me." While Lily opened her package, Jessie opened hers, to find a framed photograph of her father, a replica of one that had stood on her mother's dressing table for years. A note attached read: *To Jessie, for the sake of remembrance. Love, Mama.*

"It's a picture of my papa," she said softly.

"And look." Lily held up an identical picture. "I have one, too. And there's a note with it." She stared at the note until Jessie recovered enough from her surprise to take it from her hand and read it aloud.

"'My dear Lily, this is for you. Keep it safe, for someday it may mean something to you. With love, Catherine.'"

"Who's Catherine?" Lily asked.

"My mother," Jessie said, trying to keep her voice steady. *My dear, sweet mother. She searched her heart and found a truth there. Bless you, Mama. Bless you.*

Lily sat cross-legged on the floor and gazed at the picture, deep in her own private thoughts. Finally she looked up.

"Jessie?" Her dark eyes were solemn. "Was he my papa, too?"

Jessie froze. She and Wanda had often debated when Lily should be told. Now, with a little help from Catherine, Lily had discovered it for herself. "Yes, Lily. He was your papa, too."

With no change of expression, Lily went back to looking at the picture, tracing the face with her fingertip. Then the solemn eyes came up again. "Jessie, do you think my mama will ever come back from China?"

So there it was. Her child's faith had held out as long as it could before giving way to doubt, then at last to willingness to accept the truth. Jessie knelt on the floor beside Lily and pulled her close.

"No, Lily. I don't think she will. But I know she loved you very much, because she told me so. And you can keep that in your heart for always."

Lily sat still and silent, head bowed, leaning against Jessie.

"She told me when she gave me this." Thinking this might be the right day for it, Jessie had brought along Mei's jade pendant. Now she took it out of her skirt pocket and handed it to Lily.

"This was my mama's?" Lily asked in wide-eyed wonder.

"Yes, and it was very precious to her. Her own mama gave it to her many years ago, and she gave it to me. But she really meant for you to have it."

For a long moment Lily gazed raptly at the necklace, then at the picture, first one, then the other. Down what path her thoughts were taking her, Jessie could only guess. "I'm sad I don't have a papa or a mama," she said at last. "But I have a family just the same. Wanda's my mama now. And you're my—" Suddenly a dawning realization lit up her face. "You're my *sister,* Jessie!" In an instant she was up and twirling around the room, chanting, "I've got a sister, I've got a sister!"

"So have I," Jessie called out gaily as Lily spun past her. Soon she pulled her to a stop. "Give me back that special necklace, little sister, so I can keep it safe for you. It's time to go now. Alan's meeting us at Wanda's, and we're late already."

They gathered their things and went downstairs, Jessie carrying Mademoiselle in one hand and holding Lily's hand in the other, the two framed pictures tucked under her arm.

Once outside, she felt one more memory tugging at her. She stopped and looked back. "Bye, front door," she murmured. "Bye, steps. Bye, my room." And one last thing: "Bye, house."

It was Lily tugging at her now. "What's that you're saying, Jessie?"

"Oh, just a bit of nonsense I remember from when I was a little girl."

"But you're not a little girl anymore," Lily pointed out.

"That's very true. So let's go." Hand in hand they walked on, and this time there was no looking back.

Rounding the corner, they saw Alan coming toward them, and Lily ran to meet him. "Alan! I have a picture of my papa, and a necklace from my mama! And guess what—Jessie's my sister!"

"Really! Well, that's very nice." He shot a curious look at Jessie. "What have you two been up to?"

She smiled. "Let's just say Lily's been discovering who she is. And I've been cleaning out old memories to make room for new ones."

"Sounds like an afternoon well spent."

As they walked on, hand in hand, Lily skipping ahead of them, Jessie turned pensive. "Sometimes I look at Lily and wonder, would I ever have found her if the disaster hadn't happened? Would I have ever met you? There were so many terrible things—shocks, before and after. But there were beautiful things, too, and I think today the aftershocks have finally ended. So now we're ready for the future. *Our* future."

It seemed to her that she saw that future very clearly. Their clinic. Their home. Their children. Their dear friends Wanda, Hazel, Henry. And, of course, her sister, Lily, who would spend so much time at their house that she'd need a room of her own. On its walls would hang two framed pictures: the photograph of her father, and her own rendition of ducks on a pond, done for him when she was three. And safe in Lily's very own jewelry box would be the jade pendant from her mother.

That was Jessie's vision. Her family, moving confidently through life together, all their memories entwined. Their future, shining up ahead.

We're coming! She felt like shouting it to the sky. *We're on our way!*